Simon Benjamin is a graduate of the University of Southern California and the University of San Diego. The writing of *Scam Seduction* was inspired by true events and is Benjamin's debut. A former real estate consultant, Simon is an avid sports enthusiast who enjoys spending time with his family. He is a native of a small town in California, where he currently lives with his wife.

To my wife, Caren, and our kids.

Simon Benjamin

SCAM SEDUCTION

AUSTIN MACAULEY PUBLISHERS™

LONDON • CAMBRIDGE • NEW YORK • SHARJAH

Copyright © Simon Benjamin (2018)

Ordering Information:
Quantity sales: special discounts are available on quantity purchases by corporations, associations, and others. For details, contact the publisher at the address below.

Publisher's Cataloguing-in-Publication data
Benjamin, Simon
Scam Seduction

ISBN 9781641825030 (Paperback)
ISBN 9781641825047 (Hardback)
ISBN 9781641825054 (E-Book)

The main category of the book — Fiction / Crime

www.austinmacauley.com

First Published (2018)
Austin Macauley Publishers LLC.
40 Wall Street, 28th Floor
New York, NY 10005
USA

mail-usa@austinmacauley.com
+1 (646) 5125767

Many thanks to my wife who pushed me to write my first collection of fiction. Her keen eyes and sharp mind always seem to find a way to help improve my vision.
Special thanks to my whole team at Austin Macauley Publishers for the dedicated hard work of examining, improving, and making this all presentable.
And finally, thanks to those who lived the story.

Chapter 1

As a successful international investment banker, Herman Beringer had traveled extensively and met intriguing people from all over the world. During the 70 years of his life, he had amassed sizable wealth, but likewise, had created powerful enemies. As a result, he had become very secretive.

In January of 1992, which would unexpectedly be his final business trip, Herman Beringer was seated, by chance, next to a man in the first-class section of an Israeli El Al aircraft in a flight from New York City to Tel Aviv. This tall, heavy-set, black man, who spoke with a British accent, had introduced himself as Chief Abba Balla. After hours of conversation, Beringer had developed a profile concerning Balla. He now came to understand that Balla was allegedly running for the presidency of the Republic of Nigeria and deeply connected with Nigerian oil interests. Balla had bragged about how easy it had been to raise millions of dollars for his political campaign outside of Nigeria from 'friends' who had benefited from his 'assistance' over the years. The story was that Nigeria was preparing to transition from a military dictatorship to democracy and the man seated next to Beringer was destined to lead that movement.

The provocative conversation had passed the time quickly. As the aircraft landed at the Ben Gurion International Airport outside Tel Aviv, Beringer had assessed Balla as a potential contact for future financial transactions in oil-rich Nigeria. Beringer figured that although Balla could have fabricated most of what he had claimed, it would not be too difficult to check him out.

Who knows, perhaps he was for real.

While taxiing from the runway to the gate, Balla requested an exchange of business cards. The only card Beringer had in his front pocket was that of a close friend and occasional partner from Los Angeles. Although the secretive Beringer had not actually given Balla his name, he quickly handed to Balla his friend's card that read, ELLIOT E. STERLING. As fate would have it, Beringer soon thereafter would suffer a serious heart attack and would not live long enough to check on Balla's credentials, let alone see him again.

It was a magnificent spring day in Los Angeles. Elliot Sterling had just completed playing his routine Saturday tennis game on his court at his home in Bel Air. Although he was about to celebrate his 50th birthday, his long-time friends and tennis partners still knew Sterling as fiercely competetive and never an easy match. Of course, they all knew him as a high-achieving college student during their days at Stanford University. Sterling had come from a very poor family, earned a tennis scholarship to Stanford, and went on to graduate with a finance degree, summa cum laude. Elliot had built the city's most respected land-development company, which bore his name. This was a man of great pride. He was well-appreciated for his honesty. Competitors respected his toughness and admired his great vision.

They all knew him well for his sense of humor and his charm. Yet the people who understood him best recognized that Sterling maintained a very confidential and private side. It was as if there was a secure border one had to pass through before there could be trust.

What his friends did not realize was that his business was on the brink of collapse. Before anyone had clearly understood it, Southern California had fallen into, what appeared to be, a real estate industry depression. Housing prices had plummeted, new home sales were at a virtual standstill, and the residential subdivisions that Sterling's development firm had built throughout the county were on the verge of foreclosure by banks. Without the sales of all these newly-constructed homes, Sterling's loans would have no chance of being repaid.

The erosion of Elliot's financial position had been in progress for years. He had calculated that, by this time, the demand for new housing would finally increase. By convincing financial institutions to approve a substantial $50,000,000 line of credit, he would be able to build houses, make significant profits, and thus pay down his previous debt. The lending community had trusted Sterling and approved the loans, but the money he had signed for had a heavy price, a personal guarantee.

He knew that if his instincts were wrong, it could cost him his company, and perhaps more importantly, his own home. This was a home that Sterling had designed and built at 999 Eagle Way.

A magnificent two-story, 15,000 square-foot, French style elegant residence sitting on an acre in the heart of Bel Air. His true pride and joy. Elliot Sterling was a very confident man, but for the first time in his commercial life. His instincts were about to fail.

After the tennis match, Sterling jogged with his friends to the entry of his residence where their expensive cars were parked under the porte cochere. With a predictable air of confidence and a big smile, he told them all to come back next weekend for 'some more ass-kicking punishment.'

As Sterling was about to walk back to the house, he saw the mail being delivered and decided to pick it up. While sorting through the correspondence, his eyes immediately focused on an official-looking, yet peculiar, flimsy-feeling envelope. As he examined the envelope carefully, he observed a return address to the Nigerian National Petroleum Corporation. Sterling's curiosity had peaked.

Instead of taking a shower, Sterling walked directly to his private office in his home. Most of his work and critical thinking was conducted from this location, as he rarely traveled to the company offices. His residential office was richly decorated with special rosewoods. It felt and looked as if it were the office of an important chief executive officer of a major corporation. All of the latest equipment was available to conduct ultra-sophisticated business. As he entered his office, he was puzzled by the letter. He had never transacted business with the Republic of Nigeria. He knew no one from that country.

Suddenly it came to him. The final time he had been with Herman Beringer before his death, Beringer had told Sterling about his chance encounter with a Nigerian individual on an Israeli aircraft. Elliot now vividly remembered Beringer's comment about having given Sterling's business card with his private home office address to a Nigerian national. Beringer had told Sterling that if he was ever fortunate enough to hear from him again, he should consider it his 'lucky day and act.'

After quickly reminiscing about what a loyal friend Beringer had been, he opened the envelope.

The letter was only one page. It was on stationary entitled Nigerian National Petroleum Corporation, Tinubu Square, Lagos, Nigeria. The correspondence was addressed to Elliot E. Sterling, President, Sterling Development Company, and signed by Chief Abba Balla. The letter commenced by stating: *'We have investigated your particulars and are confident in your ability and reliability to champion the course of the business transaction we propose that requires maximum confidence.'*

The mystery letter went on to advise that the last civilian regime in Nigeria, through the elected members of the ruling party, had used their positions to formulate companies and award themselves contracts which were 'fantastically' over-invoiced in various government ministries. When the present military government overthrew the regime, 'findings and recommendations' proving the validity of these contracts were made by the new government, which gave 'its blessing' for payment of these fully-executed contracts. Although the old civilian officials were out of office, they still knew about these contracts. The problem was that these ousted 'notable party stalwarts' could no longer come forward for some of these claims for fear of being accused of defrauding the government.

The letter carried on by explaining that the Nigerians required a 'trusted overseas company' whose bank account could be used to transfer the sum of $100,000,000 US dollars. Upon wire-transfer receipt of these funds, the proceeds would be shared by giving 50% to the 'account owner' and 50% to the Nigerians. Chief Balla further explained that this transaction was highly confidential and 'purely an internal arrangement' between Balla and the chief accountant of the Nigerian National Petroleum Corporation, known as NNPC. Their side of the proceeds would be used to finance Balla's political run for the presidency of the Republic of Nigeria.

Balla went on to request four copies of Sterling Development letterhead stationery, 'signed and stamped,' along with four copies of blank 'proforma' invoices, which would be used in 'completing the application and contract specifications' to the appropriate ministry. Finally, Sterling was to advise Balla of a 'nominated bank account number, bank telex, fax, and the address of the bank.'

Assuming that Sterling could perform on the requested information, the transfer would take place 'within one month from receipt.' Sterling was instructed to 'immediately' contact Balla at a designated telephone number and communicate thereafter by fax 'as appropriate.'

Sterling slowly set the letter down on his desk, walked over to his office wet bar, and poured himself double shot of tequila. The initial thought running through his head was how Balla's proposition sure beat doing business in the United States. A few phone calls, a couple of faxes, and presto, $100 million in his bank account. This had to be too good to be true. Yet, maybe, just maybe, Beringer had worked on these arrangements for years and perhaps Sterling would be the beneficiary. Beringer was a shrewd businessman who had no designated heirs. Possibly this letter could be Sterling's destiny and good fortune. Over and over again, the image of Beringer's face was vividly pictured in Sterling's mind as Beringer told the story of his Nigerian connection. Perhaps, as Beringer had advised, this just might be Sterling's 'lucky day' and now he must 'act.'

Elliot's mind continued to wander. He had, for a number of years, been desperately searching for a resolution to his mounting financial crisis. He felt as if he had earned the position of being on top of the business world. He had never abused his power, but he liked it. To be on top and live through the fall would be humiliating. He thought of his charming and loving wife. She viewed Elliot as a man with all the answers. Would she respect him if their financial empire collapsed? How would he deal with his two children, who were both away at Stanford, his alma mater? Sterling instinctively knew that, in order to cure his financial challenges, bold steps would be required. Would this step prove to be criminal?

Like most American citizens, Sterling mastered very limited knowledge concerning Nigeria. The *Wall Street Journal* and the *New York Times* often ran stories about how Nigeria had become one of America's largest oil suppliers. The articles often alluded to the perception of how their corrupt rulers attended to the affairs of state. It seemed from these reports as if their oil revenues were so vast and their public officials' greed so high that perhaps the structure of the transaction being offered was within reason. Sterling was well-aware of his contacts in Mexico City who were fabulously wealthy from their numerous 'legitimate' business dealings with the Mexican Petroleum Industry, a government operated, yet allegedly corrupt industry. Sterling was searching for an answer.

Perhaps in oil-rich foreign nations Balla's proposed deal was simply a normal way of commercial life. Certainly Beringer had been capable of structuring such a venture. As his mind kept pushing for a direction, Elliot kept returning to the fact that everything he had in life, he had earned. He knew no shortcuts to hard work. Life had been very good to Elliot Sterling, even when he had nothing. The proposed Nigerian transaction would be totally out of character for him.

The question remained: was this a hoax? It probably was. Could this prove to be the way out of the most difficult crisis of his life? How exhilarating it would be to resolve his deep financial debt. This could be an opportunity to finally dedicate much better quality time to his precious family.

Alternatively, Elliot was facing the unbearable fear of failure, along with the consequences that came with failure. Should he proceed or not?

As with all great men, a vision of action had crystallized in his mind. Inherently there was a great risk in proceeding with Balla, a man he had never met. Nigeria's negative reputation did not warrant his involvement. Yet, for the very first time in his life, Sterling was questioning the very foundation of America's economic stability. Herman Beringer had been right. Politics and 'political correctness' in the United States had become more important than principle and common sense. His deliberation was over. Elliot Sterling would take a leap of faith and vigorously pursue this project.

Chapter 2

At ten o'clock the following Monday morning, Sterling was scheduled for an important quarterly meeting with the company's bankers. The meeting would take place at his elaborate corporate offices on Wilshire Boulevard, near his home. The plan was for Mark Goldman to first brief Sterling at a breakfast meeting, then drive him to the business engagement.

Mark Goldman had attended elementary school with Elliot. Although he had only attained a high school diploma and an honorable discharge from the United States military, he had more common sense and decency than anyone Sterling had ever known.

Goldman had no stock equity in Sterling Development Company, even though he had helped build the firm. His annual six-figure compensation with generous benefits was more than what Goldman expected. Mark was not in it for the money, he sincerely was there because of the friendship. Sterling unconditionally trusted Mark as not only his friend, but a loyal adviser. Goldman was the only person in the company to actually maintain an office in Sterling's home. Although there was limited social interaction, they saw each other five to six days a week regarding business. Effectively, Mark was the company's 'trouble shooter.' When a final decision was to be made on a business matter, Sterling would inevitably seek Goldman's opinion.

Conversely, Mark had such confidence in Sterling that he never questioned a final decision made, he simply had it vigorously implemented. Mark often referred to this as his 'blind faith' in Elliot.

As Goldman arrived at the breakfast nook of the residence, Sterling was deep in concentration. He appeared to be thinking while attempting to read the *Wall Street Journal* and the *Los Angeles Times* simultaneously. Sterling had meticulously planned for the nook to have an eastern exposure so that the morning sun rays could pierce through the dual-glazed French wood-framed windows into the spacious room. Goldman, a divorced man, was six-foot-four tall. He was ruggedly handsome and wore a mustache. This was not to be an especially comfortable briefing, due to the delicate subject matter, but Mark knew that Sterling always insisted on straight facts.

"Good morning, Boss."

"How was your weekend, Mark?"

It always amazed Goldman how Sterling could be in such deep concentration and yet able to pivot to a new conversation and take full command of the room.

"My 20-something-year-old sweetheart and I saw the Dodgers fatten up on the New York Mets and I can barely walk after all the sex I had yesterday. Just fine, thank you, and you?" Mark asked.

"Well, let's just say that my ego never gets tired of humiliating my friends at tennis. I heard through the grapevine that my wife wants to redecorate the house; and I got a letter from Nigeria."

"A letter from where?" Mark questioned with a puzzled look on his face.

Sterling made direct contact with Mark's eyes and intently instructed him to, "Concentrate solely on the bank." After an awkward silence, Sterling got up out of his chair, put his hand on Mark's shoulder, and told him that, "After the bank meeting, we'll return to the home office and chat about Nigeria."

"Fair enough," Mark responded without hesitation.

Goldman went on to describe a very bleak picture as to why the business was failing. He explained that interest rates were rising and housing prices were dropping. The company's inventory of finished housing product was not being absorbed by the consumer home buyer. It simply was a 'buyer's market' and a seller's nightmare. Goldman went on to explain that, if this trend continued, 'we will lose control of our housing projects to the bank.' Mark reminded Sterling that he had pledged the corporation's stock as collateral and was in jeopardy of losing that too. Mark closed the dismal briefing by saying that, "As you know, Elliot, these piranha bankers won't hesitate to foreclose on your house if they need to."

"How much money remains in the interest reserve account funds? How long can we continue to tap those accounts and service the debt on our loans?" Elliot asked.

"Enough to carry us conservatively for the next six full months," was the answer.

Sterling further inquired by asking whether the "bank realized how much deep shit we're in?"

"I anticipated the sensitivity of the meeting, so I made certain that our accounting people only submitted to the bank the information actually in the accountants' possession." Mark, now bursting into a big smile, goes on to say, "Since our quarterly information has not been processed and reviewed by our chief financial officer, it's not technically due until next quarter's bank status meeting. That should buy us an extra three months. In the meantime, let's pray the housing market picks up steam."

"You're good, man. Now let's go buy some time from these sons of bitches," Sterling replied with a confident voice.

It was a short drive to the Sterling Development corporate offices. Mark drove the firm's new black BMW 740 model. Sterling sat in the passenger seat wearing designer sunglasses his wife had bought for him while shopping at one of her overpriced, trendy boutiques not far from his office. It didn't take long before they arrived. The architectural style of the office building was impressive. It featured black glass and very clean lines. The water feature and sculpture at the entry had won numerous awards. They parked in a special space reserved for 'E.E. Sterling,' then quickly moved on to an elevator to the top floor. Greeting a dozen or so employees, Sterling and Mark moved directly to the beautifully-decorated main conference room. As they were walking towards the assembled bankers, Sterling stopped and looked at Mark.

"Remember, your face is your sword..." As his seriousness converted to a grin, he continued by saying, "I heard that line in an Anthony Quinn movie when Quinn played Aristotle Onassis in *The Tycoon*."

"The last time you referred to my appearance, you said that my face looked like your ass," Goldman responded without missing a beat.

As they both entered the room, three bankers immediately stood. Each of the lenders wore dark three-piece conservative pinstripe suits. They all courteously shook hands. Everyone at that meeting recognized that Sterling was a proven industry winner. A well-respected client with a perfect track record. Yet the information provided this quarter to the bank appeared incomplete. Paul Reno, the senior vice president for the bank, turned to Sterling and opened the conference.

"We're forecasting an economic downturn. Your sales, apparently, are not keeping up pace with your predictions. Elliot, you know we don't want to foreclose on all this real estate, let alone your corporate and personal stuff. I got your loans approved. I stuck my testicles out where they can get crushed. Now where the fuck are we?"

"I built the finest privately-held land-development company in Southern California. Arguably the best in the country! I've never missed a payment or any other obligation to your bank in more than two decades. Trust me, I'm not about to start now. Besides, you guys would fail miserably trying to run my business. You might even wrinkle your pretty little suits at one of the construction sites."

"Elliot, I'm not trying to bust your balls, but you got some important people in the bank concerned," Reno fired his warning shot.

"You tell your 'important' people that every house my company builds will be sold and every dollar we borrow will be paid back with interest!" Sterling instinctively understood that, by behaving insulted, he would put the bankers on the defensive. He knew that Reno desperately wanted to hear Elliot be confident about repaying his loan. Reno had heard what he needed to hear.

Sterling now realized that time had been effectively bought. With the meeting now well under control, he turned his attention to the subordinate bankers and looked them straight in their eyes.

"Unless I'm in default of my loans, the next time you fellows want to inform me about your idiotic 'economic forecast,' make sure you shove your forecasting straight up your ass before you waste my time again!"

Besides the official business of placing Sterling on notice, the two young bankers' true agenda was to witness the powerful Mr. Sterling squirm. Instead, Sterling had run circles around them both. Each now looked dazed, as if frozen in time. One looked humiliated, the other pale. Before anyone could speak or move, Sterling stood up with his hand outstretched towards Reno.

"As always, Paul, it's a pleasure to see you. I got to go make some money so that your 'important' people will keep paying you that fat salary of yours. How about some tennis soon? Good to see you, gentlemen." Without another word, Sterling, wearing his light brown corduroy coat and open shirt, had vanished. The team of Sterling and Goldman had won today's battle, but both intuitively knew that major challenges were on the horizon.

As they returned to the estate, Sterling invited Mark to his office.

"Can you close the door behind you?" Elliot requested.

"You were impressive today, Boss."

"Yeah, I know. The problem is that if I don't find a solution soon, Reno's going to be living in my home! The sad thing is that those two punks are absolutely correct about their fucking academic forecast."

"Look, Boss, I'll talk to the troops. We'll all start putting in more hours. I'll get out to the housing tracks myself during the weekends. We'll pull out!"

"I've got a better solution. Here, read this," said Elliot, handing him the letter from Nigeria.

As Goldman read the letter, it was as if he had entered a trance. When he finished reading the Balla correspondence, he slowly looked up at Sterling. "Like I said, I'll start working the subdivisions on the weekends."

"You weren't that impressed?"

"Instead of Chief Balla, maybe we can strike a deal with Batman and Robin to help us rob Reno's bank," Mark said with a straight face.

Elliot responded slowly, but deliberately, expressing that, "I know it sounds too good to be true, but hear me out."

Sterling spent the next hour explaining what had occurred with Beringer, along with the history leading up to the letter. He went on to describe what he knew about Nigeria and the parallels associated with the Mexican oil industry. By the time he had completed his convincing dissertation, Goldman had come to understand that his good friend Elliot considered this letter a real opportunity.

Perhaps the only way out.

Better than anyone else, Mark understood Sterling's commitment to succeed. He deeply understood his character. If Sterling had decided to proceed, that decision would hold his mind like a steel trap.

"O.K., Boss, let's act. This Mr. 'Chief' needs a telephone call. Let's find out if this son-of-a-bitch is for real!"

"I've checked with my contacts in London, Mark. There's a nine-hour difference. It's about noon here and 9:00 PM in Lagos. Come back to my office at midnight tonight. By 9:00 AM Lagos time, Balla should be in his office. In the meantime, find out everything you can about Nigeria. Call all those politicians we've been contributing to over the years, especially that congressman on the Foreign Relations Committee. Make sure everyone you speak with understands that your inquiry is confidential."

Chapter 3

Felicia Sterling had planned a marvelous schedule for this day. She had arranged to visit with her girlfriend for lunch at a chic restaurant in Beverly Hills. There was an appointment set at her favorite fashion boutique on Rodeo Drive. Of course, she needed to select a special outfit to wear to her husband's upcoming 'surprise' 50th birthday party. Mrs. Sterling would conclude the day by meeting with one of Los Angeles' best recognized interior decorators. She was excited to start planning the major renovation Elliot had approved for their home.

Felicia had earned her lifestyle. When Elliot was struggling to get his company off the ground, Mrs. Sterling was working long hours as a top fashion model. The money she earned helped pay for the then young couple's bills. Now in her forties, she was as charming and stunning as ever. Her stylish blonde hair and dark blue eyes were exceptionally attractive. Elliot loved her combination of a sassy quick wit and her heart of gold. Her friends admired Felicia's sincerity. There was no doubt that Felicia Sterling was smart and beautiful. She loved her husband with all of her soul and trusted his instincts. She knew that Elliot's feeling about her were reciprocal.

As she entered the trendy restaurant, Felicia spotted her friend immediately. They both ordered their favorite salads and specially brewed iced coffee. Felicia couldn't wait to talk to her friend about the details of the 'surprise' party she was planning for her husband, which was just a few weeks away.

Her friend, Rachel, could sense her great excitement. They went on to talk about how each of their children were doing so well away at college. They spoke of their commitment to Judaism and their plans to be co-chairwomen of an upcoming important fund-raising gala. These two women got along famously.

As their luncheon was drawing to an end, Rachel had built up enough nerve to ask a very sensitive question. She felt she was a close enough friend.

"If I'm out of line, please stop me."

"What is it, Rachel?"

"It's just…it's just that I've heard terrible rumors that Elliot is in deep financial trouble."

Felicia calmly reacted by saying, "That's news to me. Where did you hear that?"

Now feeling embarrassed, Rachel nervously explained by saying, "While I was having a manicure, a young woman, who is the wife of Elliot's banker, told me. She said that Elliot's housing subdivisions were failing miserably and you might lose your own home to the bank! I'm sorry, Felicia."

Without showing any emotion, Mrs. Sterling motioned for the check, and once again, calmly looked Rachel in her eyes.

"That explains why Elliot wants me to spend three-quarters of a million dollars renovating our home. When they foreclose, I guess Elliot figures he wants to turn over our home to the bank in much better condition than it is today."

As they stared at each other, they simultaneously burst out laughing.

"I wish I was blessed with your sense of humor, Felicia."

"Don't forget Elliot's birthday party. I've hired the best music group in LA. to perform."

"I wouldn't miss that shindig for anything. Let me know how the interior decorating is coming along. I love you. Call me," said Rachel.

This had been a full and successful day. Felicia's meeting with the decorator had been productive. Felicia was enthusiastic, yet concerned. She hated gossip, but she knew that often where there was smoke, there was fire. She decided to confront her husband. At least, she would be talking about financial matters and not facing Elliot with infidelity or, heaven forbid, a health crisis. She would find her husband in his office reading, as he routinely did around 8:00 PM each week night. She slowly entered. Elliot was delighted to see her.

"Tell me what a nice day you've had. Better yet, tell me about my 'surprise' birthday party."

"How do you know about that?"

"Let's just say I keep tabs on you."

"We'll talk about that later. I've got a question for you."

"Okay, shoot."

"Since I'm too old to return to modeling, are we going to lose our home to foreclosure?"

"What did you say?"

"You heard me!"

"Alright, alright. We've got a few problems. Houses don't sell the way they used to. Too damn much government bureaucracy. Got a lot riding on this real estate cycle. It will all even itself out. Where are you hearing this stuff?"

"I keep tabs on you," she responded with an innocent grin. She sensed he was troubled, but Felicia had complete confidence in her husband and grasped from his comments that he'd find the correct solution. She was smart enough to know that the conversation on this subject was over.

"Come here. Let me show you something," Elliot motioned. He handed her the Balla letter. As she glanced at the letter, she looked up at Elliot, then continued reading.

"Throw that letter away!" Felicia said as a matter-of-fact.

"This is a birthday gift, sent to me by Herman Beringer."

"I guess no one told you, Elliot. He's been dead for a while and not expected at your party."

"I'll let you know when the Nigerian funds are transferred into my account." Suddenly, he took physical control of his wife. He kissed her, then caressed her. She quickly acknowledged this and showed Elliot her affection by touching and kissing him back. She was moved by his passion.

"Shall we go upstairs?" Felicia asked as he unbuttoned her blouse. Although there was no answer, the next thing she knew they were on his couch, making love. It was apparent by the way they looked at each other that they were not just simply married, but were deep into each other's soul.

"I've got a few things yet to do with Mark tonight. We need significant preparation for tomorrow's meetings. Go on upstairs. I'll take a rain check for tomorrow night," he said to Felicia with a charming wink. "Listen closely to me. I don't want you to worry about a thing. I'm like a cat. I always land on my feet."

"I know that, sweetheart. I love you very much. Goodnight, Elliot."

Precisely at midnight, Mark was knocking at Sterling's office door. Mark had walked over from his permanent office in the guesthouse portion of the residence; where he spent about 50% of his work time. Sterling was holding the Balla letter in his hand. He had re-read it half a dozen times, looking for a weakness. So far, he had found none.

"Come in, Mark."

"There's no doubt that the Nigerian government is as corrupt as hell," Mark stated with authority. "I've had our people quietly check on the Nigerian methods of doing business. Bottom line, it's possible that Balla is telling us the truth. Basically, the way it works is this: a former Nigerian government official has a 'friend' currently in a powerful government position. The guy out of power tells the guy in power where these foreign contracts are buried. The government officer then conveniently peruses the government computers, and bingo, he locates the over-invoiced contract. We've confirmed that guys like us usually get screwed, but if you're super confidential and you're working with the right group, theoretically, we could pull this thing off. What a racket!"

"Great work, Mark. Well, the moment of truth is here, so let's find out what we've got."

Sterling adjusted the phone to conference mode and dialed the number. On the second ring, a man with what sounded like a British accent answered, "Hello. Please identify yourself."

"My name is Elliot Sterling from Los Angeles, California, United States of America. I want to speak to Chief Abba Balla."

"Yes, we've been expecting your call. One moment."

As Sterling raised up his right thumb at Mark, a man with a deep voice and British accent, came on the line.

"I am Chief Abba Balla. I am astonished as to the length of time you have wasted before contacting me. When favorable circumstances knock at your door, you must seize the moment or your advancement for progress may vanish. Do you understand me clearly, Mr. Sterling?"

"Here in America, they call that 'time is of the essence,'" Sterling quickly remarked.

"I am pleased you have called," Balla said. "As you know, this transaction has developed over many years. All preparations are confirmed on our end. We have verified that you can 'champion' this cause. We know you can be trusted. Have you settled our bank account? Are the required documents set for forwarding?"

Sterling glared at Mark, then spoke into the conference phone speaker, "You will receive the necessary information within 72 hours. I will call you in three days, precisely at this time, to confirm your receipt."

"Very well, my friend. I will inform my people of your decision to proceed. You must always remember that total discretion is mandatory. Good-bye for now."

The conversation was over in minutes, yet the results of what had been agreed upon at this late-night hour could affect Elliot and his family for the remainder of his life.

Goldman and Sterling had independently concluded that Balla was very convincing. There was no doubt that Balla had the will to transact the deal, but did he actually control the group who held the power and authority? Sterling instructed Goldman to gather the various documents the Nigerians had requested. He further informed Goldman that his first order of business for tomorrow morning would be to arrange the nominated bank account. Elliot declared that the bank routing would travel through his previously established Grand Cayman Islands account. Sterling advised Mark to meet him back at his office at 4:00 PM for processing of the assembled documents.

"Mark, you see, if I don't follow through, I'll be wondering all my life whether or not this call was for real. Go get some rest. I'll see you in the afternoon."

Chapter 4

It was an uneasy night for Sterling. He knew the stakes were high. The entire night his mind wandered and was unsettled. Everything was too easy. His gut kept telling him that if it seems too good to be true, it probably is. Yet there was something in Balla's voice and temperament that exuded confidence.

He knew that Herman Beringer was a man of great business acumen. If anyone understood how to organize an international transaction such as this, certainly it would be Beringer. By 5:00 AM, Sterling was finished contemplating. He abruptly rose from his bed and was determined to organize the only way out of his financial troubles.

After his routine workout and a light breakfast, Sterling was at his desk. He was intensely studying a file labeled 'Grand Cayman Islands, British West Indies.' Within this file lay the codes, account numbers, contacts, and other pertinent information he would require to organize the Nigerian special account. The more he studied the file, the more it became clear how to proceed. He would instruct Balla to wire the funds to Paul Reno's corresponding bank in New York City. Reno would be told to assign him a new account number in order to receive the funds. Once the monies were under Reno's control, Reno would immediately transfer the funds to a designated Grand Cayman bank account. The final distribution of the funds with the Nigerians would take place face-to-face at Grand Cayman Islands.

By 10:00 AM, Sterling was sure of himself. He was certain the banking structure was a winner, and now he had to 'sell' it to Reno. After proceeding through two separate secretaries, he finally reached Reno at the bank's Beverly Hills penthouse office. "Paul, I need you to help me arrange a bank account."

"Jesus Christ, my secretary can handle that, Elliot!"

"I mean offshore. Well, first through New York."

"Elliot, there's no fucking way we're going to allow you to park our loan proceeds offshore!"

Sterling, now laughing out loud, explained to Reno, saying, "The account is required for a new deal structure, not your loans, you moron."

"O.K., how much?"

"One Hundred million."

"One Hundred million what?"

"One Hundred million American dollars."

"What, are you in some drug deal?"

"Look, stop asking so many damn questions. This is a business transaction originally structured by Herman Beringer. Herman and I have been working this deal for a protracted period of time. I apologize for never bringing you up to date, but you know how Herman always operated in strict confidence."

"Elliot, that's a ton of money, but if Beringer was involved and you're in the deal, I'll bank it. What do you need?"

Sterling spent the next 20 minutes explaining precisely how he wanted the nominated bank account arranged in Grand Cayman.

Reno questioned why the routing went through New York. "Why not go directly to Cayman Islands?" Sterling was not prepared to admit to Reno that he did not fully trust, let alone know, the other party. In lieu of telling Paul that he needed the New York routing strictly for precautionary reasons, Elliot simply informed him that Beringer had originally arranged it that way.

Reno had no further questions.

"You'll have your New York account number in one hour. By 3 o'clock this afternoon, I'll have the Grand Cayman number. I'll call you at 4:00 PM with both."

"Paul, why are you such a pushover?" Elliot joked.

"The more money you control, the faster you're going to pay us off. Besides, I like you. I'll see you at your house for tennis on Saturday."

"I'll look forward to seeing you. Listen, Paul, I greatly appreciate your assistance. You take care now."

Sterling had accomplished precisely what he had set out to do. Once again, his reputation was placed on the chopping block. If the funds were not wired as promised by Balla, Sterling's credibility would severely suffer. He decided to plan for success and just block out any negative thoughts. What he had accomplished with Reno was now in the banking pipeline. The rest of the afternoon would be dedicated to solving problems associated with Sterling Development Company, at least until 4:00 PM.

The afternoon had gone by quickly. Sterling realized that the financial position of the once powerful Sterling firm was quickly slipping. As he studied the voluminous computer sheets forwarded to him by his accounting department, the writing was clearly on the wall. Anything short of a miracle turnaround in the Southern California housing market and the company would collapse.

Since the door was wide open, Goldman entered the office without a knock just before his appointment time. He was holding a manila legal-size file folder. Mark looked pale and concerned.

"Have a seat, Mark. You look white. What's up?"

"Remember that 350-unit condominium project we did several years ago?"

"Yeah, the one in West LA."

"That one."

"What about it?" Sterling asked.

"We've been served with a ten-million-dollar lawsuit by the homeowner's association for construction defects, breach of implied warranty, so on and so forth."

"What are you so concerned about? We've been hit before. It's part of the construction and development business. That's what we pay insurance premiums for. Don't worry about it. Our attorneys will get it under control."

Sterling could sense that Mark was worried. The look on his face was for more than a lawsuit. Goldman understood how to administer lawsuits like these better than anyone in the business. There was more going on in his burdened mind. Was it business or personal? Perhaps he was concerned about the Nigerian deal. Or did he get his young sweetheart pregnant? Sterling needed to immediately get to the root of his anxiety.

"O.K., what's going on? It sure as hell isn't the legal complaint. You eat that kind of adversity for lunch. Get it out on the table," Sterling commanded.

"Boss, I have talked to our sales director and each of our sales representatives. We're dying out there in the field. These guys tell me they can't give away a single home. I'm worried sick. I don't give a shit about the bank's losses, I care about the personal guarantees the bastards at the bank forced you to give them."

Elliot understood that this was not an employee concerned about his job. This was a sincere and loyal friend truly concerned about his pal. He also knew that Mark was right on target. After spending virtually the entire afternoon studying the accounting data, there was little doubt that his personal estate was in jeopardy. The pressure was real, and the look on Mark's face was justified.

As Sterling was just about to make some reassuring remarks to his good friend, the phone rang on his private mobile phone. "Yes?" he answered.

"Do you have a pen and paper?" Paul Reno inquired. "Your account numbers are as follows." Sterling jotted down the nine-digit New York bank account numbers. Then he quickly wrote down a 13-digit Grand Cayman bank account number.

Reno went on to elaborate, saying, "These corresponding bank account numbers are operational as we speak. You are the beneficiary on both. Our people will inform us via fax when the funds have hit your accounts. I'll track it thereafter from New York. In a few minutes, look for a confirming fax from me outlining additional account details, including bank addresses, telex, etc."

"Paul, I swear I'm going to let you beat me at tennis this Saturday. You really are the best banker in all of Los Angeles. Thank you."

"You don't need to let me win on Saturday, just pay us off. Good luck, Elliot."

As Sterling hung up the phone, he had a big smile on his face and turned his attention to Goldman.

"Look, Mark, there's very little we can do about the sale of our homes. We have no affect over what the Federal Reserve does about the regulation of interest rates and the money supply. We have no say when it comes to the federal government and the Pentagon electing to close military bases in Southern California as the Cold War comes to an end. We certainly can't control the devaluation of the Mexican Peso and how it affects our buyers. We're just a couple of hard-working guys doing our level best to do the right thing. We're entrepreneurs who want to make an honest buck. I started with nothing but a brain and the right opportunities the good man upstairs gave me. If I lose my wealth, well, I'll figure out how to get it back. Now, since there isn't a damn thing we can do this afternoon about housing sales, lawsuits, or staggering loan payments, let's concentrate on how we can make this Nigerian 'miracle' a reality! It's about time we earned ourselves a long, paid vacation."

Mark, now feeling relaxed and back to his normal demeanor, pulled out four copies of Sterling Development letterhead stationary. He further exposed four copies of blank company invoices. He then pointed with his finger to the place on the invoices where they were each stamped with the official Sterling corporate

28

seal. Goldman then asked Sterling to sign his name adjacent to the stamped seal, acting in his capacity as President. Sterling looked Mark in his eyes, took a deep breath, and signed the blank documents exactly where he requested. Just as he was signing, a fax transmission began to print.

Sterling immediately saw that the facsimile was from Reno and informed Mark that, "The timing of this fax feels like a good omen!" The Reno communication reiterated the two nominated bank transfer accounts. It defined the bank's telex, fax, and addresses, along with all the technical coordinates necessary for the fund transfer. The four invoices and corresponding letterheads with seals and signatures were settled. Within 48 hours via international courier, Balla would have everything he requested to effectuate the transfer. Sterling had now put together his end of the deal. It was time to contact the chief.

Once again, Sterling's mind moved about aimlessly. He needed Mark as a sounding board. Someone to air out some new concerns. As he was well into dialing Balla's telephone number, he abruptly hung up and began questioning Mark.

"Why didn't Balla reference the airplane flight to Israel when he met Beringer, who was allegedly me? Why didn't he at least question my voice? Could Balla be an impostor?"

"First of all, you're talking to some guy sitting in a third-world nation, most likely on some mobile phone, about 10,000 miles away. Voices are not exactly going to be clear. Hell, Elliot, sometimes I can't clearly distinguish who you are when you call from your car here in LA."

"You're right, Mark."

"Now, as for the airline flight. The guy assumes you know who he is, or why would you be calling? There's no reason to mention that flight. Knowing how clandestine Beringer was, he may have told the chief never to mention again the fact that Balla even saw him on the plane. I wouldn't read too much into that."

"All right, I'll buy that too."

"As for being an impostor. Well, look at it this way, you're Beringer's impostor. If Balla is an impostor and he can perform and you are Beringer's impostor and you can perform, who gives a damn?"

"You seem to have all the answers. Why don't you answer this: am I breaking Nigerian law or, better yet, American law by signing those blank documents? I mean, the bottom line here is that some quasi-governmental entity is about to massively overpay on this fucking contract!"

"The way I see it, Elliot, this is going to be a risk you take in order to make this kind of money. It's your price of admission. The rules of the game change when you play this kind of high-stakes international poker. If you don't have the stomach for it, pull out now. These guys have invited you into a business deal. You have nothing to do with their commercial or legal structuring. You're totally innocent. They ask you for some invoices, stationary, and a bank account number. You provide these because Beringer advised you to act on a legitimate agreement. No harm, no foul. You don't know the business customs regarding how commerce is conducted in Nigeria. How many times have you made big contributions to politicians who, in turn, voted favorably on one of our projects and you went on to make a bunch of money on that deal? Every country has their way of transacting business. You don't know what's right or wrong. That's up to their attorneys. The only concern I have is whether this son-of-a-bitch controls the group who has the authority to get this deal done!"

"O.K., O.K., I'm convinced. I'll tell you what, why don't you run the company and I'll be your lieutenant?"

This time Sterling punched in the telephone numbers with confidence. Since the international circuits, apparently, were busy, it took some time before the phone rang. As the line finally connected, one could sense that it was a very long-distance call.

A man with that familiar British accent answered, "Establish your identity."

"This is Elliot Sterling."

"Please hold. I will interrupt Chief Balla from his meeting."

"My distinguished friend, Mr. Sterling, I am a man who appreciates punctuality. I have no doubt that you are prepared to perform. I must receive your information within 48 hours. I am unduly being insisted upon by my associates to secure our trusted overseas company forthwith. If I do not receive your intelligence by the end of two days, I will no longer accept you as our associate. Do you understand me?"

"Yes, I understand you. By the way, when was the last time you were in Israel?"

"I never returned since the time we flew there together aboard the Israeli flight from New York to Tel Aviv. I took pleasure in that flight with you, perhaps we shall do it again one day."

Feeling self-assured, Sterling replied that, "You'll have the package within 48 hours."

Chief Balla now understood that Sterling was all in. He methodically instructed him to, "Listen to me carefully." Then he continued, "Once we are in receipt of your documents, you will receive further instructions via fax from David Solomon. Follow his instructions carefully. Enough has been said. Good-bye, my friend."

Sterling was now cautiously optimistic that Balla was for real. As the call finished, Goldman could not wait to tell his boss how impressed he was with the way he slipped in the question regarding Israel.

"You've got some big balls asking the chief about the last time he's been in Israel! This guy has me thinking he can do this."

Elliot, with faith that his instincts were right, told Mark to personally drive the package to the international courier's offices. He reiterated the importance of obtaining a receipt. He told him to be absolutely certain that the parcel would be delivered within two days or less. Sterling expressed to Mark that they were now obligated to play the game hard. They needed to see if the Nigerians were for real. The ball was now in their court. There would be nothing further to do for the next four days except wait for Solomon's fax.

Chapter 5

The international courier service representative in Lagos, Nigeria, knew exactly where to deliver the package. It was the only new high-rise office building near central Lagos. The area was known as Tinubu Square. Many government office buildings were in close proximity. The most impressive and important structure in the zone was the Central Bank of Nigeria. The Central Bank was equivalent to the Federal Reserve Bank in the United States. In Nigeria, the Central Bank was the second most powerful government agency, subordinate only to the military dictator. Its structure resembled a fortress with high iron picket fences. There were military soldiers everywhere the eye could see.

After passing private security guards at the ground level of the building complex where Chief Balla's offices were located, the courier entered the elevator and traveled to the 20th floor. The courier spotted the receptionist and handed the attractive young black woman Sterling's package. She signed for its receipt and the large envelope was quickly dispatched to Balla's private office. Balla's male assistant, who had previously been alerted as to the urgency of this package, interrupt Balla, who was in conference with David Solomon. Balla stopped cold his discussion and concentrated solely on the opening of Sterling's parcel. He paused, then stared at Solomon.

"Our mission has begun," Balla stated with a simper.

Solomon, a tall, handsome black man in his late thirties, observed intensely. He was well-known among his colleagues as the best dressed individual in the building. He thrived on wearing custom tailored British suits. Everyone in the facility knew that he traveled to London on business six times a year. The running rumor was that his sole mission was to return with the latest suits for Balla and himself. His colleagues considered him arrogant. Perhaps it was all the money he was making, or maybe it was due to the fact that Balla trusted him implicitly. There was no doubt that Solomon radiated with high self-esteem.

"My dear friend David Solomon, you are about to add to your fortune," Balla expressed with a coy, big smile.

"From your facial expression, we seem to have enrolled as our patron Mr. Elliot Sterling," Solomon stated with confidence.

"Yes, you are correct, my young Solomon."

"Shall we officially place him into the syndicate?" asked Solomon.

Balla thought for a moment, then responded, "Not under our normal procedures. I want this account managed differently. First, you are dealing with America. Second, you must recognize that this man, Sterling, is very smart. Our sources inform us that he is only vulnerable to our unscrupulous deception due to his deep financial stress. Handle him carefully. Do not deliver Sterling to the syndicate without first meticulously briefing each syndicate member who he will interact with. Prior to entering data into the main computer system with the syndicate, be certain to bargain for much higher fees for ourselves regarding Mr. Sterling and this account. Remember, Sterling Development Company promises to bring great rewards to our mischievous friends in the network. You must move with lightning speed to make your arrangements with our people at Central Bank. David, complete this prank quickly, as we must move on to new prey."

"Apparently, Chief Balla, you respect Mr. Sterling. I might add that you sound abundantly cautious. More so than ever before. Yet I will respect your instincts and will promptly take action on your instructions."

As Solomon departed Balla's luxurious office, he started to realize that this would not be a typical scam.

There was a reason why Balla was insisting on a 'meticulous briefing.' Benzal Oil Ltd. was a multi-billion-dollar annual revenue firm. It was organized solely to mask the true underlying identity of a corrupt, powerful syndicate. They occupied all 20 floors of the building. Their tentacles of corruption reached throughout Nigeria. Balla's screening requirement would include over 800 employees, plus corrupt officials from the Central Bank, the National Petroleum Company, and the ruling military dictatorship.

Solomon returned to his office and decided to jot down, on a yellow legal pad, all the people and strategies required for this assignment. Mr. Sterling was first on his list. He circled his name twice. He understood that Balla did not want anyone to underestimate Sterling. All the gathered intelligence on Sterling pointed in one direction. He's brilliant, but facing bankruptcy. The only clear thought running through Solomon's mind was to make sure that their staggering offer of money became so seductive, and so real, that Sterling would have no choice but to fall for the Nigerian hoax.

Solomon decided that the code name for this operation would be 'SCAM SEDUCTION.' He instantly wrote this code name in all caps at the top of his legal pad, adding two exclamation points. Solomon was ready to go to work.

The syndicate was structured fundamentally as an American corporation. It had a chief executive officer, retired General Uzman Peters, along with several vice presidents and directors. Each of the in-house lawyers was Harvard educated. The computer system was linked to the Central Bank server.

Although Benzal fronted as an oil company, it effectively functioned as a corrupt international banking institution. They had complete capacity to conduct international bank-to-bank wire transfers with a click of a computer demand. Each of their accountants had achieved finance degrees from the London School of Economics.

The syndicate understood that their opportunity to conduct 'business' with targeted victims like Sterling depended on their ability to demonstrate the syndicate's true working relationship with the current government. They needed to show how credible it was for them to partner with the government and transfer staggering sums of money with ease. To that end, a full office floor was dedicated solely to government liaison. Each of the employees in this division was previously in the Nigerian government, and some were former high-ranking Nigerian officials. These men came from either the ruling military party, the Nigerian National Petroleum Corporation, or the Central Bank. They clearly understood the day-to-day operations and mechanics of running the Federal Republic of Nigeria. There was constant close social interaction between the civilian members of the syndicate and the members of the ruling military officials.

The word 'gratification' was unwritten code for 'bribe.' There was not a day that went by without significant bribes being paid to these government officials. Gratifications in the form of money and precious gifts to civil servants had become a way of life in Nigeria. The syndicate's accountants had arranged for personal bank accounts for these officials all over the world. The officials would maintain fictitious names associated with bank accounts set up in cities such as London, Switzerland, and even New York City. The top priority for the syndicate was to make certain that key members of the ruling party were each multi-millionaires.

As Solomon continued to sketch notes on his legal pad, he kept thinking about the inter-workings of the network and his colleagues. This led him to plan how he would be able to control the taskforce leaders. Their work covered everything from private investigators to overseeing the creation of phony passports. They even had a team leader charged with staging meetings with government impostors. When Solomon noted that the taskforce ran a state-of-the-art print shop, located in the basement of the building, he marked a big red star next to this note to remind him to use this facility as needed. Any official government document, real or fake, could be reproduced in a matter of minutes. He understood how important this shop and its leader would be to him concerning the Sterling project.

The entire third floor of the building was dedicated to a sophisticated computer system. This floor was run by a former IBM employee. He was an MIT graduate and had spent a decade as a young man living in the United States learning the latest technology. Since the computer system was the best in all of Nigeria, the government often used their hardware. The syndicate charged no fee for such use, but the residual paid handsome dividends.

The head of the Central Bank of Nigeria maintained the title of governor. Of course, the network kept outstanding relations with the governor. The syndicate had arranged for several offices and a conference room, located in the Central Bank's compound, for their exclusive use. The rent was one million dollars per year, paid personally to the governor. It was well worth it, because all the victims of their various worldwide scam operations would inevitably be escorted into these offices. These preys would then mistakenly associate the syndicate as having been sanctioned by the Central Bank, and thus duped.

As Solomon continued to write, the notes rekindled his memory as to how elaborate and powerful the syndicate had actually become. For all practical purposes, the network had been granted tacit approval by the rogue Nigerian government to divert foreign contractors' payments. Benzal's scheme was simple. First, they would carefully examine government computers with the goal of locating legitimately awarded contracts they could over-invoice. This would follow by arranging for naive foreign contractors to become beneficiaries of fantastic sums of money to be hypothetically transferred into their accounts. Once in the foreigners' accounts, the funds would be split accordingly.

This was a dream for the foreign contractor, until they would be asked to put up money due to certain obstacles, such as taxes or governmental gratification. Reluctantly, the foreigner, now seduced by the delusion of receiving tens of millions of dollars, would cooperate, only to be deceived. This method was remarkably successful, for the syndicate and Solomon had decided that this would be the model that he would use to defeat Sterling.

Benzal, doing business in other names, such as the Nigerian National Petroleum Corporation, was fraudulently operating internationally with great success. They had recently made a serious strategic decision to expand the scam into America. These masterful criminals needed their best 'accounts officer' assigned to the Sterling case. Penetrating the lucrative United States market would be complicated, so the stakes were high. This is precisely why Chief Balla had handpicked Mr. Solomon.

It became clear to Solomon that the only way he could control the syndicate's information flow was by selecting an assistant. This man would help Solomon sanitize the network's dealings with Sterling.

He required an assistant who was very familiar with American business dealings. Who would take direction? His ego would need to subordinate to Solomon's orders. Yes, he had to be exceedingly intelligent, yet practical. His knowledge base regarding how the network operated was imperative. He also needed someone who was immediately available to dedicate the exhausting amount of time necessary for this complicated assignment.

Solomon knew that his assistant would be found somewhere within the computer database. He rapidly moved from his office to the computer floor. The security on this floor was tight. Solomon flashed his clearance credentials at the armed guard, then pressed his right thumb into the security scanner at the checkpoint access and was cleared to enter. Cameras were everywhere, since the area stored some of the country's top-secret information. Solomon had once described this area to a friend as similar to an American documentary film he had once seen concerning the NASA Houston Space Command and Control Center.

Solomon described his 'assistant' challenge to the manager in charge. Together they walked over to a personnel computer. The required profile was fed into a data processing system. Within moments, the candidate for 'assistant' was handed to Solomon. This included a photo and a five-page summary regarding the background and credentials of Stanley Roberts. Solomon quickly reviewed the information. Although he had never met nor worked with Roberts, he appeared perfect for the job.

It was time to meet Mr. Roberts. He thanked the manager and departed to the third floor.

Solomon walked directly to Robert's office. There sat a young black man with wire-rim glasses at his desk studying a contract document.

"Are you Stanley Roberts?" Solomon politely asked.

"Yes, and are you David Solomon?" Roberts responded with a slight grin.

"Now how do you know that?"

Roberts responded, "I make it my business to know who's the fastest rising star in our network."

Solomon, now very intrigued, said, "Are you available for an assignment as my aide?"

Without any hesitation, Roberts answered, "I'd consider it my patriotic duty. When do I start?"

Solomon answered, "Don't you want to know more about the venture?"

"As long as you are involved, Mr. Solomon, it doesn't matter to me!"

"Well, Stanley, it involves America."

"You wouldn't be talking to me if it didn't involve the United States. I'm certain you've read my profile. I have a combined law degree and MBA from Stanford University in California. I love America. One day, I wish to live with my family in America."

"Enjoy success with me on this assignment, and the syndicate will be very pleased. Maybe you'll get to America sooner than you think. I will make arrangements to free you from your current responsibilities. Report to my office tomorrow morning at 8:00 AM. I'll brief you in great detail as to our mission."

The next morning, Roberts arrived with great anticipation. Solomon was ready for him. He had developed a chart to help describe the network with clearer precision. Solomon recognized that Roberts could not do his job without first understanding how the syndicate actually functioned and who possessed the power to make final decisions. He needed to know who Solomon trusted and whom to withhold certain information from. There was a security risk in disclosing this sensitive data, but Solomon had determined that there was no choice.

Next, Solomon had formulated a thorough background file regarding Sterling and his troubled company. He then demonstrated precisely to Roberts the role he would play in this plan. They would spend the next three days working on Solomon's game plan. By the end of these 14-hour-a-day sessions, they would be prepared to make contact with the target, Elliot Sterling.

"You have learned swiftly, Stanley."

"I have a good mentor," Roberts replied.

Solomon said, "No, you have a photographic memory."

"Ever since I was a child. How did you detect it?"

Solomon, who was beginning to view Roberts as a protege, responded and said, "You absorb details like a sponge. Why doesn't your computer profile advise of this fact?"

"No one ever asked, except you."

"Stanley, are you mentally and physically prepared for this assignment?"

"Yes, Mr. Solomon, I am."

With confidence, Solomon stated, "We must now go and inform Chief Abba Balla that we have prepared for success."

As the three men sat in Balla's office, Solomon began to brief Balla on his well-designed strategy.

Roberts did not make one sound as the chief listened intently. At the end of the presentation, Balla looked at Solomon and simply stated, "Brilliant!" He agreed with all of the fundamentals of his plan of action. His only concern was Roberts' inexperience. He reminded Solomon of the importance of penetrating the American 'market' and his consistent concern for Sterling's sophistication.

Solomon vehemently defended Roberts' intellect and vast American expertise. He informed Balla that Sterling's university degree was from Stanford and that Roberts was a Stanford graduate. Solomon assured the chief that Roberts was the right man to assist him and together they would successfully accomplish their mission. Balla looked Solomon squarely in his eyes and said, "I trust you like my son. Go and accomplish your work."

Balla had given his blessing to the plan, along with a reluctant approval of Roberts. It was now time to contact Sterling. As the two were walking back to Solomon's office, Roberts was advised that their mission would commence immediately. A call would be placed to Sterling at 5:00 PM Lagos time. This would be 9:00 AM in Los Angeles. Roberts understood the importance of this communication and acknowledged that he was ready.

At precisely 5:00 PM, Solomon touched the automatic speed-dial he had programmed with Sterling's telephone number. Balla had provided him with the telephone number directly to Sterling's private home office. Within an instant, Sterling's phone was ringing.

"Yes," Sterling answered.

"I am David Solomon, an entrusted associate of Chief Abba Balla. I am in urgent need to speak with Mr. Elliot Sterling."

"You're speaking with him."

"Please be advised that Chief Balla has confirmed all arrangements to pay your contract fund. I am managing its release."

Sterling, hiding his emotions, said, "Well, that's good news. When are you going to pay?"

"The government officials at the Central Bank of Nigeria are preparing to immediately release $100 million. You must personally travel to Lagos, where you will sign before a government notary the final contract document. The signing will take place at the Central Bank and will be witnessed by a high-level Central Bank official."

"I have to what?" Sterling reacted with disgust.

"We apologize for this inconvenience. Both Chief Balla and I have appealed to the highest authorities. It is absolutely necessary for you to come. If you cannot travel to Lagos immediately, we will retract your name and cancel this contract," Solomon stated with firm conviction.

"I was never advised by Chief Balla of this requirement. Sounds to me that you are unable to perform. Why don't you tell the chief to call me directly?"

"Chief Balla is in Abuja, the new capital of Nigeria. He is engaged in an important political mission. For internal security reasons, you will no longer communicate with him. I can assure you that your contract fund is approved and ready for transfer. The international remittance department at the Central Bank reviewed your file. They found that the contract was unsigned by the principal. The official handling the file stopped the payment. We have arranged for a significant gratification to this civil servant. You must understand that the file must be in perfect order prior to the release of funds, especially with contract funds the size of yours. The moment you sign, the file will be in order. The contract is paid that same day. So, Mr. Sterling, shall we cancel with you or proceed?"

Sterling answered, raising his voice, "I'm glad you give me options. What the hell choice do I have?"

"Is your answer yes?"

"The answer is yes, under protest! You make sure and tell Balla that I'm very aggravated!"

"We sincerely regret this inconvenience. We will have you in and out of the country quickly. Tomorrow, you will receive a fax transmittal outlining the details of your trip, along with further instructions. After you have reviewed it, please contact me at any hour. I will provide you with my private cellular phone number."

"I sure hope you're not wasting my time," Sterling said with a contentious intonation.

"Let me put it to you this way. If you do not arrive in Lagos, as promised, you will have wasted mine. Please look for my fax. It is an honor to work with you, Mr. Sterling. I look forward to meeting such a distinguished American businessman. Good-bye for now."

Chapter 6

It was becoming a pattern. Elliot was finding it very difficult to sleep. He was anxious in bed the entire night. So as to not wake Felicia, he spent most of the darkness of the long night pacing the corridors of his home. Sterling was uncomfortable with Solomon's call. The rules of the game had switched. A trip to Nigeria felt risky. Perhaps even life threatening. Compounding his restlessness was the unexpected bank meeting he was demanded to attend in the morning. The bank was prematurely threatening to 'call' his loans due. They had taken the position that Sterling's financial statements, and specifically his net worth, were no longer accurate, due to the enormous downward shift in California's real estate values. The adverse tumble in home values was eroding the bank's confidence in Elliot's ability to realistically repay his loans.

The pressure seemed to be mounting by the minute. It was 5:00 AM and time to start his day. Instead of worrying himself to death, he decided to be aggressive with the bank. If he threatened the bank with legal action, Elliot was certain he would prevail in holding the loan agreements in place.

He knew he would only use this card if necessary. With this legal strategy in place, Elliot Sterling could now deal from a position of strength at the meeting. As for his unease with Solomon, he simply decided to wait for the fax. Thereafter, he would confer with Mark and make a determination as to the next step, if any.

By 7:00 AM, Elliot was in his office. Mark would be there at any moment to brief him on the latest developments concerning the bank's threats. He kept observing the fax machine. Nothing came through. As he was in deep concentration, Goldman entered the room.

"Good morning, boss. You look like you're lost in thought."

"Mark, to tell you the truth, I feel like there's a double-barrel shotgun pointed at me. One barrel is Nigeria, the other is our lender."

"Well, let me temporarily relieve you of one of those barrels. I reviewed all the loan documents. There's no way Reno and company can call in those loans. Their threat is based on declining real estate values directly tied to our asset erosion. That's total bullshit! There's nothing in the agreement that gives them any rights to pull the trigger. Our lawyers did a good job with that part of the documents. So, go ahead and tell them to shove the shotgun straight up their asses."

"I see it the same way, Mark. But that doesn't solve the problem. The bottom line is that their assessment is right. I know it, you know it. We can stop them for now, but they're going to have us up against the wall within a few months. I feel like the walls are starting to close in on me. Regrettably, it's becoming clearer. The only way out is Nigeria, yet I'm getting mixed messages from these sons-of-bitches."

"What mixed messages?" Mark questioned with a puzzled look.

"I'll bring you up to date after we meet with our paranoid banker friends. Tell me what else is going on with these guys."

Mark went on to advise Elliot that the company lawyers had confirmed their shared opinion regarding the loan agreements. From Goldman's reconnaissance regarding the lender, he had learned that the bank was about to announce a significant net quarter loss. Wall Street rating agencies were moments away from declaring a downgrade of the bank's credit rating. Federal regulators were putting enormous pressure on the lender to maintain large 'loss loan reserves.'

It was clear that the bank's stockholders were about to lose money. Regrettably, Sterling Development was on the minds of those in the important upper echelon of the bank.

After Mark's briefing, Elliot had drawn two conclusions. First, there was no way the financial institution could 'call' in his loans. At least, not at this time. Second, due to many non-performing loans, the bank itself was in trouble. This fact was causing the lender to become uncharacteristically less tolerant towards Sterling's firm.

He now understood why the bank was prematurely requesting this meeting. Effectively, the meeting was nothing more than a stern second warning shot. They had no intentions whatsoever on shooting to kill. Based on this reasoning, Elliot strategically decided that the meeting should be canceled. He instructed Goldman to arrange for a conference call in lieu of the physical meeting. The excuse would be Elliot's 'stomach flu.'

Mark returned to Elliot's office at 10:00 AM. He informed Elliot that the bankers had accepted the flu story and were awaiting his call. Elliot took a deep breath, then placed the call directly to Paul Reno's special private line.

"Is that you, Elliot? How the hell are you?"

"I've had better days."

"Well, listen. I sure appreciate you making this call. We need to talk."

"OK, talk."

"Elliot, the bank doesn't question your will to pay. They question your ability to pay. We have absolute trust in your character, but you can't pay us with good intentions. We're in deep shit here with the Feds. We're dropping fast with the stockholders. Before you know it, Moody's Investors Services, Standard & Poor's, and the rest of those pit bulls will have us downgraded. Listen carefully to me. The chairman of my bank wants to call your loans!"

"Look, Paul, I've got a major international transaction in the works. You know the size of my deal. It's been going on quietly for years. Let's keep it confidential for now. Trust me as you always have. You'll get your money."

Reno asks, "Is this so-called international deal on your financial statement?"

"No, and let's keep it that way for now."

"I'll keep the bank off your back for a while. You just make fucking sure you pay us! Thanks for the call, Elliot. Take care of that flu."

Just like that, a short-term solution was arranged. Mark was awestruck by how Elliot had mastered control away from the bank and right back into his hands. The magic act was easy. Elliot was using his well-respected reputation to hold off his creditor, even though there was nothing concrete about the Nigerian contract. Yet it was de facto Elliot's secret weapon.

He knew he had made a commitment to resolve his financial crises with a gun that just might not have any bullets. It was evident, David Solomon must perform.

It was now time to update Mark about Nigeria. This was going to be a serious conversation. Elliot quickly revealed that he was required to travel to Nigeria, based on the call he had with Solomon.

Mark immediately said, "Have you lost your fucking mind!?"

Elliot went on to dissect with Mark the conversation he had with Solomon over the phone. It was now very apparent to Mark that Lagos would be in the travel plans of Elliot Sterling.

There was simply no other option. The intense discussion had shifted to one glaring problem. Balla had met Beringer, not Sterling. Should Sterling advise Solomon that Beringer was dead, and Sterling was his designated successor?

The inherent risk could lead to a canceled deal. Elliot could not afford to take that risk. After an exhaustive analysis, they jointly concluded that there would be no such disclosure. Solomon had clearly informed Elliot that Balla was deeply involved in 'an important political mission' and was out of the picture. All of the contract documents were supposedly in Elliot's name. He had been promised to be in and out of Nigeria quickly. Assuming that Balla would not be present to identify Elliot, before any one knew better, the money would be transferred. Should the issue arise, he would deal with it while in Nigeria. Both agreed that this would be the best method to manage the risk.

Mark then attempted to speak about the physical danger of traveling to Lagos. Elliot avoided the issue. As Mark began to discuss the subject again, the awaited Solomon fax began transmitting.

The fax consisted of four pages. Goldman recovered the fax and immediately made a copy. He handed it to Elliot. They both painstakingly read each word. Elliot looked at Mark, and with an agonizing expression on his face, began summarizing the important points in the fax. Solomon had acknowledged 'receipt of the documents' sent to Balla. He went on to state that, 'Every communication will go through the person of David Solomon.' The purpose of the 'mandatory' visit to Nigeria was to sign the 'Fund Release Authority.' Without personally signing this document, 'The Central Bank would not release the funds.' The fax reconfirmed to Elliot that 'the transfer credit to your nominated bank account would occur immediately after your signature.'

Execution of the document would take place at the Central Bank of Nigeria and arrangements had been made for the Federal Ministry of Internal Affairs to issue a visa document allowing Elliot 'special entry into Nigeria.'

Elliot now turned to the suspicious and nauseating part of the fax. He was requested to 'hand-deliver USD 35,000 in cash' to Solomon upon his arrival. Additionally, Elliot was instructed to bring 'six fine gold watches.'

The fax continued with, 'The individuals involved in this transaction are retiring from their various offices and are going into politics. They require the contract funds to enable them to execute campaigns. Due to life-threatening security reasons, you must maintain the strictest degree of confidentiality. You're the person they are relying on to facilitate this arrangement.' It concluded by stating, 'Your meeting on October 17th at the Central Bank of Nigeria is hereby confirmed.'

As Elliot finished the summary, Mark angrily said, "What kind of stupid bullshit is this? They force you to travel all the way to Timbuktu, risk your life, hand over $35,000 in cash, and give these motherfuckers 6 gold watches! You have to be out of your mind to be playing ball with these guys. First, they seduce you with a bunch of money, then they start scamming you for whatever they can get out of you. Elliot, this isn't going to end well. You got to listen to me on this!"

Elliot had never quite seen Mark react to anything with such passion. He knew that his friend was very concerned. They both appeared somewhat dazed. Mark, clearly, was seeing this as a scam, and Elliot was confused. He needed to believe in this deal, but he understood that Mark probably had it right. Elliot's head was spinning with whether the Nigerian venture was just a dream or an opportunity of a lifetime.

As Elliot poured Mark and himself a shot of his best tequila, he said, "I don't know for sure whether we're coming or going with these guys. All I know is that the bank has a loaded gun at my head." As he poured them both a second shot of tequila, Elliot started calmly justifying what Solomon was asking for.

"Look, I can live with the damn fax, Mark. Our only challenge is their request for the $35,000 and the gold watches. Look on the bright side, they obviously have serious connections directly with the government. There's no other way to arrange for my entry visa."

Mark, seeing where Elliot was going with his line of thinking, said, "That, plus they're confirming their ability to get you into the Central Bank."

Mark continued warming up to the fax by asking, "Why do you think Balla is out?"

Elliot, now regaining his focus, answered, "He's the guy going into politics. Apparently, Balla can't afford to openly associate with this kind of clandestine business venture."

Elliot had decided to roll the dice. He would proceed forward with Solomon's requests and began justifying to Mark why he had made this decision. "The money and the watches must be their way of conducting business. My friends in Mexico have told me for decades about how gifts go a long way with government officials. The Mexicans call this practice 'la mordida,' interpreted in English as 'the bite.' It's the grease that skids the wheels. In America, gifts come in many different forms, including 'legitimate' campaign contributions. If we're going to transact business in Nigeria, we must remember that we're playing by Nigerian customs and rules."

Mark had known his boss and friend long enough. Elliot Sterling was going to Nigeria. No one could convince him differently. It was now time to concentrate on the logistics of this high-stakes trip, including where to purchase the watches. As Mark turned towards Elliot to express his support, Elliot interrupted him and said, "I know you have serious reservations about this deal. Believe me, they're not more than my own. Tomorrow morning, we'll call Solomon. I'll drill him on the unorthodox cash and watch request. Regrettably, the bank is ready to tear my head off. So, the only way I can plan our future is to go to Nigeria and determine the truth. Mark, I need your support on this."

"Boss, I want you to understand that if you should ever determine that it was in our best interest for me to travel to hell and back, the only question I'd have for you is what day you would want me to leave.

We'll call 'King Solomon' in the morning. In the meantime, I'll figure out where to buy the cheapest wholesale gold watches in LA."

The remainder of Elliot's evening would be dedicated to his lovely wife, Felicia. They had planned to dine together at home. Felicia, as usual, had several subjects to discuss with her husband. The most pressing topic was the magnificent 'surprise' party she had been planning for months. The party was set for October 10th, just seven days prior to Elliot's anticipated travel to Lagos. The list of guests had grown to 200.

Felicia asked Elliot if it would be acceptable to him to play the silly role of acting surprised. Or perhaps she should just leak to their friends that her husband had became aware of the party. Without deliberation, Elliot told his wife that he would 'play the game and act amazed.' As long as this event was to continue as a 'surprise,' Felicia opted to tell her husband no further details. She simply instructed him to 'show up at 8:00 PM and have the time of your life.'

Felicia could not hold back her excitement at that moment. She jumped out of her chair and embraced her husband tightly. She didn't just feel passion for Elliot, she sincerely adored him. These were two people deeply in love.

They sat on the couch in their living room kissing and caressing, then talking for hours. This was precisely the type of evening a husband and wife dreamed about. Yet it was time for Elliot to inform Felicia of his plans to travel to Nigeria. He wanted this night to carry on forever, but he promised himself to inform her this night, so he did.

"Elliot, I advised you to throw that phony letter away! I can assure you it is not genuine. Whoever these people are, their true motive is to deceive you!"

Elliot snapped back by saying, "Not any more than my American bankers and all those politicians that I support."

Felicia, who was now in tears and genuinely frightened, pleaded with her husband, "Elliot, you must call this trip off. No amount of money is worth your life!"

"Felicia, sweetheart, you know there's nothing in this world I wouldn't do for you. I love you with all my heart. I've trusted your instincts from the first day I met you. By the same token, you've trusted mine, and you know what, together we've done very well. I want you to understand that this trip is something I need to do. With God as my witness, I'll return to you as safely as the day I leave. Maybe even with a little more money. Felicia, I'm asking you for your support. I need your backing and your confidence." Elliot was now tightly holding his wife. As Felicia was wiping away tears from her swollen eyes, she faced her husband and said, "If you come back dead, I'll kill you."

Elliot cherished his wife. He was confident that she would trust him. Yet he clearly understood that she could be right. As Elliot blocked out all his thoughts, he began to slowly undress his wife. This was a person he treasured. She was the most beautiful woman he had ever encountered.

The next morning, armed with the endorsement of his wife, Elliot was now prepared to confirm with David Solomon his intentions to travel to Lagos. Mark was already sitting in Elliot's office.

Mark reiterated that he was comfortable with the fact that Solomon had enough governmental clout to send Elliot the official entry visa. He reminded Elliot how important it was to cross-examine Solomon over the cash and watch request. Elliot nodded that he would and dialed Solomon's mobile number. The now familiar British accent could be heard.

"I am David Solomon."

"Mr. Solomon, this is Elliot Sterling."

"Oh, yes, Mr. Sterling. I'm pleased to hear from you. Our people have prepared well for you. The Central Bank meeting is confirmed for October 17th. Have you made your preparations?"

"I will, after you answer this question."

"And what is that, my good friend?"

"Why would you ask me to bring $35,000 in cash and 6 gold watches? I find that request totally out of order and very suspicious. In fact, I'm very surprised you would demand something like this."

"I'm pleased that you have asked this question. In Nigeria, the money and the watches are a part of our culture. We call this 'gratification.' When you meet with various public servants, our custom is that you hand them a fine watch as a gesture of goodwill for the official acts they transact on your behalf. The immense dollar amount of our business requires a gold watch, or the gift will be considered an insult. I will guide you as to when and who is to receive these watches. As for cash, you will pay this to the official at the Central Bank after you sign the release document. Our people have invested well over one million dollars regarding this venture. We are having a difficult time currently obtaining any more American dollars. Your minimal investment shows your good faith. Be assured that, upon contract payment, you will be reimbursed for the value of the watches, the cash contribution, plus your travel expenses. Now, please do not ask any more questions!"

Elliot bought into the explanation and said, "Send me the entry visa. I'll arrive in Lagos on the morning of the 17th. I'll fax you my itinerary. I'd appreciate you picking me up at the airport."

Solomon confirmed by stating, "I will personally be at the airport. Please inform your bankers to be on the alert for the money wire-transfer on the same date. I congratulate you on your decision. We will send you by fax the official visa and final instructions. I bid you farewell for now, Mr. Sterling, and may you have a safe trip."

Elliot Sterling had sealed his fate. He soon would be venturing to Lagos, Nigeria. A place he never expected to visit, not even in the remotest parts of his mind.

Chapter 7

All the final preparations for Elliot's 'surprise' party were in motion for this night's extravaganza.

Felicia had awoken early to orchestrate the important details of what she hoped would be a heartfelt and exciting 50th birthday celebration for the love of her life. Two weeks prior, she had delegated Mark to convince her husband to spend the night at their Malibu beach home before the party. She made Mark promise her that he would deliver Elliot back to Bel Air by 8:00 PM sharp the night of the party. Felicia felt relieved that she had dispatched Elliot to Malibu, allowing her to concentrate without distraction on the beautiful party she had been planning for so many months.

As Felicia stepped out onto her bedroom's balcony, she could see the impressive yellow tent now erected over the tennis court. She was very determined that the celebration about to take place underneath that spectacular tent was going to be an evening to remember. The first meeting of the day was with her high-priced event planner. She quickly slipped on some pink designer sweatpants and matching sweatshirt, threw her hair into a ponytail, and without any makeup, made her way to the kitchen to get some coffee.

Felicia and the event planner had never worked together, so it was important to review a long checklist to assure that the ambiance for party would be just right. They talked about the lighting, the dance floor, hors d'oeuvres, food stations, and pastries. Felicia emphasized that the three bar locations were to be stocked with nothing but the best liquor. The planner assured her that everything would be perfect, including the pace of the night, the seating arrangements, and all the gorgeous flowers. They went on to discuss where to strategically hang all the enlarged photos of Elliot that the planner insisted on displaying in order to make the night special for her husband.

As the meeting concluded to Felicia's satisfaction, the planner asked, "Will your husband want to say a few words?"

Felicia thought for a moment and answered, "Yes. Let's get him up there."

The planner agreed by stating, "It makes for a warm moment and your guests will appreciate hearing from him. What about you, do you want to say a few words?"

"No. The night is his."

As Felicia finished with the planner, her mobile phone rang. The screen displayed that a 'private' caller was on the line. She thought about whether to answer, then she did. The caller identified himself as an assistant to the mayor of Los Angeles, then confirmed that 'the mayor and his wife will be attending tonight's event. We're sorry for the late response, but the mayor has moved some things around and is looking forward to spending the evening with you and Mr. Sterling.'

Felicia responded by saying, "It's our honor, and thank you for the RSVP."

What Felicia was really thinking was how rude it was to respond at the last minute, and now she was faced with the Rubik's Cube of rearranging the seating. She really didn't want them sitting at their table. The whole night Elliot would be obligated to entertain the mayor! She decided to figure out what to do with the mayor later, because the manager for the hottest musical group in LA was waiting to meet with her.

This group had performed for the biggest movie stars in the city. She knew she was fortunate to have booked them for this gig. The manager had come to examine the stage and event setting. But, in all truth, he'd come to collect their enormous fee in advance. Although Felicia understood that she was paying substantially more money than what her husband would have ever approved, instinctively she knew that the music would make the party unforgettable. So, she pulled out her checkbook and wrote the manager a colossal check.

Her two daughters, Rose and Erica, were due to fly in from Stanford University within an hour, and even though she was incredibly busy, she had promised to pick them up at the airport. Although both girls were taking stressful mid-term tests, neither one of them were about to miss their dad's 50th birthday's party. They loved and admired their father very much, and looked forward to celebrating with their beloved parents.

As the afternoon was rapidly coming to an end, Felicia was hard at work, attending to the final minutiae of what was shaping up to be an affair to remember.

Conversely, Elliot and Mark had spent the day in Malibu, wearing bathing suits and working on their tans. Obviously, they could easily have spent the day discussing at great length the complex business matters facing the company, but instead, Mark made certain that his great friend was going to spend his birthday without any stress. At least for today.

As the two lay on their lounge chairs next to the kidney-shaped swimming pool overlooking the Pacific Ocean, Elliot began reminiscing about how quickly time had passed. He talked to Mark about how one of the most enjoyable times of his life was when they played Little League Baseball together as kids. He reminded Mark that he, and not Mark, had been selected to the All-Star team.

Mark looked at Elliot and revealed to him for the first time that, "I was so mad at you for making that team that I wanted to kick your ass! In fact, I cried about it."

Elliot, now laughing, said, "You fucking cried?"

"Yeah, I cried. But it wasn't because I didn't make the team, I just wanted to keep playing ball with you. I saw you as my only friend. The guy who was a lot smarter than me, but treated me as his equal. More athletic than everyone else. The guy who made me laugh. I just felt secure hanging around you, and I wanted that baseball summer to go on forever. I guess, it's been that way for me all these years."

Elliot felt blessed to have Mark in his life. The words that he had spoken sincerely touched Elliot.

He didn't view Mark as just a friend, he treasured him like a member of his family. As he turned his eyes towards Mark, he said what came to his mind at that moment, "I love you as my brother."

Mark responded with a simple comment, "I know."

As Elliot was getting up and out of his lounge chair, he looked at Mark with that charismatic Sterling smile and said, "Christ, you're such a pansy. I can't believe you cried!" They both burst out laughing.

Conscious of his promise to Felicia, Mark told Elliot it was time to take a shower and said, "Get dressed for tonight's big shindig. After all, you are the guest of honor." He went on to hint to Elliot that it would be smart to prepare a few words, "Because rumor has it that you might just be called on to address all those aristocratic guests your wife has arranged to come celebrate you getting older."

As they walked away from the pool and moved toward the residence, Mark reiterated what time they would depart for Bel Air. Elliot then mentioned to Mark that, in less than a week, he would be off to Lagos. He reminded Mark to buy the gold watches and prepare the $35,000. He went on to tell Mark that he expected the official entry visa from Solomon to arrive tomorrow, and that upon its receipt, Mark was to proceed and purchase the round-trip airline tickets.

It was 6:00 PM and time to depart for the party. Mark wanted to make sure they left early enough, in case they got stuck in the famous Los Angeles traffic. He knew Felicia would execute him if they arrived one minute after 8:00 PM.

As Mark was waiting in his black BMW, he spotted his friend walking towards the car. He instantly noticed how sharp Elliot was dressed, wearing a black custom-made silk shirt combined with an elegant navy-blue blazer. Elliot, who hated ties, was of course not wearing one. Mark had promised Felicia he would do his best to get him to wear one, but since Mark knew that he would lose that battle, he decided not to even try.

As Elliot opened the back door to place his exquisite coat on a hanger for the trip, Mark said, "You are dressed to perfection! Never seen you look better, Boss."

Elliot appreciated the comment but confessed that he just wanted to make sure that his wife would be proud of him. He went on to express how much he hated dressing up, especially at all those events where Felicia forced him to wear a tuxedo, which he refered to as a 'monkey suit.'

Midway back to Bel Air, Mark decided he was going to disclose to Elliot what had been on his mind the whole time they were in Malibu. As he turned down the radio, Mark advised Elliot, "I'm going with you to Lagos. There is no way I'm going to allow you to go to that hellhole yourself. And I'll tell something else, I'm not accepting 'no' for an answer, even if I pay for it myself!"

Elliot calmly reacted with, "I'm glad you have no option here. Look, Mark, it's risky enough for one of us to do this. I'm not going to drag you into harm's way. I'll just go and come back. Then we'll count the money and take a long vacation."

"Not this time, Boss. I'm going! I won't be able to live with myself if anything should ever happen. I won't be able to look at Felicia or your daughters. You're not going there by yourself. Not on my watch! Nothing more to talk about."

"You drive a hard bargain, tough guy. I'll tell you what. Let's just celebrate tonight. We'll have a few drinks together. You get in some slow dancing with that sweet girl of yours and I'll give you my decision tomorrow afternoon. Sound like a plan, Rambo?"

Mark understood that there wasn't going to be any further discussion regarding this subject, so he closed the conversation with, "I don't really know how to dance all that well, but I'll assure you of one thing. You're not taking that trip alone!"

As they arrived at the residence, Mark noticed they were about ten minutes early. The estate looked magnificent. The grounds were perfectly manicured and all the bright exterior lights made the home feel like a palace. Mark, as previously instructed by Felicia, pulled up under the porte cochere leading to the home, then used his cell phone to inform her, "The Eagle has landed."

Felicia, who was anxiously waiting for the call, answered on the first ring and immediately replied, "Go ahead and bring Elliot to the tent. As you enter, turn to your right, then look for me. Make sure you tell Elliot that there're a lot of people here tonight who love him and can't wait to celebrate with him."

Mark responded with a simple, "Will do."

As they made their way down to the tent, Elliot whispered to Mark, "Thanks for watching my back all these years. I want you to know how appreciative I am to have a friend as loyal and dependable as you. Let's not just go in there and celebrate my birthday. Let's also celebrate the great friendship we've endured for all these years!" As they approached the entrance to the tent, Elliot suddenly stopped walking, grabbed Mark, and with raw emotion, gave him a heartfelt bear hug.

Elliot entered the tent and briskly veered to the right. As he advanced towards his wife, he listened to more than 200 guests roar in heart-warming unison, "Surprise!" With that cue, Felicia's high-priced powerhouse band began performing and this elegant affair was off to a magnificent evening.

Felicia, who was dressed in an Oscar de la Renta premier black strapless gown with a signature bow draped artfully at the fitted waist, simply looked stunning. She immediately embraced the love of her life, and in the incredible emotion of the night, gave her husband a long, passionate kiss, to the great delight and wholehearted applause of their guests.

As Rose and Erica began swiftly walking towards their parents, Elliot became overwhelmed with a feeling of joy and pride for his family. He spontaneously wrapped his arms around his two beautiful daughters and his gorgeous wife, then continued an affectionate and remarkable group hug with the family he dearly loved. Once again, their guests broke out clapping with an enthusiastic show of approval. This was a moment that Elliot, Felicia, Rose, and Erica would never forget.

Suddenly, all of the guests naturally begin gravitating towards the specially-designed checkered black-and-white dance floor, as they were moved by the amazing sound of music and the festive, choreographed mood-lighting. As the dancing began, everyone was feeling the genuine electricity of the evening. What a night this promised to become!

After a whirlwind of dancing, the fashionably-attired guests began taking their seats to commence eating a first-class dinner. Elliot and Felicia graciously started moving from table to table thanking everyone for attending. The mayor and his wife were seated adjacent to Dr. and Mrs. Gregory Blanchard, a well-recognized cardiologist that Elliot and the mayor mutually visited. The mayor and doctor sincerely admired Elliot as they both stood to greet him with a warm hug.

The mayor, who was famous for not holding his liquor very well and telling stupid jokes, remarked, "I know why you sat me with Gregory. You want a heart doctor right next to me to ensure that I don't kick the bucket tonight after all this dancing, drinking, and fine food. Let's face it, if I'm not around, who the hell is going to get all those Sterling projects approved? Right, Greg?"

Elliot, who was thinking to himself what an idiot this guy was, simply smiled and politely laughed. Felicia, using her eyes, signaled that it was time to move on. As they returned to their table, Mark stood, tapped his champagne glass with a spoon to get everyone's attention, and said, "To the only boss I choose to recognize and to the finest man I have ever known, happy birthday, Elliot!" Then, without any prompt, Felicia's good friend Rachel stood up and encouraged everyone to sing 'happy birthday.'

When the band and guests jointly concluded their lively version of the song, everyone started energetically tapping their glasses, demanding, "Speech, speech, speech!"

Elliot understood he was not getting out of this moment without saying a few words, so he stood to the applause and gratification of his guests and began, "Love. Without it, you live without a soul. With it, you live vigorously. I have been very blessed to find it with Felicia and my daughters.

I feel it with other members of my family. I have found it with my friend, Mark Goldman. I have, throughout the years, felt a lot of love from each of you. I know that money can come and go. Believe me, when it's time to leave this earth, it's not the money you'll be thinking about, but the the people you love.

I want to thank my wife for creating such a beautiful event for me. I love you with all my heart.

I also want to thank Rose and Erica for making the effort to leave a very busy school schedule to celebrate with their 'old man.' I love both of you very much. Finally, I sincerely want to thank each of you for choosing to be here with me and my family on this joyous occasion. I truly love all of you!

Please enjoy the rest of the night, and by the way, you're all invited back here for my next 50th birthday party."

One by one, the guests began standing in ovation for what was perceived by everyone as words spoken from the heart. Elliot was moved by the reaction and expressed his gratitude by pounding his heart with his fist, then applauding right back to his guests. Felicia, who was holding back tears of joy, remained seated, beaming with pride for her husband. As Elliot made his way back to his seat, Felicia sentimentally hugged and kissed her husband, then whispered in his ear, "I will dance with you at your next 50th birthday party. I love you." This was the night Felicia had hoped to achieve.

Even though the night was getting late, no one left. The music kept playing and the dancing was non-stop. The ambiance radiated with high energy, for the fun-loving group in attendance seemed perfectly comfortable of keeping the night going. Felicia, who decided to take a break and check on her makeup, made her way towards the large powder room in the residence.

As Felicia approached the powder room, she overheard what sounded like Sonia Blanchard, the wife of Elliot's cardiologist, loudly saying to one of Felicia's acquaintances, "I'm glad Felicia is enjoying her little shindig tonight, because rumor has it that the bank will be the owners of this place by the end of the year. I just can't stand how she's always showing off how pretty she looks and how much money she thinks she has. What a pathetic phony."

As Sonia was literally finishing her comments, Felicia entered the room, much to the astonishment of Sonia and their mutual acquaintance. She calmly faced Sonia and said, "Well, as long as we seem to be discussing rumors, I hear from from your friends that your husband, the great and well-regarded Dr. Blanchard, is having the love affair of his life with that pretty, little young nurse he hired last year. In fact, I hear he bought her a condo in Beverly Hills with a cute, little sports car to put in the garage. Oh, by the way, rumor also has it that your husband is going to dump you and your loud mouth by the end of the year. Now, I want you to do me a big favor, get your little, boney ass out of my house, take your cheating husband with you, and don't ever come back here again!"

Felicia, feeling nauseated yet happy to get rid of this obnoxious and nasty person from her life, decided to take a seat in her house to collect herself. She knew there was truth to the pending financial crisis. But she also understood that her husband always found light at the end of the tunnel. Felicia kept it simple and maked the decision to have faith in Elliot. It was now time to get back to enjoying the beautiful night and not allow that despicable woman to ruin a remarkable evening. As Felicia slowly made her way back to the tent, she also decided that there would be no mention of what occurred in the powder room to her husband. In fact, the only issue left for her was to figure out how to inform Elliot that it was time to find a new cardiologist.

Felicia returned to her table to find Elliot, Rose, and Erica laughing out loud and asked, "What's so funny?"

Elliot attempted to explain but couldn't stop laughing. Rose tried, but she was giggling so hard that she couldn't do it either.

So, Erica just burst out saying, "Dr. Blanchard and a young blonde woman were sitting at his table just casually talking. All of a sudden, Sonia Blanchard makes her way from the dessert table towards her husband holding a big plate of chocolate mousse. Then, like a possessed lunatic, she dumps it on his head! We're all going into shock thinking that Dr. Blanchard is going to kill his wife, but instead he calmly wipes the mousse off his humiliated face, licks his fingers, and unexpectedly said, 'Mmmm, that tastes good.' After that, Sonia storms out leaving Dr. Blanchard sitting at the scene of the crime with chocolate mousse dripping from his head. Now that's something you don't see everyday!"

Felicia, who was grinning from ear to ear, reacted by saying, "What a waste of expensive chocolate mousse." Jointly, they all erupted into even more laughter. As this incredible party began wrapping up and all the hugs, kisses, and gracious good-byes came to an end, Elliot, along with his family, moved from the tent to their kitchen and made some hot chocolate.

They reminisced about how life has been good to the Sterling family and how fortunate they all were to have each other in their lives. Elliot thanked his wife for making his 50th birthday one of the most memorable times of his life. He went on to tell Felicia and his daughters how much he treasured each one of them and that he looked forward to enjoying the rest of his life celebrating wonderful family moments together.

For this instant, Elliot Sterling was the happiest man on the face of the earth, even though he faced monumental challenges.

Chapter 8

The next morning, Elliot was determined more than ever to face his vast business battles. His family, friends, and the community that admired him so dearly dictated that he create a solution. The enormous success of the party served as a reminder of the kind of social disgrace he and his family would face, should he be unable to find a speedy recovery. So, he decided to start this day early in his office dedicated toward making arrangements to travel to Nigeria. As he entered his office, he immediately noticed that his fax had several pages waiting. The pages were from Solomon, which included the official entry visa to Nigeria, along with final instructions, as promised. Sterling knew that soon Mark would show up at his office demanding to accompany him to Lagos.

He realized that it was probably a good idea to have someone travel with him, if for no other reason than to witness the proceedings at the Central Bank. Mark was concerned for Elliot's safety, but Elliot was more concerned about having a witness able to testify as to the legitimacy of his dealings in the event the transaction failed. At least, Elliot would have a credible source to help explain why he went and what officially transpired in the Nigerians' government offices.

After an hour of deliberation, he concluded that the right person to travel with him would be his Harvard-educated corporate attorney, Paul Norman. Elliot knew that Mark would not approve, but this was the right decision. Out of respect for Mark, he would wait to first inform Mark before advising Solomon that a second visa would be required.

As Elliot had anticipated, Mark arrived bright and early to his office and commented, "Best party I have ever attended. Felicia is amazing. Every detail was perfect, with the exception of the husband and wife Blanchard comedy show. I'm not sure who's more nuts, your kooky doctor friend or his wacko wife. That was hilarious! Did you get the scoop on what's going on there?"

Elliot responded with a simple, "Looks like some kind of a complicated love triangle, but don't quote me on that. Now, to a more important matter. I agree with you that I should not travel alone to Lagos.

After thinking this through in detail, I have decided to travel with Paul Norman. He'll be able to review any paperwork they throw my way and serve as a great legal witness if we should ever need one in the future. It's better you stay here running our operations, and if the Nigerians do fund, I will need you here to trace and monitor receipt of the money. Normally, a wire transfer of this magnitude initiates with a 'test wire' going to the nominated bank. I want our bank to speak only to you regarding wire confirmation. Additionally, you will be the only one authorized to relay any further instructions to the bank that I may require you to while I'm in Nigeria. I don't want anyone from our company to hear about this deal, so you need to be my man on the ground right here. This is the best way to go."

Like the good soldier that he was, Mark's only comment was, "Understood. I hope Paul doesn't catch some cholera disease. He's not exactly a cowboy. He's accustomed to that Ivy League comfort zone, but there's no doubt he's as good as it gets when it comes to the legal stuff. I'll take care of the homefront, you and Norman go get us the money!"

With that conversation now settled with Mark, there were two things left to do. First, obtain an entry visa to Nigeria for the attorney. Second, meet with Norman and inform him that he was the lucky guy chosen to travel to Lagos with the boss. It was determined that once Solomon agreed to issue the second visa, it would be time to meet with Norman. Elliot decided that he would call Solomon directly in lieu of sending a fax requesting the second visa.

Impulsively, Elliot dialed Solomon's private mobile phone number. The call was answered by Solomon's assistant on the fourth ring. Elliot said, "I'd like to speak to David Solomon. This is Elliot Sterling." The man who answered the phone responded by indicating that he must interrupt Mr. Solomon, who was in a meeting.

Shortly thereafter, Solomon answered, "I'm sure you have received my instructions and the entry visa by now. Am I correct, Mr. Sterling?"

Elliot acknowledged that he had received both, but he went on to inform Solomon, saying, "My attorney, Mr. Norman, will be traveling with me to Lagos. I would appreciate if you would arrange a second visa for Mr. Norman and fax it to me immediately."

Elliot, who had anticipated resistance from Solomon, was surprised when Solomon responded with, "You will have Mr. Norman's entry visa within 48 hours. Please fax me the correct spelling for Mr. Norman's full name, along with his traveling passport particulars. We welcome both of you, and I will be certain to arrange a separate hotel room for your attorney. Now, if there is nothing further, I must go back and attend to my business.

We shall meet soon. All the best to you, Mr. Sterling."

Mark could sense that Elliot was uncomfortable with the call and asked, "Why the troubled look on your face? Sounds like you got what you asked for."

Elliot remained silent for a brief moment, then responded with, "Yes, I got Norman's visa, but Solomon didn't even ask one question as to why I was bringing Norman. In fact, he didn't even care that another witness, especially an attorney, would have knowledge of this discreet contract. I'm puzzled as to how quickly Solomon accepted that someone other than myself would be going to Lagos. Perhaps I should be satisfied that he doesn't care that I am bringing my attorney. It does give me comfort that Solomon is not worried that an American attorney would be reviewing documents and asking questions. What throws up the 'red flag' is his total disregard for my distrust in them by bringing Norman and breaking their important code of discretion. Solomon's response just doesn't feel right."

Mark is concerned as to how Elliot's words were painfully spoken and said, "Look, Boss, let's run with the idea that if Solomon was conducting a scam on us, there's no way in living hell he'd want your attorney present to witness firsthand the entire fucking crime. He seems to be sending you a message that he understands why bringing an attorney is perfectly reasonable. We probably should be feeling grateful that he's fine with your request. We either have faith that this deal is going to work out or we don't. If this is a scam, we'll find out soon. It's going to cost us some money and some time, but we'll soon find out the truth. My concern is that you come back in one piece, even if you have to leave Norman behind as a hostage. Just messing with you regarding Norman."

Elliot, who now has traded that serious look on his face with a smile after hearing the Norman's quip, went on to say, "I'm not disagreeing with you, but my gut keeps telling me that Solomon doesn't want to say or do anything that would stop me from traveling to Nigeria. There seems to be a bigger picture as to why they want me to go, even if I bring Norman. My guess is that Solomon is playing his cards close to his vest, without any expression, hoping I can't read him. So, I'll tell you what, I'm just going to stop speculating, take a plane ride over there, and call his bluff in person."

Mark responded with, "Alright, let's do this. Do you want me to inform Paul that he's going to Lagos?"

"Yes, let him know we have a special assignment for him and the dates of travel. Tell him to come to my home office tomorrow at 2:00 PM for a meeting with me regrading the specifics of the deal and the reason for traveling to such an unusual destination. Advise him to look into Nigerian law and the parallels regarding British Common law and US law. Also, ask him where a matter such as this would be litigated in the event of a legal dispute."

Mark left Elliot's office with a heavy heart. Mark felt as if he had become a cheerleader for a team that had no chance of winning. Sterling Development was on the road to failure and its president was desperate to find a way out. As he was driving to the Sterling offices to brief Norman, all Mark could think about was whether he was doing his friend a colossal disservice by advocating for Elliot's participation in what seemed like an unrealistic venture.

Upon arriving at the office, Mark understood that the 'Boss' was committed to seeing the Nigerian deal being concluded, one way or the other. He knew that Elliot would not accept any other course, so Mark decided that he should stop fretting over the Nigerian option and help Elliot any way he could. To that end, he went directly to Paul Norman's office. Norman had developed a reputation as a brilliant attorney with the uncommon ability to find loopholes in the law that most attorneys were unable to detect. He always seemed to be able to outmaneuver his opponents. Even though his young, frail physique appeared weak, this Ivy League-educated attorney, who wore wire-rimmed glasses and a bow tie, was no pushover.

Norman's door was open, so Mark walked right in and expressed, "Beautiful time of the year to travel to Africa."

Norman, who was busy at his desk, responded with, "Why, are you going there soon?"

As Mark closed the door behind him, he responded with, "No, but you are."

Norman, who was not taking any of this seriously, responded with, "Good, I always wanted to go on a safari and get up close to wild animals. Why don't you join me?"

Mark said, "No, I can't leave the shop, but Mr. Sterling will be traveling with you this Sunday."

Norman, who was getting slightly annoyed with the small talk, finally cut to the chase by stating, "If I didn't know you better, I'd say there appeared to be a modicum of truth to your suggestion. But even if there were some truth to any of this, I'm convinced that the preponderance of the evidence sways heavily in the direction that you are making all of this up as you speak."

"No, counselor. You and Elliot Sterling will be leaving a little after midnight early Sunday morning via British Airways. Your destination will be Lagos, Nigeria. You will be transacting business involving a $100 million contract. Mr. Sterling will personally brief you tomorrow afternoon at 2:00 PM at his home office. You need to allow for a total of four days on your calender, which includes travel time."

Norman looked at Mark and said, "You aren't kidding, are you?"

Mark stared back at him and wryly stated, "No. I'm not kidding."

Norman, who now realized that this was not a joke, said, "I can't go, but we'll arrange for a lawyer with international experience to travel with Mr. Sterling. My parents are having their 60th wedding anniversary on Sunday night. I must attend!"

Mark, who was now the one getting annoyed, looked up at Norman and announced, "I'm not asking you, I'm telling you. Make certain that you are on that plane with Mr. Sterling. This is urgent. The company will make it up to your parents. Besides, business always comes before pleasure."

Norman, who understood that there was no loophole with this directive, just caved in and said, "Please inform Mr. Sterling that I would greatly appreciate that the next time he selects me for an international assignment, he will sign me up for a city more like Paris or London, as opposed to the shithole city he has selected."

"I'll pass that along. In the meantime, we want you to study the different jurisdictional venues where we would have legal rights to bring an action, if necessary, regarding a Nigerian contract. Can we sue in the United States against Nigeria? What law applies? Is Nigerian law based on British Common law? Could we bring a case before the International Court of Justice at the Hague?"

As Mark stood up to leave, he sincerely said to Paul, "I'm sorry about your parents' celebration.

This situation is very time-sensitive and urgent. We'll make it up to you. We just don't have a different option. Please be extraordinarily confidential with this. We'll see you tomorrow at 2:00 PM. Thanks."

The next day, exactly at 2:00 PM, Paul Norman was standing outside Sterling's home office. He had spent most of the previous night researching law regarding jurisdiction venues in the event of a potential Nigerian legal dispute. Norman felt like his legal analysis might have been a waste of time, because he had not been briefed or privileged as to the details of this foreign commercial agreement.

Additionally, he felt very uneasy about doing business with Nigeria, a nation not known for its ethics.

"Good afternoon, Paul. Take a seat. Can I get you something to drink?" Elliot said as he greeted Norman.

"No, sir, but thank you very much," Norman responded.

Elliot, who was recognized by his employees for getting right to the point, did exactly that.

"Paul, it's no secret that Sterling Development is much challenged by the state of the economy and our lack of housing sales. It's not our fault as a company. We have designed and built outstanding homes. The market has just collapsed. Of course, construction lenders have, in good faith, lent us a substantial amount of money. But they don't care how they get paid back. They just expect to get paid back with interest. Obviously, they prefer we sell houses and pay down our debt just like the construction loan documents you reviewed say we're supposed to do. But if we can't sell houses as the source of repayment, then they expect us to give them an exit strategy for making them whole.

They look to me for that solution. This is why you and I are, regrettably, going to Nigeria on Sunday."

Elliot spent the next two hours telling the story about how this transaction was initiated by Herman Beringer. He explained in detail the events that had taken place since the day he received the now infamous Nigerian letter. After review of the Nigerian documents and listening to the full explanation, Norman looked at his boss and said, "In lieu of us pursuing travel to Nigeria, I suggest two alternative ideas. The first would be to buy a Power Ball lottery ticket. I hear the prize is over $100 million. We could pledge the anticipated winnings to the construction lender.

In my opinion, you have a much better chance of winning the lottery than collecting on the Nigerian contract. My second thought, which I like even better, is to take the cost of the airline tickets, the

$35,000, and the gold watches and donate them to charity. This is my opinion. Do I still have a job?"

Elliot, who didn't know whether to laugh or cry, started laughing and said, "You either don't understand how the international world of business works or you really are upset at me for dragging you to Nigeria right during your parents' anniversary. Since I know you better, I'm going to assume that it's the parents' thing, although I do admire you for having the balls to look me in the face and give me that speech. You're not fired, but we are going to Nigeria together and will return with the money. I don't pay you to be an entrepreneur. That's my job. You're a good lawyer. I appreciate your candor, but you'd never make it as a businessman. Now, talk to me about our legal options, just in case you happen to be right."

Paul, who accepted that his argument had fallen on deaf ears, decided to trust 'the boss' and converted the deeply pessimistic gloom to practical legal analysis. After all, Mr. Sterling was right, he was not paid to make policy or business decisions, only to express legal opinions. Fully understanding his role, Paul grabbed his briefcase, removed several yellow legal pads, and started doing what he was paid to do.

Now that he understood the deal, Norman began by informing Elliot that the agreement would be considered a binding legal contract, based on the information he had to date. Obviously, he would need to review the documents more carefully once in Nigeria at the Central Bank. The bottom line was that the Nigerians had 'invited' Elliot into a business venture that required Elliot's business knowledge and experience. Since there would be 'financial consideration' by Sterling, along with a series of other technical legal points, Norman could defend the legitimacy of the contract, even though on the optics of the deal it did not look or feel 'kosher.'

Norman went on to explain that The Hague was not the correct jurisdictional venue, because it was set up for nations to legally dispute international matters, government to government. Although the United States government could technically take on a legal matter on behalf of an American entity, it would be highly unlikely that they would pursue a matter such as this. Norman continued by confirming that, based on his limited review, it appeared that Nigerian law was predicated on English Common law, with similarities to American commercial law. Finally, Norman advised Elliot that the best and most practical method to sue the country of Nigeria would be to bring a case right here to a Los Angeles Federal

Court under the jurisdiction of a 'hidden' law known as the Foreign Sovereign Immunities Act.

He went on to quote in detail how the law defined that 'A foreign state shall not be immune from the jurisdiction of courts of the United States or of the States in any case in which the action is based upon a commercial activity carried on in the United States by the foreign state; or upon an act performed in the United States in connection with a commercial activity of the foreign state elsewhere; or upon an act outside the territory of the United States in connection with a commercial activity of the foreign state elsewhere and that act causes a direct effect in the United States...'

Norman advised Elliot that from the moment he began using telephone and fax activity in the United States for commercial purposes for the Nigerian transaction, a case using the Foreign Sovereign Immunities Act could be used against Nigeria. Norman explained that, upon stepping into the government offices to meet with government officials of the Central Bank of Nigeria along with proving financial consideration having been paid, "We have a fighting chance to win this case." He continued with a broad smile, "It's a good thing you're bringing me along, because I'm going to add to their contract, without them knowing, some simple language that will bolster our legal case in the event we need to sue to enforce the contract in the United States."

Elliot, now beaming with confidence, stood up, put out his hand to shake Norman's, and said, "Bravo. You're a fucking genius. I'm glad I didn't fire you! I know this whole deal doesn't feel right, but trust me on this. Together we'll find a way to win. My apologies to your parents. Thank you for the straight talk and all your hard work. I'll make this up to your mom and dad and to you. I'll see you at the airport on Sunday."

The results of the meeting with Norman were encouraging to Elliot. At the very least, he now clearly understood that he could bring a legal action against the Nigerians right here in Los Angeles, should this venture turn out to be a scam. Elliot saw light at the end of the tunnel. If Solomon did not honor his part of the deal, after forcing Elliot to travel all the way to Lagos to sign the government contract in the Central Bank of Nigeria, then Sterling would have recourse to bring suit against the Central Bank, the government of Nigeria, Chief Balla, and every character associated with this transaction.

The Foreign Sovereign Immunities Act, also known in legal circles as the FSIA, was turning out to be exactly what he needed as a defense to fight against the bank. Elliot's preliminary plan was simple. The Nigerians would fund the contract, or Sterling would sue the Nigerians for his share of the agreement. The bank would understand that Sterling would be party to a lawsuit involving $100 million, an asset on Sterling's financial statement that would look real and favorable to the bank's board of directors. This was the way out for Sterling.

Back in Nigeria, Stanley Roberts had prepared the entry visa for Paul Norman to enter the country. He was waiting for Solomon to arrive to his office so that he could approve Norman's visa before faxing it on to Sterling. When Solomon arrived, he immediately asked, "Do you have the visa for Mr. Sterling's attorney?"

Robert's answered, "Yes. Please review and approve, so that the visa can be sent today."

Solomon hastily grabbed the visa, reviewed it for about 30 seconds, and said, "Send it." Then abruptly reversed his instructions by firmly telling Roberts, "No! Stop. Do not send it!"

Solomon went on to say to Roberts, "I acted hastily in approving Mr. Norman's request to travel with Mr. Sterling on this trip. I should have instantaneously objected. We obviously do not want an attorney from the United States becoming privileged as to the inter-workings of the Central Bank and our relationship with it. I told Mr. Sterling that I would accommodate his request only because I did not want Sterling to become suspicious. I was concerned he would think that we have something to hide. I now know this to be a mistake."

Roberts responded by softly saying, "Do not worry, Mr. Solomon. I will make it my business to confuse Mr. Norman with many misleading comments. I will distract him with legal paperwork that he will not possibly be able to understand. I will be certain to prepare the Central Bank officials to make minimal comments while staying completely credible. It would be a colossal error to reverse your decision regarding approving Mr. Norman to accompany Mr. Sterling. My advice is to immediately proceed to fax the Norman visa to Mr. Sterling before any suspicious thoughts enter his mind."

"I will accept your advice and place faith in you that you will protect our interests. You must always remember that Mr. Sterling is gifted, which means that the attorney he chooses to represent him will be astute. Do not underestimate these people." Solomon concluded with, "Send it."

Elliot was up at the crack of dawn. It was Friday morning, the last business day before his Sunday departure to Nigeria. There was plenty to do, but there were probably not enough hours to get everything accomplished. First order of business was to meet with Mark in order to arrange for Solomon's request for the $35,000 and 6 gold watches. Goldman was scheduled to be at the home office at 8:00 AM and was to bring everything with him, including the airline tickets for the British aircraft destined to Lagos.

When Elliot entered his office, he quickly spotted a fax. He was hoping it was from Solomon referencing the Norman entry visa. It was exactly that. As he reviewed the document, he noticed that it was sent by a person named Stanley Roberts. At first he was uneasy. Why was the fax forwarded by someone other than Solomon? But, after a brief reflection, Elliot reasoned that Solomon had assistants just like any other high-level executive. So, he decided to set aside any further suspicious thoughts, especially since the visa for Norman was identical to his own.

At a little before 8:00 AM, Mark arrived holding a black briefcase. He saw Elliot and said, "I still think I should accompany you on this trip. To be perfectly candid with you, I'm really worried about your safety. We just don't know who these people are. They could be thugs. They could be international criminals or identity thieves. I'm going to be awfully upset at myself if anything happens to you. Let me go with you!"

Elliot replied, saying, "You're worse than my wife! We've talked this thing death. You need to be here in case they fund while I'm there. Nothing will happen to me or Norman. But let's say you're right and these guys decide to kidnap us or harm us in anyway. I'd much rather you be here working with the State Department and law enforcement to get me the hell out of there instead of you being trapped with with me in Nigeria. Now, do you have the money and the watches?"

"Yeah. It's all here in the briefcase. By the way, I didn't say I was concerned about Norman," Mark replied sarcastically, understanding that he was on the losing end of this argument.

Each gold watch was individually packaged in an elegant black box. The denomination of the currency was $100 bills. There were exactly 350 bills neatly organized for delivery to Solomon. As Mark handed Elliot the two round-trip British Airways tickets for Los Angeles to Lagos, he asked, "Are you going to declare to the Nigerian Customs agent the amount of money you're carrying? He will ask you whether you are carrying in excess of $10,000. You also will be asked about items such as the watches."

Elliot had previously thought about this and was prepared with the answer, "No. I will not declare any of it to Customs. The way I figure, when we arrive at Customs, we will be whisked right through by Solomon's people in the government. Solomon obviously knows that we are bringing money and gifts. I'm confident there will be no issue. I'll take that risk."

Elliot grabbed the briefcase full of money, along with watches, and asked Mark, "So where did you end up drawing the money from?"

Mark explained, "I drew it from my savings account. I just didn't want any trace of it coming from you, in the event we end up in court and this money is considered some kind of unethical payment. At least, you could say that it was not from any of your bank accounts. Since you have an attorney-client relationship with Norman, I'll arrange to loan him the money and he will officially be bringing the cash. The attorney-client relationship might come in handy down the road, should the money matter ever come up.

You can reimburse me upon your return with some of those gold Eagle coins you've been hoarding all those years. Sound like a deal?"

"That's a deal. Thanks very much for laying out the money, but I'm not going to wait until I return, I'm going give you the gold coins right now, in case your conspiracy theory of my demise becomes real. At least, you will be crying about me instead of crying about your fucking 35,000."

Mark was handed his equivalent sum in gold coins, and Elliot had everything prepared for his speculative trip. They agreed that Mark was to pick Elliot up Saturday night at 10:00 PM for transport from Elliot's home to the airport. The airplane was scheduled to depart at 1:00 AM Sunday morning. Although this meeting was over, both men realized that the probability for success was low and there would be unending anxiety until Elliot returned safely.

As Mark was heading to the door of the office, Elliot said, "I want you to pick up Norman before you pick me up to go to the airport. We'll all ride together. When we're jointly in the car, I'm going to hand Norman three of the watches, plus $9,900 to carry past Customs. Tell Norman to bring no money with him, except for what I give him. In the event that something goes wrong at the airport when entering Nigeria and the officials confiscate the money I'm carrying, at least Norman will get through Customs with enough funds so we can manage. Likewise, carrying three watches is much easier to explain than all six in my sole possession."

Mark, who was listening intently, and very pleased that his friend was being cautious, answered with, "Consider it done. See you Saturday night at 10:00 PM."

Chapter 9

Felicia and her husband spent the entire day together on Saturday. They played tennis and took a long walk through their beautiful neighborhood holding hands while talking about their daughters. They shared breakfast, lunch, and a cozy dinner with each other. Neither one of them chose to speak about Nigeria. It had simply been a delightful day until around 8:00 PM, when Elliot, who was in his spacious walk-in closet packing his bag for the trip, heard Felicia crying out loud in the bedroom. As he walked out the closet to the bedroom, he saw an image of his gorgeous wife shedding tears and gently said to her, "I have to go. I don't want to go, but I have to go."

Felicia, who knows exactly what her husband is communicating, slowly answered while trying to control her emotions, "This trip should not be about money. You don't need to do this for me. I care about you and our family. Nothing else. Nigeria is a dangerous place and the people you're dealing with cannot possibly be ethical businessmen. No amount of money is worth something happening to you, and no amount of money is worth you facing any type of criminal charges. PLEASE don't take this trip! I assure you, we'll find a way to make up the money. So what if we don't live in a big house with all our social connections? We have each other. We have our daughters. You're a great businessman and everyone loves you. We'll be alright. Call this off! I have a terrible feeling about this trip. Call Mark. Tell him you changed your mind."

Elliot, who was concerned that this outburst might happen, said, "I'm the luckiest man alive to be blessed with a wife like you. I love you and our daughters with all of my heart and soul. I sincerely know you mean every word you just said, but I still must go. Now, please hear my words. I am going to win and no one is going to harm me in any manner whatsoever. I may not fully succeed on this trip, but I'm going to eventually win. Just stick with me. When it's all said and done, I will get the money and we will be standing strong!"

Felicia succumbed to her loving husband by first tightly embracing him, then by giving Elliot the confidence he needed to hear by saying, "Okay, go get 'em!"

Those three simple, encouraging words, as colloquial and uncomplicated as they sounded, were the marching orders Elliot was hoping to hear from his wife. He understood that Felicia, against her better judgment, had deferred to her husband's request for blind trust.

From this night forward, Elliot would be driven by the great confidence that she had given him and nothing was going to get in the way of fulfilling his sacred promise to his wife 'to win.' The Nigerian deal was no longer just about money, it had become personal, and Elliot Sterling was not about to lose the money or the trust Felicia had accorded him.

It was now 10:00 PM and Mark had arrived at the Sterling residence. Norman was sitting in the car, just as Elliot had requested. Felicia knew that it was time to say good-bye to her beloved husband and accordingly hugged and kissed him while saying, "I love you and I have faith in you. I expect to see you back here in one piece within five days. Don't break your promise to me."

Elliot passionately kissed his wife and confidently told her, "I'll see you in five days. I love you."

As Elliot walked out the front door, Mark immediately grabbed his bags and placed them in the trunk of the black BMW. Elliot held on to his briefcase and sat in the front passenger seat as Norman greeted his boss with a respectful, "Good evening, sir." Sterling responded with, "I appreciate you taking this trip with me. We'll get in and out of Lagos as fast as possible. Mark has scheduled us back to LA within five days. I expect to follow that itinerary. Here is your visa to enter the country," and handed Norman the Nigerian entry visa. "I'm sure Mark has briefed you regarding the money and watches, so unless you have any other questions, I'll be giving you a total of $9,900, plus three gold watches," then Elliot reached into his briefcase and handed both the cash and the watches to Norman.

Mark began pulling out of the driveway for the short 25-minute drive to Los Angeles International Airport. He sensed that neither one of the travelers really wanted to go to Lagos, so, as he was driving, he tried to change the somber mood by saying to Norman, "Paul, I took the liberty of buying you a life insurance policy that names me as the beneficiary. My bet is that you won't make it out of there alive. Someone needs to benefit from such a tragedy, so it might as well be me!"

Norman, who was not finding this funny and was about to burst into an argument with Mark, quickly heard Mark say, "Hey, I'm just joking with you!"

Then, Elliot jumped in and said, "Mark's just trying to lighten up the moment. I've been hearing this kind of stuff for the last four decades. We good?"

Norman, who realized that Mark was coming from a good place, responded with, "We're good." Then, after a short pause, went on to gravely say, "Perhaps the policy is not such a bad idea." No one responded.

As they arrived at the airport, Mark went directly to the international terminal and pulled up to the British Airways curbside check in. Mark got out of the car and handed his boss the bags. They gave each other a hug as Mark addressed his friend with, "Don't take any risks. Follow the agenda and get your ass back here by the fifth day. I'll be on call for you 24/7. Whatever you need, night or day, just let me know. I need to be assured that you are safe and doing well, so keep me advised."

Elliot responded with a clear, "Will do." He then firmly shook his friend's hand, grabbed his bags, and walked directly into international terminal with Norman at his side.

Mark understood that the risks of this trip were high and the probability of success low. Thoughts of never seeing his wonderful friend again entered his mind. He just didn't feel good about this trip, but it was too late. So, now all he could do was hope for the best and pray for his friend's safe return. The next five days were about to become a very anxious time for Mark Goldman.

Check in with British Airways went smoothly. The boarding passes were securely in the hands of Elliot and Norman. As they waited in the airport lounge, Norman randomly asked Elliot, "Was Mark really just joking, or should I have bought a life insurance policy?"

Elliot, who was astonished by the question, responded by stating, "If you think fate has caught up with you and believe our airplane might be doomed to crash, then, by all means, buy yourself a policy. If you think you may need it due to our interactions with our Nigerian partners while we're in Lagos, well, I say save your money."

Norman looked at Elliot and said, "I'll save my money, and I apologize for even bringing that up."

Elliot responded with, "No need to apologize, just focus on how you're going to frame a legal case against the Nigerians in the event they're scamming us. You need to be 'air-tight' with the legal findings that best help us win a potential case against the Republic of Nigeria. If they don't pay on the contract, I want to be assured by you that we have a case against them under the Foreign Sovereign Immunities Act. Do I make myself clear?"

"Yes, sir. You are being perfectly clear. And just so you understand, I am going to nail them up against the wall if they so much as sneeze the wrong way. The wall I'm talking about is an American federal courthouse and they are going to be very sorry they tried to mess with you, Mr. Sterling!"

Elliot, now very impressed with the tough talk by his attorney, said, "I have a lot of faith in your words. Your conviction gives me much confidence. It's our mission to come home with the money, as opposed to preparing for a tough fight in court. Let's make it easy on ourselves by making sure that the Nigerians fund the contract and wire the funds during this trip, but we must be prepared for court."

As Elliot finished his comments to Norman, he heard the announcement that boarding was about to commence for their flight. Both Elliot and Norman gathered their belongings and prepared to board their aircraft. Once inside the plane, they were directed to the business class seating section and quickly settled in for the long journey to Nigeria. Elliot elected to sit on the aisle and Norman took the seat by the window.

The flight, which included a stop at London's Heathrow Airport, was anticipated to take over 18 hours, with a scheduled arrival at Murtala Muhammed International Airport in Lagos at 5:00 PM. The idea was simply to try and fall asleep for as much time as they could. Between sleeping, eating, and enjoying the wine, they hoped to pass the time comfortably. They both fastened their seatbelts as the aircraft was taxiing toward the runway. Before either one realized, the plane was in the air. Elliot and Norman were on their way for an adventure that neither one had ever prepared for. All they knew was that they were enroute to an unstable and corrupt country. Privately, Norman was hoping his boss knew what he was doing, and Elliot was hoping that Norman could figure out what to do legally in the event the Nigerians were up to no good. As they fly 30,000 feet in air, the moment of truth was near.

Before they knew it, the aircraft was on its final descent towards Murtala Airport. The long journey from Los Angeles to Lagos was over. As they were buckling themselves in for landing, Elliot reminded Norman that if Elliot were separated at Customs from Norman due to a money declaration or some other visa issue, he should immediately contact Mark for further assistance. Mark had prearranged for officials at the United States State Department to be prepared to assist. Paul had been fully briefed by Mark prior to the trip and stated to his boss, "I know exactly what to do, and all I can say is that I'm grateful you made all those big campaign contributions to the congressman who happens to sit on the Foreign Relations Committee. Who would have ever thought that this guy might one day come in handy regarding Nigeria?"

As they both prepared to disembark, Elliot noticed that Norman was taking a deep breathe. He was concerned that Norman was nervous and asked, "Everything alright?"

Norman, who was firmly gripping his briefcase as if he had something to hide, responded with, "For some reason I feel like a criminal in lieu of an attorney. Just not feeling like myself, but I'll be fine."

Elliot, who was a little concerned about Norman's demeanor, told him what he always told Mark before an important meeting, "Your face is your sword, but the way I see your face, you look like a kid getting ready to visit with the principal after having been caught cheating on an exam."

"I'm ready, Mr. Sterling. I don't know what got into me, but I'm definitely ready. Let's go check in."

Elliot, who now saw the color in Norman's face reappearing, said, "What got into you is that you're an honest man who is used to being in control. I want you to be you, but remember that we're in a foreign country. Stay focused on our mission. There is no room for any weakness." Elliot, who was happy that he had this little chat with Norman, continued walking forward towards the International Customs section.

As Elliot and Norman arrived at the Customs area, they both observed ten separate agent booths. They decided that it would be best to get into the same line. Norman would independently go first, then Elliot would follow.

The room was very hot and the process was slow. Finally, it was time for Norman to proceed to present his entry documents to the Nigerian official. By this time, Norman was perspiring, not because of nerves, but just because of the sweltering heat. As he approached the official, Norman handed him his credentials and the agent asked him in what sounded like a British accent, "Are you traveling for pleasure or for business?"

Norman answered, "For business."

The official then asked, "Is it private or government business?"

Norman told the truth and said, "Both."

The official continued observing the visa and appeared uncomfortable. He looked at Norman, then stared back down at the credentials and picked up his phone. Norman, who's starting to feel anxious, looked back at Elliot with a worried look on his face. Elliot, who was silently observing, calmly gestured back to Norman with a simple thumbs-up, effectively telling him to hang in there, everything was going to be okay.

The agent addressed Norman by stating, "Your visa is not in order. We need to contact the appropriate authorities in order to clear you for official entry into Nigeria. In the meantime, you will be taken to our 'Secondary Screening' area until we can determine your legal status. Please follow our security personnel."

Norman, who was trying very hard to stay cool under pressure, remembered the words Elliot had mentioned earlier and indicated to the official, "I am a United States attorney, and in the event that this matter is not resolved quickly, I hereby request that a Nigerian attorney be assigned to my case and you immediately inform the American State Department of these circumstances." The agent indicated to Norman that there was nothing further that he could do and that he should follow the guards to 'Secondary.' Once again, Norman looked back at Elliot, who was now being called forward by the same agent to present his paperwork. As Elliot walked towards the booth, he reiterated another thumbs-up.

Elliot, who was now very worried for Paul, likewise was concerned that he might be heading down the same path. He stayed calm but decided not to be weak and confronted the agent with, "Good afternoon. The gentlemen you just sent off with the armed guard happens to be my attorney. What the hell is going on?"

The agent, who was offended by the question, responded with, "This is not a matter to which I am authorized to speak with you about. Please present your credentials."

Elliot, who understood that there was nothing to be gained by pushing any further, just handed over his papers. The official reviewed the credentials, quickly stamped the documents, returned them to Elliot, and said, "Welcome to Nigeria." He then waved the next passenger in line forward.

Elliot, who was greatly relieved that he was granted entry, immediately began thinking about Paul. They had talked about their contingency plan in the event that Elliot would be held at Customs, but they had not discussed what would happen if Norman was stopped. He couldn't believe how upside-down they had this! As he was walking towards the airport greeting area where he expected to find Solomon, Elliot just couldn't stop thinking about how no questions were asked of him. Not about his purpose for traveling to Nigeria, or how much money he was carrying, or anything else. Yet, Norman, who had the identical visa credentials, was dragged away! He concluded that the only solution for Paul's immediate release was to to find Solomon and demand action forthwith. Elliot was now jogging towards the airport greeting area.

As he arrived at the international greeting area, he observed the exit sign and vigorously walked through a large, opaque glass sliding door. He instantly saw a tall man who was very well dressed in a pinstriped three-piece navy blue suit holding a sign which read, 'MR. STERLING.' Elliot went directly to this man and said, "I am Elliot Sterling. Are you David Solomon?"

Solomon immediately answered, "Yes. Welcome to Nigeria, Mr. Sterling."

Elliot, who was hot, tired, and very upset about Norman, rudely blurted out to Solomon, "Your fucking visa didn't work for my attorney. He's sitting in some 'Secondary Holding' area because of your bogus visa. You got exactly 15 minutes to get him released and legally accepted into this country before I contact my country's State Department. Now what the hell are you going to do about this?"

Solomon, who acted very surprised to hear about the failed visa, was equally surprised to be greeted with such a contentious initial greeting by his business partner and said, "Are you always this rude when you meet someone for the first time?"

Elliot, who was in no mood to be entering into small talk with Solomon, just responded with, "You got 14 minutes!"

Solomon recognized that Elliot was beyond upset and said, "We apologize for the inconvenience.

Mr. Norman will be legally accepted into the country and join you in less than ten minutes. Please wait here. I will return with your attorney shortly." Elliot did not respond to Solomon even as Solomon started walking towards the same sliding glass doors he had just passed through. When Solomon reached the doors, he went directly to an intercom, said a few words, and instantly the sliding doors opened. He then flashed credentials and walked right through. Elliot was now under the impression that this guy was not only in the government, but a very well-connected and powerful man as well.

In less than ten minutes, Solomon reappeared through the same sliding doors with Norman right at his side, just as he had said he would do. Elliot was not only relieved to see Norman, but now also had confidence that Solomon could just be the real deal.

First, Elliot went directly to Norman and said, "I apologize for the horrible experience. Are you good?"

Norman responded with a sigh of relief and said, "I know my boss would honor his thumbs-up gesture instructing me not to worry, so I didn't worry, and I'm out. I have no complaints."

Elliot then addressed Solomon by saying, "Thank you. Now let me start over. My name is Elliot Sterling and it is my pleasure to meet you, Mr. Solomon. We look forward to a mutually beneficial relationship and the seamless and successful completion of our business dealings."

Solomon then extended his hand towards Elliot, and as they shook hands, Solomon said, "On behalf of Chief Abba Balla and the government of Nigeria, we welcome you and Mr. Norman to our country. We will work hard to make your stay comfortable, and more importantly, profitable."

As Sterling and Norman gathered their bags, they were escorted by Solomon toward the exit of the baggage area. As they were walking, Solomon briefly stopped and said, "I owe you both an explanation as to what happened to Mr. Norman at Customs. The internal codes which were transmitted from our Foreign Affairs Agency to Customs did not match the codes on Mr. Norman's visa. This is why the Customs agent could not approve Mr. Norman's visa. He had no choice but to send Mr. Norman to 'Secondary.' This was an internal error committed by a member of our staff. Upon return to my office, I will personally terminate this man from his employment. We apologize to you, Mr. Norman, and to you, Mr. Sterling, for us having placed your attorney into an unnecessary and stressful position."

Elliot responded with, "Apology accepted, but you don't need to fire your employee."

As soon as they all reached the sidewalk, a brand-new black Mercedes-Benz arrived at the curb to pick them up. A driver got out of the car and placed their bags in the trunk as Solomon stepped into the front seat. Norman and Elliot climbed into the back. The driver was then assisted by airport security traffic personnel, allowing the Mercedes to maneuver through very congested airport traffic. Elliot's fate now rested in the hands of David Solomon as they drove to the Meridian Hotel in the center of Lagos.

The driver of the Mercedes was introduced to Elliot as Stanley Roberts, a high-level assistant to both Solomon and Abba Balla.

Elliot was informed that he could speak 'freely' while in the presence of Roberts, due to the complete trust Abba Balla and Solomon had in him. Solomon then went on to advise Elliot and Norman that they would be picked up at the hotel by Roberts at exactly 9:15 PM.

They would be taken to the personal residence of Nigeria's Minister of Finance. They were invited to eat dinner with the minister and would discuss protocol for the next day at the Central Bank, where Elliot would be signing the agreement. Solomon went on to brief Elliot about a 'test wire' that was routed by the Central Bank earlier in the day to Sterling's designated financial institution. The 'test wire' was sent for the purpose of officially determining whether all the financial coordinates previously submitted by Sterling were in fact accurate. The Central Bank successfully determined that they were. Additionally, Sterling's bank had acknowledged to the Central Bank their official receipt of the 'test' and wired back a confirmation indicating that they were prepared to accept USD 100 million from the Central Bank of Nigeria.

Sterling responded to Solomon's briefing with, "I'm delighted to hear that the transfer is ready to go.

I will do my part tomorrow at the Central Bank and then work with you to coordinate the appropriate distribution of the funds regarding your share. It will be my honor to meet the minister of finance. We will be ready for Mr. Roberts at 9:15 PM."

As their car pulled into the hotel's main entrance, Solomon said to Sterling, "Mr. Roberts will assist you in obtaining your rooms. They are prepaid by us with no charge to you. He will accompany you to your suites and will enter the room with Mr. Sterling. Once in the room, please deliver the $35,000 along with the gold watches to Mr. Roberts. We will be certain to distribute these gifts correctly as the customary protocol for 'gratification.' The initial gift will be presented tonight to certain individuals who assisted in arranging for tonight's dinner. We thank you for your cooperation regarding this part of the operation."

Sterling, who was feeling very good about everything he had heard in the car, simply said, "Okay."

Roberts stopped the car at the entry of the Meridian Hotel. Everyone exited except for Solomon, who stayed in the front seat of the Mercedes and said, "I will see you later tonight, and welcome to Lagos."

The receptionist who checked Sterling and Norman into their rooms was in a special VIP office at one side of the general reception area. She was very pleasant and had introduced herself as Fola Paji, assistant general manager of the hotel. She immediately confirmed that the rooms were prepaid and, 'Two of the best rooms in the hotel.' Norman asked for and received Fola's business card and placed it in his pocket as the bellboy took their bags and escorted them to their respective rooms.

After the bellboy left, Sterling delivered the money and watches to Roberts without any hesitation.

Roberts placed the funds and the gold watches into a black leather briefcase that he had grabbed from inside the room from the closet of the master bedroom area of the hotel suite.

He explained, "When we prepaid for the room, we took the liberty to inspect the suite, then left the briefcase in your room for me. I trust you are not offended by our actions, Mr. Sterling?"

"Not at all, so long as you can assure me that you didn't take the liberty to do anything else to the room," Sterling responded sarcastically, yet seriously.

"May I ask what you are referring to?" Roberts shot back, somewhat insulted by the insinuation of Sterling perhaps suggesting the use of a listening device or some other devious trick.

"I'm not referring to anything, Mr. Roberts. You just need to get to know me a little better, then you'll start to understand my humor. So, you now have what you came for, we'll see you in the lobby at 9:15 PM. Please thank Mr. Solomon for the superb rooms."

"Thank you, Mr. Sterling. Get some rest, and I will return as indicated to pick you up."

Roberts went directly to the Mercedes, where Solomon was waiting for him. Solomon asked whether everything went as planned. Roberts just handed him the briefcase and answered, "Perfectly."

Solomon, who was now beaming with a smile on his face and had an air of confidence as they drove away from the hotel, said to Roberts, "Our entire plan is working to perfection! Sterling and Norman were so impressed by the way I got Norman out of Customs with a snap of my fingers. Little did they know that we were the ones that set up Norman with the 'Secondary' problem in order to impress them with our powerful relations with the government. I'm sure Sterling would be very upset if he knew that a part of the money he just gave us was used to pay off our friends at Customs. I was such a good actor when Sterling told me that Norman was held up in Customs. As they say in America, that worked like a charm."

Solomon went on to boast and explain how much Sterling and his attorney would now trust them, based not only on the Customs matter, but the 'test wire' and the finance minister meeting as well. He discussed, "The prepaid rooms show our 'good faith' and hospitality, even though Sterling was of course paying for all this out of his own pocket. When he finishes with the finance minister tonight and walks into the Central Bank tomorrow, he will do anything we ask from him, because he will be so impressed by the reality of our power to perform and the seduction of the $50 million Sterling expects to earn, that he will have no choice but act as we request. I love this scam!"

In the meantime, back at the hotel, Sterling felt exhausted, yet exhilarated, with what now felt like favorable probabilities of receiving the funds and settling his financial nightmare. He had already spoken to his wife, assuring her that he had arrived safely and that he had a good feeling about things.

To add to his optimism, he had also spoken to Mark, who had verified that Paul Reno, from their bank, had unconditionally confirmed to Mark that the $100 million 'test wire' was in fact a legitimate wire from the Central Bank of Nigeria. Paul Reno was set to receive the funds and act per the instructions Sterling had earlier given. As Sterling finally settled into bed in order to get some rest, he couldn't help but think that this all seems too good to be true. He really wanted to believe it, but there was a little voice telling him to be careful as he quickly dozed off into a deep sleep.

After a couple of hours of sleep, the telephone rang and the operator informed Sterling that this was the 'wake-up call' he had requested for 8:30 PM. He slowly got out of bed and walked directly to the shower to get ready for his important meeting with the minister.

At 9:10 PM, Sterling knocked on Norman's door and found Norman dressed in a navy-blue suit. As they both made their way to the lobby, Sterling advised Norman, "It is remotely possible that our rooms may be 'bugged' with some kind of electronic eavesdropping device. Don't take any risks, just assume that it is happening, and take all precautions when speaking out loud."

Norman, who was somewhat alarmed and confused, asked, "What gives you that impression?"

"Just a hunch. I could be wrong, but I might be right, so let's just err on the side of caution."

At precisely 9:15 PM, Roberts walked into the lobby and was greeted by Sterling and Norman with a routine handshake. Roberts, who was dressed to perfection wearing a black silk suit and solid red tie, asked, "Are you prepared to proceed to the minister's home?"

Sterling said, "Well, unless you have something more important to do, let's go meet the minister."

While entering the Mercedes, Sterling asked Roberts, "How long does it take to get to the minister's residence?"

"About 45 minutes," he answered, then Roberts continued by telling Sterling that he had attended Stanford University and had earned joint degrees in law and finance. He emotionally stated, "It is my life's goal to move my wife and children to America and live out my years in Palo Alto, California. I want to pass the State Bar of California and become a legal citizen and practice law."

Sterling, who was very impressed with his education, said, "I graduated from Stanford. I consider our alma mater one of the best universities in the world. If you ever need any help getting to America, please let me know. I'll help you make it happen." The Stanford University bond between Roberts and Sterling had the immediate effect of lowering Sterling's guard. He was falling deeper and deeper into the confidence of the Nigerians just as he was arriving at the minister of finance's home.

Roberts drove up to a security guardhouse located in front of a palatial estate with tall iron fencing surrounding the entire property. Sterling counted five armed guards with automatic weapons standing at the entry point to the driveway leading to the home. All Roberts did was lower his window, then wave at the guard in charge, and the heavy iron gate electronically opened. It was apparent that the guards not only knew Roberts well, but they were expecting them.

Once inside the gates, Roberts drove a short distance on what appeared to be a cobblestone and granite private road leading to a huge, circular driveway where six brand-new Mercedes vehicles were parked in front of the massive residence.

The home was lit with floodlights accentuating the grand, opulent architecture of the lavish estate. Sterling intuitively understood that he was about to meet someone very high powered in Nigeria just as Roberts said to him, "Mr. Solomon is waiting for us at the front door, and he told me to express to you that your life is about to change."

Chapter 10

Just as Sterling, Norman, and Roberts were getting out of the car, they were met by two armed guards who said that they would accompany them into the residence.

As they were about to enter the home, Solomon opened the front door and greeted them by saying, "Welcome to the home of Sani Odibo, Minister of Finance for the Republic of Nigeria. Minister Odibo will meet us in his private study within the next 15 minutes. The minister has requested to meet you in person prior to our official gathering for dinner in the Banquet Room. Please do not talk to Mr. Odibo unless you are spoken to. When the minister walks into the study, you must stand up as a sign of respect. Mr. Norman will not be allowed to accompany you to the private meeting with the minister. I will take Mr. Norman to the Banquet Room while you are meeting with Minister Odibo."

The home felt almost like a museum, with its very high ceilings, magnificent oil paintings, and marble sculptures lining the wide hallways. Sterling noticed the amount of servants but saw equally as many armed security personnel. All Sterling kept thinking about was how a public civil servant living essentially in a third-world nation could amass such enormous wealth. Either he was wealthy prior to government, or this 'guy' had stolen one hell of a lot of money throughout the years while in government.

The private office was enormous. Sterling noticed a mahogany wood desk, along with four couches.

Solomon told Sterling that he should take a seat on the couch closest to the desk and wait for the minister to arrive. Solomon informed him that he would now be leaving the office so that the minister and Sterling would have an opportunity to engage in a private conversation. Solomon then went on to say that he would accompany Norman to the Banquet Room, where he and Norman would be seated separately. Sterling would be seated as the guest of honor alongside the minister.

"We thank you, Mr. Sterling, for making this long journey to Lagos. Good luck with your conversation with Minister Odibo. I shall see you imminently."

Within minutes, the minister entered the private office through a side door that appeared camouflaged along the wall. He was a heavy-set black man and exquisitely dressed in beautiful traditional Nigerian garb. The clothing was tailored perfectly and consisted of a wide-sleeved floor-length white robe, known as an 'agbada.' The sleeves were very long and were folded up to expose the hands. Additionally, he was wearing a traditional headpiece, a round cap commonly referred to as a 'fula.' This man wore his clothes with pride as an indicator of status and wealth.

As Sterling rose to his feet, the minister extended his hand and in a big, booming voice said, "Welcome to Nigeria and welcome to my home! I am Sani Odibo, Minister of Finance for the Republic of Nigeria. You have come to us well-recommended by Chief Abba Balla. He graciously welcomes you and apologizes for his inability to join us here tonight. Chief Balla will soon be the duly democratically-elected president of Nigeria. And you, Mr. Sterling, will have assisted him in accomplishing this extraordinary moment in our nation's history. To this we all owe you a debt of gratitude."

Sterling, who wanted to say something, could not get a word in. All Sterling could do was keep nodding his head in approval, hoping, without success, to say anything. When the minister completed his monologue, Sterling was about to thank Odibo, but two men abruptly walked into the office and went directly to Sterling, saying, "Please have a seat, Mr. Sterling," as the minister took his seat at his desk.

"Tomorrow, you will go to the Central Bank of Nigeria for a 10:00 AM appointment. You will be asked to present two forms of identification. Please show your passport and your California driver's license.

You will then be handed a Bible, upon which you will place your hand and swear to the legal authorities present that you are in fact Elliot Sterling, the beneficiary of the $100 million agreement. Are you prepared to officially swear to this effect, sign the contract before a notary, and conform to our internal understandings?"

Sterling answered with a firm, "Yes," the only word he had been able speak so far.

Odibo then ordered the aides to show Sterling the actual contract he would be signing at the Central Bank.

The first thought that crossed Sterling's mind related to the importance of Norman being brought to the office to review the agreement. Norman would perhaps be able to add something to the contract that could strengthen the potential legal case in relation to the Foreign Sovereign Immunity Act.

Sterling was handed the agreement and immediately saw his name as the beneficiary. As he thumbed through the pages, he additionally read about the $100 million payment due for 'goods and services rendered.' Sterling noticed the provision that stated that 'stipulated payment was to be paid only upon the physical presence of the beneficiary at the Central Bank of Nigeria.' The initial review of the agreement, at least on the surface, appeared in order, with the exception of a short paragraph indicating that all associated taxes with this contract would be 'paid in full, prior to release of the contract payment.' Although the paragraph seemed unusual, especially given the fact that taxes are normally paid after there are earnings, as opposed to before, Sterling assumed there was an easy explanation, which he would later obtain from Solomon. The more pressing issue was how to get Norman to the office.

After Sterling's hasty reviewed of the document, he said to the minister with a poised expression on his face, "To quote Abraham Lincoln, a man who represents himself has a fool for a client."

The minister answered with, "Since our lawyers represent you and us as partners, are you insinuating that we are fools or are you concerned that we are trying to deceive you?"

"Neither. Just a businessman doing what I do on every agreement that I sign: the attorney reviews, then I sign. Why else would I have brought Mr. Norman here? Let me put it to you this way, if you were in Los Angeles being asked to sign my agreement for a housing development partnership, I'm pretty sure you'd insist that your attorney review my contract." Sterling went on to say, "As another one of our American presidents once said, 'Trust, but verify.'"

Odibo then responded with, "Very good. Very good, Mr. Sterling. I'm impressed. Alright, I will agree to allow Mr. Norman to review the contract, with two conditions. Condition one is that he will have a total of 15 minutes to do so, and condition two, he will do such a review now, before we eat. Agreed?"

"Yes, with one condition. If he recommends a clarification or an amendment to the contract, you will reasonably incorporate such an amendment into the agreement. And to demonstrate how fair I am, I will even allow you more than 15 minutes to review such an amendment. Acceptable?"

Now, with a serious look on his face, and without answering Sterling's request, he instructed his aides to, "Escort Mr. Norman to my presence."

Shortly thereafter, Norman entered the office and just by looking into Sterling's eyes, he knew what to do.

Odibo's assistant handed Norman the contract and stated, "The minister and Mr. Sterling have jointly agreed that you will take the next 15 minutes to review this agreement. You and Mr. Sterling will be allowed to stay in the minister's office during your evaluation. We shall return at the conclusion of this time period." The minister and his aides then stood in unison and marched out of the office without another word said by anyone.

Sterling pulled a paper and pen from his pocket and wrote to Norman, 'We may be on camera and they will probably be listening, so when I talk to you, I'll be speaking in code or I'll write a note. You may be allowed to add an amendment to this contract, but if you can, keep it simple. Focus on the Foreign Sovereign Immunity Act (FSIA)!! Everything looked good to me, except for the tax paragraph, which I think we can bring up directly with Solomon in lieu of now. GOOD LUCK.'

Norman read the note and winked at Sterling, acknowledging his message, then began speed-reading the agreement. After ten minutes of silence, Norman took Sterling's notes and wrote a few of his own, starting with, "We need to add your address in Los Angeles, amending the contract in order to establish jurisdiction in California. This is NON-NEGOTIABLE!! The tax provision leaves us wide open to being responsible for a tax payment before the funding of the contract. Your call as to whether we strike this tax provision now or speak to Solomon later tonight. We meet the 'commercial activity' requirements and the Nigerian government's involvement regarding the FSIA. If you add your California address, we have a FSIA case against them! We can live with the rest of the agreement."

Sterling looked at Norman and responded out loud, "Sounds good. I am certain that I will always call California my home state, and we'll speak to Mr. Solomon later tonight." Just as Sterling was making his comments, the minister and his assistants re-entered the office and Odibo said, "I trust you are hungry, because my chef has prepared a magnificent feast for us. Shall we proceed to the Banquet Room?"

"Yes, Minister Odibo, I am famished. But we do have one minor clarification that I believe was overlooked in the agreement that must be added," said Sterling.

Odibo, now looking and acting impatient, curtly responded with, "And what is that, Mr. Sterling?"

"The contract is missing my address. That's all we need," Sterling said in his charming manner.

Laughing out loud, Odibo responded with, "That is your amendment request, Mr. Sterling?"

"Yes, that is my amendment request."

"I would have agreed to that 15 minutes ago! Your address will be amended into the contract before you sign the agreement tomorrow morning at the Central Bank. Now let's go eat and drink!"

Everyone now felt content and the cloud of distrust seemed to have eased, at least for the moment.

The Banquet Room looked magnificent and was fit for a king. The lighting sparkled from an elegant Baccarat Crystal chandelier. The white cotton tablecloth was exquisitely set with gold leaf fine china dinnerware and silver utensils. Towards the center of the elegant banquet table were two extraordinary 25-inch gold candelabras; the velvet-burgundy drapery hanging at the French glass doors could easily have been found in Buckingham Palace.

Twenty people were seated at the table. Sterling sat at the head, adjacent to the minister, and Norman was seated towards the middle, near Solomon. Although the dinner was served formally in multiple courses, Sterling was completely unfamiliar with what he was eating. He found himself joining in with a lot of laughter, even though he did not understand Odibo's jokes or stories. Sterling just kept hoping the last course could be served so he could get the hell out of there. Finally, as desert was being distributed and the night appeared to be coming to a close, the minister stood and decided to address his guests.

"This has been a special celebration. We are recognizing the importance of conducting business with America, a nation which prides itself on capitalism. We are acknowledging one of America's best businessmen, Mr. Elliot Sterling. He has come all the way to our great country to show his devoted commitment towards conducting commerce with Nigeria. He has performed on his contract as if he were a naturally-born Nigerian citizen looking after the national interests of Nigeria. To this, Mr. Sterling, we owe you our gratitude and our respect. So, tomorrow when you go to the Central Bank to complete your faithful work here in Nigeria, please always remember that we are your brothers!" Without another word, the minister shook the hand of Sterling and walked out of the Banquet Room to the applause of everyone, including Sterling.

To the delight of Sterling and Norman, dinner was over and it was time to go get some rest before tomorrow's important meeting at the Central Bank. Solomon confirmed that he would be driving them back to their hotel, along with Roberts. As they were walking back to the Mercedes, Sterling asked the question that had been on his mind the entire night, "Why does the agreement have a provision which obligates the beneficiary to pay taxes on the payment of the funds prior to receipt of the funds? It makes no sense that we pay taxes on money we have not even earned."

Solomon responded clearly but in a very soft tone, "I see that you have read the contract, my distinguished friend Mr. Sterling. For the last 20 years all of our contracts have had this type of tax provision inserted into their agreements. The theory is easy to understand. An offshore contractor, such as yourself, can contractually be paid, but you may never pay the associated tax due for the income received. Therefore, we would have to bring a legal proceeding against you in Nigeria to collect the taxes due. The government does not want to have to legally pursue you in the United States in order to collect their taxes, so they just automatically insert the tax paragraph in all offshore contracts, theoretically enabling the government to automatically collect their taxes. Now, the good news is that this type of tax has never been collected or enforced regarding the class of contract you will sign tomorrow."

As the tax explanation by Solomon concluded, Sterling and Norman were listening and trying to read between the lines as to whether the tax provision was real or imaginary. Just before they entered the car driven by Roberts, Norman asked Solomon, "Who is going to guarantee us that the tax won't be collected?"

As they all entered the Mercedes and started driving towards the hotel, Solomon answered with, "Don't worry about it. I told you, the tax is never collected. I assure you that if the Central Bank demands the subject tax payment, we will pay or arrange to pay for it."

Sterling then asked, "How much is the tax amount?"

Solomon responded with, "Two percent."

Norman quickly stated, "Two million dollars!"

Solomon then asked Norman, "Why are you so surprised? Don't you pay taxes in America? I have been told that you pay much more than two percent taxes on your gross income. Please, no more talk of taxes. I have not been informed of any tax to be paid tomorrow, but if there is a tax due, it will be paid by Chief Abba Balla."

Roberts, who had not said a word the entire car drive back, said, "I will pick you up tomorrow morning at 9:15 AM. Our appointment at the Central Bank is for 10:00 AM. Please wait for me in the lobby of the hotel. Mr. Sterling will need to bring his passport and his California driver's license. Mr. Solomon will be meeting us at the Bank. We want to assure you that all the arrangements have been completed on our side, guaranteeing for the proper execution of the contract in accordance with the laws of the State of Nigeria. We expect that the entire contract fund of $100 million will be transferred tomorrow to the designated bank Mr. Sterling has selected. Upon your confirmation that the funds have been successfully received by your bank, Mr. Solomon, along with myself, will swiftly travel to meet you in person at your bank to make face-to-face arrangements to transfer our share of the funds to the financial institution we designate. We wish luck and a very good night."

Sterling and Norman said good night and exited the car.

As they were walking towards their rooms, Sterling looked at Norman and stated, "I hope we don't get fucked with the taxes! Something tells me that the tax provision is real and the government is going to have its hand out to collect what they are entitled to. Solomon says that the chief will pay, if required, but I'm not buying it."

Norman suggested, "We'll just need to see how it goes tomorrow. Obviously, we didn't bring a check for $2 million, so they're not going to get it out of us. We'll just deal with it as it comes."

Sterling responded with, "Now, how did you get so smart?"

Norman said, "Best mentor in the business."

Sterling, who was sincerely worried about the taxes, showed no emotion and told Norman, "Go get some rest. We got a big day in front of us tomorrow. Be ready to kick some Nigerian ass! I'll meet you for breakfast at 8:15 AM. Have a good night."

Chapter 11

It was 8:15 AM and Sterling had already been sitting in the restaurant for over 30 minutes reading the *New York Times* and drinking coffee while waiting for Norman. Although he had slept for a few hours, most of the night had been dedicated to calling his wife and assuring her that he was fine. He additionally spent time speaking to Mark, briefing him on the possibility of the fund transfer taking place later this afternoon, Nigerian time. Sterling had confessed to Mark that his instincts were telling him that the fund would be held up due to a tax issue, but he did let Mark know that there still remained the possibility that the Nigerians would just 'pull the trigger and send us the funds!'

Norman arrived for breakfast and said, "I was so exhausted last night that I forgot to compliment you on what a superb job you did to get Minister Odibo to accept adding the California address to the agreement. Job well-done!"

Sterling, who was perturbed by the tax issue, simply replied, "I hope that those sons-of-bitches added the language as promised. I don't think I did such a good job. Believe me, if I had done a good job, I would have insisted right then and there to strike the tax provision in its entirety from the agreement!

Instead, I let it slide. I'm pretty sure this mistake is going to come back to bite us on the ass."

Norman responded with, "Well, my view on the matter is that you did the right thing by avoiding the subject, because I believe that Odibo would have taken offense to a request to delete the tax paragraph and you would have put our California jurisdiction issue in jeopardy. The minister probably would have given you the same speech Solomon gave you regarding tax provisions: that they are in all of their offshore agreements and are unenforced. Look, your 'mistake' only cost us $2 million."

Sterling sipped his coffee, looked at Norman, and responded with half a smile, "Very funny. You're a funny man. Now order your breakfast and let's get the hell out of here before I sue you for malpractice."

Norman, who quickly converted to his 'serious lawyer' mode, informed Sterling that they needed to make certain to confirm the California address and request a copy of the agreement. At minimum, they should obtain a copy of the first page and the signature page. Additionally, it was imperative to request a 'contract number' assigned to the agreement, so that they could eventually refer to the contract in any potential FSIA legal proceedings.

It was approaching 9:15 AM and Sterling signed for the breakfast bill and walked with Norman to the lobby, where they immediately spoted Roberts standing there, as previously arranged.

Roberts greeted them with, "Today, Mr. Sterling, will be a day you will never forget. It will change your life forever. Please know that you can rely on me for anything you need. I will help you."

The car ride to the Central Bank took about 30 minutes. The side streets were congested not only with automobiles, but with bicycles and people. The boulevards were dirty, trash along the curbs, and the aura was that of a third-world country's. As Roberts was about to arrive at the Central Bank, he informed Sterling that they would enter the official parking garage and undergo a security clearance. Upon approaching the Bank, Roberts pointed to an 11-story building with black glass and a black iron fence around the entire circumference of the impressive facility. Sterling turned to Norman and said, "It's game time."

As the car stopped at the iron gate where the armed guards were patrolling the Bank, a young soldier with an automatic weapon at his side asked Roberts, "Who are you here to visit, and what is your name?"

Roberts stated his name and continued with, "We are here to visit with Stanley Ecke, vice-governor of the Central Bank. I am accompanied with the distinguished Mr. Elliot Sterling and his attorney Mr. Paul Norman from the United States of America. We have an appointment at 10:00 AM."

The guard then asked Roberts for his government security clearance credential and for Sterling and Norman's passports and California driver's licenses. All the documents were then taken to a small guardhouse and scanned for authenticity.

The guard went on to make one phone call and returned to the Mercedes with a clear voice and said, "Proceed, and welcome to the Central Bank of Nigeria."

The gates opened and Roberts moved straight into the parking structure and parked in a space reserved for, and labeled, 'Minister of Finance.' They all exited the car and followed Roberts through a beautiful patio with an elaborate water fountain made of marble. As they entered the building, once again, they went through a thorough security check, then accessed the elevator to the second floor. As they departed the elevator, they were greeted by two armed guards who took them through thick glass doors and into a very large conference room. Roberts informed Sterling and Norman to take a seat at the conference table and that David Solomon, the vice-governor, and the attorney for the Central Bank would be joining them shortly.

Within a moment, Solomon's now familiar voice was heard saying, "Welcome, Mr. Sterling and Mr. Norman. It is my great honor to introduce you to the Honorable Stanley Ecke, vice-governor of the Central Bank of Nigeria."

Sterling and Norman stood and shook the vice-governor's hand, stating, "It is our honor and pleasure to be here, and we thank you for inviting us to the Central Bank."

Ecke, who was a distinguished looking elderlyman, responded with, "We trust that your stay in our country has been comfortable, and we invite you to return as often as you can. Please advise your government and your business leaders that Nigeria is open for commerce. This is a nation starving for trade and investment. Americans have the know-how, but now, Mr. Sterling, you have Nigerian know-who!"

The vice-governor moved directly to Sterling and shook his hand, then extended his hand to Norman. Before Sterling said anything further, Ecke stated, "We thank you for your business, and we consider you a friend of the Republic of Nigeria. The Central Bank's attorney, Mr. Onogo, will, from this point forward, be authorized to disburse the payment due under the contract. Please follow the requests and directions of Mr. Onogo. We wish you safe travels back to America, and we look forward to our next transaction."

As quickly as Ecke had entered the conference room, he had now vanished. Onogo then addressed Sterling and said, "Please provide me with your verification credentials. We will accept your passport and your California driver's license." Sterling handed them over without one word said and without any expression. Onogo promptly delivered the credentials over to his assistant, who left the room with the documents. Attorney Onogo then pulled a legal file from his briefcase and handed Sterling the contract for his review. Right after, Sterling handed the contract to Norman, who started reviewing it.

The room was dead silent. It felt more like a serious medical surgery in lieu of an upbeat conclusion to a major business deal. Onogo's assistant re-entered the room and delivered back to Sterling his personal documents. He went on to inform Onogo, "We have verified that we are dealing with the person known as Elliot E. Sterling, and you may proceed with all the required signatures, which the Central Bank is prepared to notarize."

Onogo addressed Norman with, "Have you completed your review?"

Norman just said, "No."

Onogo, who had an authoritarian, stern personality, responded, "We do not have all day! I will give you five additional minutes to conclude your futile review. The contract has been approved by the government of Nigeria. There will be no amendments. You will either sign the agreement as it is presented or you will not. It is pointless for you to continue to waste all of our time."

Norman, who was irritated by the arrogance of Onogo, sarcastically answered, "If you were legally representing vice-governor Stanley Ecke, I am certain that you would advise him that it is 'ignorant' to review a legally binding contract. In fact, based on what you're telling me, you probably would inform the vice-governor that it would be a 'waste of time' to try and understand the legal context of a $100 million agreement Mr. Ecke was about to sign. But since you are not representing Mr. Sterling, and I am, I'll take as much time as I need before I advise Mr. Sterling to sign this document. Do I make myself clear, Mr. Onogo?"

Onogo did not respond to Norman, but instead handed Sterling a one-page summary of the specific Central Bank wire instructions verifying the bank account numbers that Sterling had previously established with Solomon and asked, "Are these instructions correct? We have sent a second 'test wire' to your bank and they have confirmed the instructions to be flawless. If you agree, please sign your acceptance of these instructions to be true and accurate."

Sterling took the document and read it carefully, then told Onogo, "This is correct." He then handed Norman the document and jokingly told him, "Cut 30 seconds off Mr. Onogo's deadline and review these instructions while you're at it." Norman smiled, while Onogo pretends not to have heard a thing Sterling said.

Approximately ten minutes later, Norman indicated to Sterling that he had completed his review and discreetly pointed at the contract with his finger, indicating to Sterling that the vital California address had in fact been incorporated into the final agreement. Sterling winked at Norman and said, "Very well, Mr. Onogo, my attorney has completed his review and we are prepared to sign the contract, contingent upon a very minor request. So please listen to Mr. Norman for a moment."

Norman then addressed Onogo directly and articulated, "Mr. Sterling is prepared to sign the contract and the wire instructions document, with one condition. We request a copy of the agreements fully executed by both parties. We additionally request that you provide us with the official contract number that you have assigned to this contract, as indicated in the agreement. If agreed, please bring your notary, so as to commence executing the documents."

With a conspicuous glare at Solomon, the attorney for the Central Bank begins shaking his head in disapproval, as if to be saying, 'How dare you question the integrity of the government?' Onogo then reluctantly said to Solomon, "We will provide you, Mr. Solomon, with a copy of the contract signed by both parties. Once Mr. Sterling signs before the notary, I will take the agreement for signiture directly to Mr. Wole Obasanjo, governor of the Central Bank. Mr. Obasanjo is the only authorized government official with the authority to sign an agreement that will disperse the amount of $100 million. Once the governor's signature is witnessed by the notary, we will stamp on the first page of the contract the government's certified and registered contract number. If Mr. Solomon decides to release a copy of the contract to you, Mr. Sterling, well, that will be his decision, not mine. Now, enough said on this subject. Are you prepared to sign the documents?"

Sterling glanced at Norman, then asked Solomon, "Will I get a copy of the fully executed contract?"

Solomon nodded his head with approval, and Sterling said to Onogo, "I will honor the integrity of your government, let's proceed with your Bible swearing."

Shortly thereafter, the notary appeared, and Sterling signed where the notary pointed. The entire process took less than five minutes. Upon signature by Sterling on all the required documents, the notary handed the agreements to Onogo. By this point, Onogo had everything he needed from the Americans and all the power had shifted to him. He then looked at Solomon and stated, "I will have the contracts signed by the governor within the hour. The transfer of the funds to Mr. Sterling will take place immediately after the governor's signature. Of course, there will be no transfer until the Foreign Offshore Contract two-percent tax has been paid. Please be certain to provide the receipt indicating that the $2 million tax has been paid in compliance with the recently issued presidential decree enforcing tax collection for offshore contracts. If you have the receipt, you may give it to me now, or you may go to the Revenue Collection window on the third floor to make your payment."

Solomon did not look surprised at the tax request, but he did appear nervous. Sterling had the look of a man who had just been deceived by the seduction of money. All Sterling could think of was that he should have known better. This was just too good to be true. The Nigerians now had his signature on a $100 million contract that they had the power to fund, pay themselves, and cut him out.

This was no time to show weakness, so Sterling confidently said to Onogo, "Mr. Solomon had assured me that such tax provisions in your offshore contracts are never enforced. Obviously, you are quoting some new presidential decree that none of us were privileged to know about. But Mr. Solomon has personally assured my attorney, Mr. Norman, and of course myself, that in the event that such a tax was required as a prerequisite of the Central Bank's funding, Mr. Solomon would pay the tax. So, please be assured that Mr. Solomon will pay this tax as specified in the contract and you, Mr. Onogo, will be transferring my funds immediately thereafter. I am sure that your taxes may not necessarily be paid today, but very soon. Please set aside my funds, make sure that Governor Obasanjo signs my contract, and make us an appropriate copy. Mr. Solomon will be bringing you the tax receipt forthwith."

Solomon, without emotion, responded with, "Just to clarify a few points. First, it is not me who will be paying the tax. It will be Chief Abba Balla. Second, it will be several days before Chief Balla will be in a position to organize and pay a tax of this size in United States dollars. And third, I did not learn of the presidential decree regarding this tax until now. I say to both Mr. Onogo and Mr. Sterling, do not worry, the $2 million tax obligation will be settled speedily."

Onogo reacted with, "Fine. The Central Bank will set aside the $100 million for a period of one week. I will have the contract signed by the governor today, contingent upon the taxes having been paid in full. Please bring to my office the tax payment receipt and we will fund immediately thereafter. On behalf of the Central Bank of Nigeria, we thank you for conducting business with the great sovereign nation of Nigeria. Good day, Mr. Sterling."

With that final statement, the disappointing meeting was over. No further words were spoken until Sterling, Norman, and Solomon had exited the Central Bank and were back inside the car with Roberts.

As the doors to the Mercedes closed, Sterling blurted out, saying, "You people either think I'm stupid or naive! It's not possible that you, Mr. Solomon, had no knowledge whatsoever that the taxes must be paid. It is black and white in the contract that taxes are due prior to funding. Then, presto, out of nowhere, a fucking presidential decree appears, making it official that we must pay taxes. What a scam!"

"It sounds like you are calling me a liar, Mr. Sterling."

"No, worse. A con artist. You bring me all the way to Nigeria. You take my money and my gifts. You show me all the powerful government relationships you have. Then you get me to sign a bullshit contract that is not worth the paper it is written on. But worse, you want me to believe that the chief is going to fund $2 million in cash to pay taxes based on a phony presidential decree. Wow, you really think that we're dumb!"

"Are you finished, Mr. Sterling?"

"No, I'm not. I will be leaving today for Los Angeles. I demand that you return my money and the watches and never contact me again."

"As you wish, Mr. Sterling. We will return your money and the watches in exchange for your notarized signatures surrenduring all your rights and interest in the contract you just signed at the Central Bank. You will have no beneficial interest in the contract upon your assignment, and we will never contact you again. Likewise, you will never contact us again, because legally you will give up all your rights to the $100 million contract. Do we have a deal?"

Looking at Norman, a cautious Sterling said, "I'll give you my answer when we arrive at the hotel."

After nearly 20 minutes of silence, Sterling proposed that Solomon and Roberts join him and Norman for a drink at the hotel lobby bar. Without any hesitation, Solomon responded with, "This sounds like a good idea."

Upon returning to the hotel, they all departed the Mercedes and moved directly to a quiet corner in the hotel bar lounge where they took their seats. Sterling, anxious to express himself, started by saying, "I apologize for my outburst in the car. I'm not quite certain what made me express those words, other than frustration. I sincerely felt that we had concluded our business and were just moments away from the successful transfer of funds. Of course, it was very disappointing to hear that the tax issue, the very issue that I feared would stop the transfer, actually stopped the transfer. I felt as if you had deliberately deceived me by not knowing about the new tax decree. Please accept my apology."

Solomon, smiling and then laughing, said, "Of course, my good friend Mr. Sterling. I accept your explanation, and I accept your apology. Believe me when I tell you that we are more disappointed than you are to see the contract being held up by the Central Bank. I think we need the money for Chief Balla's political campaign much more than you need it."

A relieved Sterling reacted with, "I'm glad you comprehend what I have said. Now let me clarify my position a little further. You do not need to return my money or the watches. I will not be releasing any of my interest in the contract. And lastly, I expect Chief Balla to honor your commitment to me that all taxes due will be paid in full before the seven-day deadline Onogo enacted is up. Do we agree?"

Before Solomon got a chance to agree, Norman added, "You must also assure Mr. Sterling that you will provide us a copy of the fully executed agreement, which includes the stamped official contract number."

Solomon reacted with, "First, I do want you to understand that this presidential decree was completely unexpected by any of us. This type of decree is rare, although it does happen. It just came at a terrible time for us. We will pay the tax. The biggest challenge we have is not the tax, it's the seven-day deadline. Since the contract funds transfer is in US dollars, the tax must be paid in US dollars. I reiterate, the $2 million tax is not the problem. We will have that. The problem is putting together United States dollars instead of using our Nigerian currency. There is a scarcity of US dollars in the country and it is difficult to exchange our currency, the Naira, for US dollars. Under the worst of circumstances, we will request and receive an extension of time from the Central Bank. And yes, Mr. Norman, we will get you your certified copies."

Sterling then reached across the cocktail table and shook Solomon's hand while saying, "We have ourselves a deal! Please do everything you can to settle the tax payment as quickly as possible. Mr. Norman and I will be returning to Los Angeles on the first available flight tomorrow. I would appreciate if Mr. Roberts could take us to the airport tomorrow morning. I will inform him on his cell phone later this evening as to what time our flight will be departing."

"Yes, of course, Mr. Roberts will arrange to transport you to the airport. And please be assured that Chief Balla will honor his commitment to settle the tax payment. As soon as the Central Bank transfers the funds, I will meet you at the designated bank in the Grand Cayman Islands to collect our share of the proceeds. Please take into consideration that the accounting of our share will include the $2 million advance we will make for the tax payment. I'm sorry that you are returning to America without the final transfer of our funds, but we have made much progress and soon will be celebrating our successful venture. We will be in constant communication with you. I wish you safe travels. Farewell, Mr. Sterling and Mr. Norman."

Sterling, who formally said good-bye, was now exhausted from all the tension of the day. He then sat back in his chair and told Norman after they had gone, "I don't know whether this guy, Solomon, is the world's finest bullshit artist or he's telling us the truth. I really have no idea. I guess, for the time being, I choose to believe him. What do you think?"

"He's pretty convincing. Especially that exchange in the car about giving us our money and watches back but insisting we assign our contract rights to them. Very shrewd move. Let's see if they pay the tax, send us a copy of the agreement, and more importantly, transfer the funds. In the meantime, let's get the hell out of here. By the way, Mr. Sterling, I want you to know that you're brilliant under pressure."

"I thank you for the compliment, Paul, but I should have fought harder with Minister Odibo to strike that damn tax provision from the contract!"

Norman, sensing that his boss was suffering with the tax issue, said, "That's water under the bridge. You handled everything like a champion. Every move you've made since we've been here has been perfect. We're on their territory, and you've been nothing short of spectacular. I can't wait to get them on our territory. We're going to get that fund transferred, one way or the other."

Sterling, who was very appreciative of his counselor's support, responded with, "Something tells me you're right. Thanks for snapping me out of my malaise. We're going to win this fight!"

Anxious to get home, Norman informs Sterling that he will take the initiative and work with the hotel's concierge to assist him in booking the next best flight back to Los Angeles. He was hoping to set up a 1:00 AM flight later that night. This would be the same travel schedule they had previously booked, just 48 hours earlier. Once set, he would call Roberts to confirm transportation to the airport.

Sterling thanked Norman for handling the airlines and told him that he was going to his room to call his wife and Mark. He asked Norman to keep him informed.

Norman spent the next hour arranging for the 1:00 AM departure later that night. He was also successful in confirming with Roberts that they were to be picked up at the hotel at 9:45 PM. The travel arrangements were set and Sterling had been briefed as to the schedule.

With the agenda set, Sterling first called his wife and then Mark, indicating to both that the trip had been a success, with the exception of the tax provision. He told them he couldn't wait to get home and that he would brief them in detail upon his return. Mark had volunteered to pick them up at the LA International Airport, which Sterling welcomed.

With the calls completed and the travel agenda confirmed, Sterling set up a wake-up call for 8:00 PM, which would give him plenty of time to get some rest, pack, and settle the hotel bill.

It seemed that as soon as he fell asleep, Sterling was already getting the wake-up call. Still exhausted, he took his time getting out of bed, and then into the shower. The packing was quick, and before too long, he'd be going home to see his beautiful wife. His mind was acutely aware of the major risks associated with the Nigerian contract, and he was also realistically in tune with the grave circumstances facing him with his bank at home.

With all the bags packed, Sterling carried them himself to the front desk cashier to settle his bill with the hotel. The cashier said that the bill was prepaid in full and he was free to leave at his will. As he left the cashier, he saw Norman and Roberts walking towards the restaurant where they would all join up.

Since there was a half hour to kill before they needed to depart to the airport for the 1:00 AM flight, the restaurant seemed like a logical place to sit and have some coffee. Sterling addressed Roberts by saying, "Please be certain to thank Mr. Solomon and Chief Balla for paying for the hotel. I also want to thank you for moving us around Lagos during our stay and for agreeing to drive us to the airport tonight on such short notice."

"It has been my honor, Mr. Sterling. You will be the man who will help Chief Balla become Nigeria's future president. Throughout your visit to Nigeria, you have championed your business dealings intelligently and with grace. I admire your ability to adjust to our way of conducting business, but challenges remain before your business will be completed with us. I want you to know that I will help you clear those challenges. But I want you to help me too."

"And how's that, Mr. Roberts?" asked Sterling.

"I want to move my wife and my children to live permanently in America. I want either to eventually practice law as an American attorney or be a professor at Stanford University, perhaps specializing in Nigerian or African political science. I want you to assist me in accomplishing this goal. In exchange, I will assure you that your fund will be transferred as planned. You still face many obstacles to have your funds transferred. Nigeria is facing a serious devaluation of the Naira. It is going to become very difficult for Chief Balla to organize $2 million to pay the taxes."

Sterling, who was quietly listening, said, "So, what can you do about it?"

"I am one of the only government officials with top security clearance jointly at the Central Bank and the Ministry of Finance. I am privileged to have access to the restricted wire-transfer codes required to send the $100 million fund to you. Additionally, I have special classified authorization to search the Central Bank and Finance Ministry databases. This means that I can obtain a copy of the notarized contract you signed and the official contract number, in the event you need it. You should also understand that I have the complete trust of Mr. Onogo. So, as you can see, I could be very valuable to you! But, I come with a gratification price."

"Now, how do I know you're telling me the truth? Everyone I meet here says the same thing. Everyone seems to have all the power, but when it's time to act, things always have a way of not getting done," Sterling said.

Roberts responded gravely with, "There will be a time when you will need me," as he handed Sterling a piece of paper. "On this paper is my highly confidential and secure private cell number. There are very few people who have it. If you find yourself needing me, and you decide to trust me, please feel free to call. Should you decide that I can assist you, I will further disclose my gratification requirements at that time. Until then, I will of course remain your friend. As for this moment, let us now proceed to the airport."

Not very much was said enroute to the airport. Sterling kept thinking about the currency devaluation that Roberts had mentioned. He was concerned about Roberts' confident statements regarding 'the challenges' that seemed to be inevitable. He kept worrying about the doubt that Roberts had cast on Balla's ability to pay the taxes. Assuming that Roberts was real, Sterling felt that it would be smart to leave behind in Nigeria an 'inside man,' especially since Roberts had just unconditionally assured him that 'the fund will be transferred as planned,' with Roberts' assistance.

As they arrived at the airport curbside baggage, Sterling extended his hand towards Roberts and, as he shook it, said, "I trust you, Mr. Roberts, and I will call you in the not-too-distant future. Once again, thanks very much for the ride. By the way, I believe that you will make an outstanding professor or attorney in America. I'll be in touch."

With a smile and a wave to Roberts, this long and fascinating trip to Nigeria came to close. As he was smiling and waving, Sterling couldn't help but think that much had been accomplished, yet his other perspective was that he was no closer to receiving the money today than when he had first departed Los Angeles for Lagos. The only thing that seemed for sure was that everything remained uncertain.

Chapter 12

The long flight back to Los Angeles was the end of emotionally-packed few days. Both Sterling and Norman felt dead-tired. They had spent a lot of the flight home discussing what they had experienced. But they had allocated the most amount of time trying to read between the lines regarding Roberts' tangible offer to throw the Nigerians under the bus in exchange for 'gratification' and moving his family to America. Norman was cautiously confident that Roberts could perform as he had indicated. Sterling was not completely convinced.

As the aircraft touched down at Los Angeles International Airport, they both acknowledged to each other that Roberts could, in some way, be able to assist in getting the money successfully transferred.

The question remained, at what price and when.

It was good to be back home. Everything just felt right again. Although traveling outside the country consistently seemed exciting, there was always that little sigh of relief upon returning to the United States. As Sterling handed the Customs agent his credentials, the agent reviewed them and with a friendly smile said, "Welcome home."

Norman and Sterling picked up their bags and made their way up the ramp in order to exit the International Customs area. As they arrived at the top of the ramp, Sterling spotted Mark, who had been patiently waiting for them to exit. A big smile came onto Mark's face when he saw his friend Elliot.

Likewise, Sterling was now beaming at the sight of seeing Mark and displayed a thumbs-up.

Mark, grateful that his friend had returned unharmed, hugged Elliot and said, "I've had plenty of nightmares concerning this trip. I'm a happy man to see you back here. Wow did I worry about you gentlemen! Well, not so much about you, Norman. Hey, I'm just kidding. How the hell are you guys?"

Sterling, who sincerely was in high spirits to be back and to see Mark, said, "This has been, without a doubt, the most intriguing experience of my life. It's the kind of stuff movies are made up of or books are written about. I think we can get this thing to go our way. However, we're going to face a whole bunch of challenges along the way. We just have to be smart. But, as long as our team consists of people like you and Paul Norman, we're going to kick these guys' asses!"

Mark, who saw that his boss was worn out, said, "I'm all in. So, here's the plan. No more talk about this trip or business. I'm going to get you back to your lovely wife. You and Paul get some well-deserved rest. We'll get back together tomorrow afternoon and set up a plan for Nigeria."

"Sounds like a plan. I'd like both of you to meet me at my office at 2:00 PM. Now, get me home!"

Mark made record time getting from the airport to Sterling's home in Bel Air. He knew that Elliot was eager to see his wife. As they drove up to the residence, Felicia was actually standing outside in the front yard waiting for her husband to arrive. The moment Mark stopped the car, Elliot opened the door and embraced his wife. Mark unlocked the trunk, grabbed Elliot's bags, then placed them at the front entry door. Without any further words necessary, Mark simply got back into the black BMW, started the ignition, and drove off.

Elliot, holding Felicia's hand while walking towards the house, said, "See, I told you there was nothing to worry about!"

Felicia, now tearing up and angry, said, "I worried every second you were away! I never want you to put our family through something like this again. Promise me that you will never make me agonize like this for the rest of my life. I cannot accept this type of risk to you, our children, or me. Never again!
Do you understand me, Elliot?"

Looking at the sincere conviction in his wife's face, Elliot said, "I promise you I won't ever make you feel like this again." Then smiling, he said, "Does this mean I can keep your share of the money?"

"I love you, Elliot. The thought of your kids being left without a father and you making me a widow is too much to ask. So if I got to trade you for money, I'd take you."

Elliot, who was worn out and fatigued from his complicated Nigerian travel, responded with, "I completely understand what you felt, but you also need to appreciate my situation and what I've just been through. I face serious business matters that require bold actions. A part of who I am is having the respect of the business community. It's hard for me to be me without that respect. I know that it is insane to risk my life for business success, but on the other hand, I have spent my entire life making our name in the business world. You, better than most people I know, realize that in order to win, you gotta take risks, or there will be no reward. So, trust me on the risks I take, and I guarantee you that we're going to win!"

"I've always trusted you all my life. I'm not about to stop now."

Elliot gently grabbed his wife's hand as he led her upstairs to their bedroom, where he had no other plans but to stay with his passionate and stunning wife until the next day.

By 10:00 AM the next morning, Elliot was back in his office studying all the bleak emails Mark had forwarded to him regarding the bank's threats to take legal action to enforce their rights over Sterling Development and the loans that seemed impossible to repay. At exactly noon, the fax machine started ringing and a long fax transmittal commenced. The fax was from Solomon with more bad news. The Nigerian currency, the Naira, was officially devalued against the US dollar by over 20%. Instead of reading the fax further, Sterling allowed the fax to continue to print and walked to the front entrance of his home where the *Wall Street Journal* was delivered daily.

He picked up the *Journal*, walked to the kitchen in his home, and poured himself a cup of freshly-brewed coffee just made by the housekeeper. As he took a seat in the breakfast nook, Sterling rapidly started searching for a lead story regarding the Nigerian currency devaluation. Buried on the third page of the newspaper was a tiny headline referring to a major devaluation of the Nigerian Naira. The article focused on the fundamental and technical reasons for the devaluation, but more importantly for Sterling, the newspaper, unfortunately, confirmed that the currency had lost 20% of its value overnight.

Sterling was very concerned how the heavy devaluation amount would place enormous pressure on Chief Balla to come up with the taxes due. Effectively, the $2 million due for taxes had just become $2.4 million. Instantaneously, $400,000 had been added to the amount Chief Balla would need to raise in order to clear the taxes payable to the Central Bank. Sterling just kept thinking about how Roberts had predicted this precise scenario. It was as if Roberts had been tipped off by a very powerful insider with access to top secret information.

Sterling's concerns were compounded by the pressure to pay the taxes to the Central Bank within the time frame established by Onogo. Would Onogo grant a reasonable time extension to pay the taxes? All of this was weighing heavily on Sterling. While Sterling was in Nigeria, the United States bank had become very aggressive with Mark. The Nigerian business dealings were very unstable and the American lender was about to legally strike, leaving Sterling with very little choice but to fight back. Sterling retreated to his office to prepare for the 2:00 PM meeting with Mark and Norman.

Once back in his office, Sterling thoroughly read the three-page fax from Solomon. It not only discussed the serious devaluation, but it went on to outline various scenarios regarding the pending tax payment. Solomon was clear to state that, even though it would cost approximately $400,000 additionally to settle the taxes due, Chief Balla was committed to honoring the payment. The fax raised the interesting rumor that, in light of the devaluation, the government was considering waiving the taxes due under the decree in their entirety. Solomon continued by stating, 'it might be wise simply to do nothing until the government tax waiver is determined.' Solomon went on to admit that, 'it is only a rumor, which could take months to sort out the truth behind the hearsay.'

Solomon plainly explained the scarcity of US dollars throughout Nigeria. The government, corporations, and wealthy individuals were all competing to trade the devalued Naira for dollars in order to continue with their business dealings. Solomon warned that, 'the extra money now required due to the devalued currency might take as much as three months to raise.' He continued by requesting that Sterling loan Chief Balla the $400,000. The theory was that this would be a 'practical way' of getting the $100 million funds transferred 'expeditiously.'

The fax closed with an aggressive option that suggested that Sterling should consider wiring the Central Bank the entire $2 million in full, thus saving the extra $400,000 in its entirety. 'This would assure the transfer of the $100 million fund within one hour of receipt.' Sterling understood immediately that the fax from Solomon represented trouble. Nothing in this communication indicated swift conclusion to the transfer of funds. Every option Solomon outlined had serious challenges. If it wasn't a timing issue, it was the financial risk being placed squarely on Sterling. Pressure seemed to be rising from all sides. The American bank was demanding its money, and the Nigerians were, for all intent and purposes, also insisting on money.

Both alternatives represented a horrible nightmare. Regrettably, the better solution still seemed to be the Nigerian risk, even though it was a terrible option. The only consistent thought running through Sterling's mind was, 'What a mess!'

At 2:00 PM, Mark and Norman arrived at Sterling's office, as scheduled. The next three hours were spent detailing what had transpired in Nigeria. Sterling and Norman went over painstaking details, writing notes while simultaneously bringing Mark up-to-date on what had occurred. Norman was of the opinion that the funds and their transfer were real. In fact, he was very sure that Sterling would win a FSIA court case in America against the Nigerians. But, more importantly, he was of the belief that the Nigerians were just as hungry to get the funds transferred as they were. Sterling was much less optimistic than Norman.

After listening to the long story and staying virtually silent for three hours, Mark said, "What a fucking amazing trip! Jesus Christ, the next time you guys decide to take a trip like this, you make sure I'm in on it!"

Sterling then remarked, "Hold on, cowboy. These guys are playing hardball with us. By design, they've shown us enough to get seduced by all the government trappings, but what they really want is for us to take on all the risk. Here's what's gone on since we got back. And, Paul, I want you to listen carefully to what I've got to say, because, collectively, we're going to need to make a very tough decision."

Sterling then pulled out the Solomon fax and began laying out the sober reality of the Nigerian contract tax problem being tied to the Naira devaluation. "Here is what's happening, and these are our options. First, the Naira has been devalued by 20% of its value against the US dollar. This means that in order for Chief Balla to convert Nairas into dollars, he needs an extra $400,000." Sterling then showed Norman the *Wall Street Journal* article confirming the extent of the devaluation.

Sterling continued by explaining that Solomon had heard a serious rumor that the presidential decree forcing offshore contractors to pay the two-percent taxes was possibly going to be rescinded in its entirety. The problem was that it could take months before that could officially take place. Yet the possibility, according to Solomon, appeared real. Obviously, that would not only save them a total of $2.4 million, but it would solve the issue of Sterling being required to lend the tax money. The timing of this option was very uncertain.

Sterling then dejectedly looked at Mark and Norman and said, "Now, from here, the options get worse."

Sterling proceeded to explain how Solomon described the shortage of dollars in Nigeria and how expensive it was to trade Nairas for dollars, due to the devaluation. The 20% devaluation was effectively adding $400,000 to the required $2 million taxes due. Sterling then stated out loud the punchline of Solomon's request by saying, "This son-of-a-bitch wants me to put up $400,000 as a loan to Balla so they don't need to go out and raise the extra cash. I guess their thinking is that it will be faster and easier to raise $2 million as opposed to $2.4 million. Solomon goes on to warn that it will still take at least three months or more to raise the total due. These guys have some real chutzpah!"

Sterling then looked at his two confidants and said, "If you think the last option is risky, wait until you hear this last proposal!" He then told Norman and Mark that Balla requested that Sterling seriously consider loaning Balla the entire original $2 million. The concept was proposed to, in theory, save the $400,000, plus, even more importantly, 'The fund would be transferred within one hour from receipt of the money by the Central Bank.'

Mark, looking at Norman, said, "This is going from worst to worst. I thought you said you liked the probability of the transfer. These guys sound like a low-level JV team. Besides, how the hell are we going to entrust this kind of money with complete and total strangers?"

Norman responded with, "I'm not advocating to send the money, as requested under the proposal, I'm simply telling you that these people are serious about wiring this money out of Nigeria. And I'll beat them in court if they don't. There is only one positive in wiring them any money on the record, we document serious financial 'consideration' for our FSIA legal case."

Sterling looked at Mark, then at Norman, and said, "If the tax decree is revoked, we don't need to send these bastards anything. Paul, let's say you're right and the Nigerians want the 100 million as much as we want it, why not just put the pressure on them? Either they put up additional money or they get the president to revoke the tax decree. I say let's wait them out. Worst-case scenario is we send them money later, which only helps our FSIA case. Best-case scenario is they transfer funds without us putting up any money."

Norman then asked, "What are we going to do with the pressure our bank is putting on us?"

Sterling responded with, "We wait it out too! We keep negotiating with them. We buy as much time as we can. As soon as we determine when the bank decides to legally strike against us, we take legal action against them. We bluff the bank by informing it that we will tie up the the properties in bankruptcy and by any other legal rights and remedies at our disposal. In the meantime, we'll keep a close eye on the Nigerians' ability to pay the taxes. If push comes to shove, we'll hit the Nigerians with the FSIA case you tell me you're going to win. Gentlemen, this is going to be big league fight. Either the bank wins, the Nigerians win, or we win. I have every confidence that we are the ones who will come out on top!"

Mark, who was ready to follow his boss into battle anytime and anywhere, simply said, "Ooh rah!" the battle cry common in the United States Marine Corps since the mid-20th century.

Norman, who clearly understood Sterling's directive, responded seriously with, "Game on!" Then, he advised Sterling to fax Solomon a letter requesting a copy of the contract, along with the contract number. Additionally, Norman informed Sterling to make certain that Onogo granted Solomon at least a 30-day extension regarding the date by which the taxes must be paid. He suggested that Solomon tell Onogo that the tax decree was about to be revoked and an extension was in order.

Sterling acknowledged that this was the correct next step and said, "Go ahead and write that up for me and I'll fax that to Solomon today. Just add to the letter that we will be sending no further money and we choose to wait for the tax decree to be rescinded. In the meantime, proceed with the rough drafting of the FSIA case and preliminary legal action against the bank. If you need additional financial resources for all this work, just let me know. You are going to have your hands full with all of this shit!"

Norman stood to leave and said, "I'll have the letter for you in an hour. I also want you to know that I'm not going to let you down on any of this. We'll hold off the bank, and we will defeat the Nigerians in court if they don't pay us first."

Sterling shook Norman's hand and said, "I appreciate your conviction, and I have complete confidence in you. Now, go get 'em!"

Mark, who remained in Elliot's office, said to his friend, "You might as well change the name of our company from Sterling Development to Sterling Law Offices. If these guys don't transfer the fund, we are going to be legally fighting for years to come. We better put away a war chest of money to fight all these legal battles, because neither the bank nor the Nigerians are just going to roll over and let us beat up on them. They will both come at us with everything they've got."

"Well, at least we're swinging for the fence. One way or the other, I am certain the Nigerians are going to pay us. Look, we have the contract and they have the money. It's going to take some time and a lot of legal strategy, but the Nigerians are going to pay and the bank will be settled."

"I'm all in, Boss. I'll keep tabs on the bank. I'll let you and Norman know what it's up to at all times."

Sterling then asked Mark to arrange a meeting with the congressman on the Foreign Relations Committee that, "I have been paying campaign contributions to for the the last decade. Tell him I'd like to have lunch with him as soon as he gets back to the Los Angeles area. I think he might be able to give us some insight as to the current Nigerian political situation, including Chief Abba Balla."

Mark answered by saying, "Just so you know, the name of the guy you're talking about is Congressman Jared Baron. He's considered an expert in international relations and is currently second in seniority on the Foreign Relations Committee. He loves to eat at the Beverly Hills Hotel on Sunset Boulevard. I'll make reservations there as soon as I can confirm which day works best for him. By the way, he's due for a campaign contribution. I'm sure he'll be grateful if you remember to bring him a little something."

As Mark was walking out the door of the office, he commented, "I don't know who is more corrupt, the Nigerians or our guys. Everybody's got their hand out. Whatever happened to the concept that politicians are nothing more than public servants? They serve at the will of the people, not the other way around. I hope we can get back to that one day. Anyway, I'll be in touch soon."

Just as Norman had promised, he faxed the proposed letter Sterling had agreed upon to send to Solomon.

Norman had organized a well-written communication that brilliantly commenced by stating, 'What a pleasure it was to meet in person at the home of the minister of finance and the next day at the Central Bank of Nigeria.' This statement could help win a FSIA court case by tying the government directly to the contract. The fax continued by clearly outlining the importance of forwarding a copy of the contract and associated contract number. Norman made it a point to state that there would be no further monies sent, in hopes that the presidential decree would be rescinded. The letter went on to insist that Mr. Onogo grant a 30-day extension regarding the tax due date. Sterling signed the letter and sent it.

It didn't take long for Solomon to respond to Sterling's fax. It was almost as if Solomon had a premonition as to how Sterling would respond. Solomon's fax indicated that Mr. Onogo had agreed to a 30-day extension 'due to the uncertainty of the presidential decree.' He went on to indicate that Onogo would release the contract copy and number upon the settlement of the tax matter, and not before. It was puzzling to read from Solomon that he totally agreed with waiting for the possible presidential tax decree to be rescinded. Solomon went on further by saying, 'We agree that it is best to withhold paying any further money towards the tax funds until the tax decree is settled.'

Sterling was skeptical with the response and immediately forwarded a copy of Solomon's letter to Mark and Norman for their review and comments. Essentially, the Nigerian business deal was placed on hold for 30 days.

Norman was the first to react, he indicated, "I'm delighted to hear that Solomon was silent regarding our meetings with the minister of finance and our visit to the Central Bank. Effectively, Solomon was confirming that there was in fact a face-to-face meeting through his silence on the issue. Also, I'm very happy that we got the 30-day extension by Onogo. We'll just sit tight until the tax is paid to get our hands on the fully-executed contract. I'm suspicious about why they agreed to wait on the tax rescission."

Mark's response came in right behind Norman's comments. He was brief, and said, "They caved in on everything. What a bunch of pussies. I don't trust them, but I guess we'll just wait out the 30 days!"

Chapter 13

As Sterling was seated in the swanky Polo Room Restaurant of the Beverly Hills Hotel waiting for Congressman Baron to arrive for lunch, he kept thinking about how little had changed over the last 30 days. Solomon continued to insist, with no results, that the presidential tax decree would be revoked. The American economy remained anemic. Sterling's lenders kept threatening to sue him, but they took no such legal action. In the interim, Norman was busy every moment of every day preparing to legally go to battle against the bank. Simultaneously, he was organizing a very expensive and sophisticated Foreign Sovereign Immunities Act case against Nigeria. Elliot just kept thinking to himself, *What a pathetic life I lead!*

The congressman, now running about 20 minutes late, finally entered the room and said, "Elliot, how the hell are you?" Sterling stood and responded with, "I've had better days, Jared."

The congressman sat and stated, "I've heard back in Washington that Sterling Development is about to bite the dust. Is all that shit true?"

"Well, let me put it to you this way, you guys in Washington aren't doing anything to make the economy any better and the bank has got me by the balls."

"So, what's that mean, Elliot? Are you dead or alive?"

"I'm alive, but no thanks to the American system. I've got a major deal going on in the Republic of Nigeria."

Sterling immediately got the congressman's full attention, he asked, "How major?"

"One Hundred Million Dollars. Now, Jared, who do you know in Nigeria?"

"I'm the chairman of the Subcommittee on Western African Affairs, which includes Nigeria, Cameroon, Chad, Benin, and the Niger Republic. Nigeria is the most populous black nation on earth, with well over 100 million people. They are in transition from military rule to having a democratically-elected president. I personally know the head of state, Yemi Muhammadu. CIA tells us that the leading contender to win the open election is a guy by the name of Chief Abba Balla. Are you building houses over there?"

"Fuck no, I'm not building houses in Nigeria! It's an old oil deal started by a partner of mine. My partner passed away and I inherited the contract. Do you know Abba Balla?"

"Never met him, but I'm scheduled to meet Balla and Muhammadu next month as a part of my travels to Western Africa, along with a couple of other congressman on my committee. By the way, you've picked the right business to get involved with. The petroleum industry in Nigeria is the largest on the African continent. Their oil industry is of vital interest to the national security of the United States, and we pay very close attention to Nigeria specifically because of that petroleum. Now, what can I do for you?"

Sterling quickly understood that Baron knew exactly what he was talking about, and more importantly, he knew precisely the right Nigerian actors, so he said, "Chief Balla is my Nigerian partner. He owes my partnership a tax payment of approximately $2.4 million. Once he pays that obligation to the Central Bank of Nigeria, the $100 million contract will be wired to my bank immediately. I just returned from Nigeria. I met personally with the minister of finance at his home, and I have executed all contract documents in the Central Bank offices. I want you to tell Balla to his face that if he cannot cover the entire tax obligation himself, I will put up $400,000 in order to help him settle the taxes due. Tell him I will accommodate him if you can personally assure me that Balla is prepared to pay his share of the $2 million towards the taxes. He will understand exactly what you're talking about. If he agrees, I will wire my funds while you are physically in Nigeria."

"How in hell did you become partners with the next president of the Republic of Nigeria? By the time he completes his presidency, he'll end up a billionaire, if he's not assassinated first. How did a schmuck like you pick up a partner like Chief Abba Balla? I'm really impressed, Elliot!"

"It's the same way a schmuck like you became a congressman. I'll tell you the rest of the story the next time we get together, when we have little more time. Now, can you get this done for me?"

Baron, who was way overweight and had his professionally-dyed blond hair combed straight back, answered with, "What's in it for me?"

Sterling didn't see that coming, he replied, "Friendship. Political support."

"I got that as we spoke. No, Elliot, your little request is going to cost you $300,000. Just consider it a cost of doing business."

Sterling, who now realized that Baron was getting greedy and turning into his poisonous scorpion self, said, "I guess all those campaign contributions over the last decade didn't mean all that much?"

"Sure they did, Elliot. You got this meeting, didn't ya? Now, let's stop fucking around here. I've got to get going! Do we have a deal or not?"

"Nope. No deal. I'll work this out myself with Balla. I don't need you that much. Why don't you go on to your next bullshit meeting? Go earn your living as a congressman."

"Hey, listen, Elliot, I didn't mean it the way it came out. You're my friend, and I appreciate every campaign contribution you have ever made to me. Don't get so bent out of shape. Let's work this out like gentlemen. What's fair?"

"One hundred thousand dollars upon the successful wiring of all the funds to my bank account. That equates to about $5000 a minute for the 20 minutes you'll dedicate to this. I think that's abundantly fair."

"You got a deal at $200,000, you son-of-a-bitch."

"We'll pay you $150, but you're going to receive it in Nigeria from the Nigerians as a form of their 'gratification' to you for your 'consulting' work. I'll guarantee your fee, but the man you will receive it from is David Solomon immediately upon confirmation that the funds are in my account. Agreed?"

"David Solomon. Balla's top lieutenant. Man, you really do get around. You got a deal, Elliot," said Baron as he shook Sterling's hand, confirming their arrangement. "I'll call you before I leave for Lagos. Rest assured, I'll get you your money. Good doing business with you, Elliot. We'll talk soon."

Sterling felt like he had just made an arrangement with the devil. The positive was that he had confirmation that Balla and Solomon were the real deal. Additionally, Balla would understand that Sterling was well-connected in Washington and that there would be consequences to Balla if he failed to perform. The negative was that Baron was a slippery slope. Sterling was concerned that a guy like the congressman might sell out to the highest bidder, including the Nigerians. The Baron deal was done, so Sterling just decided to hope for the best.

As Sterling was walking through the magnificent lobby of the iconic Beverly Hills Hotel, he couldn't help but wonder how many clandestine deals over the years had been made in this very building. He kept wondering to himself, *If only these walls could talk, what a story they would tell.*

The hotel was only 20 minutes away from Sterling's home. As he pulled into his driveway, he immediately saw Mark and Norman's cars parked in the porte cochere. There was no scheduled meeting, which led Sterling to figure that either something very bad or very good had happened. His initial gut feeling was that he was about to hear something not so good. He hurriedly made his way to his private office, where both men were waiting for their boss.

"From the looks on your faces, I don't think you're here to visit with me on a social basis. What's up?"

Norman responded, "The bank has gone nuclear on us. It wants everything, including your home!"

Sterling showed no emotion and asked, "Did they file a lawsuit? Did they send us a formal demand letter?"

"It's a serious lawsuit. They are claiming rights to all the Sterling Development subdivisions and all of our vacant property for future developments. They are demanding all of the company stock that was pledged as collateral. These bastards want your home and virtually anything that has any value to pay back their outstanding loans. Effectively, they're calling in all their loans. The bank doesn't want to arbitrate or mediate, it's going right to court and they want to kick our asses. There is no arbitration clause in the loan agreements. We struck that provision from their contracts because you instructed me to go straight to court in the event of a default. They have formally issued their default notice, and they mean business!"

Sterling, who was not at all surprised, said, "I'm amazed it took them this long. If I had been them, I'd have filed months ago. Paul Reno knows we don't have the money to pay them back. I'm sure he was waiting to see if the Nigerians were going to fund. That was Reno's last best hope. He just couldn't hold back the main bosses any further. I don't really blame Paul for this. The fucking Nigerians have just taken way too long, assuming they are real. But, since I really don't have any other option, I've got to continue to believe they're real. Alright, so now what?"

Norman looked at Mark, then confidently looked at Sterling, and responded with, "I'm ready for them. We'll answer the complaint, then we will counter-sue them for bad faith dealings, along with everything else I can think of. I have a long list to choose from. I'm going to tie them up in court for years. By the time I'm done with them, Reno will probably have retired. And I'm not even talking bankruptcy. We'll buy you as much time as you need to figure out how to pry the money out of the Nigerians, including taking the Nigerians to court on the FSIA case. Mark has done something very clever, so I'll let him explain it to you."

"Norman and I understood that this day was going to come, so we needed to bolster up his countersuit against the bank. I had our accountants enter the Nigerian contract into our financial statements as an asset with the value of $100 million, even though we are only entitled to $50 million. Since the Nigerian agreement is silent in regarding the Nigerians as our 50% partners, we are entitled to enter the contract at its full value, which we did. Therefore, we are very capable of paying our obligations to the bank, but they must be reasonable and have patience. Any court of law will understand that these are difficult economic times, and since we have the assets, the bank owes it to its stockholders and has a responsibility to reasonably work with us to assure that their loans are repaid at 100 cents on the dollar, as opposed to 20 cents on the dollar. Now, of course Reno was fully informed about our Nigerian asset, because he set up the accounts and the bank transfer routes. The bank and Reno will have a hard time denying that fact. So, a judge, and eventually a jury, should be able to comprehend that the math works in our favor and our intentions were always good."

"Bravo! Well done. You two really do have my back. I guess I should stop complaining about how much I pay you guys. Now, let me ask you, Paul, is it really going to be that simple to keep the bank off my back? What about my home?"

Norman responded with, "Yeah, we'll keep these guys busy for years. Of course, it's not going to be simple, but they're not going to lay a glove on you. Don't worry about your home, we'll get that segregated as a personal asset, even if we need to negotiate a discounted lump-sum payment to release your home from the entire business encumbrance. You'll get your house, but make no mistake, the bank will eventually win regarding the Sterling Development assets if we don't get paid by the Nigerians. But we have a protracted time frame of many years to figure out how to get the Nigerians to pay or win the FSIA legal case against them. Even the FSIA case should be enough to convince a court to hang in there and wait for us in good faith while we legally fight for what is rightfully ours from the Nigerians."

"O.K. I understand. You just gave me a lot of clarity and peace of mind. The only goal is Nigeria. $100 million. All my efforts will be dedicated towards pressuring them to transfer the money. Nothing else will save us. By the way, Mark, who gave you the authority to place the Nigerian contract on our books?"

Mark, who figured that question might come up, said with a smile, "I read your mind."

Sterling glanced concurrently at Mark and Norman and said, "I've been doing some work too. I met with that piece-of-garbage Congressman Jared Baron. I made a deal with him that I'm not so proud of, but nonetheless, the deal is done. Here it is. The asshole gets $150,000 upon the successful transfer of the Nigerian funds. He'll meet in person with Chief Abba Balla in Nigeria within three weeks. Baron will inform Balla that we are prepared to forward up to $400,000 to cover the tax shortfall. Once he assures me that Balla has his $2 million ready, we'll send our commitment. Baron has agreed to receive his 'gratification' directly from Solomon while in Nigeria. Although Solomon will actually pay the fee to Baron, we will guarantee that it gets paid in full to him."

Norman responded with, "Great! That $400,000 tax payment is exactly what I need for my FSIA pleadings regarding our money contribution towards the contract. So, if you do end up wiring the money, this will be the perfect financial consideration we need on the record. I realize it's very risky to send out this kind of money, but it sure helps perfect our legal case against the Nigerians."

Mark then spoke up with, "I don't trust that back-stabbing son-of-a-bitch Baron. Elliot, this guy will throw you under the bus. He cannot be trusted. This bastard will sell his grandmother to the highest bidder. Any way of getting out of that deal?"

"Not without it being suspicious. We can't afford Baron going rogue on us and poisoning the contract. Baron is not only meeting with Chief Balla, but he is scheduled to meet the Nigerian head of state, Yemi Muhammadu. He also knows that Solomon is closely associated with Balla. So, the way I see things, it's good that Balla and Solomon understand that we have serious connections with Washington. It might keep them a little more honest. So, we're stuck with the arrangement I made with Baron. We need to let Baron do his thing. Remember, the 'good congressman' doesn't get paid without first the $100 million being parked in our bank account. Believe me, I don't trust him, and frankly, I can't stand Baron, but maybe his greed will help us win."

"I understand your thinking, Boss. I just hope Baron doesn't screw us with our 400,000 tax contribution. This guy is capable of playing both sides against the middle. When Baron gives us the green light to send our share of the taxes, I can't guarantee he'll unconditionally know the truth about whether Balla will actually have his share of the money ready. We'll just have to go with your instincts on this one. But I hereby register my protest."

"Short of me going back to Nigeria in person, I've determined that this is the best way to proceed."

Understanding that the decision was going to stick, Mark said with his sarcastic humor, "I recommended a small campaign donation to Congressman Asshole and you end up setting up his entire pension fund! Hey, I'm just kidding. This might be the best move of this entire ordeal. Worst case, we blow $400,000 and Norman gets to play FSIA lawyer for awhile. Best case, Balla funds."

Norman, who had been just listening to the conversation, joined in by saying, "I don't like what I hear regarding Congressman Baron, but I assure you that the moment we contribute our tax consideration, we will have shifted the FSIA case heavily in our favor, especially if they elect not to fund. We will become the victim, and they will become the thief. Anyway, I am going to excuse myself, because I have a ton of work to do. I'll leave you both with this thought, one way or the other, we've got an excellent fighting chance. That I am willing to guarantee."

"Thanks, Paul. You give me energy and inspiration. Together with you and Mark, we're going to get through this. Keep us informed. Now, go fight like hell, and don't take any prisoners!"

Mark stayed with Sterling to discuss how to organize the upcoming $400,000 wire-transfer to Chief Balla, along with the mechanics of how to get Baron paid the promised $150,000.

About halfway through their discussions, they heard the fax ringing. Mark moved over to the fax and instantly noticed that it was from David Solomon. He removed the pages from the fax and began reading out loud the important part of the message from Solomon.

"The presidential decree regarding offshore contractors and taxes due will continue and not be revoked. In fact, the decree has been amended, raising offshore contractor taxes by an additional half-of-one percent, for a total of two-and-a-half percent. Our contract will be 'grandfathered-in' at the old tax rate of 2%, so long as we pay our taxes within 30 days from the new decree."

Mark continued reading by going right to the punch-line, he said, "Chief Abba Balla requests your assistance in wiring the $400,000 shortfall required to settle the requisite taxes due. Furthermore, please forward the funds we request as soon as possible, but no later than the 30-day time frame we have under the amended presidential decree. Our $2 million are prepared and only await your funds to arrive. The Central Bank has been informed that we will pay the taxes due within the 30-day 'grace period,' provided we receive your funds on time. Mr. Onogo, the Central Bank's attorney, has guaranteed us that the $100 million transfer will be wired to the designated bank account on precisely the same day the full tax obligation is paid. We urge you to send your funds forthwith. If you have any further questions or require any clarifications, please call me at your convenience."

Mark handed the fax to Elliot and said, "These guys are the greatest con artists in the history of con artists. I mean, we couldn't hire a Hollywood script writer to write a better con than the one these motherfuckers are perpetrating on us. These scoundrels are good! Now, the sad part about all this is that we need them, whether they're lying to us or not. If they're stealing from us, well, that's good for our legal case against the government of Nigeria. If they are for real, they just screwed their own government out of $100 million. Wow! You can't make this shit up."

Elliot, who couldn't help but laugh at the ironic truth behind Mark's words, said, "That fax is exactly why I hired Baron to settle this in person. It takes a crook to know one. So, we'll let him figure out the truth."

"I'm glad you don't need to go back to Nigeria, Elliot. It was very astute of you to get Baron on board. I think you should call Solomon and confirm that we are going to accommodate their request. You need to let him know that Baron will be authorized to speak on our behalf when he sees him in person. I also think you should give him an earful regarding how very uncomfortable you are sending the money."

"I agree. I'm going to call him right now," Sterling said as he dialed the phone number.

After the typical delay of waiting for the long-distance call to finally go through, a man answered, "May I assist you?"

"My name is Elliot Sterling, and I want speak with David Solomon."

"Yes, sir. Right away."

The familiar voice of Solomon said, "I take it that you have received my fax. It is with a sense of humility and deep regret that we were forced to send you that fax. Chief Balla has set aside $2 million but cannot raise any more United States dollars. The dollar is next to impossible to get our hands on. Because of Chief Balla's

117

presidential campaign, he is under extreme scrutiny by the government and the press. Every move he makes is carefully observed. His hands are tied. We sincerely apologize, but we need your assistance."

"You expect me to accept your explanation, even though you looked me in the eyes and assured me that you would be solely responsible for any taxes due. Now, you take out your violin and start playing me some stupid melody that this is going to cost me $400,000. You haven't even guaranteed me that you actually have your $2 million or, for that matter, that the Central Bank will fund. This is a very good poker game you're playing, but the problem is that all the cards are stacked in your favor!"

"As we speak, I will be sending you a fax showing you that our $2 million are on 'set-aside deposit' with the Central Bank, specifically earmarked for our contract. All that is pending is your wire for the balance due. When you receive my fax, please notice that Mr. Onogo, the attorney for the Central Bank with whom you met, has signed the receipt for our funds credited towards the taxes due. Let me be clear with you, Mr. Sterling. If you do not wire the Central Bank the shortfall taxes due within the deadline, we will be forced to remove you as the beneficiary, and we will involuntarily replace you with one of Chief Ballas' trusted offshore business partners. We have no other choice. If you want to continue as our partner, then send us the money, as any good partner would do under the circumstances. You stand to make $50 million with very little invested, are you in or out?"

"I'll give you my answer in a moment. Your fax is coming through. So, hold on, let me read it."

"I will wait for you, Mr. Sterling."

Sterling and Goldman read the fax carefully and simultaneously nodded at each other, indicating their independent approval to proceed with the deal.

Sterling grabbed the phone and said to Solomon, "I don't know why you didn't send me Mr. Onogo's confirmation letter along with your first fax. You could have saved us this whole conversation. Please advise Chief Balla that I will be wiring the Central Bank the $400,000 shortfall we need to satisfactorily pay the taxes due, but here are my conditions for sending you the money. First, I want you to fax me a copy of the new amended presidential decree, for my records. Second, please re-fax me a copy of Central Bank's receipt for the $2 million posted by Chief Balla, the contract number on Mr. Onogo's receipt is unreadable. I need to clearly see the number. And last, I want you to wait for my 'representative' to arrive in Lagos within three weeks. He will meet you and Chief Balla in person. I will wire the funds the moment my 'representative' confirms that he has met with you and has reviewed the original documents you will fax me. Do we understand each other, Mr. Solomon?"

Solomon quickly responded with, "Please disclose the name of your representative."

"His name is Jared Baron. He is a member of the United States House of Representatives in Washington, D.C."

"I know exactly who he is. Chief Balla is soon scheduled to meet with the congressman. How much does Mr. Baron know about our business dealings? And what is your relationship with Mr. Baron?"

"The congressman is my friend. He knows only that our business transaction has been developing over many years and that it is finally ready to fund. He is a very powerful man in Washington. His influence regarding American and Nigerian diplomacy is respected at the highest levels of our government. Let me put it to you this way, the president of the United States listens to Baron's opinions when it comes to Nigerian foreign relations and foreign aid."

"Why do you want us to meet with Mr. Baron? Our business dealings with you are highly confidential. We do not want anyone becoming privileged with our business."

"It's too late. Mr. Baron is my confidential representative. If he advises to send you the money, I'll send you the money that same moment. If he tells me this matter is a scam, I'll send you nothing. These are my conditions. So, Mr. Solomon, are you in or out?"

After a brief silence, Solomon confidently answered with, "We look forward to our meeting with Mr. Baron. Please prepare your $400,000 wire. We are very sure that your 'representative' will be authorizing the funds immediately after our meeting. I will inform the Central Bank to expect the balance due in taxes within three weeks. I will make it my business to ensure that the Central Bank will be prepared to fund our contract immediately upon receipt of your wire. And finally, I will notify Chief Balla regarding your decision to accommodate our request. We thank you for your continued cooperation and patience. We are now very close to the successful conclusion of what we trust will be the first of many business arrangements with you. I will next speak to you immediately following our meeting with Mr. Baron. Farewell, Mr. Sterling."

Chapter 14

Three weeks had passed since Sterling had last spoken to Solomon. Those 21 days had been the slowest in Sterling's life. Due to the lawsuit with the bank, he had virtually removed himself from the day-to-day operations of his development company. For all intents and purposes, Mark was managing Sterling Development and Norman was fully engaged in defending the bank's litigation. Time seemed to be moving at a snail's pace. The only interesting progress during this period was the size and scope of the countersuit Norman had orchestrated against the bank. Norman had aggressively demonized the bank as an evil institution with bad intentions to destroy the Sterling empire.

As Sterling was about to leave his home office and take a walk around the neighborhood, his private mobile phone rang. The phone display indicated that it was Congressman Baron on the cellphone. Sterling, who was anxious to speak with Baron, grabbed the phone and said, "When the hell are you leaving for Lagos?

Baron responded with, "Well, that's why I called. I'm scheduled to leave tonight, but I need to discuss our fee arrangement before I leave."

"What about our fee arrangement?"

"You need to understand, Elliot, that I can only ask so much of these Nigerians. I mean, well, you know that if I ask them for something regarding you, then they'll think they can take something away from the United States government. I need some money up front. For all I know, you could be in some kind of weird-ass deal here and the next thing I know I'll be brought up before the House Ethics Committee or thrown out of Congress. Hey, look, we all need to to be looking after each other. I'm going to give you the bank account number to my favorite charity. Just wire half of my fee there, they'll know what to do with the money. The other half, well, I'll just pick it up from Solomon in Nigeria.

You good with that?"

"Fuck off, you piece of garbage!"

"Now there you go again, getting all pissy on me. You've got to understand all the pressures I'm under. I'm not a multi-millionaire like you. I got a lot of overheads to keep up with. Private schools for the kids. A wife who wants everything that all the other politicians' wives buy. I've got to support two houses, one in Washington and one in LA For Christ's sake, Elliot, be fair!"

"You need to listen carefully to my words, Jared. I don't need you. I will honor my deal with you, but I don't need you.

If you modify our deal by even a penny, take our deal and shove it up your ass. Do you grasp what I'm telling you?"

"Sounds like you don't like my proposal?"

"Good. You learn quick. If you want out of our arrangement, believe me, you're hereby released."

"Now I understand why the bank fears you. You can be mean. It was just a proposal. I'll live with our deal, but just remember, I want to be paid the same day you get your funds. Do we agree?"

"Nothing has changed on my end. I get funded, you get funded. All you have to do is make certain that Balla has put up his end of the taxes and that the Central Bank is prepared to release the contract funds upon my wiring $400,000 to them for the balance due on the taxes. When you have confirmed these two facts, call me, and I will immediately wire my funds, based on your word."

"Alright. You win again, Elliot. I leave tonight for Lagos. I will call you at precisely 9:00 AM, your time, three days from today. Wait for my call. I will either say wire your funds or I will advise you to pull out of the deal. I still think you're short-changing me on our arrangement, but you win some and you lose some. Don't forget, I'm a very powerful man. You won this exchange, but you never know, you might need me in the future, and I'm going to remember our little conversation here today. Look for my call."

"Now look who's getting pissy! Just for the record, Congressman, I think you ought to be doing this for zero fee.

Safe travels, Jared. My regards to Chief Balla and David Solomon. I'll await your call."

As Sterling hung up, he couldn't help but have a bad feeling about the call. It was clear that the congressman would sell out to the highest bidder. The question remained whether Sterling would actually be the highest bidder. In all the years that Sterling had known Baron, he never saw him as blatantly corrupt, until now. The next three days were going to be treacherous, but there was nothing further to do than wait.

Baron, along with two other members of Congress on the Foreign Relations Committee, flew the entire night and some of the morning in order to participate in their Nigerian meetings. They were greeted at the Lagos airport by the Nigerian president's diplomatic attache. The congressmen were rushed through International Customs and taken by motorcade to their hotel near the Presidential Palace. They were informed by the attache that they would be picked up the following morning at 9:30 AM for transport to their meeting with the Nigerian head of state, Yemi Muhammadu. Thereafter, they were scheduled to meet with Chief Abba Balla, who, by all measures, was anticipated to become the newly-democratically-elected president of Nigeria.

Baron asked the attache, "Will Chief Balla's advisor David Solomon be present at the Balla meeting?"

"I do not know, but I can easily find out if you would like me to obtain a confirmation," he was answered.

"Yes. I would like a confirmation. Thank you."

Immediately thereafter, the attache grabbed his cellphone and called his office to get Baron his answer.

Within minutes the attache had his answer and told Baron, "Mr. Solomon will be attending the briefing with Chief Balla and all of the rest."

Baron, who had not yet smiled on this trip, grinned as he heard the news on Solomon and said to the attache, "I want you to please inform Mr. Solomon that I need to speak to him privately once the Balla meeting has concluded."

"Yes, sir, Congressman Baron, I will arrange for Mr. Solomon and yourself to privately meet following your briefings with our head of state and Chief Balla. Consider your request done. I will return tomorrow at 9:30 AM. We welcome you to Nigeria and wish you a productive and pleasant stay."

The trip to Lagos was long and tiring for Baron and the two congressmen. They agreed to relax and catch up with some sleep at the hotel. They decided they would have dinner together later that night, but for now, all they wanted to do was sleep.

The rest of the afternoon and evening went by quickly. The congressmen knew that the next day would be long, so they all agreed to go to sleep early in anticipation of getting some rest.

The next morning, Baron and his delegation were ready to meet with Muhammadu and Balla. They had discussed some strategy over breakfast and were leisurely drinking coffee waiting for the attache to arrive. At exactly 9:30 AM, the attache entered the restaurant at the hotel and encouraged everyone to start moving towards his car, 'Because the surface streets are exceedingly jammed, we must move now, or we will be late for our important meetings.'

As they arrived at the Presidential Palace, the congressmen were taken to the front doors of the Palace, where they were introduced to the heavily-armed guards as 'Our visitors from America.' Within seconds, the congressman were whisked through security and requested to wait in a small office.

Twenty minutes later, the attache arrived at the office and said, "It is time for us to meet."

The attache escorted the three congressmen down an ornate and spacious foyer leading to an ostentatious office.

Baron, who had been in this office before, told the other congressmen, "This office is the equivalent to the White House Oval Office, so treat it with the highest degree of respect."

Moments later, the ruling military leader and head of state of the Republic of Nigeria entered the room and said, "Please, gentlemen, take your seats. How is my great friend Congressman Jared Baron?"

"I am well, General Muhammadu. The president of the United States sends his warmest greetings. He extends an invitation to the White House whenever your schedule and that of the president can be arranged. My colleagues and I also bring greetings from the chairman of the board of our largest petroleum company. They are currently negotiating with the Nigerian National Petroleum Corporation to enter into a joint venture. We are here to respectfully request your cooperation in approving this business venture. Of course, we will be very grateful for your continued cooperation, and I've been personally told by the chairman that he would like to show his appreciation to you in person as soon as you will be gracious enough to meet with him."

"Please advise your president that I accept his invitation and we will work out the details as soon as time will permit.

Additionally, inform the chairman that I have already approved the joint venture. Tell him further that we will expect him here in Nigeria, one week from today, so that the agreements can be signed and our business can commence. Of course, he should arrange to visit with me first before any agreements are executed in order to settle a few incentives.

I hope you enjoy your stay while visiting Nigeria. If there is anything you need from the government, well, you know where to reach me. We wish you a safe return, and please visit Nigeria again soon."

Everyone quickly shook hands, and the meeting with General Muhammadu was over within minutes. All of Baron's goals were met regarding this conference. His congressional colleagues were very impressed with what had just been accomplished. One congressman simply said, "You have the wrong job. You need to be secretary of state!"

Baron understood that the meeting had gone perfectly, but now it was time to get an immediate payday for himself. With that in mind, Baron asked the attache, "Where am I meeting Chief Balla?"

"You will be meeting him at the Central Bank of Nigeria in Governor Wole Obasnjo's private conference room. I will call him now and inform him to meet you in 30 minutes. I have made arrangements for your colleagues to be driven back to the hotel, and I will drive you personally to the Central Bank."

"Very good. Let's not keep Chief Balla waiting."

All the important government buildings were located within a short distance of each other. It didn't take more than 15 minutes to arrive at the Central Bank. They made their way straight to the top floor of the building and into the conference room where Chief Abba Balla and David Solomon were sitting and waiting for Baron.

As he extended his hand to Baron, the chief said, "I am Chief Abba Balla, and this is my senior advisor, David Solomon. It is my pleasure to finally meet you in person. As you know, I am about to become the first democratically-elected president of Nigeria. You must inform your president that I need his help. I am also here to inform you that I need your help and that of the US Congress. I will make history. Join me in that history!"

"You are a courageous man, Chief Balla. Our president and the United States Congress understand the enormous risk you have undertaken to transform a country under military rule to a civilian democracy. We know that you are about to make history, and we are all determined to assist you in succeeding. What can we do to help you?"

"First, please inform your government that the transfer of power between General Muhammadu and myself will be without bloodshed. The general has informed the Nigerian military to cooperate with the orderly transition to a civilian leadership. We have organized a sophisticated voter fraud prevention mechanism in order to assure a fair result. I realize that there is opposition to me from the old Nigerian elite who want the system to remain the same.

These people have made fortunes under our current way of life, but masses of the people are suffering, and I will help them. Second, we will require serious financial commitments from America. We need new infrastructure and schools. Let me put it to you this way, my dear friend Congressman Baron, we need new everything. Please help us create an important democratic and diplomatic alliance between the United States and Nigeria."

"I serve on the powerful Foreign Relations Committee. As soon as you're elected president, I will introduce a measure to increase foreign aid to your country. After you have created your national budget, please contact me directly and I will get you all the money you need. We want to do business with Nigeria, we want access to your oil, and we want a US military base set up right here in your country. You are now going to be promoted by me as exceedingly important to the national security interest of the United States. Your democracy, tied to your sweet petroleum, is a combination that will take your great country very far with us. You can count on our support!"

"Thank you, Congressman. I trust your words, and I will say nothing further. I leave you now with my loyal assistant, David Solomon, so that he can discuss a few other particulars with you. Enjoy your stay, and I want to personally request you to please return to Nigeria for my inauguration as president."

"It will be my honor to attend. Best of luck to you, Chief Balla."

Now that everyone had cleared the room, it was Baron's turn to concentrate on his goal of cashing in on this trip. All the lip service was over, and it was time to get down to business with Solomon.

"I understand that Chief Balla and you have a pretty major deal going on with Elliot Sterling. Is that right?"

"Yes, Congressman Baron, you are correct."

"Okay, so did you pay the $2 million for the taxes? I just need you to show me your proof and a couple of other minor details. After that, I'll call Elliot and tell him to wire you the $400,000 you need. Then, you'll get, whoever you need to get, to wire the $100 million to Elliot. And when that's all done, you'll pay me my $150,000 and we all get to go home and tell our wives what a nice day we had. So, Mr. Solomon, do you have the proof I need?"

"No, Congressman Baron, we do not. We felt that it was in the best interest of our partnership with Mr. Sterling to advise him that we had paid the $2 million on deposit with the Central Bank, because Mr. Sterling was pressuring us to pull out of the deal. Chief Balla has a commitment for the $2 million, subject to us showing proof of the 400,000 in our possession. We are running a very expensive political campaign and we cannot be using funds for anything but the campaign. The money we will be receiving from our large contract with Mr. Sterling will be used to fund the chief's national campaign.

"I can assure you that the moment we receive Mr. Sterling's funds, our $2 million will be ready to go. The $100 million will be wired to Mr. Sterling that same day. Mr. Onogo, the Central Bank's attorney, is prepared to confirm all of this to you, if you do not trust my word."

"Are you telling me you lied to Sterling?"

"No, we just did what was in the best interest of our country. Mr. Sterling has almost nothing invested in this venture, yet he stands to make $50 million. We will make the critical decisions, not Mr. Sterling. Now, Chief Balla will be very grateful to you if you do something for us. Tell Mr. Sterling that you have seen all the proof and advise him to send us the $400,000. We will pay your $150,000 gratification in cash.

In fact, you will be paid the instant we receive Mr. Sterling's money. You won't need to wait for the Central Bank's transfer to Sterling. This way you can take the cash back with you. If this is not agreeable, then no one will get paid!"

"I know firsthand how arrogant and stubborn Elliot can be. I agree with you, sometimes what you don't know can't hurt you. Besides, knowing Elliot, he'll most likely tell you to go to hell, and I won't get anything. I'll put my trust in Chief Balla and you. I don't need to talk to your Mr. Onogo. Let's do this deal! I'll call Mr. Sterling at 9:00 AM California time and tell him that everything is in order. He will have his bank wire you the 400,000 by 10:00 AM California time. Please have my cash, in $100 bills, delivered to my hotel room by 1:00 PM tomorrow. Thereafter, I'll be leaving for the airport back to Washington. We're good, we have a deal."

Solomon then looked Baron in the face and said, "Yes indeed, we have a deal. You are a very wise man, Congressman Baron. Chief Balla will be immensely appreciative of your decision to cooperate with us. Something tells me that we will be enjoying an exceptionally beneficial relationship with you. We thank you for your collaboration. I am quite certain that you are going to make yourself a very wealthy man during Chief Balla's presidency."

"I will call Mr. Sterling at 9:00 AM, his time. You will have your money very soon. Please call me on my private mobile number when you are in receipt of Sterling's funds. I will await your call."

"As soon as we receive the wire transfer, we will arrange for your gratification fee to be delivered to your hotel.

We will be happy to transport you from the hotel to the airport."

"Great! Thank you, and we will speak soon."

As this meeting adjourned, the attache greeted Baron at the door of the conference room. They walked together back to the car and drove on to the hotel. Baron spoke very little, because his mind was preoccupied with the correct manner in which to structure his words to convince Sterling to wire the funds. Baron was not thinking about the ethical ramifications of lying to Sterling. He was just trying to figure out how to get Sterling to transfer the money. After all, $150,000 was just about equivalent to his entire annual congressional salary, tax-free at that.

Upon arriving at the hotel, Baron informed his two colleagues that they would all be returning to Washington tomorrow, at around 1:30 PM. He then retired to his room to efficiently plot how he would deceive Sterling.

Chapter 15

Back in Los Angeles, Sterling had been awaiting the all-important call from Congressman Baron. The bank was very aggressive with their lawsuit, placing severe personal pressure on Elliot. He had been informed by Norman that a subpoena had been issued demanding his deposition. Sterling was hoping that Baron would have some good news for him. Just as had been discussed, the phone rang at 9:00 AM. It was Baron calling from Nigeria.

"How the hell are you, Elliot?"

"I'll be doing much better when you tell me the truth about what's going on over there."

"We are good to go, my friend! Pull out that huge checkbook of yours and send some money our way. We're all about to get rich, so pull the trigger and send us the wire. I can assure you that the Central Bank is ready to fund the $100 million. I have spoken to Chief Balla, David Solomon, and Mr. Onogo at the Central Bank. I still don't get how you put together this deal, but it's real, and it's going to fund the minute the Central Bank is in possession of your $400,000 tax payment.

"Tell me more, Congressman."

"I've seen the amended presidential decree. It is authentic. I've reviewed Balla's $2 million receipt for the taxes. And that too is authentic. The receipt clearly indicates your contract number. Mr. Onogo, the attorney for the Central Bank, and I have spoken at length.

Send the tax funds and you're going to see a big chunk of money sitting in your bank account very soon after. Mr. Onogo has promised to get me all requested copies of these documents upon your funding of the $400,000. I trust he will keep his word. Don't wait any longer. Wire the funds!"

"Is Chief Balla fully aware of the contract?"

"More than you think, Elliot. Balla is going to be the next president of Nigeria. He needs his share of the $100 million to help finance his presidential campaign. So, in a way, he needs this money about the same, or more, than you need yours. He's not fucking around. Get this man his money ASAP!"

"What about Solomon? Is he full of bullshit?"

"Solomon is fiercely loyal to Chief Balla. He's a serious guy and I trust him, but don't mess with him. My impression is that he will tear your head off if Balla gives him the okay. My gut feeling is that significant business remains to be conducted by us and them. I think this deal is peanuts compared to the commerce waiting for us in the future. I reiterate, get these people their money!"

"Hey, Jared, if this was your money, would you really send it?"

"In a heartbeat, Elliot, in a heartbeat. These kinds of opportunities don't come around that often. You got a good thing going here. Besides, your bank isn't going to have any mercy on you. So, get your ass in gear and send out that wire now before they change their minds!"

"Why doesn't Onogo give you the clean copies of the documents we've requested?"

"He feels absolutely no obligation to do it. He will give us copies, but only when you show your good faith with the wire. To be honest with you, I don't think this guy likes you all that much. But, he is willing to give us the copies once you've performed. By the way, did you piss Onogo off when you were here?"

"Yeah, just a little. I suppose we can wait on the documents."

"So, Elliot, you ready to get filthy rich?"

"I hope I don't live to regret what I'm about to do. Alright, get Solomon to fax me the fucking wire instructions to the Central Bank. I'll send the $400,000 within 30 minutes of my receipt of the instructions. We'll get your fee paid as soon as I receive my bank confirmation regarding the $100 million. I sure hope you know what you're talking about, Congressman."

"You're doing the right thing, Elliot. I wouldn't misguide you. I'll call Solomon now. He'll get you the wire information within ten minutes. Call me when you get your money. I'll pop a big bottle of champagne for us! Take care, Elliot."

"Thanks, Congressman. I'll be in touch."

Baron had been genuinely convincing. Yet, Sterling was very uneasy wiring this kind of money based on the word of scoundrels. The options were atrocious. Sterling simply had no choice, given the gravity of the bank litigation. It really just got down to which poison he was going to take. The bank definitely wanted to hang him, and the Nigerians probably wouldn't hesitate to steal from him. Since nothing good was going to come from the bank, the decision seemed clear. Take a colossal risk with Baron and the Nigerians and hope that he had not been seduced into a scam.

At worst, Norman would have the 'money consideration' needed to seriously assist him in winning the FSIA legal case against the Nigerians.

As Sterling was deliberating his final decision on whether to forward the money, the fax machine started ringing. It was the wire instructions from Solomon regarding the Central Bank's coordinates. Well, it was now game time. Yes or no.

Without any further hesitation, Sterling got on the phone and instructed his private banker to wire $400,000 to the Central Bank. This painful decision was done.

Within one hour of Sterling's instructions to send the funds, Sterling's banker called to confirm that the money had been wired to the Central Bank. Now, it was time to wait for the $100 million to arrive into Sterling's bank.

These were going to be a stressful few hours anticipating the results.

In the meantime, Baron had been packing in his hotel room so that he and his fellow congressmen could make their way back to Washington, D.C. The trip had been a grand success, and Baron stood ready to collect his fee in cash.

At approximately 1:15 PM, Baron's phone rang in his hotel room. It was Solomon on the line, he announced, "I just spoke to Mr. Onogo, and he confirms that Mr. Sterling's $400,000 wire has been received by the Central Bank. Mr. Onogo's staff is in the process of verifying that the funds received by the Central Bank are in fact 'good funds,' available for application towards the taxes due. He estimates that verification will take about an hour. We have your gratification fee ready as we agreed, but I am not authorized by Chief Balla to release it to you until Mr. Onogo gives us his final approval. So, we have prepared a minor contingency plan."

"What the hell kind of contingency do you have in mind, Mr. Solomon? Look, I've done my job. I'm not happy with what I had to do to convince Sterling to pay, but I did it, and now I want my money. This is starting to piss me off!"

"Do all of you Americans have such a thin skin? Perhaps you did not hear me. You will not receive your money until we can confirm that we have ours. Maybe my English is hard to understand. Please listen to our amended plan.

You will not receive any money at your hotel room. We want you to check out of the hotel. We have a driver and car waiting for you at the hotel. Our driver is going to take you to the airport. Once you arrive at the airport, you will be escorted directly to the private First-Class Passenger Club area for your airline. We have arranged for a private room inside the Passenger Club where you will be handed a small carry-on luggage which will contain the entire gratification in cash. Of course, you are welcome to count it, should you choose to do so, but I assure you, all of your funds will be there. Do you understand?"

"Yeah, I hear you. I still think that's total bullshit. You obviously don't know Elliot Sterling. Those funds sitting at the Central Bank are as good as gold. This man doesn't play around when it comes to money. You really are pulling my chain. I don't really like what you're doing here, but you aren't giving me much of an option. As my granddaddy once taught me, when in Rome, do as the Romans do. So, here I am in Nigeria, and I guess I'm going to have to act like you Nigerians."

"I must abide by the wishes of Chief Balla. You will have your money later this afternoon at the airport."

"Your first name is David, right?

"Yes, sir."

"Okay, David. Now it's my turn. You tell Chief Balla that if I don't get my money at the airport, Nigeria is not going to receive a fucking dime in foreign aid from the United States government. Is my English clear, David?"

"Yes, Congressman Baron. Your English is clear."

"Very well. I'll look for your little courier at the airport. Tell him not to be late. I want to have enough time to count my money. Not that I don't trust you, but now I've got to be little more careful. Business is business. Good luck, David."

As previously arranged, at 1:30 PM, Baron's two colleagues were waiting for him in the lobby with their luggage ready to proceed to the airport. They were met by a slender-looking man who introduced himself as one of Chief Balla's official chauffeurs. Baron instantly smelled on the drivers breathe that he had been drinking liquor.

While walking to the car, Baron mentioned to his colleagues that he smelled alcohol, yet they didn't seem to care.

Baron said it again, "Our driver may have had one too many drinks. Let's just get our own transportation."

"Listen, Jared, by the time we get a reliable driver, we're going to be late for our flight. Besides, I thought you had some special meeting at the airport with some last-minute government official needing to meet with you privately. Let's just roll with this guy. I really don't think we have anything to worry about."

"Yeah, I do have a meeting at the airport. This 'drunk' is supposed to escort me to where the meeting is taking place. Alright, let's drive with him, but I still think he's over the legal blood-alcohol driving limit."

"Well, maybe by American standards, but I'd be willing to bet that he's fine by Nigerian levels. I just don't think that our Nigerian government contacts are going to send us a drunk Nigerian to drive us to the airport. Lighten up, Jared!"

As they got into the car, the driver said, "Please forgive me, but you will notice that this automobile has no seatbelts, except for the driver's seat. This was the only car that was available, due to the worldwide oil conference Nigeria is hosting today. Our government official who routinely uses this auto ordered that each of the passenger seatbelts be removed, due to comfort. He feels restricted wearing a seatbelt. So, please try to move very little during our travel towards the airport."

Baron just rolled his eyes while his colleagues displayed facial expressions showing concern.

Right from the beginning, the chauffeur appears to be driving way too fast. As he pulled up to what is known as the A1 highway, the speed perception gave way to reality. This chauffeur was driving out-of-control crazy just before entering a long, dark tunnel built right into the side of a mountain.

Baron demanded, "Slow this car down! I order you slow this vehicle down, NOW!"

These were the last words Congressman Jared Baron of California would ever utter. Just as he finished speaking, their car accidentally swerved ever so slightly, bumping into the automobile next to them. This caused the two vehicle drivers to immediately lose control, which provoked both vehicles to instantaneously flip. Within moments, there was a chain reaction of cars horrifically crashing into each other. The congressman's car was upside down and on fire. The A1 highway tunnel had become the scene of an unmitigated disaster. This dark tunnel was now illuminated by flames. A horrifying sight. A picture straight out of hell.

It took the authorities well over an hour just to arrive at the scene of the impact where the three United States congressmen and their driver lay burning to death. By the time the fire had been extinguished and the first responders found Congressman Baron, it was too late. His body, and that of everyone in the vehicle, had been burnt beyond recognition. Of course, the only thing left to do by the authorities was to finish their investigation, which included pictures of the scene of the accident, and transfer the four dead men to the nearest morgue for identification.

As the bodies of the congressmen arrived at the morgue, two of General Muhammadu's officials were already waiting.

One official flashed his credential and stated to the morgue employee, "We are now in charge of this matter…"

The morgue employee was intrigued by the fact that no one could possibly have understood who these dead people were.

They were unrecognizable, and it would be impossible to determine which vehicle they were extracted from, since the car was effectively totaled, along with its license plates. So the employee decided to put up a little resistance by asking, "How do you know who the deceased are? Besides, we cannot turn over the bodies without legal paperwork signed by a judge. These men are dead. We will only release them to their lawful relatives. Besides, we're certainly not going to release them to you without written authority. Thank you, and good day."

"We are acting under the authority of General Yemi Muhammadu. We are not asking you, we are demanding you to release the three men to us!"

"Why only three? There are four men here."

"The three men identified as having been taken from the backseat of the Mercedes are from America. They are United States congressmen. We are responsible for their safe return. We must transport them to the United States Embassy for immediate return to their country and their families. We had them under our surveillance when visiting Nigeria. We know they were in the accident, because we were trailing them. Now, we've told you much more than we need to tell you. Under the demand of General Muhammadu, we hereby instruct you to do the following. Clean these people up to the best of your ability. Place them all in your best caskets. Have this done by no later than two hours. We will pick them up for transfer to the US Embassy and onto a military airport. We need these people out of the country. Stop wasting any more time. Move, and move now!"

"Of course, we will abide by your instructions. Should we send you our bill?"

Sterling was completely unaware that Baron was dead. In fact, he was in a panic, because his bank was unable to confirm any wire transfer from the Central Bank of Nigeria. All Sterling could think about was that he had been scammed by Baron and the Nigerians. He tried to phone Baron three separate times, with each call directed to voice mail. The phone sounded as if it had been deliberately shut off.

To make matters worse, Solomon would not accept his calls either. The assistant picking up the calls would inform Sterling that, "Mr. Solomon is in a meeting and cannot be disturbed."

Something was dreadfully wrong. The Nigerian business deal had just gone from promising to a nightmare.

Mark began calling on Sterling's private phone line. As soon as he picked up, Mark, as if he were out of breathe, hurriedly said, "Elliot, quickly turn on your TV. Go to CNN. Baron is dead!"

"He's what?"

"He died in a car accident in Nigeria on his way to the airport. Turn on your television!"

"Mark, you need to get over here now. And tell Norman to come with you."

Sure enough, CNN confirmed that Congressman Baron and two other congressmen had 'perished in a fiery car accident' while on their way to the Nigerian airport, according to the US State Department.

Within 20 minutes, Mark and Norman arrived at Sterling's private office. They found Sterling at his desk drinking Scotch and listening to CNN on the television. Instead of acting nervous, Mark asked, "Can I get some of that Scotch?"

Elliot responded with, "Sure. Take some, and give Paul a glass. I guess we'll toast our farewell to Congressman Jared Baron. Go ahead, Mark, you have the honors."

"Well, gentlemen, raise your glasses to one arrogant, greedy son-of-a-bitch. Not sure we're all going to see you in heaven, but wherever you're going, have a good trip. That's it."

Sterling looked at Mark and said, "That's it?"

"Yeah, that's it. Now, on my way over here, I had the chance to reach a good friend of mine who works in the State Department in Washington. He shared with me what the Department knows so far. First, it is true that Baron, two other congressmen, and the driver were killed in a horrific car accident in a highway tunnel just outside Lagos. They literally burned to death. Second, they were definitely in transit to the airport with intentions to fly back to Washington. The airline has confirmed their names as officially registered on their passenger list. The Nigerian government also collaborates this story. Apparently, the Nigerian head of state had these guys under surveillance the entire time they were in Lagos. Third, Baron was traveling in a car issued by the Nigerian federal government."

As Sterling took a sip of his Scotch, he looked at Mark and asked, "Why would Baron be on his way to the airport without having collected his promised $150,000 fee from me? The only way he was getting paid by us was after our $100 million had been officially received by us. So, why was Baron going to the airport without communicating with me?"

Mark answered the question, "Apparently, he made a better deal with Balla, except Balla had no intentions of paying our poor-schmuck friend, the late Congressman Baron. Instead, he figured out a way to kill him! And Balla keeps the entire $400,000 we wired to the Central Bank. In fact, Balla is looking to keep all the contract money!"

Sterling, now holding his head with two hands, said, "These guys seduced me with all this money and then they scammed me! So far, these bastards have really kicked my ass. It's time we teach them a lesson! Okay, let's figure this out. Either Balla wants the money all for himself or he's found himself a new partner in General Muhammadu. All they need to do is kill off anyone who knows anything about the deal. I think Balla, and probably Muhammadu, ordered the assassination of Baron. The other two congressmen and the driver were just collateral damage. I could be next. This is getting dangerous!"

Norman, who was, as usual, just listening, entered the conversation with, "I've got the solution to all of this. Tomorrow, I head into a federal court. I will file our FSIA legal case against Balla, the Central Bank, the finance minister, and any other John Doe we can name, including General Muhammadu. By taking this move, we will stake a legal claim to the money due by Nigeria to Mr. Sterling. Additionally, we will now put a notice to the world that this is legitimately our contract and our money. The Nigerians will need to think long and hard before they're going to want to harm you with the knowledge that our legal system and our government are now watching. By the way, you just placed the odds in our favor with that $400,000 consideration you sent them. I'll file the case tomorrow. We'll get these guys!"

Sterling reacted by commenting, "We have no choice. Go ahead, file the case. I mean, look at this situation. You got three dead American congressmen. I may have personally lost $400,000, plus the watches and and the other cash we gave them. I have no partner to speak to in Nigeria regarding our $100 million deal. The

American bank wants to take over my business and my home. And now I need to be concerned that some fucking Nigerian official might decide to put a price on my head. Yes, Paul, file the case!"

"Please remember, Mr. Sterling, that litigation is very slow. I think we'll win. But, if they decide to defend, which I think they're going to do vigorously, the FSIA case will take years to decide a final resolution. So, unless we can come up some other business angle to pressure the Nigerians into paying the contract without a legal battle, I'll file the case tomorrow morning in federal court. By the way, we're going to concurrently ask the court to freeze $5 million in Nigerian assets, to be held in the United States under the jurisdiction of the court. In the event we prevail, the collateral will be released to the plaintiff. This can consist of a Nigerian airplane sitting at JFK airport in New York or cash parked at Chase Bank. It will be whatever assets we can find. I have plenty of legal precedent for this."

Sterling stood and said, "I understand that court cases take forever. I just don't want to start one if you can't succeed. I know you're going to be successful, I can see it in your eyes. So, go win! I can't wait to see their faces when you freeze $5 million of their assets!"

Sterling then looked at his confidant, Mark, and said to him, "I happen to agree with you, Baron definitely sold me out! If he was leaving the country without speaking to me first about collecting his money, he had just found a better source to get his fee. I also agree that Balla and Solomon have no intentions of funding our contract. No doubt it, they're crooks."

Chapter 16

Three long months had passed since Norman had filed the FSIA case now known as Sterling v. the Republic of Nigeria. The case had been filed in the Ninth District Federal Court and was assigned to Judge Anthony Fernandez.

The Nigerian government had retained a high-powered international law firm with offices in Los Angeles. A team of four attorneys were assigned to defend the Nigerians. They denied each and every claim brought against them by Norman.

In fact, they were counter claiming that Sterling was attempting to defraud the Nigerian government using a 'fictitious contract.' They asked that the case be thrown out of court, due to the 'preposterous idea that the plaintiff expected to be paid $100 million in exchange for having invested just $400,000." The defendants additionally stated that the alleged people Sterling claimed to be transacting business with were simply impostors renting office space at the Central Bank of Nigeria.

Of course, Norman painted quite a different picture, one that indicated that Sterling was conducting a legitimate business transaction in which he was invited to participate by the Nigerians. Norman argued that it was irrelevant how much money was invested by Sterling. He stated that the facts would clearly show that there was a legally-binding contract executed by both parties, and that Mr. Sterling had been defrauded. The evidence would show, beyond a shadow of a doubt, that the Nigerians had breached their contract with Mr. Sterling. Norman further brought forth that the preponderance of the evidence would demonstrate 'bad faith' dealings conducted by high-level officials in the government of Nigeria.

Along with many other serious claims, Norman asked the court for a, 'prejudgment writ of attachment in the amount of $5 million, based on the plaintiff demonstrating meritorious allegations, fraud in the underlying action, and that the defendant may attempt to dispose of or hide United States assets from the court.'

The Nigerians had requested that Judge Fernandez dismiss the case, indicating that the Ninth District Court in the United States had 'no jurisdiction over the matter.' They asked the judge to, 'dismiss the case and to send it back to Nigeria, where it should in fact be legally adjudicated. After all, the commercial activity had all been conducted in Nigeria, as opposed to Los Angeles, California, United States of America.'

Today was the day that Judge Fernandez was to rule on the jurisdiction matter, along with whether the case had merit, and if it had merit, whether the court would accept or deny the prejudgment writ of attachment. Oh, what a day this was going to be for Norman! His client's financial life hinged on these decisions. Anything less than a positive decision on behalf of the plaintiff regarding the merit and jurisdiction could prove devastating to the plaintiff.

These critical rulings at the Ninth District Federal Courthouse, in Los Angeles, by 9:00 AM were still pending. Norman had asked that Sterling be present to hear firsthand what the judge had to say. All four lawyers for the Nigerians were also present. The tension was high. No one acknowledged or looked at each other. Everyone sat stone-faced waiting for the judge to enter. Sterling had been prepared by Norman for the worst, but there was a feeling of optimism that the judge might see the merits of the case, predicated on the fact that Sterling had established a very good reputation as a serious businessman in Los Angeles.

At 9:15 AM, the court bailiff announced, "All rise, Judge Anthony Fernandez presiding."

Just as everyone was about to take their seats after the judge entered the chambers, Mark Goldman walked through the door and sat next to his old friend, Elliot, and whispered, "Couldn't resist not being here. Just wanted to see these overrated, high-priced, prick LA attorneys, in their $2,000 suits, get their asses handed to them by Norman. I assure you, Boss, we got these guys."

A subdued Sterling looked at Mark with a less-than-confident smile and said, "Thanks very much for coming. Let's see what the judge has to say."

Norman, who was sitting at the attorney's table directly across from the four Nigerian counselors, turned his head back towards Sterling and clenched his fist, symbolizing a message of confidence.

Moments later, Judge Fernandez began to speak, "I appreciate the exemplary briefs submitted by both the plaintiff and the defense counselors. Your legal work is a praiseworthy model for our legal community to take note. I have carefully reviewed the arguments on both sides of of this case, and I am prepared to make a ruling on the three matters before this court. Let me begin with the issue of jurisdiction. The Foreign Sovereign Immunities Act of 1976 is a United States law that establishes the limitations as to whether a foreign, sovereign nation, or its political subdivisions, agencies, or instrumentalities, may be sued in US courts, federal or state. It also establishes specific procedures for service of process, attachment of property, and execution of judgment in proceedings against a foreign state. The FSIA provides the exclusive basis and means to bring a lawsuit against a foreign sovereign in the United States. Again, after careful consideration, this court finds that the plaintiff has demonstrated sufficient facts within the framework of the FSIA to merit jurisdiction in this court. The defendant's motion is hereby denied."

The judge continued with, "Regarding the defendant's Motion to Dismiss, this court finds that the Motion to Dismiss is denied."

"And finally, regarding the plaintiff's Motion for Prejudgment Writ of Attachment, this court finds sufficient evidence to order a $5 million attachment against the defendant, and herewith issue a prejudgement writ of attachment regarding the two bank accounts located in New York City that were cited in the plaintiff's brief. The court will follow with a written judgment regarding these matters. A week from today, we want you all back in court, at which point we will be setting our schedule, leading towards a final court date to litigate this case."

And with the sound of the gavel, the judge rose, then left the room while everyone was standing.

The defendant's attorneys were shocked, yet they showed absolutely no emotion, except that they all appeared to have seen a ghost. Norman couldn't hide his emotions. He walked directly to his client, not smiling, but literally shedding a tear of joy for his boss while he hugged him with pride in his heart. Elliot, who had already gotten the wind knocked out him by Mark's hug of joy, saw the tears in his young attorney's eyes and became overwhelmed with emotion. Sterling put his hand on Norman's head, similar to how a father puts his hand on his son's head with pride when a son does a good deed, and with a crackling voice said simply, "Well done, Paul, well done!"

As they emotionally composed themselves and started walking towards the court exit, the lead attorney for the Nigerians approached Norman and said, "Can I have a word with you?"

Norman answered with, "Sure."

"I don't think you and I have formally met. My name is Neil Roberts," he said as he extended his hand to greet Norman.

"I'm Paul Norman. What can I do for you?"

"Nice job in there, Mr. Norman. When this legal stuff is all said and done, you might want to consider coming over to my law firm. We can always use a sharp legal mind like yours. Very impressive. Anyways, there's not much you can do for me, but you might be able to do something for you client."

"And what's that, Mr. Roberts?"

"Look, I wouldn't be celebrating too much. We're going to run you guys crazy. We're going to make you more broke than you already are. Not that you're looking for my advice, but here it is anyways. Tell Mr. Sterling to quit this case. You're never going to win. First of all, we're going to emergency-appeal Judge Fernandez's preliminary rulings. Even if you defeat me regarding my appeal, we're going to bring every motion conceivable against you. We're going to depose Mr. Sterling and we are going to prove that he got into this fabricated Nigerian contract because he is on the verge of bankruptcy. You and I both know that his only way out is to collect on this bogus contract, and in doing so, defraud the Nigerian government out of $100 million. At the end of the day, no judge is going to believe you, including the Ninth District Court of Appeals, which we are prepared to take you to even if you win a final verdict here with Judge Fernandez. So, if you don't take my advice, please prepare yourselves for a long, drawn-out battle. I trust you have anticipated a sizable war chest for legal fees and expenses. Don't forget, my client is a country, and they just print as much money as they need to."

"For a minute there, I thought you were going to offer some kind of a settlement. But now, you're sounding like a sore loser. Here's my response to you. I'm thrilled that your corrupt-nation client has the ability to print the equivalent of $100 million so that you can pay us our contract. Oh, excuse me, after today's writ of attachment, you only need to print $95 million. By the way, we'll be demanding to depose the governor of the Central Bank, Wole Obasanjo, along with the minister of finance, Sani Odibo. You see, I personally met with these characters. I know what they promised my client. So, on the contrary, Mr. Roberts, I suggest you advise your client to settle this case now, because if you don't, we will ask the court to enforce the RICO provisions of the law, which will probably triple our award. Now, here's my advice to your client, pay us what you owe us under the contract. Or, have fun explaining to them why Mr. Sterling, by order of the court, now controls $5 million of their money. Nigeria is playing on our home field. Mr. Sterling is as reputable a businessman as you will find in America. He has an enforceable contract with the Nigerians, and you are going to lose. I promise you, this case is going to get worse for your client as each day advances. Good day, Mr. Roberts." And without shaking Roberts' hand, Norman walked away to meet up with Elliot and Mark.

Mark spotted Norman and said, "From a distance, that didn't look like it was going so well."

Norman quickly responded with, "No, actually, we were able to send a pretty good message to the Nigerians. Neil Roberts is a senior partner at his firm and is the lead attorney on this case. He tried to strongarm us, but it backfired on him. I'll tell you all about it at the celebration lunch that our boss is about to invite us to attend. Let's go, I'm starving!"

Sterling had selected his favorite steak restaurant, located on the 400 block, Canon Drive, in Beverly Hills.

The staff at the upscale eatery knew Sterling well and were very eager to cater to his wishes. It started with immediate seating at the best private booth in the house. Without a word, the waiter brought a bottle of Sterling's favorite wine and three glasses to the table. Even before the menu was passed out, a second waiter brought a mouth-watering antipasto consisting of olives, anchovies, cheeses, and meats. This was the lifestyle and level of respect Elliot Sterling had become accustomed to living in.

As Sterling raised his glass, he said, "To my brilliant lawyer. A man who has dedicated himself to legal excellence. A reliable counselor who understands the art of winning. Job well-done!"

Mark followed with, "To Paul Norman, my friend and colleague, you have just saved all of our asses! We look forward to returning right back here after you win our case. You are the man! Now, go get us our money!"

Norman picked up his glass and said, "To my boss. Thank you for entrusting me with this case. I will not rest until we win, and make no mistake about it, we will win! And to you, Mark, I want to thank you for the big-league support you have given me. You quietly go about your business always doing the little things that never show up in the box scores but assist in the wins. Today's court rulings would never have been possible without your devotion towards our cause."

These three men were about to take on a country. This was a team with depleted resources but hell-bent on victory.

The classic Biblical story of David and Goliath.

Throughout the course of their meal, Norman explained how Roberts had promised to out-spend Norman at every level. He warned Sterling and Mark that Roberts would be bringing every legal proceeding conceivable. He spoke about the real possibility of an appeal. Norman made it clear that he expected Roberts to frame Sterling as a criminal desperate for money. He prepared Elliot for the eventuality of a myriad of questions, leading to a hard-hitting deposition. It was important that Sterling understand that this case was about to cost a small fortune, including a costly discovery period.

Sterling's response to Norman's warnings was clear and direct, "Play to win!"

With that simple mandate from his boss, Norman went on to give him insight as to what to expect in the weeks and months to come. He explained that although Roberts would most likely block the deposition of Governor Wole Obasanjo, claiming that we would have to travel to Nigeria to serve him a subpoena, Norman explained his trap. "Obasanjo is due to arrive in Washington, D.C., next month at the annual meeting of the International Monetary Fund and the World Bank Group. Delegates are government officials of the member countries of the IMF and World Bank Group executive directors. The annual meeting is by invitation only. Guess who one of the featured speakers is this year?"

Sterling, with a big smile splashed across his face, answered with, "Governor Obasanjo!"

"Bingo! And guess who else is invited to attend?"

Sterling said, "You're making this way too easy. The answer is Sani Odibo, minister of finance for Nigeria."

"Right again! We're literally going to hand them their deposition subpoenas as they arrive at their hotel in Washington. They will have no choice but to comply, because Roberts will previously be sitting on our demand for the deposition of these two guys while continuing to inform Judge Fernandez that we can only serve them in Nigeria. As soon as they receive their subpoenas, I will be on my way to Washington to conduct the formal deposition of two of the highest-ranking government officials in the Republic of Nigeria. Roberts will have no choice but to join me! These depositions are the key cornerstones of our case. We will be able to demonstrate to the court that the Nigerian government was unconditionally aware of the legally-binding contract. We will prove, without dispute, that the government, through the Central Bank of Nigeria, demanded that taxes be paid as a prerequisite of the release of the $100 million contract. We will also be able to identify, beyond reasonable doubt, that we met with both the minister and the governor, as opposed to impostors, as they allege."

Mark looked up at Norman as he was finishing eating his favorite Ghirardelli Chocolate Mousse dessert and said, "We're not going to ask you how you found out that these two bastards are going to be in Washington, but however you did that, you're definitely getting a raise. Jesus, you're good!"

"Before we finish this delicious lunch, I have two other quick topics I'd like to address. The first is the RICO Act, or simply RICO. I have requested that our judge consider this law as a part of our case. RICO is a United States federal law that provides for extended criminal penalties and a civil cause of action for acts performed as part of an ongoing criminal organization. A RICO judgment can double, even triple, an award, but it could be dangerous to Mr. Sterling."

Sterling, who was listening intently, asked, "What makes RICO dangerous to me?"

"It is dangerous because you are gravely alleging that the government of Nigeria is engaging in organized criminal behavior. You are asking a federal court in the United States to find, before the world, that the Republic of Nigeria and the Central Bank of Nigeria are corrupt. Effectively, they are ruled by a military dictatorship, and I don't see a hell-of-a-lot of jurisprudence over there. So, if you're about to prove that the Nigerian head of state, Yemi Muhammadu, is a crook, you might want to think about the ramifications of such a claim. Bottom line, they're not going to sit around and let that happen without all-out war. Just look at the three congressmen who quickly found themselves dead. Maybe that was an accident, and maybe not."

The always-decisive Sterling responded with, "Go after these guys with everything you got. Pressure them with RICO, bad public relations, and anything else that comes to that brilliant mind of yours. Strength is the only thing they're going to understand. I'm not worried, just push them as hard as you know how!"

"Okay. At least, we had the conversation. Now, I just have a couple of other points I'd like to discuss. I'm going to need some help fighting the bank. Everything is well under control, but my full attention needs to be on the FSIA case that we have with the

Nigerians. It's a full-time effort. So here's what I recommend. We bring in a third-party law firm to buy as much legal time as possible until we get the Nigerians to pay us. I'd like to hire this firm as soon as possible and instruct them to paper the bank to death with legal maneuvers. We will need to allocate at least $200,000 in order to retain them. Do I have your permission to bring them on board?"

"What do you mean by 'at least' 200,000? Is that just the beginning or is that our budget for the case?"

"That will get us to the point where we should have Judge Fernandez's court ruling regarding the FSIA case. I'm talking about the initial court case that we are now litigating with the Nigerians."

"I used to think I was a pretty wealthy guy. I mean, in the old days, $200,000 wouldn't phase me, one way or the other. But the way I'm going lately, that seems like a lot of money. I got to be careful with the allocation of my funds. Before you know it, I won't have any. So, here's my deal. I authorize $100,000. I want you to hire the smartest young attorney you can find. I want this guy to work in-house with you at our offices. You direct him, but let him do all the work. Get an attorney who understands banking and financial law, then paper these bastards to death. That's the best I can do. Can you work with that?"

"Sure, I can work with that. I know just the guy. We're going to drive the bank crazy. I'll especially enjoy messing with your friend, Paul Reno. Can't wait to ask him at his deposition why he didn't take into consideration the $100 million Nigerian contract on your financial statement. Especially given the fact that he had personally organized the bank account number for the sum."

Sterling then asked, "Is that everything?"

"No, just one more thing. The victory we had today was glorious. But, it is just the beginning. We have a long fight in front of us. In the long run, we should win the Nigerian case on its merits. The challenge is that it will take us years, including appeals, to finally get our money. The rulings we won today will be brought up on emergency appeal to the Ninth Circuit Court of Appeals. We will win, and then we will eventually go to trial in Judge Fernandez's court. We can expect to win that trial, but they will appeal that decision to a higher court. Hell, this thing could end up at the Supreme Court over jurisdiction and the fine points of the FSIA law. You see, even if we're right, which we are, the Nigerian attorneys are going to pursue the case. They're going to 'milk' this for as many fees as they can. Their client is a country, and they can print as much money as they want to keep paying legal fees. These attorneys have zero incentive to advise their client to settle with us at a reasonable point. They represent a corrupt foreign country, and they don't give a damn, one way or the other. On the contrary, the Nigerian lawyers have huge overheads with their big offices, elaborate homes, and fancy cars."

Sterling interrupted Norman and said, "Sounds like doomsday. Should we quit now?"

"No, sir. We're not going to quit. On the contrary, I'm going to run a truck right up their ass. I'm going to pressure them at every level. At some point in the proceedings, we will win the RICO argument and it is going to become apparent to their attorneys that they're looking at a serious problem. Your job is to determine when the United States government is looking to fund Nigeria's foreign aid package. You also need to know when a major American oil company is preparing to sign a monumental petroleum exploration deal in Nigeria. When the timing is right, we will threaten our Nigerian friends with exposing the RICO findings we have on them to not only the United States government, but to the oil companies themselves. No CEO of a publicly-traded oil company will want to explain to their stockholders why they're doing business with a rotten and corrupt government. And Congress is not going to be quick to release foreign aid to a country deceiving American citizens."

Sterling, impressed yet again, said, "Boy, you have really given this thing some thought!"

"Yes, I have. But, there's just one more thing."

Sterling responded, "I can't wait to hear this. Shoot!"

"I want you, Mr. Sterling, to make a business deal with the Nigerians yourself. Not me, or through the attorneys. And not the politicians or the big oil executives. It's got to be you, at the perfect moment in time. I will get you that perfect moment, and then you, and only you, will get our contract paid, as originally intended. Just be ready to act when the timing is right. Now, here's your clue. Make your deal with Stanley Roberts, David Solomon's main assistant. He is motivated and has access to all the right people. Remember, he has the Central Bank codes for fund transfers. We know him, and he confidently told us he that can get this done. At the end of the day, he's our man!"

Sterling and Mark looked at each other, then Mark said, "You mean the court case is just a front to expose Nigeria as an organized crime syndicate under the disguise of a legitimate nation?"

"Exactly correct. Little by little, we will prove our case. It will be evident that we have them on criminal behavior, and they're going to fold. I just don't want to rely on their attorneys, our government, or oil company executives to get us our money. I want that part in our hands. Our judicial system will eventually do it for us on our case's merits, but we don't have the luxury of the time or money to wait for justice. So, Mr. Sterling, we do it ourselves. We understand each other?"

Sterling just kept glancing at Mark, and then said to Norman, "Either you are a terrible attorney who really doesn't know what the hell he's doing with this case or you belong on the Supreme Court as a justice. But after what you've accomplished so far, I think you belong on the Supreme Court. So, we're going to play this exactly as you say. All you need to do is tell me when to pull the trigger and I'll be ready with Stanley Roberts."

Chapter 17

Several weeks had passed since the 'victory luncheon' with Norman and Goldman. Since that time, Norman had hired a Stanford University law professor, on leave of absence from the University, to work in-house with Norman on the banking lawsuit. Just as Norman had predicted, this case had become a procedural nightmare for the bank. Conversely, the FSIA case was becoming a procedural nightmare for Norman.

Around 3:00 PM, Mark called Sterling and said, "I've been thinking about this Stanley Roberts call that Norman wants you make. I think you should call him now and get a preliminary reading on what he's thinking. Additionally, I recommend that you tape the call with Roberts and get him to show criminal intent and disloyalty towards the Nigerian government. We will then use that tape to get Roberts to act on our behalf at the Central Bank. But, you didn't hear this from me."

Sterling replied, "You understand that taping someone without their knowledge is considered inadmissible evidence in our court?"

"Of course, I know that, but I'm not talking about using it in our court, I'm talking about using it in Nigeria with high-ranking officials to effectively blackmail, I'm sorry, persuade Roberts into doing what we ask of him regarding the transfer of our money."

"I see, you want me to use FBI, or is it Mafia, tactics to get this guy on the record. I mean, you actually want me to persuade Roberts into incriminating himself on a taped recording, then play it back to him so that he is so terrified that he funds our contract. Where did you come up with this shit?"

Mark, now very serious, responded with, "I'm not asking you, I'm telling you. Do this, and we are going to win. I've never been so certain in all my life as I am now. Do it, Elliot. I'm telling you, this is going to work. From what I understand, this guy wants out of Nigeria. Not only are we going to get him and his young family out of Nigeria, but we're going to offer him money and a job in the good old USA. Believe me, he's going to find a way to wire us our money, or we're going to kick his butt with our tape recording. He can play ball with us, or he faces a long jail sentence, or even death, for treason. I'll bet my life, or should I say his life, that he's going to choose us!"

"I didn't think you were such a mean bastard."

"Hey, these guys are doing everything they can to rip us off. I wouldn't be surprised if they outright had Baron knocked off. These guys are bad 'hombres' and this is the only way we're going to defeat them. Hell, I don't want to wait five or six years before we find justice in our courts. So, I say take no prisoners and play it my way."

"Alright. We'll explore your way. I think it might work. The question is, how much money does Roberts want for his fee to do the job? Also, is he still capable of performing? I guess we'll find out once we call him. The last thing he told me before I left Nigeria was that he knew the Central Bank codes to wire the money. He told me, in no uncertain terms, that he could get the money out. Let's find out if he's for real. Come on over. I'll call him and you can record!"

It didn't take Mark much time to get to Sterling's office. As Mark made his way into the office, he saw that Sterling had already set up the recording device and was ready to act on the scheme. Sterling spotted Mark and said, "This trick might work. I've just got to get Stanley comfortable. I think he's going to sing like a bird. If you're ready, I'm going to call him on my speaker phone so you can hear the conversation. All you need to do is flip the recorder switch to the 'on' position and we'll hang this son-of-a-bitch."

Sterling then proceeded to dial the private cellphone number Stanley had handed him in Nigeria before he left. After a short delay and the now-familiar international dial tone ring, a man answered the phone and said, "Who is calling me from the United States?"

"Hello. This is Elliot Sterling. Am I speaking to Stanley Roberts?"

"Yes, Mr. Sterling. What a pleasant surprise to hear your voice. I am very puzzled as to why you waited so long to contact me. You almost waited too long. But, as you Americans say, 'better late than never.' Much has occurred since we last spoke. I'm quite sorry about your congressman friend and his colleagues. Tell me, what would you like me to do for you?"

"First of all, I hope you and your family are doing well. As to what I'd like you to do for me, well, let's get right to the point. I

148

want you to arrange for the Central Bank to immediately wire my contract funds."

"I was quite certain that this was the motive of your call. Of course, you've complicated things by virtue of you filing your lawsuit against my country and the Central Bank. And you didn't help your goodwill with Nigeria when you attached five million of our dollars. You know, United States dollars are hard to come by here in Nigeria, and you just grabbed $5 million of them. You are not exactly the most popular man in Nigeria."

"Well, I'm sure you know, Mr. Roberts, that I sent the Central Bank $400,000 in order to assist Chief Balla in paying the taxes due. You probably know who stole my money and why I didn't get paid. So, why don't you start off by giving me a brief explanation as to what the hell is going on here! Then, when you're done with your explanation, continue on with how you're going to get my contract paid."

"O.K. I'll tell you the truth as it was explained firsthand to me by David Solomon. General Muhammadu and Chief Balla conspired to kill Congressman Baron. The other congressmen just happened to be, as you Westerners say, collateral damage. Now, before you get too upset with the general and the chief, keep in mind that Baron had just double-crossed you. He decided to accept a gratification from Balla in the amount of $150,000, to be paid in cash to Baron upon his arrival at the airport just before he was to return to the United States. Balla and Solomon used Baron to convince you to wire the$ 400,000. Since Baron was so tragically killed in a car accident, Balla had the good fortune of keeping for himself all the 'tax' money you wired."

"How sure are you that this is true?"

"It has been collaborated by Muhammadu's top aide, who has directly spoken to me about these facts and the truth."

Sterling silently looked up at Mark while shaking his head and asked Roberts, "Why did Muhammadu want him dead?"

"Congressman Baron had been privileged to confidential information. He knew that the general was about to receive a major gratification from an American oil company that was to be granted the rights to lease thousands of acres of land set aside by the Nigerian government for petroleum exploration. Those rights are worth billions of dollars of revenue to the oil company and Nigeria. It is rumored that Baron had settled with the American oil company the amount of $25 million dollars, payable to Muhammadu at an European bank. The congressman was responsible for arranging the oil company's CEO's, Mr. Jorge Blanco's, visit with the general in Nigeria so that they could settle the details regarding Muhammadu's gratification, and specifically, the bank account number he would use in Europe. Thereafter, they were going to sign agreements granting the oil rights to the American oil company."

Sterling interrupted by saying, "So, what's wrong with that? The general was about to receive $25 million bucks. That doesn't sound like a death sentence to me."

"Well, that's just half the story. The other half is associated with Baron's ability to influence the amount of foreign aid coming to Nigeria from Washington. Congressman Baron was to serve as the Nigerians' advocate. This year's budget for foreign aid was to be the largest package in the history of the United States and Nigeria. Baron understood the dirty little secret that the general and his cronies would end up with most of the money."

"Alright, I hear you, but I still don't understand the harsh decree on Baron."

"When Chief Balla and the general met in person, Balla had boasted to the general how he had scammed the 'important Congressman Baron' into taking a gratification from Balla instead of an American businessman, even though it was on the same deal. Effectively, Baron had 'sold out' to Balla simply because it was a better deal for Baron. Well, right at that moment, General Muhammadu told Balla that Congressman Baron could no longer be trusted and he must be eliminated. The general went on to say that Baron, at some point in time, would turn on the general or Balla. After all, if he could sell out Sterling, Baron might just close his eyes and decide to blackmail the Nigerian government based on all the salacious information he had. So, rather than face potential extortion, they just decided to kill him. Problem solved."

Sterling responded with disgust in his voice and said, "We hear about this type of behavior in dictatorships all over the world. Absolutely no respect for human rights or due process of the law. It's just a narcissistic thug deciding what's right, even though most of the time they are wrong. What he did to those three American congressmen is despicable. As corrupt as Congressman Baron was, they had no right to take his life. What comes around, goes around. My instinct tells me that Balla and Muhammadu will get paid back with some tragic ending. Thank you for your candor. By the way, what did you mean when you said I almost waited too long to get back to you?"

"I'm leaving the country with my family. I have been accepted for citizenship in the United States of America. I will be leaving my government job here and expect to be granted my official 'green card,' granting me and my family immigration as lawful permanent residents with immigration benefits, including permission to reside and take employment in the United States. I expect to leave Nigeria within the next three to six months. I have been working on this project for more than two years. I remember telling you, when you were here, that this was my dream."

"Congratulations, Stanley. I'm happy for you. Well, I guess you and I have some unfinished business to settle before you leave."

"Thank you, Mr. Sterling, and I'm proud to say that I will be leaving Nigeria in good standing."

"I'm glad to hear that, Stanley, because you're going to need every bit of that 'good standing' to get my money wired out of Nigeria before you retire from your government job. Do you still have access to the codes, along with the authority to wire funds out of the Central Bank? Can you still get this done for me?"

"Yes, I have the access codes, but things have changed since we last spoke. First, everyone knows that I will be retiring from government soon. Second, General Muhammadu and Chief Balla have had a major falling out. It looks as if the general wants to postpone the democratic elections for a one-year period, perhaps two years. Balla told the general to go to hell on the proposed delay. The general wants to keep the government under military power and the chief insists that it is time for the government to move towards an open election with a democratically-elected president. David Solomon has told me that he and Chief Balla are very nervous about what the general might decide to do next."

"Do you think the general is going to volunteer to step down? Or is he going to stay in power?"

"Let me put it to you this way, Mr. Sterling. Right now, things in Nigeria are very dangerous and volatile. The citizens who speak out against the government are being rounded up and jailed. Some have been killed, and some have never been heard from again. What I'm saying is that the general has created a perception of turmoil and unrest. I think Balla will lose the power struggle with Muhammadu and the general will remain in power for at least a year or more. There will be no elections. So, there may be a small opportunity to get your money out before the general calls off the election and as long as I remain in the government."

"Well, great, let's get my contract paid immediately!"

"It's not that easy! If I get your money paid and I'm blamed for costing the country $100 million, I could get hung for treason. So, if I'm going to help you, I'm going to make sure I help myself. I want a lot from you in exchange for the successful transfer. Keep in mind, I'm retiring from government in the highest regard and with distinction. For me to potentially be killed, go to jail, or be considered a traitor to Nigeria, well, that's going to cost you some serious money. I can walk away from Nigeria within three months in great regard, although relatively poor, or I can help you, and walk away wealthy. I'll help you, but I must walk away wealthy, or it's not worth it to me. You might not even have to pay anything to Chief Balla. Can you imagine, you're probably going to get to keep the entire $100 million. Now you understand what I can potentially do for you, so what are you going to do for me?"

Sterling, who was reluctantly understanding the argument Roberts was making, looked at Mark, then crossed his arms across his chest, and said, "Let me hear your proposal."

"Fine. I'll give you my proposal, with one condition. Don't answer me tonight. Think about it, then tell me tomorrow."

"It doesn't sound like I'm going to be very happy with what you're about to tell me."

"Well, hear me out. Then let's talk tomorrow at around this time. Agreed?"

"Alright, let me listen to your proposition."

"I will wire your contract funds from the Central Bank of Nigeria to your designated bank account in exchange for your guarantee to me of three things. Number one, $5 million deposited in a British bank of my choosing. Second, a fully-paid home in Palo Alto, California, in a neighborhood near Stanford University. The home must be valued at a minimum of $1 million. My wife and I will select the home and you will pay $1 million towards the purchase. We both know homes are very expensive near the University, so I've tried to be fair on my budget. And third, I need you to arrange for the University's International Relations Department to hire me as a professor of Nigerian and African Political Affairs. I will accept their lowest pay-scale for an incoming professor. As you know, I hold a combined law degree and MBA from Stanford University. Of course, you will be able to vouch for my high-level Nigerian government service."

After looking at Mark and shaking his head in disbelief, Sterling quickly responded with, "You want the equivalent of a 6% fee on a $100 million contract. Plus, you want one of the best teaching jobs in America, at one of the best universities in the world. Maybe your fee is worth 1% on a transaction the size of ours!"

"I thought you and I agreed that you would wait at least until tomorrow before you would insult me like this."

"I'm not insulting you. I just want you to understand how unreasonable your proposal sounds to me."

"Well, Mr. Sterling, you may not have a choice. I think I bring more value to you than you bring to me. I can live without the money, but I don't think you can. I want you to throw all your American fee formulas out the window. Let's face it, I'm your best bet and perhaps the only way out of your financial troubles. You may eventually win in a court of law, but from what I hear from our government, your legal proceedings may take upto seven or more years. As a lawyer, I'm going to give you some free advice. There are no guarantees of a legal victory. Maybe you win, after all of the appeals, but perhaps you lose. Even if you win, have fun collecting the court's award. Collection is not as simple as you think from a foreign sovereign nation. Even though your court has attached $5 million dollars for you, it could take you years to obtain the remaining money. So, as we agreed, please think about my proposal overnight."

"Sometimes people think they are holding much better cards than they actually have. And sometimes people way overplay their hand. The latter is exactly what you are doing, Mr. Roberts. So instead of telling you crudely to go straight to hell, I will honor my agreement to call you tomorrow at this time. Now, I'll leave you with this thought, your value to me is greater if you can fund my deal without Balla. Let me know tomorrow if you can. In fact, let me know for sure that you can actually perform as you say you can, because if you have any doubts, you have no value to me. I will call you tomorrow. Have a good night."

Mark immediately said, "I got this all on tape. This guy is a dead man. Either he does what we want or you'll be able to stop his immigration to America, perhaps get him killed by his own government or he'll end up in a Nigerian jail. Brilliantly handled, Boss. We need to talk honestly about the value he brings to the table, then make the right deal."

Sterling said, "I agree that we have him, but as a practical matter, we still need him. Without his cooperation, voluntarily or involuntarily, we still need him to make the actual wire transfer. Without Roberts, there's not going to be a wire transfer. There will only be a legal fight. On the one hand, he thinks he's got us, but he doesn't know that we have him. So, do we tell Roberts we have him on tape and that we are prepared to use the tape against him? Or do we wait until the perfect moment to advise him that he has no choice but to do it our way?"

Mark, who was looking somewhat puzzled, remarked with, "Give me an example of the perfect moment."

"One month before he tells us that his green card has been issued and he's preparing his family to move to America. If he's still working for the government, we will have leverage over him to make the wire transfer, or we will stop his immigration by exposing the tapes to both our governments."

Mark, who liked how the boss was thinking, said, "I like playing hardball with this guy!"

"I agree, and timing is everything. It's probably best to give him our counter-proposal and settle a deal with him, if possible. Now, if he's downright stubborn, well, we'll just say no. Then we will wait for the right timing to lower the boom with the tapes. Bottom line is this, we need to make a deal with Roberts while he remains in the government. He's obviously no good to us once he leaves his government position. For the moment, let's not tell him about the tapes. We'll just counter him with a deal we can live with; if we can't make a deal, we'll stay in touch with him and wait for the perfect moment to strike. If that sounds like the best way to go, let me hear your thoughts regarding the counter-proposal."

"Yeah, let's wait on the tapes. The only thing that worries me is that this guy could lose his job without us realizing it or he's just plain thrown out. I mean, anything could happen over there. They could have a revolution, the Central Bank could change its personnel, including the governor. Hell, they could easily run out of US dollars. There's just no guarantee that Roberts will be in the government to pull the strings when we need him. If he won't make a deal with us now, we really need to keep in close touch with him. He's our ticket to a fast-track victory, so let's not lose him."

"Sounds more like you want to make a deal now."

"I don't want to way overpay this son-of-a-bitch. Yet, Nigeria is unstable. Their political situation could collapse. My instinct is to make the deal with him now, because he still has the power to do so, as opposed to rolling the dice on the future of his job in order to save money on his fee."

"I appreciate your point of view. I'm not going to wait too long with this guy, but if we can save three or four million dollars on his fee, I'm willing to do some negotiating. I have the same concerns as you do, but let's work him a little bit. After all, you and Norman are going to need a few bucks out of this deal, and believe me, I'd rather pay more money to you and Norman than to this asshole," Sterling said with a smile.

"I get it. Here're my thoughts. We pay Roberts $1 million bucks if we need to partner with Balla. We pay him $2 million if Balla is out. We contribute $500,000 towards the purchase of his home. He can get a mortgage for the rest. Go ahead and talk to your buddies at Stanford and get him him some teaching gig for minimum pay."

Sterling looked up at Mark with an amused facial expression, as if to say, 'We got this!'

Mark, who knew his friend like nobody else, realized, just by looking at Sterling's expression, that they were on the same page.

With nothing further to say on the subject, Sterling told Mark, "So, come by tomorrow around this time. We'll call Stanley and inform him what we think. I'll just leave the taping equipment right where it is and we'll record what he has to say. If we make no deal tomorrow, I agree with you, we'll get back to him in a few days and keep the dialogue going until we make a deal. See you tomorrow."

As Mark left the office, Sterling sat on a couch and just started thinking about how complicated the Nigerian matter had become. He reminisced back to the very first day he had received the, now infamous, letter from Chief Abba Balla. He thought about how his precious wife had begged him to 'throw the letter away' and how Mark had all but laughed off how unrealistic the contract appeared to be. He just kept thinking about how dangerous his travel to Nigeria actually was and how he had risked Norman's life by taking him along.

The government was definitely involved in this scam. It just seemed amazing that a country could be organized to perpetrate frauds on ordinary citizens, yet it could operate as a foreign sovereign nation. It made him mad to think that a government had bilked him out of more than $400,000. And every time he thought about Jared Baron's wife and kids, along with the other two congressmen's, it just made him furious. If nothing else, Sterling's mind clearly understood that he was not about to accept defeat, but quite on the contrary, he was determined to win. It was evident that the only man who could bring him that victory was Stanley Roberts.

Sterling had gone into such deep thought that he had literally dozed off to a sound sleep right on the very couch he was sitting on after Mark had left. He was so heavily asleep that when Felicia came to visit him, she did not wake her husband for fear that it would

155

startle him. She knew he was under a lot of pressure and wanted him to get some uninterrupted rest. So, she went upstairs to their bedroom and brought down a hand-knitted blanket she had personally made. With tears running down her cheek, Felicia placed the blanket comfortably over Elliot, kissed him on the forehead, and whispered, "Sleep well, my love."

Chapter 18

The next day, Mark arrived back to Sterling's office for the follow-up call with Roberts. As he entered the room, Sterling asked, "Any change of heart regarding Roberts? I mean, should we stay with the lower proposal or should we just give him what he wants?"

Mark, who knew this question was coming, answered with, "Let's test him today, but the sooner we settle with him, the closer we are to receiving our money. Obviously, a big assumption remains as to whether this bastard can actually do what he says he can do! If you can save a few million bucks by playing him the right way, then do it. Just remember, the whole reason for dealing with this putz in the first place is to get the money now, versus waiting for a long court battle. I want the savings as much as you do, but I don't want to lose this guy. Get to a fee agreement with this man as fast as you can."

"Well, let's make the call. Just flip the tape on when he gets on the line so we can record his reaction."

As Sterling punched in the cell number for Roberts, he jotted down some final notes for the call.

Roberts answered the call with a simple, "Hello. Is this Mr. Sterling?"

"That's correct, Mr. Roberts, this is Elliot Sterling."

"I trust, Mr. Sterling, that you have had an opportunity to reconsider my most generous offer to risk my life in order to make you a rich man."

"Let me ask you, Mr. Roberts, how sure are you that you can even get my contract funded by the Central Bank?"

"I am 100% sure that I can wire the contracted funds."

"And what makes you so certain?"

"Because the Central Bank believes that the contract is legitimate. They are under the impression that the funds are going to Chief Balla or his designated entity. Balla and David Solomon have been working on this venture for many, many years. It's all approved, and the Central Bank is in on it. As far as the Central Bank is concerned, you are just a front for Balla or his family. Your name means nothing to the Central Bank. You're just the guy whose name appears on the contract in order to get the money out of the Nigeria. As soon as the timing is right, your name will be removed and replaced with a newly-designated foreign company. I am positive that I can perform, because the Central Bank has written instructions from Balla directing them to fund the contract upon my direction. The only reason it's not funded is because Balla is working on your replacement, which requires new signatures at the Central Bank, similar to what you have already experienced. Keep in mind that currently there is much tension between Balla and General Muhammadu. Fortunately for you, this tension has slowed down assigning your contract's replacement."

"Can you wire the funds to a different bank account other than what is currently designated?"

"Yes, I can. I have the authority to wire the funds anyplace in the world. I just cannot exchange the beneficiary without the official documents you signed in the Central Bank. Remember, I have the authority, along with the official codes, to effectuate the wire transfer. I could walk into the Central Bank right now and get those funds wired. So, why don't I? The answer is, there's nothing in it for me. I'm not going to risk my immigration to America, going to jail, or, for that matter, my life just to make you or Balla rich!"

"Very convincing, Mr. Roberts. Very convincing. Let me tell you what I can do for you. I will guarantee you an entry-level teaching job at Stanford University, even if I need to endow a Teaching Chair on your behalf. I will also allocate a $500,000 allowance towards a home of your choosing. I will assist you in obtaining up to a $500,000 mortgage towards your home. I will pay you a fee of $2 million for securing the wire transfer to a new bank of my choosing. Chief Balla will not be a participant with me, due to his grossly negligent behavior. Is this an acceptable offer?"

"Thank you for your offer. You are $3.5 million short on your proposal. My home allocation is $1 million. Not $500,000 plus a mortgage. My cash fee is $5 million. Not 2 million! You are not listening to me, Mr. Sterling. I am not going to make you rich while I face a death sentence. What I am insisting on is the equivalent of a life insurance policy. The beneficiary of that policy will be my wife and my children. That is my final offer to you. A word to the wise should be sufficient. Be careful with your timing. The political environment in Nigeria is boiling. Anything can happen here, including civil war. Do not ruin your timing. You risk receiving nothing from your contract. I might not receive a fee, but I will have my freedom and the hope for a good life. My answer is no to your offer. What is your answer to my mine?"

Sterling, who was in constant eye-contact with Mark, rolled his eyes, then answered Roberts' demands by saying, "You seem to value your life a lot more than mine. Do you think for a moment that if you wire my contract funds to a new bank account, whereby Chief Balla gets nothing, that Balla will simply write it off as just another business deal that didn't go so well? Or do you think Mr. Balla is going to be angry? In fact, so angry that he might even put a price on my head? I'll be willing to bet $50 million that Balla is going to place a target on my back. So, you're not the only one who needs life insurance. The difference here is that this is my contract, not yours. You are a government employee. Your job is to pay off my legitimate contract, not to extort money from me! Now, let me tell you something else. It is not easy to make it in America. If all I offered you was a decent job at Stanford, that was probably enough. Do you have any idea how hard it is to buy a home in the United States and qualify for a mortgage? Not only do I guarantee you a home, but I offer to place $2 million into a bank account of your choice. You, my friend, are not only greedy, but you might even be stupid. My answer is not only no, it's hell no!"

"That's a very long lecture, Mr. Sterling. It almost sounded rehearsed. You can save all those words for your employees, but not for me. You will receive nothing on your contract without me. So, you can talk all day long, but the bottom line is, you need me. Without me, you lose. With me, you win. You may think I'm greedy and stupid, but from where I see it, you're the one who fits that description. Remember, even if you defeat us in court and actually receive a judgment, after six or seven years of legal entanglements, I'm very confident that you're going to have a terrible time collecting on your award. I wish you well with your life and sincerely thank you for considering my offer."

Sterling, who was mesmerized with the consistency of Roberts' demands, said, "Call me if you change your mind. Then again, who knows, I might even call you if I change mine. Good luck, Stanley."

As Mark clicked off the recorder, he said, "This piece of shit is not bluffing! Actually, I was surprised when he played his 'you need me' bullshit card and you didn't kick his ass with, 'We got you on tape, asshole.' Either pay this guy what he wants or tell him we got the tapes. Your choice, Boss, but tell him!"

"I thought about disclosing the tape card, but by instinct, I held back. My gut tells me that there will be a more effective time to use the tape threat. I'm just waiting for a more precise moment to ensure the best result. I'm going to trust my instincts on this one. We'll give him a few days to see if he blinks. If he doesn't get back to us within a week, I'll either give him what he wants or I'll aggressively shove the tapes down his throat."

"I wouldn't wait a week, Elliot. This guy could disappear in a heartbeat. Either make nice with him or let's bury him. My advice is get Roberts onboard now!"

Just as Mark finished his message to Elliot, the private office line started ringing. Elliot picked up the phone and answered with a polite, "Hello."

"Mr. Sterling, this is Paul Norman. How are you, sir?"

"I'm well, Paul. What's new?"

"Everything is good, sir, except I just received a call from the FBI field office in Los Angeles. They want to talk to you tomorrow. The FBI agent implied that the White House has directed an investigation into Baron's death."

Sterling, who was confounded by Norman's comments, said, "Why the hell does the FBI want to talk to me?"

"Apparently, the FBI obtained access to Congressman Baron's cellphone records and flagged a call Baron made to you, while in Nigeria, shortly before his death. They want to know why he was calling you and your explanation about what he was doing for you in Nigeria. Additionally, the FBI has been informed by the White House and are familiar with the fact that we are suing Nigeria under the FSIA for our $100 million contract. Our lawsuit, along with your cell call with Baron, is what is prompting the FBI to want to speak to you."

"I really feel like I should avoid this. I'm in a no-win here. There's no way in hell I'm going to disclose to the FBI that I hired Baron to confirm the legitimacy of my deal with the Nigerians. I can't tell the FBI that I was going to pay Baron a substantial fee for my work while he was simultaneously conducting official business on behalf of the United States.

Between you and me, Paul, it appears that Baron was killed by the Nigerian government. I have hearsay knowledge of this from Roberts, but I'd prefer not to disclose it at this time. So, how do I avoid the FBI meeting?"

"Well, if you want to look suspicious, I'll weasel you out of this, but I think that would constitute a big mistake. I would advise that we set up the meeting with the FBI. Answer their questions truthfully, but be smart. Only answer their questions with a 'yes or no' if you can. Otherwise, keep your answers short. You've done nothing wrong. Simply inform the FBI that you have been a friend of the late congressman for a long time and that he was to speak face-to-face with the Nigerians in order to confirm the timing of the release of your contract. If you are asked whether you were to pay a fee to the congressman, just say no! Technically, the Nigerians were the ones responsible for paying the fee, not you. If asked about the contract, just say that it was many years in the making and started by your partner."

"I suppose I can do that, but I'd really prefer not to take that meeting. To tell you the truth, I think these guys are trying to figure out whether I offered Baron, or perhaps the Nigerians, money in exchange for influence to get my contract paid. I'm drawing the conclusion that the FBI is investigating whether I paid a Nigerian official a bribe while using Baron as my liaison. Have you heard of the Foreign Corrupt Practices Act? This doesn't feel right to me."

Norman, who was carefully listening, yet simultaneously thinking, responded with, "Of course I know what the Foreign Corrupt Practices Act says. This is a United States federal law known primarily for two of its main provisions, one that addresses accounting transparency requirements under the Securities Exchange Act of 1934 and another concerning bribery of foreign officials. And you are correct, the US Department of Justice is the primary enforcer of FCPA."

Sterling responded with, "Bingo! These guys could be telling you that the White House is launching an investigation into Baron's death, blah, blah, blah, but in reality, I may be the focus of the investigation! It's possible I'm a bit paranoid here, but my instinct said, watch your ass!"

Norman reacted with, "I don't think so, but I'm not going to dismiss it as absurd. You need to step back and look at this through the eyes of the government. Three American congressmen didn't just vanish in a foreign country. The federal government owes it not only to their grieving families, but it owes it to the American public to determine the facts associated with their deaths. The sooner the government can determine the facts regarding how the congressmen died, the sooner they can go resume diplomatic relations with Nigeria. American oil companies have powerful influence over the White House. Baron's death needs to go away so that Nigerian oil can start shipping to the USA."

"I hear you, Counselor, but what if I'm right and you're wrong?"

"Even if I'm wrong, Mr. Sterling, I assure you the FBI will not be able to prove anything. Fortunately for us, when the congressmen had their tragic car accident, all the evidence they were carrying was destroyed in its entirety at the scene of the accident during the the ensuing car fire. Your congressman, the late Mr. Baron, had an obligation to assist you with your business transaction, as his constituent. The FBI will be unable to prove any form of a bribe or any other such form of payment, because there was no such payment by you. There are no witnesses in America. There are only Nigerian government witnesses, and they have no firsthand proof, nor are they privileged to any conversations you may have had in private with Congressman Baron. Besides, no one is going to believe them anyways. I really do insist that you talk to the FBI. If you avoid them, you look like you have something to hide. Go in strong. Don't worry, we got these guys."

"Alright. Okay, I'll do it. But if I end up behind bars, my wife is never going to forgive you. Will you be in the room with me?"

"Yes, sir, I will."

"Where are we meeting and at what time?"

"We'll meet tomorrow morning at 10:00AM. I made arrangements for a private law firm's conference room. These are the lawyers we previously used to defend our construction defects case, which we won. A neutral location felt right."

"Yeah, that location is just right. Why don't you pick me up tomorrow, say 9:00 AM? As we drive, you can brief me in more detail about how to best handle these guys."

"I'll see you in the morning, Mr. Sterling. This is going to be a lot easier than you think. Before the interview is over, you're going to have them eating out of your hands."

The balance of the day went by quickly, it included a very long conversation with Felicia about their future and how Elliot was determined to bring peace and respect back to their lives. His wife just kept emphasizing, throughout the evening, that as long as they had each other, their children, and their health, everything else was going to be alright.

Felicia kept saying, "Follow your good instincts. Keep battling, and I assure you things will turn out right for us."

These words of encouragement, along with the confidence she expressed in her husband, were the inspirations Elliot needed to hear. It was like shots of adrenaline.

So, when Norman picked up his boss the next day, Elliot Sterling was pumped and ready to win.

Norman, who was wearing his standard, lawyer-looking dark gray pinstriped suit, greeted his boss with a simple, "Good morning, Mr. Sterling." His boss, who sensed the seriousness of the FBI meeting, was uncharacteristically dressed in a conservative navy-blue blazer, gray pants, and a white-collared buttoned-down shirt.

He responded to Norman by saying, "Indeed, it is a good morning! You have advised me well to attend this meeting. It's the right thing to do. I'm ready if you're ready."

Norman, sensing a bullish Sterling, said, "Something tells me you're more than ready for this."

As Sterling got into the car, he responded with, "I'm the victim here, not the guy on trial. The crook, may he rest in peace, was Baron, not me. And the scam artists are the Nigerians, not me. Whatever these guys want to ask me, I'm ready. On the contrary, the FBI should be assisting me and interviewing the bastards in the Nigerian government. I'm not afraid of anything. In fact, I'm going to get these guys to assist us in our legal case against Nigeria. So, yes, it is a good morning."

The car ride to the lawyer's office was upbeat, with very little said about the meeting. They just spoke about the future and what lay ahead once this chapter in both of their lives was complete. Before they knew it, they were walking into the conference room where they were immediately greeted by two members of the Federal Bureau of Investigation.

Both FBI agents looked as if they had been cast in a movie. Each were tall, with that 'superman' look to them. Each had that classic 'square jaw,' short hair, and a somewhat strong physique dressed in the typical FBI black suit, black tie, and long-sleeved white shirt.

The agents extended their hands to Sterling and Norman and addressed them separately by name, even though they had never met. Obviously, the agents had studied their photos and knew exactly who each was. The first agent identified himself and stated, "I'm James Levinson. I'm in charge of the field office here in Los Angeles, and this is FBI Special Agent Jerry Flynn from our Washington, D.C., office. Special Agent Flynn is the head of our task force dedicated to international fraud and money laundering schemes."

Sterling decided to go right after the agents by looking directly at Levinson, then Flynn, and saying, "Well, let's get right down to the point. What do you need from me?"

Agent Flynn responded quickly by stating, "You can tell us everything you know about the late Congressman Baron and his relationship to Nigeria. Why did he call you from Nigeria? And why did he call you prior to his trip?"

Sterling confidently responded, "That's easy, but I'd appreciate if you could answer something first."

"I thought we were the ones asking the questions, but alright, what's your question?" Agent Flynn said.

"What are you specifically investigating and on behalf of which government agency?"

Flynn, with a smirk on his face, answered, "That, Mr. Sterling, is two questions, but okay, I'll give you the answers to both. Once I do, we'd really appreciate if you could just simply answer our questions. Sound like a plan?"

"Yeah, sure, Agent Flynn."

"Members of the House of Representatives don't simply vanish from the face of the earth. Usually, there's something behind the why, especially when there is not one trace of evidence regarding their mysterious, sudden deaths. The federal government wants to investigate why these men are dead. The White House initially asked us to get to the bottom of this. Later, the State Department and the Speaker of the House of Representatives formally demanded this inquiry."

"Fair enough, Agent Flynn. Thank you for shedding some light on my questions. Well, I'm sure you understand better than I do that Congressman Baron was a very influential member of the Foreign Relations Committee. He had great power and influence over many countries in Africa. He seemed to understand Nigeria well and had taken a great interest in the Republic of Nigeria, as a nation. Mr. Baron was always referring to the great potential of Nigeria and understood the enormous financial power they were developing due to vast oil reserves located in their country. He knew the head of state on a personal level and he made it his business to meet with the most influential governmental officials. The congressman used to brag about how many major American petroleum companies solicited his assistance regarding making oil partnerships in Nigeria."

Agent Flynn rudely interrupted Sterling by saying, "Yes, we know all that, but how does this relate to you?"

"Well, wait a second here. A moment ago, you asked me to tell you everything I knew about Baron and his relationship to Nigeria. Now, did you change your mind or am I just boring you?"

"No, you're right. I did ask you that, but to tell you the truth, I know everything you're telling us, so I can make this visit a little shorter if you concentrate on why this man called you from Nigeria and why he called you just before he departed for Nigeria on that faithful trip."

Sterling, who was now annoyed with the arrogance of the agent, responded with, "Are all of you FBI agents so fucking cocky? Or is it just you, Mr. Flynn? I'm here voluntarily. I've got better things to do than to be talking to a conceited asshole like you. So, you can subpoena me if you want or we can do this respectfully while on the same team. Your choice."

At that moment, Sterling wasn't sure if he had infuriated Flynn or whether he had put the FBI agent in his place. The consequence of having provoked Flynn could easily bring a federal indictment on Sterling just because Flynn might have been insulted by his comments. On the other hand, Flynn could possibly have realized that Sterling had nothing to hide and that it would be best to cooperate with each other. As the silence in the room was, to say the least, uncomfortable, Sterling looked over at Norman, whose facial expression was a mixture of shock with a smidget of 'you have some big balls.'

Agent Flynn broke the ice with, "I apologize, Mr. Sterling. I meant no disrespect. I guess it's my unfiltered way of getting to the heart of why we are here. Are we good?"

"We're good. Go ahead with your questions."

Flynn, with a more conciliatory and relaxed tone of voice, asked, "Congressman Baron's phone records show that right before his travels to Nigeria, he called your phone. Is this true, and if so, what was the purpose of his call?"

While looking at Norman, Sterling answered, "This is true. But the purpose of the call requires better foundation so that you can correctly understand the reason for the call. I'll try to keep this simple. I currently have a major business transaction in Nigeria. The contract that I am involved with was started many years ago by a friend and long-time partner of mine who has since passed away. There were many delays and complications that kept holding back the final payment of this contract. The final obstacle for the release of funds associated with my contract came down to one point. I was obligated to wire transfer to the Central Bank of Nigeria a total of

$400,000 in order to settle some taxes, due to the government, related to a foreign contractor, which was me. I was amazed that I was responsible for paying taxes on my contract proceeds even before I had received a dime. So, this is where Congressman Baron came into play. I had heard that the congressman had excellent connections in Nigeria. Since I was his constituent, I felt it was appropriate to request his advice regarding the legitimacy of the Nigerians' request for the tax funds in advance of their actual funding of my contract. Over lunch, I explained the details of my business dealings in Nigeria and requested that he assist in confirming that the tax was real. Mr. Baron eagerly accepted the task of checking this matter out for me and disclosed that he actually had a long-standing trip to Nigeria within weeks of our luncheon. He promised to personally speak to the appropriate people in Nigeria and confirm, one way or the other, whether the tax request was real. His call to me before his travels to Nigeria was simply a courtesy telling me that he had not forgotten about my contract and that he would call me from Nigeria after he determined the facts. I expressed my sincere appreciation for the call. I wished him safe travels and told him I looked forwarded to hearing from him with the truth. That's why Baron called me before he left to Nigeria."

Both Agent Flynn and Agent Levinson had taken copious notes on a yellow legal pad as Sterling told his story. Flynn then looked up at Sterling and slowly said, "I understand. I understand." Then, he thought for a moment and went on to say, "Okay, our phone records further indicate that the late congressman had called you from Nigeria. Can you confirm that the call actually took place?"

"Yes. My recollection is that he made a call to me, about three days later, from Nigeria."

"And what did he tell you?"

Sterling responded with a stern and unforgiving voice, "Baron told me that he had completed a thorough due diligence regarding my contract. He assured me that the contract was real and that I should have absolutely no reservations in wiring the $400,000 tax payment directly to the Central Bank of Nigeria. The congressman encouraged me to send my money immediately, due to the fact that the Central Bank was prepared to wire my contract funds instantaneously upon receipt of the tax payment."

Flynn, who was fascinated with Sterling's story, blurted out loud, "And did you wire your funds?"

"Yes, every last dime!"

Although Flynn already knew the answer to the next question, he proceeded to ask the follow-up question, anyway, for the record. "And did the Central Bank send you your contract funds?"

"No, sir. I wired the money in good faith based on the firm assurances that the late congressman made to me. The Central Bank sent no wire. To make matters worse, my Nigerian business associates ceased any further communications with me. The next I heard, Baron and the two other congressmen had been killed in a terrible automobile accident. Effectively, I have been scammed by a very seductive and sophisticated crime syndicate tied directly to Nigeria's government. The Central Bank is in on it. This reaches to the very highest officials in Nigeria. In fact, I wouldn't be surprised if the Nigerian head of state has something to do with all of this."

Flynn, incredibly intrigued, asked, "Can you prove that?"

Sterling, feeling more and more confident that he was convincing the FBI that he was a victim, answered by saying, "You bet your ass that I can prove it! I have filed a $100 million lawsuit in federal court here in Los Angeles against the Republic of Nigeria and many of their government officials. We are expected to start the trial soon. The reason we are so confident about the probable outcome of this case is because my attorney, Mr. Norman, and I traveled together to Nigeria. We met in person with the minister of finance, the governor of the Central Bank, and other high-level officials in the Central Bank's offices. I signed my contract in front of a government notary inside the Central Bank and before witnesses, such as Mr. Norman, and high-level government agents. We will prove our claims and we will win this case, because that is what justice will mandate. And one other fact I want you to be aware of is that the judge in our case has already issued a $5 million prejudgment writ of attachment. We have $5 million of Nigerian funds, attached in two New York banks, and the trial hasn't even started. As you can see, the court means business, and so do I."

Flynn then looked up at his fellow agent, Levinson, then stared at Norman for a moment. He looked down at his handwritten notes, then at Sterling, and stated, "I believe every word you're saying, Mr. Sterling. I'm sorry you have been going through this ordeal. Quite frankly, before this meeting, we thought you had a nefarious relationship going on with either Baron or officials in the Republic of Nigeria. We were aware of your travels to Nigeria, but we couldn't quite understand why a Los Angeles-based real estate developer would travel to a third-world country. Now we understand why. Okay, so long as we're sharing vital information, let me tell you something you don't know. Congressman Baron was an FBI target regarding a major international money-laundering operation. We think the main country involved is Nigeria. Again, until today, we thought you were deeply involved in the operation. That perception is now clearly rejected."

Sterling, who was getting more and more upset by each word uttered by Flynn, said forcefully, "Are you telling me you had me under surveillance?"

"I'm sorry, Mr. Sterling, but since this matter is under investigation, I am unable to comment."

"Did you pricks wiretap my phone?"

"Please, Mr. Sterling, don't ask us any more questions. I can't comment any further, period!"

"How do you expect me to cooperate with you guys? I don't know if you're taping me. Hell, I don't even know if you're going to use my comments against me. This is total bullshit!"

Flynn then paused a moment and said, "Here's how you know. We're going to recommend that we close our file on you. As far as the FBI is concerned, you are off the hook regarding our investigation, pending sign-off by my boss in Washington. We apologize for the mistrust. We're just doing our job."

"When will I know whether your boss signed-off on your recommendation?"

"Consider it a fait accompli. We'll call Mr. Norman with the final confirmation. You don't need to think about it.

We appreciate you voluntarily meeting with us. Let's keep in touch. Cooperation may prove to be mutually beneficial. Off the record, I wish you lots of good luck with your lawsuit and I hope you nail those bastards!"

Chapter 19

Nearly three months had passed since the FBI meeting. Yet, no one had gotten back to Norman confirming that Sterling was officially 'off the hook.' He couldn't help but conclude that he was probably not off the hook. In fact, he started to wonder whether the FBI had actually wiretapped Baron while speaking to Sterling prior to departing to Nigeria. That conversation was dangerous, because the congressman had discussed fee compensation for his services to assist in the release of funds to Sterling. Perhaps that dialogue could be construed as a serious crime, even though it was Baron who was insisting on the compensation. Although this was a deep concern, Sterling kept telling himself that if the FBI really had this wiretap, they most likely would have had it prior to the meeting with Flynn and Levinson. Even though Sterling had considered Norman contacting the FBI numerous times, he just kept deciding that it would be best to let the FBI sleeping giant sleep.

During these three months, Norman had successfully conducted the deposition in Washington, D.C., of Wole Obasanjo, governor of the Central Bank. Additionally, he had deposed Sani Odibo, the Nigerian minister of finance. The actual moment the subpoenas were handed to the high-level Nigerian officials, they had made national news. The governor and minister had both traveled together from Nigeria to attend the International Monetary Fund annual meetings in Washington.

As they walked into the ritzy hotel where the conference was to take place, newspaper photographers from around the world were snapping photos of the foreign dignitaries as they arrived. To the astonishment of the Nigerian governor and the minister, several photographers had captured the very instant Norman had arranged to hand the startled officials their subpoenas. Needless to say, these pictures and the terrible optics of 'distinguished' high-level government officials being handed their subpoenas made it into newspapers around the world.

What had made matters even worse for Governor Obasanjo was that the pictures included an attractive young woman at his side checking into the same hotel room as him. This embarrassing photo showed Obasanjo with one hand receiving the deposition subpoena and with the other, instinctively, yet accidentally, placing a Central Bank file marked 'CONFIDENTIAL' over the young woman's face. The British and American newspapers had a field day with that photo, with one of the papers featuring a front page headline that simply said 'AWKWARD!'

That photo had made Sterling laugh for days after it was published, and it was probably the funniest moment since this long Nigerian saga had begun. The depositions went on to prove that the governor and the minister were both in Nigeria precisely during the time that Sterling and Norman had visited Nigeria. Yet, both Nigerian officials denied ever having met Sterling or Norman, testifying that neither had visited the Central Bank or the finance minister's home. Of course, this testimony would come back to haunt them when Norman, who was an American attorney, would submit an affidavit swearing to the contrary. Additionally, phone records, hotel records, travel visas, surveillance cameras at the Central Bank, wire transfer records, along with other witnesses' testimonies, would be able to piece together the credibility of Sterling's story, as opposed to the outright lies of the governor and the minister.

The deposition and the great 'awkward' photo were the highlights of this twelve-week period. Everything else seemed off track. Sterling had tried at least twice a week during this period to reach Stanley Roberts. The calls went directly to voice mail with absolutely no attempt to return the call. This was a great disappointment to Sterling, because it was very apparent that the legal case was going to take forever. It was also evident that the Nigerian government had decided to play hardball. The thought of the FBI potentially dragging Sterling into a criminal investigation, tied to Roberts having gone AWOL, and the prospects of a drawn-out court case were becoming a horror story for Elliot.

The days went by slowly for Sterling, even though he was actively fighting very difficult opponents. The bank wanted its money, the Nigerians had an endless pit of funds to fight in court, and the FBI had the power of the government. The odds seemed insurmountably stacked against Sterling. It was abundantly clear that, without Stanley Roberts, it was just a matter of time before Sterling would financially collapse. Mark had been right when he insisted that Elliot make a deal with Roberts, despite overpaying him in order to make a quick deal. As Sterling sat in his office on an overcast, rather gloomy day, he realized what a terrible mistake he had made with Roberts. Contact with Roberts had fallen apart. There seemed to be no method of communicating with the only man on earth who could save his empire. Where the hell was Roberts? Did he leave his government position? Was he living in America? Could he be in prison, or was he even alive?

While Sterling was deep in thought, the phone rang, which pulled Sterling out of his trance as he answered, "Yes, hello?"

"Elliot, this is Mark. Turn the fucking television on! Balla is dead! Solomon is dead! They've been assassinated! It looks like General Muhammadu had them taken out. I'm on my way over to your office."

Sterling, who was shocked and unsure as to what this dramatic turn of events meant to him, responded to Mark by saying, "Contact Norman and tell him to call Agent Flynn at the FBI and insist on as much information as he can get out of Flynn. Then, tell him to get his ass over here as soon as he can. I've got CNN turned on with the 'BREAKING NEWS' caption and their lead anchor chronicling the events as they are unfolding. This is outrageous!

What the hell is going on here? Mark, did you hear anything concerning Roberts. Is he dead or alive? Who else was assassinated with Balla and Solomon?"

Mark arrived at the private home office and found Sterling glued to the television, which was showing a short documentary regarding the rise of Chief Abba Balla as a 'promising champion for democracy in Nigeria.' Chief Balla was a favorite of the American State Department, because they saw him as the best hope for an open, democratically-elected president in Nigeria, as opposed to continued military dictatorship.

The storyline continued by reporting that Balla had been 'gunned down in broad daylight at a political rally just outside of Lagos.' The network went on to describe how the assassins had specifically targeted Chief Balla and his long-time adviser David Solomon. No one else was killed or injured in the plot. Just as Sterling was going to turn off the television, General Muhammadu came on the air, speaking from his desk in the Presidential Palace, and said strangely, "First, I want to assure the Nigerian people that, contrary to rumors circulating from person to person, I, or anyone in my government, had anything to do with the tragic murder of my friend and colleague Chief Abba Balla and his adviser David

Solomon. These were two great men whom I admired. It was no secret that I enthusiastically endorsed Chief Balla to become the democratically-elected president of Nigeria. This is an enormous loss and a sad day for our country. For the stability of the nation, I will continue on as the head of our beloved country. Although democratic elections in Nigeria will be called off at this time, do not give up hope in open, democratic presidential elections. They will return soon to the great and sovereign people of Nigeria."

Mark rolled his eyes and said, "That son-of-a-bitch general was definitely in on ordering Balla and Solomon's death. He sounds like a serial killer who was astonished at the news that someone in the community was found murdered."

"Did you speak to Norman?"

Norman walked into the office just as Sterling asked Mark this question. Sterling was anxious to hear what Norman had to say and immediately asked, "Did you reach the FBI?"

Norman, slightly out of breath, replied with, "Yes. I spoke to Flynn. He confirmed that Chief Balla and Solomon were the only officials murdered. He also verified that four Nigerian armed guards were killed guarding Balla. The FBI's preliminary intelligence indicates that the military, along with old, ultra-conservative business and petroleum interests, conspired to assassinate the chief. They simply want the status-quo military dictatorship to continue. Their fear is that the general population might revolt against the oligarchy that controls the government, business, and the military. Additionally, Flynn said that it would be hard to believe that Muhammadu wasn't in on the plot. In fact, they think he may have even been the mastermind."

Sterling looked at Mark and said to Norman, "I just heard this guy on TV call Chief Balla his friend and go on to praise him. The power structure in Nigeria is ruled by an economic elite that is totally corrupt. Chief Balla never had a chance. They just used him to show the people that Nigeria was transitioning to democracy. Just a whole bunch of bullshit! Did Flynn say anything else?"

"Yes, he did. He said his boss closed the file on you, Mr. Sterling. Their working theory is that Congressman Baron was in bed with the Nigerians. They believe that Baron had accumulated too much information on government corruption and was pushing them too hard. As a result, they had him eliminated. You're off the hook!"

"That's great news, and I'm thankful. Now, what the hell are we going to do about my deceased, asshole partners?"

Norman quickly responded, "That's easy. Locate Roberts. If he's still in the government, make a deal and get him to send us our money through the Central Bank. If we can't find him, we're going to need to get the FBI to testify for us in our FSIA trial. We need the FBI to be our witness in demonstrating the corrupt dealings of the Nigerian government officials. This will help persuade the judge of our pleadings. The fact that Balla is dead makes things more difficult, because he was such a material witness. After all, he was our partner. We must clearly show that the government is intertwined in private and public corruption and that Mr. Sterling is an innocent victim. Agent Flynn's testimony would go a long way towards showing these facts. Our massive challenge is that I don't know if the FBI would ever allow Flynn to testify at our trial. What's even more complicated, I'm not sure if we'll ever find Roberts!"

Mark, who was listening carefully, spoke up and said, "Look, from a business standpoint, conditions have changed in favor of us. We no longer have a business partner to share a $100 million with. We're going to keep all of it. Second, Balla is no longer a threat at replacing us with a substitute partner. Third, Balla is no longer a threat to come after us in any capacity, since we own the rights to the contract and he's no longer around to contest anything. Let me put it to you all this way. No one, except us, knows where the 'bodies are buried' regarding our contract. For Christ's sake, I should have had these guys shot myself! Forget about Flynn, we have got to scour the earth and find Roberts.

Let's all pray he's still in the government!"

Sterling reacted by saying, "You guys have this situation read exactly right. I should have listened to you, Mark, when you all but begged me to quickly make a deal with Roberts when we knew he had the power to order the transfer. This was a big fuck-up by me. The only redeeming quality is that Balla and Solomon are now both dead, leaving no partners. I apologize, but I'll find Roberts for us! In the meantime, Paul, see what you can do to get the FBI to play ball."

As Norman stood to go back to his office, he shook Sterling's hand and said, "I'll do everything in my power to convince the FBI to allow Flynn to testify for us, but Mark's right. We must find Roberts. If he can effectuate our wire transfer, we win on every level, including the bank litigation. Think about this. No partners and $100 million in working capital. We won't need the Sterling Development Company. We'll just give the bank the troubled real estate and the rights to our company. We walk away. They get the headaches, and we start a brand-new development firm. Simultaneously, I withdraw the lawsuit against the Nigerians and life is good again! Mr. Sterling, find this guy!"

"I'll find him, but push hard to get Flynn onboard anyways. Remember, when I find Roberts, there remains a real possibility that he is no longer in government or he no longer has the authority to approve sending the wire transfer. So, don't lower your guard on the FBI. The Nigerian FSIA trial might still end up being our only way out. Do you understand me, Paul?"

"Yes, sir. Very clearly."

"Good. Now, let's all go to work! Mark, I want you to stay here so we can brainstorm how to find this bastard."

Mark moved to sit in a chair next to Sterling's desk and said, "This is going to be worse than finding a needle in a haystack."

Sterling, who seemed to have reinvigorated his mojo, said, "Well, let's just start by calling Roberts in Nigeria."

Mark said, "That's as good as any start, but my hunch tells me it's not going to be that easy. In fact, we may need to hire a private investigator to find this man. But, go ahead, give it a shot. Call him."

With great anticipation, Sterling dialed the number, and after a pause, an international operator stated, via recording, "All lines are down due to an usually high call volume, please try back later."

Sterling frowned with disapproval, hung up, and said, "Do you know the name of an international private investigator? Unfortunately, given the danger in Nigeria, none of us can go over there ourselves and find this son-of-a-bitch. I think you're right. We're going to need to hire a private eye to go to Nigeria and find this guy."

Mark responded saying, "We'll need someone better than Sherlock Holmes! I mean, the guy we hire is going to be entering into a somewhat paranoid country. Anyone snooping around government offices in Nigeria is quickly going to be detected. Our investigator will need to be very experienced and shrewd. I'll start looking for the right man today. I'll call some of our contacts in the LA Police Department. They may point me in the right direction."

"That sounds good, Mark. Hey, let me bounce something off you."

"What's that, Boss?"

"Is there a possibility that Roberts is right here in the United States? After all, he did tell us that he was waiting for his final immigration papers for his family and himself. If he's already here, my guess is that he's somewhere in California. Remember, he graduated from Stanford, and he knows his way around this neck of the woods. Perhaps he still has ties to someone at the Central Bank that can get our deal done. Money carries a big stick in Nigeria. It may cost us a huge gratification to get that done, but it will still be worth it. So what if we need to pay $5 million to get our funds out? As long as we have no partners, we've got plenty of money to spend on someone inside the Central Bank that can help us, if Roberts can no longer do it himself."

"I think you're onto something, Elliot. I know an immigration attorney with deep connections at the State Department.

He knows immigration practices inside and out. If Roberts is already here, this lawyer will track him down. This guy won't work for free, but I think he'll be worth the money."

"Great! Go hire him. Do what you need to find Roberts. In the meantime, I'll keep trying to call him. I'll also start calling my contacts at Stanford. If he's here, or he plans to come here soon, my guess is he'll try to solicit a job at Stanford, just like we had spoken. Maybe something will come up there. This is not going to be easy, but keep pushing hard. We're going to find him."

The next day came and went, as did the entire week, with not a trace of Stanley Roberts. The phone calls remained unanswered. The private investigator had come up with zero, and the immigration attorney, who had demanded a big retainer, had nothing to add about Robert's whereabouts. The University had received no curriculum vitae regarding Stanley Roberts. It felt as if he was no longer living on the planet.

Until one quiet Friday afternoon.

Sterling was sitting in his office when the housekeeper knocked at his door and said, "Excuse me, Mr. Sterling, there is a car at the front gate requesting, through the intercom, a visit with you. I told him to wait while I asked permission."

Sterling addressed the housekeeper by saying, "Maria, is it a man or a woman?"

"It is a man, Mr. Sterling."

"And what is his name?"

"His name is Mr. Roberts."

"Excuse me. What did you say?"

Maria, who rarely saw Mr. Sterling flustered, answered, "His name is Mr. Stanley Roberts. Would you like to see him through the intercom camera?"

Without uttering a word, Sterling suddenly popped out of his chair and walked briskly towards the intercom camera. Maria, who was running to catch up with her boss at the camera location, asked, "Should I grant him permission to enter?"

Sterling was simply baffled. He couldn't believe his eyes. Yet, he was smiling from ear to ear as he answered very softly, saying, "Yes, Maria. Yes, Maria. Open the gate and tell Mr. Roberts to proceed to the front door."

"Right away, Mr. Sterling."

Maria informed Roberts that she would open the gate. The housekeeper went on to instruct him to park his car in the porte cochere, then proceed to the front door of the residence. Within moments, Robert's automobile was parked where instructed.

He slowly got out of the car while admiring the beautiful grounds of the estate. As he walked towards the entry door, Roberts saw Sterling come out of the front door. Sterling, feeling very concerned about the dangerous security risks associated with Roberts at his home, said, "How the hell did you find this place? What the fuck are you doing here?"

Roberts, who was somewhat startled by the greeting, responded with, "Yes, and I'm happy to see you too."

Sterling, who realized that he was being rude to the one man who could actually save him, changed his tone as he extended his hand out to shake the already-extended hand of Roberts.

"I'm sorry, Stanley. I'm just so astonished to see you. Let me start over. Welcome to my home. Please come in. May I offer you something to drink?"

"Certainly, I'll have a drink with you, Mr. Sterling, but more importantly, we need to talk."

"Come in. Let's walk to my office and we'll be able to speak privately. Now tell me, how did you find my home?"

"Before I left Nigeria, I went into the Central Bank files that stored a copy of Chief Balla's original letter addressed to you at this address. So, I wrote down the address, hoping to find you here. I came to Los Angeles to escort my eldest daughter as she enrolls at UCLA. She is an honors student and she was accepted into the University as a foreign student even though my family and I will be moving permanently to California within the next 12 weeks. I knew that the University was located near Bel Air, so I decided to visit with you in person because we have unfinished business. Fortunately, or perhaps unfortunately, I left Lagos for this trip several days before the tragic assassinations of Chief Balla and David Solomon. I have it on very good authority that General Muhammadu ordered their killings. The general and the ruling oligarchy are simply not ready to give up power, especially to a democratically elected President. That is why they are dead. The good news for you is that the ensuing chaos presents a perfect opportunity to get your money out of Nigeria!"

Sterling, who handed Roberts a glass of 18-year-old Macallan Scotch, said, "I'm listening."

"I will be leaving Nigeria to reside in America with the rest of my family within 12 weeks. All the official immigration papers are approved. I am formally scheduled to retire from government and the Central Bank within ten weeks from today. Eight weeks from today, I will, for the final time in my career, be designated the official responsible for all wire transfers coming into the Central Bank and departing it. I will have sole responsibility to release funds to designated foreign contractors approved by the government for payment, such as yours. To make matters even better, the previous presidential decree requiring that taxes be paid by the foreign contractor prior to release of funds has been deleted in its entirety. Your fund is sitting and waiting to be released by me, and me alone, eight weeks from today. That is the day I will make you a very rich man. Do not miss your date with destiny!"

Sterling looked at Roberts and said, "I think you meant to say, 'very rich men,' as opposed to 'a very rich man.' I'm pretty sure you came here with high expectations of being one of the men associated with 'rich.' Am I right?"

"Yes, Mr. Sterling. You are right. Proportionally rich, but not greedy."

Sterling, who was now in tough negotiating mode, responded curtly, "Okay, let's hear it. What do you want?"

"First of all, Mr. Sterling, I suggest you change your tone of voice. You seem to think you're doing me a favor. I see this as a business deal where both parties have something to gain. You know, as well as I know, that you're never going to see your money without me. If you want to go to your courts here in America, go ahead. Maybe, within a decade or so, you might get an award. Or maybe you'll lose. Or even worse, you'll win but would have no way of collecting your court award. Let's face it, I am your best bet, period, no further discussion. Now, I will acknowledge that I won't receive anything without your contract being funded. So, let's make a deal!"

"I'm annoyed with you, because I feel like you are trying to take advantage of me. This is my contract. You are a government employee. You should just do your job and fund my legitimate contract without shaking me down for money."

"Well, since you seem to be insulting me once again, I'll do my best to educate you as to why you will pay me what I tell you to pay me. The contract is not legitimate. Chief Balla and some of his powerful allies in government effectively made it up. It was their way of funding Balla's expensive presidential political campaign. The Nigerian government will be able to prove that in court, even though some government officials might get seriously incriminated by this. You might get a sympathetic judge who will say you were scammed. But you also might get a judge who will conclude that you were in on it, that you were greedy and that you too have dirty hands. We just don't know, do we?"

"Look, Stanley. You didn't come to my house to give me unsolicited legal advice. You came to my house because you are smart enough to know that in order to live in America with your family, you need money. I'm your ticket to that money. Please don't bullshit me with all your long and stupid theoretical lectures. Alright, let's get down to it. What do you want?"

"Given all your tough talk, you still need to know that I can break you by denying your wire transfer. I know that you and your company are on the verge of collapse. My lectures are neither theoretical nor stupid. They are factual. So, allow me to lecture you with one final critical fact previously discussed. My life will be in danger for as long as I live. The transfer I am prepared to make for you will always be perceived as an act of a traitor. As you have witnessed firsthand with Balla and Solomon, General Muhammadu kills people, and he certainly will not hesitate to kill me. I will never be able to live with peace of mind. All I'll have is the money you will pay to me. So, believe me, Mr. Sterling, you will pay me, and you will pay me handsomely."

"Define handsomely."

"Well, given that your partner is dead and there's no one to replace him, I'd say you're lucky that I don't force you to substitute the deceased partner's share for me. But, since I am a reasonable man, my fee will be substantially less.

Here's what I want: $5 million deposited at my bank, plus a teaching job at Stanford University."

Sterling, who put his poker face on, responded with, "Is that it?"

"Yes, that's it."

Sterling put his hand to his chin, then thought for a moment, and said, "I'll give you $2.5 million, plus the teaching job at Stanford. I may need to offer Stanford a financial endowment in order for them to offer you a job, but I'm willing to do that. You'll have money and a job. What more do you want out of your new life in America?"

Roberts, who remained very calm, said, "I think you and I have had this conversation before. I remember the results of that conversation. Do you? Well, in case you forgot, there was no deal! Look, Mr. Sterling, at some point you must stop thinking about what annoys you concerning me and start thinking what incredible value I bring to the table. I assure you that, if I walk away from this discussion without a meeting of the minds, you are going to hate yourself everyday for the rest of your life. So, here is my final offer: Five million in cash and I eliminate my request for the Stanford teaching job. I will pursue my own position at Stanford. What is your decision, Mr. Sterling? Yes or no? I really do need to return to my daughter at UCLA."

Sterling, who showed no emotion, got out of his seat and asked a question in lieu of providing an answer, "Can you change my bank routing instructions?"

Roberts, who was starting to look a little bit pale, answered, "Not a problem. Just give me the formal instructions in writing. I will remove the old wiring instructions and replace them with your new bank."

Sterling, who realized he didn't have many good options, looked at the floor, then stared out the window as he was thinking about whether to threaten Roberts with the incriminating tapes Mark had previously recorded or, alternatively, just make the deal. Sterling locked eyes with Roberts and said, "Okay, Stanley, you win."

Roberts, who was now wearing a big smile on his face, said, "You've made a very good decision, Mr. Sterling. After all, what's $5 million as compared to the $50 million you would have been required to pay Chief Balla. I have a specific date for you as to when I will disburse your funds. The date will be precisely November 2nd, 8 weeks from now. After today, you are not to contact me again. Not by phone, fax, or any form of communication. I will never see or talk to you again. My life depends on your solemn oath to uphold this pledge to me. Do I have it?"

"Yes, of course."

"Two weeks after I wire you the funds, I will officially retire from my government position. Thereafter, I will be leaving Nigeria for my new life in America. If anyone should suspect that I wired you the funds due to our collaboration, I will be hunted down like a lion and killed. The first thing the government officials will check are my phone records. They will investigate me from every angle. What they will find is that I was just doing my bureaucratic job. No records will exist that anything clandestine took place between us prior to the wire transfer or after it.

"Everyone in my department knows that I had a long-standing plan to escort my daughter to UCLA. Additionally, everyone understands that I am about to retire and move to the United States. The Central Bank has a lengthy file, developed by Chief Balla and Solomon, regarding the 'legitimacy' of your contract. The only clue an investigator would have is proof of our communication immediately prior to the transfer or anytime after the wire. For the sake of my wife and my children, do not contact me ever again. Besides, if they link me to you, they will not hesitate to kill you too. Do we understand one another?"

"I hear you, Stanley. Now, let me ask you some questions. First of all, how will I know if anything changes? How will you tell me if the November 2nd date changes? And how will I pay you?"

"First, there will be no changes. The Central Bank posts all personnel assignments regarding officials' duties months in advance. I am assigned for November 2. Count on this date. Your money will be wire-transferred on this date. All of the prerequisite work will be concluded prior to November 2. I will literally be pressing a key button and your funds will be sent to the designated bank at that moment. You will of course know that the funds are transferred, because your bank will confirm that $100 million have been credited to your account.

Today, you will provide me in writing the new bank designation, along with the specific wire instructions. I want you to backdate the new designated bank to the date you were in Nigeria. I will insert these written instructions regarding the substitute bank into the file at the Central Bank as if you handed them to Solomon when you were physically in the Bank with Mr. Norman. As to how I get paid, I will provide you with that information right now."

"Sounds like you've thought this plan through quite meticulously."

"Yes, Mr. Sterling I have. Now, we're at the moment in this plan where you call your attorney, Mr. Norman, and he comes here to write me your personal written guarantee, esuring me that you don't accidentally forget to pay me. As we await Mr. Norman, I want you to please gather your new bank wire instructions so that Mr. Norman will be able to hand me the new document I require for the records at the Central Bank. In the meantime, I will prepare my instructions regarding where you will deposit my funds. Are we now reading from the same page, Mr. Sterling?"

"You're smarter than you look, Stanley. Yeah, we're on the same page. Norman will be here within 20 minutes."

Sterling excused himself as he left his private office in order to call Norman, and then Mark, without Roberts listening. He speed-dialed Norman on his phone and was impressed by how quickly his attorney picked up the call. Sterling calmly said, "As improbable as this may sound, believe it or not, Stanley Roberts is sitting in my office at my home."

Norman responded, "Excuse me, who is sitting in your home?"

"You heard me, Stanley Roberts!"

"Shit! He can't help us anymore if he's living here and out of the government! Damn it! Tell that bastard to go to hell."

"Relax, Paul. Everything is good. He's not out of government. His daughter is entering UCLA. He's just dropping her off here in Los Angeles. More importantly, he's going to help us. It's going to cost us a whole bunch of money, but he's going to help us. I need you to get over here ASAP. We're going to document our understanding in writing, so bring your laptop and let's get this done. I'll brief you in detail when you get here."

"Wow! I'm speechless. Either you've been praying really hard or you're the luckiest guy on earth. I guess it doesn't matter, Mr. Sterling, he's here, that's all that matters. Amazing. Just amazing! I'll be right there."

As he hung up with Norman, he immediately called Mark, and just like Norman, Mark picked up on the first ring and said, "I can't find this fucking Roberts. This guy has just plain disappeared. I'm pulling my hair out. I'm really at a dead end!"

Sterling, who was listening to Mark ramble on and on, finally got a word in and said, "I found Roberts."

Mark asked, "Is he dead or alive?"

"He's very much alive. In fact, he's sitting in my office at home."

Mark responded with, "Get the fuck out of here! What do you mean he's in your office?"

"Look, I don't have much time. He dropped his daughter off as a new student at UCLA. He's here and I made a deal with him. I'm going to pay him five million bucks and he's personally going to wire us the funds on November 2nd.

Norman's on his way over here to document the deal between us. I wanted you to know what I'm doing, but you can't come over here because Roberts doesn't want anyone else to see him here except for Norman, who has lawyer-client confidentiality oaths. I'll honor Robert's request to keep you out. But I just wanted you to know that you were right all along to get this guy in the loop. We now have a deal with Roberts. We're going to get paid, Mark. We're going to get paid! I'll call you later."

"Unbelievable! Good luck! Go get 'em, Boss!"

The next step for Sterling was to call his bank in Israel. For more than a decade, Sterling had quietly maintained a foreign bank account in Tel Aviv. His Israeli banker was his college roommate and close friend at Stanford. So, even though it was 2:00 AM in Tel Aviv, and 4:00 PM in LA., Sterling had no choice but to call for the bank wire details.

As Sterling dialed the international call to his Israeli friend and banker, Benjamin Yaalon, he was worried that Yaalon might not pick up, due to the late hour. He could even be out of the country. But, finally, on the fifth ring, Yaalon, who was half-asleep, answered at his home in Tel Aviv by saying, "Elliot. Is that you? Are you alright? It's two o'clock in the morning here!"

"Yes, Ben, everything is fine. I'm so sorry to disturb you. As we speak, I am ready to sign an agreement for a major deal. I cannot close on the contract without wire instruction details, along with a bank account to receive the wire transfer. We're going to be wiring your bank $100 million on November 2nd. I sincerely apologize, but I need the bank instructions right at this moment. Later, I'll explain to you why the urgency and what the business transaction entails. In the meantime, I sure would appreciate your accommodation."

"Say no more, my friend. I will immediately fax you all the bank instructions you require. You'll have them within the next 20 minutes. I'm walking over to my private office and computer here in my home. When you wire the funds, we're going to deposit them into your existing checking account because we don't have time to set up a new bank account. We will properly invest the money after the wire successfully hits your account. Call me tomorrow. I'm dying to hear your explanation as to why you're sending me a $100 million bucks and what your urgency was to tell me about it in the middle of the night!

By the way, you're going to need to explain to Miriam, my wife, that it really was you calling me at 2:00 AM and not some girlfriend! All kidding aside, I understand exactly what you need. Consider it done. My best to Felicia. We'll speak tomorrow. Shalom, Elliot."

"Todah Rabah. Thank you very much. You're a good friend, Ben. I apologize for the late call. Good night."

As Sterling was walking back to his office, he heard Norman's voice engaged in conversation with Roberts. It sounded like a couple of long-term buddies catching up on old times. When Sterling stepped into the private office, both Norman and Roberts simultaneously spoke, interrupting each other. Then, Norman asserted himself and said, "Stanley has briefed me on the deal structure. Assuming you have the new bank routing instructions and you're willing to provide Stanley with a personal guarantee, I think we have ourselves an achievable deal."

Roberts jumped in and said, "I only have one minor clarification that I'd like to discuss with Mr. Sterling."

Norman responded with, "I trust you are not going to alter the agreement in principle, because, if you are, don't even bother speaking!"

"No, I'm not going to change the deal in principle. I want to maintain the right, in writing, to assign my guarantee to any third party of my choosing, and I'll tell you why. If for some reason Mr. Sterling chooses not to pay me my $5 million, I'll have no other recourse but to take Mr. Sterling to an American court to collect on the guarantee. I myself, for obvious reasons, cannot do that. Nigerian government officials will hunt me down and murder me once they see evidence of a lawsuit. Please believe me when I tell you that they will find out if I go to court against Mr. Sterling. So what recourse do I have left other than my assigned third party bringing Mr. Sterling to his senses?"

"And who do you propose to be this assigned third party?" Norman asked.

"My attorney, Ibrahim Adewole. He practices in San Francisco. He was my classmate at Stanford University. I would trust him to discreetly collect for me in the unlikely event that Mr. Sterling decides to do the wrong thing."

Norman looked at Sterling and said, "This is totally unacceptable to me, but it's your call."

Sterling thinks for a moment, then said, "Of course I can't agree to your Mr. Adewole. Here's why: I don't know him. Suppose he decides to blackmail you. Or, even worse, he decides to blackmail me. He can decide that $5 million is a whole lot of money and why shouldn't he get some? In fact, he might even decide that $100 million is a shit-load of money, so what's an extra 5 million for him? Absolutely not, Stanley. The answer is no! We have a deal. No one is to be brought into your confidence other than Mr. Norman and myself. I have to trust that you will fund my money on November 2nd, and you must trust that I will pay you the $5 million I owe you. That's it!"

"Very well, Mr. Sterling. I will expect my money to be wired to my account within three working days from the receipt of your funds. My recourse will be to either take you to an American court, at the risk of exposing both you and myself to our Nigerian friends, or have you killed. Don't look so offended, Mr. Sterling. I'm just kidding on the 'killed' part.

Look, I am certain that you are going to pay me, but I will reserve the right to sue you if you don't. I may lose my life, but at least my wife will collect what she deserves. Your penalty will be that the Nigerians will understand that you paid me a gratification to get your money out of Nigeria. Good luck to you with that bit of information in their possession. Well, enough of this catastrophic talk. You will be paid on November 2nd, and I trust that you will pay me pursuant to my guarantee, as stipulated.

More important than the written agreement is whether I have your word. My research on you says that your word is as good as gold. Do I have your word, Mr. Sterling?"

"You have my word, Stanley."

"Alright, Mr. Norman, go ahead and write up the documents. Again, these are deal points. First, I will wire the $100 million on November 2nd. Second, Mr. Sterling will provide you with new bank wire instructions. These instructions will be backdated to the actual date of the original instructions previously submitted to the Central Bank. I will remove the old instructions from the Central Bank's file and insert the new instructions in their place. Third, I will provide you with my bank wire instructions indicating where to deposit the five million dollars from Mr. Sterling. Finally, Mr. Sterling will hand me his personal guarantee regarding my $5 million dollar fee."

Sterling nodded his head in agreement with the terms and directed his hand towards Roberts as they shook. The deal was done, and it was up to Norman to draft the documents. As Norman opened his laptop, the fax machine began to ring.

Sterling then walked confidently towards the fax machine, very certain that this would be the bank wire instructions from Benjamin. Sure enough, they were, and without even pausing to read them, he simply handed the instructions to Norman, unequivocally trusting Benjamin to have written them perfectly.

Norman looked up at Sterling and asked, "The money is going to Israel?"

Sterling confirmed with, "That's right. It's going to Israel."

Norman, with a glimmer in his eye, said, "Okay, gentlemen. I'll have all the documents ready in one hour. Stanley, let me have your wire instructions for the 5 million. I'll start writing the guarantee. We'll sign in about an hour."

More than two hours had gone by when Norman finally said, "Sorry this took so long, but I just wanted to be certain that the documents were correct. I'm confident they are ready for signature. Here is your copy, Mr. Sterling, and here is yours, Stanley," as he handed them each a set of documents. "Please review the agreements, and if they are in order, go ahead and sign them."

Within 15 minutes, Stanley said, "You're an excellent lawyer, Paul. Everything is correctly documented. I'm prepared to execute the agreements." Sterling continued, "I have no changes. Let's sign."

Within moments, the agreements were signed by both parties; the countdown to November 2nd had officially started. Sterling addressed Norman by saying, "Perfectly done, Paul." Then he faced Roberts and said, "I understand the risk you will undertake to wire my funds. I want you to know, Stanley, that you can count on me to pay you what we've agreed upon. Do not worry about your fee, just concentrate on every detail necessary to successfully transfer the money to my Israeli bank account. Let me walk you to your car."

When they arrived at the car parked in the porte cochere, Roberts extended his hand towards Sterling, but instead of shaking Roberts' hand, Sterling gave him a hug and whispered in his ear, "You have my word that I will pay you. Just make sure you pay me. I wish you and your family great prosperity in America. Good luck with your life."

"Do not worry, Mr. Sterling. I will deliver on my promise. Farewell, and it has been my honor to meet you."

Chapter 20

It had been two weeks since Roberts had left Sterling's home. The legal matter against Nigeria had been relatively silent, as was the bank's case against Sterling. Aside from occasionally speaking to Norman, Mark, and Benjamin, very little went on concerning Sterling's business life, until today.

By noon, Norman had contacted Sterling three separate times by phone regarding the bank's litigation against Sterling. The topic of discussion was a written order issued by the judge instructing the bank, as the plaintiff, and Sterling, as the defendant, to hold a formal pretrial settlement conference. The judge had demanded that both sides submit written settlement offer terms, if any, for the judge's preliminary review. The judge's goal was to determine if the bank and Sterling could find the common ground necessary to achieving an equitable solution, thus avoiding a long and complicated trial.

Norman advised Sterling that this would be the perfect time to structure a settlement with the bank. The big remaining question was whether Roberts would actually wire the funds on November 2nd. If he did, a settlement, guided by the judge on the record, would favor Sterling immensely. Norman went on to explain to Sterling that, "So long as the bank does not hear about the proposed wire transfer on November 2nd, I am certain that we can convince the bank into believing that we are desperate to maintain ownership of your home. If the bank thinks we're never going to get paid by the Nigerians and you and your wife are in distress regarding the potential loss of your home, I believe the bank will make a deal for the Sterling Development Company's assets. The agreement I would recommend proposing to the judge would be along these lines: first, we agree to release all of our interests in the Sterling Development Company, including all of our housing subdivisions and our corporate stock. Second, the bank releases your personal guarantee on your Bel Air residence. Third, the bank releases any claim it would have regarding your Nigerian $100 million contract. Finally, the bank releases all personal claims it might have against you, whether they are known at this time or discovered at a future date."

Sterling, who was listening intently, said, "Brilliant. Just brilliant! You're going to get the judge to serve as our mediator, formally settling all the disputes between Sterling Development and the bank. So, let me get this straight, we're going to have the right to collect on the $100 million wire-transfer while legally prohibiting the bank from touching our funds. On top of that, our company, which is a sinking Titanic, gets dumped on the bank for effectively 30 cents on the dollar. Now, if I'm hearing you right, the bank releases my personal guarantee regarding the Bel Air residence. Wow! Incredible! We get our $100 million, I get my home back, the bank gets the title to the Titanic, and we never have to deal with the bank again!"

Norman responded by saying, "Yes. That's exactly what I'm telling you! Obviously, this is all contingent upon Stanley Roberts wiring us the funds on November 2nd."

"Paul, I think you can pull this off. The bank has no confidence in us getting paid by the Nigerians. They think the litigation is going to go on forever with appeal after appeal. They assign no value to the Nigerian contract. They also know that I have an emotional attachment to my home and that I'll fight to get back my residence free and clear of the bank's liens. It's easy for the bank to quantify and value the Sterling Development assets, and although they will only get back pennies on the dollar, it's an asset they can control. If we legally fight the bank, they realize that we can tie them up for years on appeal and potential bankruptcy. Paul, they're going to settle! We just need to be certain to time the judge's settlement precisely around Roberts' November 2nd wire confirmation."

Norman, shaking his head in agreement, said, "I am confident that we can make this deal, so long as the bank and the judge remain oblivious as to what Roberts is about to do for us on November 2nd. With your permission, Mr. Sterling, I'll write up the settlement proposal and forward it to the judge. I'll request that the judge schedule a settlement conference with the bank within the next two weeks. The tricky part will be to juggle a final settlement agreement synchronized with the timing of Roberts wire transfer."

Sterling, with his charismatic look in his face, said, "The sooner the better! Get this plan on track, but I want you to make one minor amendment to the plan."

"And what is that, Mr. Sterling?"

"I want you to ask the bank for $5 million to be released to me from Sterling Development's cash reserves. Inform the bank that we insist on their release of these funds. Advise the bank that we are faced with significant professional fees, along with other expenses, once we reach an agreement. Let them feel sorry that I have lost the development company. In effect, the bank would be setting aside the $5 million dollars we'd pay Roberts for the fee he negotiated. Hell, the bank will spend well over $5 million with their own legal outside counsel."

"I will of course add your request, but you just made our settlement agreement more difficult!"

"I'm very confident that you're going to get us the extra five million. We must ask for the moon, then settle for as much as we can get!"

Norman, who looked uncomfortable, said, "I'd just like to go on the record with you expressing my sincere reservations regarding the five million dollars. I think we're pushing the envelope. Not only will it be a deal breaker, but we may piss them off so badly that the bank may make things worse for us out of spite."

Sterling contemptuously responded by saying, "Like what?"

"Like, they won't release their guarantees regarding the Nigerian contract. Since you signed a personal guarantee and we also added the contract onto the Sterling Development books as an asset, the bank has us personally and commercially! Or the bank decides to punish you regarding your personal residence. Is it really worth the risk?"

"I sincerely appreciate your thinking, but let me share my opinion on this matter. The bank will consider me stupid for giving up Sterling Development Company in exchange for the Nigerian contract asset, which they consider a scam. They know we will be fighting for many years before we will see any money from a court battle. Effectively, the bank thinks that the only thing I get out of this deal is my home released from the guarantee, plus the $5 million from the Sterling reserve account. Not even in their wildest imagination would they comprehend that we may actually receive the Nigerian wire transfer on November 2nd. Look at this practically from the bank's financial analysis. They no longer face the threat of our bankruptcy. The court case will be dismissed, saving them a ton of legal fees. The bank will own all of Sterling Development Company, including the subdivisions. Plus, they would start removing a bad loan off their books, which the bank regulators encourage. All they have to do is release my home, along with my personal guarantee, then hand us $5 million. Since they don't have a clue as to what Roberts is about to do at the Central Bank on November 2nd, they'll probably take the deal!"

Norman glanced at Sterling and simply said, "You're the boss, Mr. Sterling. We'll follow your instincts. I'll insert the five million demand into the proposed settlement agreement brief to the judge. I'm not very optimistic as to our chances of getting this part of our proposal approved by the bank and the judge, but hey, you never know unless you ask. Of course, I could ask to manage the Los Angeles Dodgers baseball team, but I'm pretty sure I won't be managing them." After a little bit of awkward silence, Norman added, "That's just a joke. Very bad humor. Sorry, anyways, I'll take care of this."

Sterling, sporting a smile on his face, said, "You're never going to make it as a stand-up comic, but you're one hell of a great attorney. Look, all kidding aside, get this settlement conference with the bank scheduled as soon as you can. I'm very confident that things are going to go our way."

Norman spent the next two weeks drafting, then submitted to the judge and the bank a thoughtful and well-prepared proposed settlement agreement. It took a while, but he was finally able to secure an agreement with the judge to hear Sterling's settlement proposal on a specific date that came almost two weeks from the judge's original request. All parties were anxious to sit down face-to-face with the goal of getting a settlement accomplished.

On the morning of the settlement conference, three bankers arrived along with their two lawyers. Sterling entered the federal courthouse with Mark and Norman and immediately took a seat in one of the conference rooms at the court. The bank brought the two arrogant young bankers who had originally met with Sterling when all of them had come together to discuss Sterling Development's complicated challenges. Interestingly, Paul Reno, Sterling's long-term banker and friend, was nowhere to be seen.

The moment Mark spotted the arrogant young bankers wearing their pompous pinstriped navy blue suits, he whispered to Elliot, "I can't wait until you kick the butts of those two condescending pricks."

Sterling whispered back, "Don't worry, I got these two guys, but first let's see where they're coming from. Once they have exposed their hand, I'm going to get their foolish egos to believe that the bank will be trading my home and the release of their rights to a worthless Nigerian contract in exchange for obtaining the title to our Sterling Development stock, along with our land holdings. Once the bank shows they're vulnerable, we'll kick their little asses back to their hedonistic college days."

Mark responded with, "I'll be patiently watching. I really can't stand these two assholes."

"No worries, we're going to enjoy having the last laugh on these two guys. Just follow my lead."

Mark, who had been following Elliot's lead most of his life, simply winked at Elliot with his sign of approval.

As everyone settled into their seats, the judge opened by stating, "There is no right or wrong proposal here this afternoon. What I'm looking for is common ground. If we can find some common ground on just one point, I'll consider our work very encouraging.

Now, I'm going to release the final version of each of your proposals and we're going to stay here all night, if necessary, to resolve this case. If we can avoid a trial, you're all going to save yourself a lot of grief. I will help arbitrate this settlement conference for as long as the court can see the possibility of a reasonable settlement agreement. If we can come to a fair arrangement, I will issue a court order enforcing compliance of your mutual agreement. If there is no consensus, we'll see all of you in court."

"Thank you, Your Honor. My name is Clarence Levy. I am the bank's corporate counsel, appearing on behalf of the plaintiff. I am joined by the bank's representatives, Mitch Johnson and George Walsh. With the court's permission, Mr. Walsh will make some preliminary comments."

The judge said, "Please proceed, Mr. Walsh."

"We would like to express to the court that we greatly appreciate the opportunity to lay out the facts regarding this matter, and with the assistance of the court, look forward to its resolution. The court will soon find that we are ready and willing to find common ground regarding the reasonable resolution of this dispute. We welcome your vast experience regarding matters similar to this and sincerely look forward to a speedy resolution. Having said that, I will express our outrage at the initial draft by Mr. Sterling. The defendant's request is preposterous."

The judge responded by saying, "And what steps did you take to draw your conclusion?"

"We carefully and thoughtfully read the settlement agreement, Your Honor."

"Alright, Mr. Walsh, why don't you explain to everyone why the defendant's claims are worthless to you?"

"First of all, to ask us for $5 million is insulting. Mr. Sterling owes us a serious amount of money. We do not owe him, he owes us. We're not here to fund a charity case. We strongly reject this one-sided request in its entirety!"

The judge, who had a confused look on his face, responded with, "Well, if you mean what you just said, why are you here, Mr. Walsh?"

"We attended at the request of the court."

"The court requested your attendance with good faith intentions of potentially settling this litigation without going through a trial. The moment you say that you reject the proposed settlement agreement in its entirety is the moment I conclude one of the following. Either you and your counsel do not understand what you're doing or you're acting in bad faith. We did not bring you here to waste the court's time, and we certainly did not ask you here to exaggerate your feelings about how terrible the proposal sounds to you. So, if you have nothing further to contribute to these deliberations, then I suggest we adjourn and just chalk this up to a textbook waste of time!"

Walsh, who had turned the same shade of white after Sterling had put him in his place many months ago, responded with, "I apologize, Your Honor. With your permission, I'd like to try this again."

"Proceed, Mr. Walsh."

"Thank you, Your Honor. First, we will agree to release all interest in the Nigerian 100 million dollar contract. Should Mr. Sterling prevail in his court case against the Nigerians, or in the unlikely eventuality that Mr. Sterling should collect on his contract, we will agree to stipulate our release concerning any associated funds."

Sterling, who was delighted to hear Walsh's opening concession, did not make an expression on his face and did not say a word. Norman and Mark did not even look at each other over concerns they might reveal to Walsh that he had just made a critical error in his negotiation tactics. As the judge made a note on a yellow legal pad, he said, "Please continue, Mr. Walsh."

"We will demand Mr. Sterling's unconditional release of all his assets regarding the Sterling Development Company.

Simply put, the bank will become the lawful owner of all stock holdings in the company held by Mr. Sterling and his family. All of the firm's real estate assets, including, but not limited to, the current housing subdivisions under construction, will come under the bank's control and legal possession. We will be entitled to the Sterling Development brand name and will operate without Mr. Sterling's direction."

The judge interjected with, "So, if I've heard correctly, Mr. Sterling is to release all interest in his company to your financial institution, is that right, Mr. Walsh?"

"Yes, Your Honor, you heard that right."

"Alright, what else, Mr. Walsh?"

"We will pay zero to Mr. Sterling regarding his demand for $5 million in cash, requested to be drawn from Mr. Sterling's interest reserve account currently held by the bank."

"Anything else, Mr. Walsh?"

Although Mr. Sterling never actually mortgaged his personal residence to the bank, we have segregated, for accounting purposes, the sum of $2.5 million allocated toward his home as a portion of his personal guarantee granted to the bank regarding the commercial loans we made to his company. The bank will agree to accept one lump-sum payment from Mr. Sterling in the amount of $2.5 million for the unconditional release of any personal guarantees the bank has assigned to his personal residence. Upon the signature of all parties to this proposed settlement agreement, the bank will immediately be prepared to release the personal promissory note and associated personal guarantee back to Mr. Sterling. That's it, Your Honor."

The judge looked right into the eyes of young Mr. Walsh and said, "From what I've heard, we are many miles apart. Not even close. But, since I'm not Mr. Sterling, I'll let him speak for himself. So, Mr. Sterling, would you like to address the court or would you prefer to see all of us at trial? Your choice."

Sterling slowly got out of his chair and said to the judge, "I've got a few things to say. I'll be brief, even though it has taken me decades to build my company, probably longer than Mr. Walsh's life, but I'll be brief. First, I will remind Mr. Walsh and his bank that federal bank regulators highly encourage banks to find settlement measures to remove bad loans from bank books. It allows for the banks financial statements to look better to its stockholders, but perhaps even more importantly, the banks are no longer required by the federal regulators to set aside substantial loan loss reserves to cover potential losses such as a Sterling loan. A successful settlement agreement will actually help Mr. Walsh's bank because we are informed that they have many major loans currently on their books that appear to fall into the category of 'troubled.' The bank has an opportunity to solve this matter right now in lieu of fighting us for years in court. And even if they should prevail after appeal, they still will face our legal right to file for protection under the Federal Bankruptcy laws. So, with that in mind, I will state our final and best offer to settle this matter."

The judge, who understood exactly where Sterling was going, interrupted and said, "Do you literally mean final offer?"

Sterling softly responded, "Yes, Your Honor. This is our final offer."

"Okay, Mr. Sterling, let's hear your final offer."

Sterling, without any notes, began by speaking, "Although we accept that the bank will release to us all of its interest in our Nigerian agreement, including litigation rights tied to that agreement, the court should note that this is not a generous concession made by the bank. In fact, it's no concession whatsoever, due to the fact that the bank assigns zero value to the agreement on its accounting books."

The judge jumped in and said, "As a point of clarification, when you refer to including the litigation rights tied to the Nigerian agreement, I gather you are referring to a possible future legal judgment, if any, awarded by a court of law?"

"That is precisely what I am referring to, Your Honor."

"And what is your next point, Mr. Sterling?"

"As you know, Your Honor, I started the Sterling Development Company from scratch. Until recently, it had been recognized as one of the most successful real estate development firms in the nation. I didn't just get lucky and create an exceptional company. It took many family sacrifices and countless hours of dedicated hardwork. Along comes young Mr. Walsh and says that he wants effective ownership of my firm. We accept to release our interest in Sterling Development to the bank. But please note, Your Honor, that this is the definition of a meaningful concession. The only condition I place on that decision is that the bank be obligated to accept any and all liabilities tied to my firm."

Once again, the judge interrupted and said, "Yes, Mr. Sterling, the moment the bank agrees to accept your company as a part of this proposed settlement, they will be agreeing to own both the assets and the liabilities. Alright, now what about your $5 million cash request? Where do you stand on this?"

Sterling looked straight at Mr. Walsh and stated with clarity, "You know full well, and I know even better than you, that your bank will spend every penny of my $5 million interest reserve fund to service the monthly interest payment on our construction loan. That is precisely why we set up an interest reserve fund: to pay the interest on the construction loan. If we settle now, that $5 million reserve will not be spent because you're going to own my company and you also own the bank. The $5 million will become a windfall to your bank.

Now, let's get real here. If I fight you legally, your bank is going to spend every last dollar sitting in the interest reserve, plus some more, just to keep its loan current and satisfy the bank regulators. If you release the $5 million interest reserve now to me, you'll settle your lawsuit, take the title to my company, and get this loan off your books. You're going to lose the $5 million either way. You might as well pay it to me and get this ordeal behind us. So, Your Honor, that's a long explanation, but here's my answer to your question. To settle this lawsuit, we will take not one dime less than the entire $5 million we have requested."

The judge took over by saying, "Okay, that gets us down to the personal residence matter where Mr. Sterling agrees to pay back to the bank $2.5 million and the bank releases Mr. Sterling's personal guarantee."

Sterling addressed the judge and said, "Your Honor, I am prepared to pay back to the bank a total of $2.5 million allocated specifically towards the unconditional release of any and all liens the bank may have assigned to my personal residence. Of course, my personal guarantees will become null and void. The only conditions I would insist upon is that this settlement agreement be fully executed on or before November 2nd of this year. If everything I have outlined is agreed upon by the bank, then we have ourselves a deal."

The judge put down his pen, looked at Walsh, and asked, "Do we have an agreement, Mr. Walsh?

Walsh, who appeared nervous, stated, "I do not have authority to accept the arrangement Mr. Sterling has proposed. I ask that the court provide for a 30-minute recess while I consult with the people who can either accept or deny the proposed deal on the table."

"Sure, Mr. Walsh, I'll give you some time. We'll reconvene in 30 minutes."

As Walsh gathered his papers to depart the court facilities, Sterling approached him and whispered, "Tell Paul Reno that I can still kick his ass in tennis!" Walsh just barely grinned and kept walking towards the exit to find a secure area in order to make a call seeking approval from his superiors, which included Reno and some other bank directors.

As Walsh left, Sterling, Mark, and Norman proceeded to the hallway of the court facilities. Mark then said very quietly, "Your argument was perfect. I'm pretty sure you understand bank economics far better than these bank idiots. You may have convinced the bank to take the deal! How great would that be? The bank picks up our massive debts and liabilities, the personal guarantees vanish, and we get to receive $100 million from the Nigerian government without any accounting to the bank. The bank and the judge will forever believe that we got the raw end of the deal, even though it's precisely what we wanted. You get your home back without liens. The bank pays you $5 million in cash, and all we need to do is pay them $2.5 million. Here's my comment: brilliant proposal!"

Without making any eye contact, Walsh made his way into the court chambers. He sat down and nodded his heads as if to say to Sterling, 'I think we can do this.'

At precisely 30 minutes from the time the judge had called for the recess, he returned and asked, "Alright, Mr. Walsh, where do we stand?"

Walsh began by saying, "We thank you for the time you granted us, Your Honor. Management has authorized me to settle this matter almost as proposed by Mr. Sterling. All settlement deal points are acceptable, except one. We have ourselves a deal if Mr. Sterling will agree to split the difference with the bank regarding the $5 million interest reserve fund. Mr. Sterling has requested all of the $5 million, we are prepared to pay him 50% of his request. We will release $2.5 million dollars of the reserve to Mr. Sterling and we will retain the remaining money. If this is agreeable to Mr. Sterling, we have a deal. We consider this proposal as our final offer. If rejected by Mr. Sterling, we are prepared to proceed to court and we ask that you set a date to start the trial. Thank you, Your Honor, for conducting these settlement discussions. The ball is in Mr. Sterling's court, no pun intended."

The tired-looking judge said, "Very well, Mr. Sterling, you heard the gentleman, what's your answer?"

Sterling responded with, "Your Honor, you gave the bank 30 minutes, I ask that you give me five minutes to discuss this with my attorney and my associate."

"You got it, Mr. Sterling."

Sterling, Mark, and Norman got out of their seats and convened just outside the courtroom conference area. The first to speak was Norman, who said without any hesitation, "Take the deal! We got everything we could have expected. I never thought the bank would give up any part of the interest reserve. Mr. Sterling, take the deal!"

Sterling looked at Mark, who stated, "You just kicked their asses! They're going to hand over $2.5 million out of the interest reserve, which you're going to turn around and hand right back to them in order to pay off your lien on your home. The bank is giving you the money to pay off what you owe it. You're getting your house back for free! Take this deal and run as fast as you can."

Without any further comment, Sterling turned around and simply walked back to the court to face the judge.

Norman and Mark walked immediately behind him in single file. No one uttered a word until the judge returned back into the room. Once the judge was seated, Sterling stood and said, "I have my answer, Your Honor."

The judge, who had just about had enough, said, "No reason to keep us all in suspense, Mr. Sterling. Yes or no?"

"My answer is no, with one strict condition."

The Judge, who just couldn't wait to hear what possible condition Sterling had in mind, sarcastically snapped by saying, "I didn't ask you for a yes or no with a condition. I simply asked you for a yes or a no. Now what's going on here, Mr. Sterling?"

"Nothing is going on here. It's just a condition. My answer is no, I agree to our settlement agreement with the strict condition that our agreement must be fully executed and approved by the court on or before November 2nd, or either party shall have the right to cancel the settlement, maintaining the right to proceed to court."

The judge, who was processing what Sterling had stated, glared at Walsh, then addressed Sterling by saying, "I don't really have any problem with your little condition, but I do want you to explain the foundation of your prerequisite."

Sterling stood and said, "Oh, that's easy. I need to plan for my new life as the former owner of the Sterling Development Company. Either I plan for the surrender of my company to the bank or I prepare with my attorney to fight for my company. I'm not going to play around with a long, drawn-out negotiated agreement that can't seem to find the right language for a final settlement. As I said, I need to get on with my life. So, by November 2nd, we either have a deal signed by all parties, including you, Your Honor, or I'm going to reserve the right to take the bank to court. This strict condition,

Your Honor, is not negotiable. My answer is 'no' with my condition."

The judge stared at Walsh and nonchalantly said, "Alright, I can live with that. What about you, Mr. Walsh?"

Walsh quickly responded to the judge, stating, "We can live with November 2nd, but we're not paying out $2.5 million to Mr. Sterling."

The judge snaps at Walsh and says, "You've got five minutes to call your boss and make this a deal. Now, go convince him on the merits, and let's get this over with!"

Walsh responses with, "I'll do my best your Honor."

With no one leaving the area, Walsh walks to the corner of the room with his cell phone in hand. Within minutes he returns to face the judge and simply says, "We have a deal your Honor. We have a deal!"

The judge, with an uncharacteristic smile on his face, addressed Walsh and Sterling and declared, "Very well done, gentlemen. We've got ourselves a settlement agreement. I will, for the record, now summarize what the agreement must incorporate. First, the bank will release any and all interest in the Nigerian contract held by Mr. Sterling. This will include any funds that might be released by the Nigerian government directly to Mr. Sterling or a legal judgment Mr. Sterling may obtain against the Nigerian government in his pending case.

Second, Mr. Sterling will agree to release to the bank all his legal and equitable rights regarding his ownership of Sterling Development Company. This includes all assets and liabilities.

Third, the bank agrees to release to Mr. Sterling the $5 million interest reserve account currently held by the bank. For clarity, that means Mr. Sterling will receive a net $2.5 million from the bank since Mr. Sterling agrees to pay the bank $2.5 million for the bank's unconditional release of the lien the bank holds on Mr. Sterling's personal residence.

Fourth, all personal promissory notes and personal guarantees will be released by the bank to Mr. Sterling without any further effect.

And finally, the settlement will be fully executed by both parties on or before November 2nd. In the event the agreement is not signed by all parties, including myself, the plaintiff or the defendant may request to proceed directly back to court for trial. I intend to hold both the plaintiff's and the defendant's attorneys to the highest degree of good faith dealing and legal ethical practices concerning the goal of reaching the November 2nd deadline. I congratulate both parties for agreeing to this settlement. I wish you all good luck with all your future endeavors."

With those words stated for the record, the judge stood and left without another comment. The deal was done.

As Sterling and his entourage were heading towards the exit of the court facilities, Walsh caught up with Sterling and said, "Just wanted you to know that it was Paul Reno who argued hard to find a way to settle with you. The rest of the directors wanted your head. Paul convinced each one individually to get this matter settled with you. Even at the end, with the interest reserve challenge, it was Paul who said 'get the deal done'. He told me that because of your sense of fairness we should take the deal. Oh, by the way, he also told me that after the settlement agreement is fully executed, he wants to come over to your house and kick your butt in tennis. Don't shoot me, I'm just the messenger."

"Tell Paul I'll be waiting for him on my court anytime after November 2nd. While you're at it, let him know that I'm pretty sure that the reason he went all-out to convince the directors to settle with me and split the interest reserve account was solely due to the fact that he knew I wasn't bluffing on any of my threats. As the consummate professional that Paul is, he wasn't doing me any favors. Reno was just looking after the best interest of the bank, as he should. Now, as long as you're running messages, tell him that the only ass that's going to be kicked is his own. By the way, make sure we sign this agreement on or before November 2nd, or I promise you we'll be back in court. Ask Paul if you don't believe me. Have a good day, Mr. Walsh."

Sterling then walked over to Mark and Norman standing near the elevator and said, "What can I say, I had to call an audible! Just followed my instincts and I got lucky this time.

Hey, listen, I've got to run. My wife has prepared dinner for me at home. Come on over tomorrow at 1:00 PM. We need to figure out the next step with the Nigerians. I think we should settle with them too. Anyways, give it some thought. The sky is going to be the limit for us! You guys are awesome!"

Chapter 21

Sterling and his wife had spent a delightful evening having dinner the night before. Elliot candidly informed Felicia the results of the settlement conference with the bank. He told her that he had lost their company to the bank, but that he had secured their residence without any further liens. All personal guarantees to the bank were to become void. Effectively, he advised his wife that Mr. and Mrs. Sterling were about to start all over again, with one exception. The exception was that this time he and his wife would start off with $100 million in cash deposited in an Israeli bank. They spent much of their evening discussing the merits of whether to live in Israel or Los Angeles, even though they would own their home in Bel Air, free and in the clear. They openly talked about the social ramifications of living in a high society environment like Los Angeles without the prestige of being the proud owners of a company like Sterling Development. Although Felicia was not thrilled about moving to Israel, she wasn't opposed to it either. Her biggest concern was not the social aspect, it was the proximity to her children.

Felicia kept reiterating that she didn't really care where she lived, so long as it was together with her husband and their children. She explained to Elliot that a home with absolutely no debt in Bel Air, along with $100 million in the bank, 'will buy you a whole hell of a lot of social.'

They went on to conclude that evening that if the Central Bank of Nigeria released Sterling's funds on November 2nd, they would stay in Los Angeles. They would build a new life together with their kids staying right in their home in Bel Air. Felicia understood that her husband would come out on top. Elliot was reminded once again that his wife was a one-of-a-kind loyal and loving soulmate. Now, it was up to Elliot to flawlessly execute his plan.

Sterling was keenly aware of the fact that if Stanley Roberts failed to wire the Nigerian contract funds on November 2nd, he would be in deep trouble. There was no way to know for sure. All

Sterling could do was plan for success. That's why he settled with the bank, but the Nigerian litigation was drawing too much attention onto Sterling's contract funds by Nigerian government officials and the Central Bank.

The concern swirling through Sterling's mind was that the Nigerian litigation would prohibit Stanley Roberts from wiring the funds to Sterling. It was becoming evident that the Nigerian court case would need to be dropped in order to take the attention away from the contract funds. The big risk centered around dropping the Nigerian legal case prior to Roberts' funding through the Central Bank. What a disaster that would be! Not only would he let the Nigerians off the hook, but Sterling would have given up his company without a fight. This risky decision was about to become the most important business decision of his life. He would never recover from this wrong determination, yet the right judgment would financially settle him and his family for many generations to come.

At about 1:00 PM, Sterling made his way to his home office, where he found Mark and Norman sitting on the couch waiting for him to arrive. Mark and Norman stood to greet their boss. Sterling instantly told them both, "We've got a huge decision to make here today that is going to affect all of our lives, especially if we fuck up and make the wrong decision."

Norman jumped in by saying, "I know where you're heading with this. Roberts is standing by to release our funds on November 2nd. The bank is done and it won't be able to touch the $100 million. The dilemma is that we're suing the Nigerians. Consequently, there is no way they are ever going to wire us our funds while we're suing them. Their whole legal defense is to prove to the court that no such contract exists between the Nigerians and us."

Sterling, who respected how well Norman understood the challenge, just said, "Go on."

Norman looked straight at Sterling and said, "We've got to get rid of the case! Roberts needs to be free to wire us the funds from the Central Bank without any intervention by some Nigerian legal authority preventing him from acting. The trick is to settle the case, yet allow for the contract to be lawfully funded even after the Nigerians have discovered that we have been paid. We must be certain that our settlement agreement with the Nigerians allows us to keep the funds in our possession after Roberts wires them to us. In other words, we must be absolutely certain that once we have the

100 million in our bank, the Nigerians cannot sue us and take it away. I got this. I can do this!"

Mark, who was listening carefully, said, "Look, I agree with everything you just said. The issue here is timing. Any way we want to play it, we're going to have two agreements in place. One with the bank and one with the Nigerians. The bottom line comes down to this: if Roberts doesn't fund, we're fucked! The bank will own our company and we no longer will retain any legal recourse against these Nigerian bastards! All these legal arrangements are great, but why sign away all of our rights with the possibility that Roberts could fail to fund? We got to talk this through some more."

Norman acknowledged with, "You're right, but we have no choice with the Nigerians. Our settlement agreement with them must be signed at least one week prior to November 2nd in order to ensure that there are no obstructions stopping Roberts from funding. We can't wait until the last day to sign the settlement. The best I can do is insert some language allowing for a seven-day rescission period while being ambiguous as to Lagos or Los Angeles time. The problem with the rescission is that either party can pull out of the agreement during the seven-day period, leaving the settlement open to cancellation. This is not something I can recommend. Although I can throw in many provisions that perhaps allow us to challenge the settlement agreement in Court, I think we'll lose that challenge. But if Roberts is explicitly prohibited by the Nigerian authorities from funding our contract, I do believe we would prevail in bringing back the case. I'll enter verbiage along the lines that the contract must be allowed to be paid without any interference by any government authority even after the settlement agreement is signed. In the eventuality that Roberts is prohibited from funding due to the government stopping him, I think we'll win! I'm very confident that we'll be able to bring back the FSIA court case against Nigerians. Mark, you should have been a lawyer."

Mark reacted with, "No thanks, I'll leave that tedious and monotonous deskwork to you. Just one other point regarding the bank deal: I suggest we don't sign our agreement until November 2nd, when we get confirmation that Roberts' wire has hit our account. Make sure that you insist that the bank signs first. Make up some legal reason for why they need to sign first, like Estoppel Certificates, or stock transfer, or whatever. Just make sure they sign first. Once the bank has signed the settlement, tell them to send it to you for Elliot's signature. Although Elliot will sign technically for the record, demonstrating that he has signed before the wire transfer was confirmed, we will not release the settlement back to the bank until we are positive that our funds have arrived. This way, just in case Roberts is stopped, we will not have officially released our interest in Sterling Development to the bank and we will maintain our rights against Nigeria to bring back the legal case against them."

Sterling, now very impressed with Mark, said, "What law school did you go to?"

Mark responded with his standard answer for anytime he was asked about his school, "The University of Hard Knocks."

Sterling understood well that he had just been provided with very seasoned and wise advice by the two business associates he trusted blindly.

He addressed them both by saying, "As usual, you guys have got it exactly right. If we can thread the needle precisely as we have discussed here today, we're going to get to the mountaintop. This requires perfect legal work by you, Paul. You need to outsmart your counterpart, Neil Roberts. We must also be very precise as to the timing that Mark has so astutely outlined. If we outwork and outthink the bank and the Nigerians, we're all going to benefit. Each of you will receive $1 million as a bonus from me within 3 business days of receipt of the Central Bank wire. If you choose to leave your funds in Israel, I'll have my personal banker, Benjamin Yaalon, set up accounts for you. If you want your funds wired someplace else, just provide me with your bank instructions. In addition, we are going to start an international hedge fund based out of Los Angeles but with close ties to Israel. My friend Benjamin Yaalon is already preparing the business plan. You both are invited to work in the new company, as well as invest in the fund as equity partners. November 2nd is exactly 30 days from today. Execute now as if there is no tomorrow. This is the final game of the world championship. Winner takes all. You are the men I'm entrusting to go to war with me. Let's do this!"

Norman responded gratefully and said, "Thank you for such a generous bonus and job offer. There is no one I would prefer to work for other than you, so I accept your job offer. It will be my honor."

Mark, having trouble holding back his emotions, hugged his friend and just said, "You can always count on me."

Norman picked up his briefcase, headed towards the door, turns toward his boss, and said, "I know exactly what to do. Don't worry about a thing. We'll have the Nigerians and Neil Roberts eating out of our hands. As far as the bank settlement goes, we won't sign that agreement until we can confirm that the Central Bank has wired us the funds. I will have the agreement ready by the middle of next week. Trust me, this is all going to be a piece of cake! In fact, let me call Neil right now. I'll set up a meeting for tomorrow so that we can get the ball rolling."

Sterling simply replied with, "Please do. Let's find out where we stand with these guys!"

"Okay. Here goes," said Norman.

On the third ring, Attorney Neil Roberts answered his cellphone with, "I've been hoping you'd call me. Frankly, I was going to call you. How about you and I have lunch tomorrow at the Italian restaurant on the corner of Canon Drive and Brighton Way in Beverly Hills. The name escapes me, but their food is second to none!"

Norman, who was flabbergasted, answered with, "Sure. What time?"

"I'll see you there at noon."

"Alright. Noon it will be. By the way, what do you want to talk about?"

Attorney Roberts answered with a sharp wit by saying, "Same thing you want to speak to me about."

Norman, who didn't want to give the Nigerians' attorney any heads-up about the topic, just said, "I'll see you at noon."

Norman hung up the phone and said to Sterling and Mark, "Here I am calling Neil to set up a meeting to tell him that we're effectively ready to quit the Nigerian case, and before I can tell him anything, he tells me he wants to meet. I ask him about what. This guy evades the answer, then tells me he wants to meet about the same thing I want to talk to him about! What the hell? Are these guys listening in on our conversations? Weird call!"

Mark asked, "Well, what did you tell him?"

"I agreed to meet at noon tomorrow. The crazy thing is, he doesn't know why I was calling and I haven't the foggiest idea why he wants to meet. All I know is, we're going to get together."

Sterling jumped in and said, "I'll bet you they want to settle with us. Some stupid offer, but it's going to be an offer."

Norman was silent for a moment, then he responded with, "Mr. Sterling, I think you got this exactly right. A Los Angeles newspaper has been trying to get me to comment on the upcoming Nigerian court case and I'm reasonably sure that the newspapers have been in touch with Neil too. They don't want the potential bad publicity that may come from a long legal battle. Especially when articles will go into detail and implicate high-level government officials, including the head of the Central Bank and the minister of finance. These will be bad stories for them, especially since you have a top-level local businessman getting scammed by a foreign country. Yeah, they want to get rid of this!"

Sterling added, "I've read in major newspapers that Nigeria is inviting our American oil companies to go there and search for crude oil. Our government has a lot to say about the approval process. Bad press favors us. They'll settle!"

Norman, shaking his head in agreement, said, "I'll meet with Neil tomorrow and I'll tell him that we're going public with our story. Not just to the LA papers, but to every newspaper and television network that will listen to us. I'll set the trap and wait for him to make us a settlement offer. Assuming he bites, what number do you authorize me to accept?"

Sterling thought for a minute, then said, "Tell our good friend Neil that you might reluctantly recommend a settlement to me in the amount of $7 million. I'll tell you why I chose that amount. We're going to owe $5 million to Stanley Roberts, and I will owe you and Mark $1 million each. If they settle for the $7 million, we'll be able to keep the full $100 million intact and available for our new hedge fund business. Make sure you blend into the conversation that we will reserve our rights to pursue payment of our contract without any interference by the Nigerian government. He'll instantly cave into us maintaining our right to pursue our contract, because he thinks our contract is some delusional dream. Your job is to keep him thinking that way while convincing him that you're going to have a hard time getting me to accept such a low-ball offer to drop our FSIA legal case against them."

Mark, now laughing out loud, said, "You heard the man, your job is to collect $7 million from the Nigerian attorney while simultaneously preserving our rights to pick up another $100 million from the Central Bank. So, in case you're not as good at math as you are at the law, your financial target is not a $100 million, it's $107 million dollars. Just like you said, Paul, this is going to be a piece of cake."

As he got ready to leave, Norman shook Sterling's hand, then with a confident voice, said to Mark, "If I were you, I wouldn't bet against me. But, either way, I promise to let you know tomorrow how I did!"

The next day at noon, Norman was about to enter the restaurant where the meeting was to place with Attorney Neil Roberts but found himself in the middle of paparazzi. There must have been at least 50 independent photographers trying to take pictures of a high-profile celebrity apparently getting ready to exit the Beverly Hills restaurant. As Norman was doing his best to maneuver his way into the facility, he instantly recognized the celebrity as none other than Mick Jagger of the famed Rolling Stones. It was remarkable how much chaos and commotion one human being could bring to a quiet restaurant on Canon Street in Beverly Hills. As Jagger was whisked away in his shiny, black Cadillac SUV, the paparazzi disappeared like cockroaches exposed to light and the pandemonium was replaced with tranquility.

Norman finally entered and immediately spotted Neil seated at a quiet table towards the back of the restaurant. Neil stood to greet him and joked, "I didn't realize what a celebrity you were. I thought all those photographers were here because of you."

"No, actually, that was Mick Jagger, but if we don't get our lawsuit settled up, that's the kind of coverage you can expect everytime we arrive at court, especially when we call as a witness the minister of finance or the governor of the Central Bank of Nigeria. Or maybe we'll get lucky enough to bring your head of state, Mr. Muhammadu. After all, you never know, he might be a material witness! Just kidding, Neil. How's everything?"

Neil, somewhat taken aback by the comments, said, "Feisty this afternoon, Mr. Norman. Did I say something to offend you?"

"No, Mr. Roberts, it's not you. It's the people you represent. Now, here's your courtesy warning: settle or I go public!"

Roberts responded with, "We haven't even sat down and you're already threatening me. I can't wait to see what happens by the time we get to drinks. In fact, at this rate, we're not even going to get to drinks! I suppose you and I are talking to the same newspaper reporters. Of course, I dismiss them, but by the tone of your assault on me, it appears you're taking them much more seriously than I am. Now, the reason I wanted to speak to you is related to the fact that it's probably not such a good idea that our clients be dragged through the sewer with all kinds of 'he said, she said' stuff. You know how it goes; we'll say your guy is a liar trying to get rich off the government of Nigeria using some fake contract as his pretext. Likewise, you'll be playing the violin disclosing what horrible people my clients are. For every accusation you bring up, we're going to drag you through the mud with our own. Hell, there's just no end in sight to this shit. So, I thought we'd get together in the interest of our clients and agree to stay away from all this press nonsense. You guys stay silent and we agree not to comment to the press. In other words, we just allow the court to make a judgment on the legal facts, as they are presented. Now, if you agree, why don't we order some drinks, have a good meal at the expense of the Republic of Nigeria, and battle each other in court on the legal merits. What do you say, Norman?"

"Here's what I say, Neil: go fuck yourself! First, we're going to the press so that the whole world is going to know exactly what your criminal government is up to. Then, I'm going to kick you and your clients' asses in court on the legal merits. You don't understand, Neil, your clients lie through their teeth. I personally traveled to Nigeria. I know the truth firsthand. Your clients are guilty of every single charge we have brought forth against them. You're not only going lose in the court of law, but you're also going to lose in the court of public opinion. Your loss is going to hurt you big time. Not only are you going to owe us a whole hell of a lot of money, but all those joint venture partnerships with American petroleum companies, well, I'm not so sure they're going to want to make those deals with criminals!"

Neil, who was now sizing up the seriousness of Norman's words, responded with, "Sounds as if you don't like my news blackout proposal."

Norman continued by saying, "I'm reasonably sure that you understand the gravity of what I'm saying. Now, it's my turn to give you some unsolicited advice, just like you gave me the first time we met. You and your firm are going to look very bad defending a criminal government against a first-class and well-respected man like Elliot Sterling. We are going to tell the truth to the media about how we met in the home of the minister of finance and how we met with the highest levels of the Central Bank. By the time we're finished with Nigeria in the newspapers, no one is going to want to conduct business with Nigeria. You and your firm are not only going to end up representing a bunch of thugs, but you're also going to lose. That can't be good for such a prestigious firm like yours. Cut your losses while you can, Mr. Roberts. This will be the last chance we'll give you."

Roberts, who had come prepared to settle the case precisely for the the reasons Norman had mentioned, said, "How about we give you guys $1 million for all your efforts and legal fees? Dismiss the case, we all just go away."

"How about you offer us ten times that amount and agree to a few conditions we have."

"Are you nuts, Paul? We're not going to give you $10 million dollars!"

Norman looked at Neil and said, "I knew we weren't going to make it to drinks. You have a fair warning that we're going to the press. I've advised you what it costs to settle this case. Now, should we order drinks or should I leave?"

Neil responded with, "Let's order drinks and some food while you tell me more about your conditions."

Norman said, "Our conditions are very simple. I'm going to lay them out for you right now. If you can live with what you hear, then we'll order those drinks and food. First condition, Mr. Sterling will drop his case against you, so long as he retains the legal right to reasonably pursue the payment of his Nigerian contract. Second, no Nigerian government official or agency will legally obstruct Mr. Sterling's unconditional right to collect on the contract. Third, if the contract should ever be paid in the future, the Nigerian government will consider the payment to be valid. The funds will have been earned by Mr. Sterling. Effectively, Mr. Sterling will be granted legitimate right to the contract funds without the threat of any Nigerian legal obstruction, collection efforts, liens, or future legal ramifications, in the event the Nigerian contract funds were to be eventually paid. Our proposed settlement agreement will contain language which would grant Mr. Sterling the automatic right to renew an FSIA legal case against your client in the event of evidence showing a breach of these conditions. Your client will be required to acknowledge that right, understood?"

"Okay. It's time to order."

"Do we have a deal?"

As Neil was flagging down the waiter so he could start ordering, he said, "Look, as far as I'm concerned, you're never going to get paid. My client says the contract does not exist. In fact, their sworn testimony, through depositions and submitted legal documents in opposition to your case, clearly indicates that your guy is lying. So, let's order!"

"Very good. We agree on the conditions. Now, who has the authority to sign off for the Nigerians? I'm not going to wait months for an approval and a signed settlement agreement. If we decide to settle with you, well, this needs to be done forthwith. Either we're advancing the case against you or we make this deal. Can we get our agreement executed by next week?"

Neil responded with, "Let me answer your second question first. Maybe we can sign by next week. That's contingent upon whether my client will approve your outrageous dollar demand of $10 million. On the other hand, I have been granted authority to settle with you for $5 million. If you agree to the $5 million, we have a deal and I will assure you that we will sign by next week."

Norman, who realized that Neil's offer was outstanding, tried to stay cool while he processesed whether to just accept or play hardball for more money and said, "Look, I'm authorized at ten million. Best I can do is tell you to wait for our answer. I'll get back to you within a couple days. I can't assure you of anything except that I will present your low-ball offer to Mr. Sterling."

As Norman was saying the words 'low-ball' he detected a slight weakness in Neil's facial expression and decided he'd play hardball by continuing with, "Let me save you some time. We're never going to accept $5 million. There's no deal here!"

Neil, who was looking distraught, quickly turned to Norman and said, "I'll tell you what, here's our best and final offer. We'll settle this case for $7.5 million, including your conditions!"

Norman, who was having a very difficult time maintaining a poker face while not demonstrating a huge smile, calmly said, "I thought you just said a minute ago that your authority was $5 million maximum!"

With a twinkle in his eyes, Neil responded with, "That's true, but I chose to withhold from you that I also had authority to go all the way to $7.5 million. Hey, look, we're negotiating. Do you approve it or not?"

"Sure, I approve it, but that doesn't mean a thing. Like I said, my authority is capped at $10 million. Only Mr. Sterling can agree to your final number."

Neil, who was feeling somewhat abused, responded with, "Well, call the son-of-a-bitch! Excuse me, I mean, call your client. I need your answer. I don't want to be playing around with this. Either I'm going to go to war against you or we're settling. Now get me a yes or a no! Call him!"

Norman, who was thrilled with the settlement but didn't want to call Sterling for fear of perhaps a misunderstanding over the phone, thought quickly and said, "Alright, I'll call Mr. Sterling. I'll get you your answer."

"Good. Get me my answer. Hell, you need it too!"

Norman pulled out his phone and called a fake phone number, only pretending to contact Sterling and went on to say, "Hello, Mr. Sterling. I'm here with Mr. Neil Roberts, senior attorney for the Nigerians on our FSIA case. We have been discussing the possibility of finding a resolution to our litigation but we're not quite settled yet. Well, I should rephrase that. The conditions are agreed too, but the money is below your rock-minimum amount. They offer us $7.5 million. That is their best and final offer...Did you say that this is out of the question? I know. I know, the bottom line is $10 million. Okay, we'll decline their offer...Excuse me, Mr. Sterling, I didn't hear your last question...Yes, the conditions are approved. Yes, we can get this signed by next week. You want me to hold. Okay, I'll hold."

Norman looked at Neil with a straight face and said, "He wants me to hold, but I don't think this sounds so good. Please bear with me for a moment while I get you the final answer."

Continuing to play out the charade, Norman said out loud into the cellphone receiver, "Okay. Yes, of course. I'll inform Mr. Roberts right now. Yes, sir. Thank you, sir. Goodbye."

Neil, who had no idea as to the final decision, nervously asked, "Alright, what the fuck is the verdict?"

Norman responded with, "Let's order dinner and drinks. Mr. Sterling has accepted your offer. We have ourselves a deal! Let me summarize our settlement agreement. Your client will pay us $7.5 million and will agree to our conditions. We will fully execute the agreement by no later than one week from today. I will forward to you a draft agreement for your review within two days. You have two days to review and red-line the draft with any proposed revisions. I will then finalize the agreement and we will sign by the end of next week."

Neil, who was surprised but relieved, said, "You sure had me guessing on the decision. Great job, Paul. Shall we order?"

Norman, who was astonished at himself regarding how well the fake call just went, continued right along with his successful manipulation of the Nigerians' attorney by inventing more concocted fiction, "Neil, you're simply a better negotiator than I am. I never thought it would be even remotely possible to come to settle at $7.5 million. We're suing you for $100 million. Mr. Sterling told me that he would never settle for less than ten million. No, it's you who has done a great job. I hope your clients will appreciate your work. You settled for $2.5 million below our bottom line and you saved them the embarrassing news stories that were about to be written. Alright, so let's get started here, Neil. I'll have a double shot of the best tequila they have in this place. Then, I'm ordering their famous chopped salad, followed by purportedly the best Angel Hair Pasta in Los Angeles. How about you, Neil?"

"Well, first of all, thanks for the compliment. When I was retained to represent my client, they insisted that no such contract existed in Nigeria. They instructed me to take this case all the way to the Supreme Court of the United States. They informed me that they were prepared to outspend you ten-to-one if required. In fact, they adamantly informed me that we would never settle with you for any amount of money. So, no, Paul, I don't think this settlement goes down in my legal career's highlights reel. The only thing that matters is that we have a settlement. Let's get it down on paper and get the principals to sign it. Now, to the more important things, I'm going to follow you by starting with a double shot of tequila. Then I'll go with a classic Caesar salad, followed by their famous Chicken Cacciatore."

"There you go again, Neil, outdoing me with the food. That really sounds great, let's order!"

The meeting and settlement could not have gone better for the Sterling team. They got what they wanted, plus some.

The food was superb, and the two lawyers got along exceptionally well throughout their luncheon. They had hashed the entire settlement agreement terms and conditions right down to the details of how the Nigerian settlement payment would be made to Mr. Sterling. They seemed to have understood each other well and as they were just about ready to stand up and leave, Neil asked, "When do we advise Judge Fernandez that we have reached an agreement?"

Norman paused a moment and said, "Now. Judge Fernandez must be informed now."

Neil quickly responded with, "Alright, I'll stipulate you informing the judge of our joint agreement to settle the case. Please do so as soon as possible."

Norman responded with, "I'll get on that right away!"

As the bill for the lunch was delivered to the table by the waiter, Neil grabbed the bill and said, "This one is on us. The next one, if there ever is a next one, will be on you. By the way, Paul, what's it going to take to get you to come over to our law firm?"

"Well there, Counselor, I'm pretty sure you have a law license to practice in the state of California. In fact, I'd be willing to bet that you are very aware that if I were to respond to that question, especially to an opposing attorney during an ongoing case, I might damn well lose my license. So, why don't you rephrase the question a little more like, 'What are your plans should you ever decide to depart the Sterling organization?'"

The thought that kept swirling through Norman's mind as he listened to Neil's unsolicited proposal was that perhaps this son-of-a-bitch was trying to set him up for some kind of an ethics charge with the State Bar of California. Such a charge could have the effect of potentially causing the reversal of the settlement agreement and its payment. Since Norman was unwilling to take the risk that the employment offer was completely bogus or sinister, he instantly decided he'd just play along with Neil without revealing his hand. If Neil was convinced that there could be a chance at either the employment association or the State Bar charges becoming a reality, at least Neil would work hard to ensure that the settlement agreement got signed no matter what his true motives were.

Based on Norman's request that Neil rephrase the question, Neil said with a smirk on his face, "So, Mr. Norman, should you ever decide to depart your current association with Mr. Sterling's business entities, would you ever be interested in becoming an associate at a large law firm similar to ours?"

Norman, who was listening to Neil's bullshit, gave a brilliant answer, "We'll see."

Neil responded with, "What's that mean?"

Norman looked at Neil and said, "That means, we'll see."

Neil looked right back at Norman and reacted with, "I didn't hear a no!"

Without addressing the subject further, Norman shook Neil's hand and said, "You'll have our draft agreement shortly. I'm glad we were able to come to a meeting of the minds regarding this settlement agreement. I'll never forget how you were able to make $2.5 million within 5 minutes. Hell, you should remind your client that you are a bargain charging only a thousand dollars an hour. I'm not so sure the Nigerians are going to understand or appreciate how good of an attorney you really are. By the way, if you ever need a reference in the future concerning some other FSIA case, I'll recommend you. Thanks very much for your continued cooperation. Good choice on the restaurant. You'll hear from me soon."

The meeting was over. Norman's strategy had been executed to perfection. Now, it was time to call Mr. Sterling, of course this time for real, and inform him of the good news. On the first ring, Sterling answered the phone and asked, "Did they take the bait?"

"Not only did they eat the bait, but they ate the fishing rod and swallowed the entire boat! You now have enough money from these guys to not only pay Stanley Roberts his $5 million, but you can pay Mark and me and still have an extra $500,000 left over!"

Sterling computed the math quickly and excitingly said, "You got $7.5 million out of them?"

"Yes, sir. Plus, all of our conditions!"

"Remarkable! Now, all we need to do is pray hard that Stanley Roberts performs. In the meantime, get your butt over here! I'll call Mark and let's celebrate!"

Chapter 22

Sterling was ecstatic with the news from Norman. While he waited for Norman and Mark to arrive, he grabbed a high-priced bottle of Remy Martin Cognac from a shelf above his desk and poured himself a drink. As he was serving himself, Mark walked in and said, "I hope you weren't going to finish off that big bottle all by your lonesome self. Leave a little bit for the employees!"

Elliot, who was all smiles, looked up at Mark and said, "I got plenty more from where that came from," and poured a generous amount of Cognac for Mark into an elegant crystal glass.

Shortly after Mark's arrival, Norman came walking through the door of the office and went directly to Sterling, commenting, "We are one step closer to starting our hedge fund business! With that said, Mr. Sterling, I'm going to pour myself some of your expensive Cognac and do my level best to catch up with the two of you."

Sterling, who was emotionally over the top with what Norman had extracted out of the Nigerians, collected his thoughts, raised up his glass, and addressed Mark and Norman, "I propose a toast to the job phenomenally well done by Paul today. And to you, Mark, for all your wise advice and counsel leading to this successful moment. Don't ever think for a minute that I have ever taken my relationship with either one of you for granted. I will never forget that both of you have been very loyal to me, even though it would have been easy to walk away. You are my guys, and together the future looks very bright! L'chayim! To life!"

Mark, who always got very emotional when he heard his lifelong buddy speak with passion like this, decided to respond with the first thing that came to his mind, "Paul and I are not in this with you for the money. Well, let me slightly correct that, we do like the money, but we love and admire our boss more. Of course, I'm personally very impressed and grateful that Paul was able to drag 7.5 million bucks out of those bastards. But let me soberly remind all of us that that $7.5 million won't take us very far in the capital-intensive hedge fund world. So, I'm going to drink to today's victory, but let's get real, I'm not going to sleep well until Stanley Roberts funds our bank account two weeks from today on November 2nd!"

Elliot responded with, "You are absolutely right! Today was an important battle won by us. But we didn't win the war. We still need Stanley Roberts to wire us the $100 million in order to scream victory. I am very aware that anything can still go wrong. Paul understands this too. But, right now, just for a moment, we're going to celebrate this hard-fought battle. Then, in a few minutes, we'll outline each of the steps required to get to November 2nd. Okay, now raise your glasses, because this final toast goes to Stanley Roberts. May your life's path lead you to the Central Bank of Nigeria on November 2nd and may you successfully transfer our funds on time!"

Mark cheered with, "Hear! Hear!"

Then, Norman shouted, "L'chayim, Stanley!"

Sterling, with his charismatic look on his face and his steady, familiar voice, settled into business by firmly putting down his drink and saying, "Alright, this is the last stretch. We're not going to get another chance to get this right. Let's make sure that when Stanley funds, we don't fuck up on our end. Okay, Paul, lay this out for us."

Mark, stopping Paul from speaking, said, "Before you start with your briefing, I need to update you both on the latest information I have regarding Nigeria."

Sterling interjected with, "Why don't we concentrate on Paul's things-to-do list, then we'll get to your news flash a little later."

Mark, who was now more emphatic, blurted out, "Because without my news flash, that fucking to-do list might need to change its priority!"

With a worried look on his face, Sterling said, "Go on."

Mark composes himself and starts by saying, "Excuse me for being a bit melodramatic, but this is important. I have been in day-to-day communication with the State Department in Washington. My contact there is the highest ranking man at the Department of State on West African Affairs. His name is Alexander Laurence. They refer to him as Special Representative Laurence. He is a retired senior Foreign Services officer with a wealth of Nigerian experience, including most recently as the US Ambassador to Nigeria. Additionally, he was the Deputy United Nations Special Representative of the Secretary General regarding West African affairs. This guy knows his stuff!"

Sterling, who was getting more nervous by the second, said, "Okay, you got our attention. What the hell is going on here?"

Mark got right to it and said what no one wanted to hear, "Nigeria is on the brink of civil war. Special Representative Laurence expects a coup d'etat within the next 30 days."

Sterling, who was somewhat dazed by the information, angrily said, "Dammit, Mark, why didn't you tell us this when you first got here?"

"I didn't want to mess up the victory celebration. I'm sorry, I should have. In fact, I should have told you this as soon as I heard it. I just wanted to be absolutely sure before I got anybody riled up with the news. I apologize."

Sterling gets a hold of himself and said, "Although your timing stinks, great work on getting us the information. At least, we understand the urgency and the new risk. Look, we can't do a thing about Nigerian political realities. All we can do is be prepared on our end. We need to complete our settlement agreement with the Nigerian government immediately. There may not be anybody with authority to sign that agreement if we aren't careful. So, Paul, that's your number one priority. Get that settlement done ASAP before Neil figures out what's really going on in Nigeria. Do you understand me, Paul?"

"Yes, sir, I understand you. I'll push Neil. We'll have the settlement signed by next week. Hey, Mark, we're really fortunate you did this surveillance work for us. Superb job. This kind of information, although late, may just save us.

Any chance that Mr. Laurence could be wrong?"

"No chance. The Department of State, as we speak, is drafting an official travel warning to Americans traveling to Nigeria. A major international petroleum conference in Nigeria is about to be canceled. Nigeria is in deep shit!"

Sterling, who was again feeling pressure, remained cool and said, "We believe you, Mark. It just would have been nice to have this information last week in order to be ahead of the game. I just hope this doesn't come back to bite us in the ass. You needed to give us a heads-up, as opposed to a surprise. We're fighting for our financial lives here. We need to know everything you know, the second you know it. The error is water under the fucking bridge now. Learn from the mistake, Mark. Don't ever let something like this happen again."

Mark, who was very upset at himself, looked at Sterling and commented, "I own this error, and it will never happen again."

215

Sterling, who had felt the need to call out Mark on this mistake, gets back on track and said, "Okay, enough of that bullshit. Let's go beat up on the bad guys. As I said, Paul, get the Nigerian settlement fully executed immediately.

Mark, stay on the State Department guy as if your life depended on it. If you need to to go to Washington, D.C., and take that special representative to dinner, do it!"

Mark was sincerely grateful that his friend and boss had decided to use the opportunity as a teaching moment in lieu of shaming session and responded, "I'm ahead of you regarding Laurence. I'm scheduled to meet him for dinner in Washington, Monday night. I'll report back to you with the latest as soon as I hear it."

Sterling then placed his attention on Norman and said, "Now, listen carefully, Paul. The way I see it, we got another hot spot. We need to settle with the bank with the same urgency as the Nigerian settlement. We must be careful that the bank does not renege on their deal with us, especially if they see any kind of weakness. Let's get their settlement signed right away. Can you handle the workload? Should we bring in another attorney to help?"

Norman responded with, "Sure, I could use another attorney, but by the time I get that person up-to-date, it will be too late. I'm going to camp out in my office with my top legal assistant and crank these agreements out by next week. You've trusted me this far, rest assured I'll get the job done."

Sterling put his hand on Norman's shoulder and said, "I don't have any doubt that you will. Now, get the hell out of here and go write those agreements!"

Norman responded, "Mark, please let me know if there's anything new with the State Department. Unless you say differently, I'll assume I have at least all of next week to get these deals signed, even though I'm aware that every minute counts."

"Will do, Paul."

As Norman left the office, Sterling said to Mark, "Stick around, let's talk about a few things."

Mark sits back down and said, "Shoot."

"Do you think we should reach out to Stanley Roberts and get him to fund prior to November 2nd?"

"No, Elliot. He specifically asked that there be absolutely no contact with him after your last meeting. You'll put his life at risk. Believe me, this dude is going to run away faster than a jack rabbit if we communicate with him."

Sterling, with a frown on his face, said, "Yeah, I know you're right, but if government offices start closing due to civil unrest, Stanley may never make it to the Central Bank. And then what?"

Mark answered the question by saying, "You end up with $7.5 million from Nigeria, your wonderful home will be free and clear of any debt, and all the Sterling Development headaches, including your personal bank guarantee, will be gone forever. It's not 100 million in cash, but it could be a lot worse."

"So, here's what you're saying, Mark, sign the settlement agreements with both the Nigerians and the bank. I don't even need to hold off on signing the bank settlement until after confirmation of the Nigerian wire, because we're going to settle with Nigeria and the bank whether we receive the 100 million wire or not. In other words, we're no longer going to sue Nigeria or litigate with the bank. That's it, we're done!"

"That's exactly correct. If Nigeria goes into some form of civil war, then we're going to have one hell of time calling government witnesses. I can't even image how difficult it will be to attempt to collect from a broken down, war-torn country. If Stanley fucks us, we'll just have to be grateful for what we get out of Nigeria and the bank. And just for the record, if we don't collect the $100 million, you don't need to pay Paul or me a million bucks."

Sterling responded with contempt by saying, "I get it. We'll just need to start with a much smaller hedge fund consisting of $7.5 million as opposed to a $100 million. Ninety plus million short!"

"You started with a hell of lot less than that, Elliot! No fear. Just smart and hard work. The rest we'll leave to destiny."

With his eyes wide open, Sterling said, "Alright, just like old times. Let's push Norman to get the Nigerian and the bank settlement agreements signed by next week. On November 2nd, we're either going to be working with $100 million or $7.5 million. Either way, Sterling Hedge Fund will be open for business!"

"You are the man, Elliot Sterling! You're going to make a fortune with 7.5 million. I can't even imagine how much money you're going to make for all of us if you start with a $100 million. We're going to come out just fine either way. In two weeks, we'll know. Remember, Stanley Roberts has five million bucks riding on successfully wiring us our funds. That guy is going to move mountains to get us our money. Comparatively speaking, he needs this to happen as much as we need this to happen. So, if there is any way to get this done, rest assured that he will find that way. Now, am I going to suffer for the next two weeks worrying about whether he'll pull this off? Yeah, you can bet your ass I am. But let Norman and me do the worrying. You keep coordinating with your Israeli buddy, Benjamin Yaalon. Get the Sterling Hedge Fund entity ready to go by November 3rd. I'm going to help you build that company into the biggest fund in the world!"

"Man, you're getting me all fired up and ready to go. I haven't felt this kind of adrenaline since I did my first deal at Sterling Development. Well, since we're talking about the new hedge fund, let me give you a little heads-up on what's happening on that front. Benjamin has hooked me up with a major armaments dealer in the Middle East. The Israelis make a superstar rifle known as the Savor. The public has been vaguely aware of it for a few years now. The rifle is admired for its military service with the Israeli Defense Forces and its innovative form. The Sterling Hedge Fund is going to be financing a major distribution of the Savor throughout the world. We're going to have an equity position in all of the sales. $7.5 million makes us a lot of money, a $100 million makes us filthy rich!"

"Holy shit, Elliot! You're not messing around here. You really do mean business. Military arms dealer. Wow! I knew you were going to take us to a new level. This idea is just over the top. Superstar. That's what you are, a superstar! I can't wait to get started. What can I do to help you prepare?"

"Stay close to your State Department guy and gather as many new contacts as you're able to make in Washington, especially at the Department of Defense. Shift your emphasis in Congress to members of the Senate Armed Services Committee. This is the committee of the United States Senate that's empowered with legislative oversight of the nation's military, including the Department of Defense's military research and development. In addition to the senators, get to know members of the US House of Representatives Committee on Armed Services. The House is responsible for funding and oversight of the Department of Defense and defense policy. These are the people who will provide us with leads and information that we'll require in the future. Stay close to these guys. Contribute to their campaigns, attend their Washington high society parties, and do the power lunches. Over time, these relationships will pay off massive dividends. Do you grasp what I'm telling you, Mark?

"Perfectly. We're going into the future's business. We need to know where the emerging markets are heading, specifically those that relate to military armaments. The more insight we have into the future, the more money we're going to make. One thing I do know about hedge funds is that they face less regulation than mutual funds and other investment vehicles. I think I'm going to love the hedge fund business!"

"Mr. Mark is right on track! You're going to be great at this. Inquire about new government contacts, starting with your upcoming Laurence dinner. Don't be too concerned about regulations. I think we'll base Sterling Hedge Fund in Israel."

Mark, who was clearly excited about the new venture, said, "As far as I'm concerned, you can base the hedge fund out of Mars. Wherever you go, I go."

"So, now that you've caught a glimpse into the future, let's get back to the present. As soon as you meet with Laurence, call Norman first, then call me with the update status regarding Nigerian internal politics. Make sure you read Laurence right. We have no room for any errors. You need to able to calculate whether there will be enough time for Stanley Roberts to enter the Central Bank and make the transfer on November 2nd before any serious insurrection. Ask Laurence whether he has any information concerning the Nigerian Central Bank. We want to get a handle as to whether the Bank is functioning normally at this time and what typically happens to the Central Bank if the country is thrust into civil war. He may be able to give us some valuable historical insight regarding whether the Bank continues operating on an international basis even during a civil unrest crisis. If he doesn't know, tell him to dig into this deeper. I'm sure he can help. Alright, so go get some rest, then have a safe trip to D.C."

Mark, understanding the seriousness of his mission to the nation's capital, responded with, "I'll get you the answers. I know we got a lot riding on this, but we're going to come out of all this like champs. I'm positive. Take care of yourself, Elliot. You'll hear from me soon."

With Mark on his way, Elliot turned his mind towards concentrating on the strategy and urgent timing of Norman's final preparation of the pending settlement agreements. There was not even a second to be wasted. He got on the phone and called Norman, asking, "Have you heard anything from the bank or the Nigerian attorneys regarding a potential Nigerian uprising? What? What did you say?"

Norman repeated himself, "The bank is ready to sign the settlement agreement. They mentioned nothing concerning the Nigerians. But, we got a serious problem brewing with the Nigerian attorney. Neil has put me on notice that he may not be able to deliver on the Nigerian settlement documents. Our agreement appears dead, due to the civil unrest."

"I was afraid I heard you right the first time. This is bad news. What did you tell Neil?"

"I told Neil to advise his bullshit clients that we hope they don't sign our settlement, because my client doesn't even want to sign the agreement. I let him know that I convinced you to stay with the agreement only because we had accepted the deal at the restaurant. He was informed that you're going to enjoy humiliating them in a United States courthouse and that you much prefer to wait a few years to collect $100 million, as opposed to $7.5 right now. By the time we obtain our judgment in court, their civil problems will be long gone. And finally, I told him that we're going to work mighty hard to convince Judge Anthony Fernandez to put out an order to freeze Nigerian assets totaling as much as $100 million in their United States bank accounts, which would include cash or even a Nigerian commercial jet sitting at JFK airport in New York."

Although disappointed, Sterling responded with, "It's amazing how well you put them on the defensive. You gave him a lot to think about. You probably ought to pile on some more by telling Neil that you'll be surprised if he's going to get paid by a nation on the brink of a civil war. It would be smarter for his firm to get the settlement agreement signed and his final bill paid. Neil knows that in federal court an attorney cannot just walk away from their client. He could end up billing a shitload of legal fees that might never get paid. It's in his own best interest to get our deal fully executed before it's too late! So, Paul, is this settlement going sideways?"

"I'm sorry, Mr. Sterling, this doesn't look good for us. Neil sounds genuinely concerned. His Nigerian government counterpart is not responding to his questions regarding the settlement agreement. He has requested a conference call with that representative to formally get an official position regarding our agreement, but until then, I'm very pessimistic. Based on this guy, Neil thinks the civil war could only be days away. Nobody really knows for sure, but the defeatist attitude I detect in Neil's voice leads me to believe that a serious rebellion is near for the Republic of Nigeria."

Sterling, who was not happy with a word Norman was telling him, said, "Now what? Do we tell the bank to go to hell on our settlement agreement? Do we sign with the bank even though it sounds like I've got a better chance of hitting the lottery than getting

Nigeria to sign our agreement and pay us? This just got really complicated! Where do we go from here?"

"I'll finish the settlement agreement with the bank, then I'll get them to sign. This way, we are done with them just in case things dramatically turn with the Nigerians. I'll sit on the bank's signed settlement agreement until we get clarity from Neil. Once I get the bank's signatures, I'll tell them you're out of the country and will be returning shortly to sign all of the agreements, which require a notary's certification. They'll be fine with the excuse. Just stay out of the public's sight for a few days while we sort this all out."

A slightly relieved Sterling said, "Sounds good, Paul. In the interim, we'll see what Mark finds out from the State Department and what Neil comes back with. As you say, at least we'll have the bank settled, even though we won't have much money left over for the Sterling Hedge Fund! We'll just stay calm for a few days and see what happens."

Norman responded with, "I agree, and please don't worry about the hedge fund. If we sign with the bank, at least you'll own your home free and clear. You won't owe anybody anything!"

A more optimistic Sterling said, "Well, maybe I'll just mortgage my home. It'll get us a bunch of money that way in order to start the fund. Yeah, that's what I'll do. Okay, that will be Plan B."

"Whatever works best for you and your family, Mr. Sterling. I'll get the deal with the bank done and ready for your signature. Then I'll get with Neil within the next few days to determine the direction the Nigerians will be going. Of course, let me know if you hear anything from Mark concerning Laurence."

"Under the circumstances, sounds like we're on the right track. If I hear anything from Mark, I'll advise forthwith. Let's stay in touch."

"By the way, Mr. Sterling, Neil clearly recognizes that he might not get paid by the Nigerians. He is our biggest advocate to get the settlement agreement signed, sealed, and delivered. Hopefully, he'll use his experience, brains, and greed to get our deal done. Please stay out of the public's sight for a few days here as we get closer to the finish line with the banks. I'll be in close communication. Have a good evening."

As Norman hung up, Sterling couldn't help but think about how fortunate he was to have his loyal friend Mark and a trustworthy lawyer like Paul Norman at his side. He realized right then and there that even if the Nigerian settlement were to fall apart, he was going to sign the bank settlement, then mortgage his home to start the Sterling Hedge Fund.

Three long days had passed since Sterling had heard a word out of Norman or Mark. Felicia and Elliot spent the time talking, and eating, and talking, then eating some more. They even played board games like Scrabble and Monopoly. Heeding to Norman's advice to 'stay out of the public's sight' while the bank's settlement paperwork was being completed, Sterling had effectively become a recluse to the outside world. He even took up learning how to play the card game Gin Rummy from Felicia, who had learned to play the game from her grandfather. Although he treasured his time alone with his supportive wife, it was time for the moment of truth regarding his complicated business and legal affairs. Just as Sterling was completely worn out doing nothing, his cell phone rang, with the screen name indicating Mark Goldman.

"Mark. Talk to me! What do you hear from the State Department?"

"Listen, Boss, this doesn't look good. Laurence predicts a civil war in less than 30 days. They think Muhammadu is going to fall. Many official government offices have begun to close, with no government employees at work. We need to sign the settlement agreement with Nigeria yesterday! Elliot, you need to make this happen ASAP!"

"Have you spoken to Norman?"

"Yeah, I just got off the phone with him. He understands the urgency. Norman told me what's up with the fucking Nigerians and Neil. I told him to stop making excuses and get this done now!"

"I don't know that he can, Mark. It's out of his hands."

"I just told Norman to call Neil and immediately get in touch with his Nigerian legal contact. I insisted that he schedule a conference call with their highest-level Justice Department Cabinet member so that they can arrange to grant Neil a power of attorney authorizing Neil to sign our settlement agreement on behalf of the Republic of Nigeria. Simultaneously, Neil should be working with the Nigerian Embassy in the United States to officially notarize Neil's signature on the agreements. Laurence informed me that United States oil companies that find themselves unable to get their deals done are using this mechanism to get their business agreements signed. I am convinced this is the break we needed, so, please, get off the phone and push Neil. This may be our only way out!"

"Yeah, wow! Alright, I'm on it. When are you coming back?"

"I'm taking the red-eye tomorrow night. I'll wait to hear from you regarding Norman's progress before I leave, in case you need something in Washington. While I'm here, I'll continue to reach out to members of Congress who may be helpful for the new hedge fund business."

"Great job, Mark. Thank you."

"Don't thank me, just get Neil to do exactly what I just said. This will be the differential as to whether we win or lose."

"Okay, I'm getting off the phone. I'm calling Paul. I'll be in touch as soon as I hear something. Tell me if you hear anything further. The power of attorney idea is going to save us. Let's get this done!"

Mark signed off by saying, "I have always had blind faith in you. I know you're going to get this done. I'll wait to hear back from you. Good luck, Boss."

Before Sterling could even dial Norman's cell number, it was Norman calling Sterling, saying, "Did you speak to Mark?"

Sterling, who was very uneasy, said, "Yes. Now what do you need to do to get Neil to settle the power of attorney?"

"I just spoke to Neil. He has vaguely heard of something along the lines of what Mark's talking about. He doesn't think the Nigerians would grant him a power of attorney, because this is the first time he has represented them. Neil's firm was a referral by a friend in New York City who recommended Neil due to the fact that he is based in Los Angeles, where our case is being litigated. He has arranged for a conference call with his Nigerian contact for tonight at midnight, Los Angeles time, which is 8:00 AM in Nigeria. Nigeria is eight hours ahead of LA. The good news is that he finally got a hold of the Nigerian legal contact. The bad news is Neil thinks this is a long shot."

"Here's what I want you to do, Paul. Tell Neil that you insist on participating in the conference call. Tell him that the United States Department of State is fully aware that American petroleum companies are getting agreements signed with Nigeria exactly by the method we are proposing. You tell them that we expect the same courtesies extended to the oil companies. Let them know, in no uncertain terms, that if we are not granted this same courtesy, we are going to expose Nigerian government officials' names who have authorized the power of attorney. If oil companies are getting preferential treatment due to some bribe, or as they like to call it, gratification, I'm pretty sure those government officials will not want to have their names exposed. Paul, we clear on what I want you to do?"

"Yes. I understand the idea perfectly. We're going to play hardball. Of course, the downside is that they will tell us to go hell. The upside is that they will be bluffed into pushing our settlement through. Kind of like a last-minute presidential pardon."

"Yeah, I think you got it, except for one point."

"What's that, Mr. Sterling?"

"I'm not bluffing. So, you go tell Neil that our State Department high-level contact is prepared, upon our instructions, to expose the names. Advise Neil and his piece-of-shit Nigerian legal contact that we mean business. And tell them something else. We're not paying a single penny in gratification! If Neil wants to pay a bribe out of his own fees, tell him to be our guest. We pay nothing. Pressure these guys. This's the only way you're going to win."

An apprehensive Norman responded with, "I'm going to call Neil as soon as we hang up. I'll explain exactly what we want him to do, he'll understand our playbook perfectly. Then I'll work my way into the conference call. You may not hear from me until after 1:00 AM or later tonight. Should I call you tonight or wait until the morning?"

"Call me the moment you leave Neil's office. I'll be waiting."

"Just one last question, Mr. Sterling. What answer do I give Neil if he asks why we're now in such a hurry to get this done? After all, I did tell him you hoped they didn't pay so that we could kick their butt in court."

Sterling responded with, "Tell him we changed our mind since the whole fucking country is about to collapse for an indefinite and totally unpredictable amount of time!"

"Good enough. I'll call you as soon as I'm done. This is going to be a precision bombing mission. I think Neil will appreciate the ammunition we'll be giving him. I can't predict the outcome for you, because I don't know anything about Neil's contact other than he's the guy who approved the $7.5 million settlement with us. I'll be honest with you, Mr. Sterling, this could go either way."

Sterling, who was detecting some weakness in Norman's voice, decided to challenge his attorney by saying, "Look, I appreciate that you think you have an almost impossible assignment to convince these people to do this our way. I just want you to know that I wouldn't ask you to take on this challenge if I wasn't confident that you will find the words and the strategy to be successful. We need this win to survive. Mark my words, you are going to win this battle, then we are going to win the war. Not only will we get paid the $7.5 million, but my gut says Stanley Roberts will wire us the $100 million. The stakes have never been higher. Perhaps as high as it will ever be in your life. But, I choose you. I choose the man that I trust can win for me. So, don't think for even a second that we won't win. We are going to prevail, because you are going to rise to this occasion and get us the power of attorney. I know you can do this, now go with confidence and win!"

Norman, listening to this passionate speech, replied, "I've read about legendary Coach Vince Lombardi's famous motivating talks to his football players and President John F. Kennedy's words inspiring a nation, but you got them all beat! I'll get us a working solution one way or the other! Thank you for your trust in me."

Feeling like he had connected with his attorney, Sterling reacted by saying, "You don't need to thank me for anything. You've earned my trust. I'll never ask you to do something I don't sincerely believe you can handle. So, you know what, just go out and handle this. I want to remind you of something I've always told Mark when we have gone into critical business meetings throughout the years. I may have even mentioned it to you on some other occasion, but it has worked to perfection every time. Remember that your face is your sword. Neil will be sizing you up the moment he greets you entering his office to have this conference call. Neil must feel your confidence. It's imperative that he be conscious of your strength and leadership. Neil must understand that we're going to pull the trigger on the Nigerian officials if we don't get our way regarding the power of attorney. Paul, this is your moment. Draw all your vast talents together and win. Call me with good news!"

As Sterling was about to say goodbye, Norman politely cut his boss off and commented, "Yes, sir. I promise you that if there is a way to get what we want, I'll get it for us. Look for my call."

"That's all I could ever ask of you. But, I still don't have any doubts. We'll talk later."

The balance of the day went by in an instant. It was 15 minutes before midnight and Norman was in the elevator moving up to the highest floor in Neil's Wilshire Boulevard high-rise building in Beverly Hills. Norman had spent the entire time after he had finished speaking with Sterling preparing for this moment. He had spoken at great length with Neil regarding the game plan. Paul had sold him on the fact that Sterling was about to hang out to dry as many Nigerians as he could if the power of attorney idea was rejected. Neil clearly understood that Sterling meant business and was prepared to go to battle against his own client, if for no other reason but to collect his huge legal fee.

Earlier in the afternoon, Neil had disclosed that his client owed his law firm in excess of $250,000, which included expert witnesses and professional consultants. Up until now, he had never thought for a single moment that a foreign sovereign nation would ever stiff him. His motivation was very high. At a minimum, Neil wanted to get his firm paid, and if feasible, take care of Sterling in the process. He instinctively understood that Norman's game plan to pressure the Nigerians by exposing their shenanigans might just work. He clearly understood from Norman that Sterling 'would not pay a cent towards gratification.' In fact, Neil's worry was that his Nigerian counterpart was about to shake him down for a hefty bribe, to which Norman had earlier responded with, "Welcome to the club!"

As Norman walks into the perfectly-decorated Beverly Hills law office, he was greeted by Neil, who joking remarked, "We have got to stop meeting like this in the middle of the night."

Norman, who had been coached well by Sterling, didn't laugh at his comment. Instead, he extended his hand with a serious look on his face and simply said, "Let's go to work."

Neil, who sensed a very cold and no-nonsense opposing attorney, responded with, "I thought you liked me."

Norman wryly said, "Depends on how you do tonight."

Neil, who was rapidly getting the picture, understood that Norman had come to his office with a dead-serious temperament of taking no prisoners and said, "Alright, we'll call this guy in a couple of minutes. I prefer you don't say a word. I think if he knows you're in on the conference call, he'll just clam up and reject any power of attorney solution. I have already laid the groundwork. The way I see it, this call is going to cost my firm a big shit-load of money. As we're all getting to know very well, Nigerians don't do a thing outside the ordinary unless they receive money for their goodwill. You'll quickly determine whether this call is going as planned if this asshole states he needs to pay 'gratification' to someone else in the chain of command. In reality, the gratification, also known as a bribe, goes to him, but they always say it's for someone else, if you know what I mean. Anyways, I'm sure I don't need to education you on gratification. So, without objection, I'll talk and you stay silent. I'll attempt to get my firm's fees, and of course, your money too."

Norman, who was very uncomfortable remaining silent on the call, vigorously raised his objection by first responding with, "You come across as an expert on Nigerian bribes." Then saying, "What the hell am I doing here if I can't talk!"

Neil, who knew that Norman had no leverage with him at this point, said, "To be honest with you, Paul, I just invited you into this call so you could witness firsthand what their final position was going to be concerning this matter. I didn't want you to think this call never took place. Believe me, once you gave me the war plan, I knew what to do. They hear your voice, you might as well kiss your money good-bye. Just shut the fuck up and let me handle this. Agreed?"

Norman, disgusted with Neil's response but knowing he was in checkmate, angrily responded with, "Yeah, I agree, you piece of garbage. Play it your way. I hope you know what you're doing, because if you fuck this up, I'm going to cause you and your gangster clients so much misery that you will, for the rest of your life, wish you had given me the liberty to speak. Do you hear me, Neil?"

"Calm down, Mr. Norman. I got this. Let a master do his thing. Just sit back and enjoy the ride."

Listening to Neil speak was disgusting. Norman couldn't help but instantly think about how his boss would be disappointed in him for having been ambushed in the manner Neil had just accomplished. Norman was faced with making a serious split-second decision: should he stay or should he go? If he stayed, at least he'd find out the results in real-time. If he left, Neil could use the Sterling game plan to leverage payment for only his firm's legal fees, thus potentially cutting out the Sterling funds. There was no choice but to stay, so Norman responded with an outraged voice, "It's your show. Proceed, you prick."

And with that prompt, Neil speed-dialed his Nigerian legal counterpart.

"Good day. You're speaking with Mallam Sanusi, Ministry of Legal Affairs."

"Minister, this is Attorney Neil Roberts in Los Angeles. How are you?"

"Very well, Neil. Very well. How can I assist you?"

"I'll be brief, Minister. I know that the Republic of Nigeria is going through a very difficult challenge at the moment. I have every confidence that all will be stabilized soon and everything will get back to normal. In the meantime, we do have a settlement agreement approved by the federal court here regarding the Sterling matter. As you instructed me, we successfully settled that case for a fraction of its worth. I suggest we sign that settlement now before they change their minds. Mr. Sterling has asked that he withdraw from the settlement, but I have petitioned the judge to force Sterling to honor the deal. Although this is a bad time, you will not regret when this matter is settled forever."

Minister Sanusi responded, saying, "My good friend Neil, I'm so sorry, please remind me, who is Sterling?"

Norman, listening to Neil lie about petitioning the judge, then hearing Sanusi ask for clarification regarding Sterling, just stared at Neil and put his hands up in the air, as if to signal defeat. But Neil, who didn't pay attention to Norman, answered the question by saying, "I recognize you're very busy, Mr. Minister, but he is the principal in the Los Angeles legal case we recently discussed regarding the Foreign Sovereign Immunities Act."

After a brief pause, Sanusi responded, "Oh, yes, yes. That's the case involving our Central Bank governor and finance minister. Of course, of course. Too many cases for me to keep up with! Please remind me once again, what is the financial settlement amount?"

"Yes, sir. The amount is as follows. We pay out a total of USD 7.5 million, which will resolve the case in its entirety. This is a serious legal and public relations nightmare for the Republic of Nigeria. We face legal jeopardy that could end up totaling well over $100 million, plus legal fees. Right now, our legal fees are just over $250,000 and growing by the hour. As we previously concluded, it is best to immediately sign the settlement agreement, pay off Sterling, and stop incurring further legal fees. Minister Sanusi, this is the smartest option."

Without any delay, the minister responded, "Of course, this is the intelligent decision. The problem is not the money. We have set aside the funds to settle this matter and pay your fees. That's not the issue. The demur, or should I say, my dissent, is due to the current presidential decree that creates an official government moratorium regarding the signing of any new agreements. Our government is facing complicated civil unrest. We are simply not entering into any new obligations. As you can see, Neil, my hands are tied. Call me back once we settle our challenges here in the Republic of Nigeria. It shouldn't be that long."

Neil, now starting to get a little agitated, said, "I hear you, Mr. Minister, but this is not a new obligation. The settlement is already approved at your highest levels of government. It just needs a signature. As you said, the money and my firm's fees have already been set aside. So, how do we get the signature?"

After a long pause, the minister finally reacted with, "Technically, you're right. There is a possibility that I could send the approved settlement agreement to our embassy in Washington, D.C. Theoretically, our ambassador could sign the settlement. He does have the power of attorney to sign on behalf of the nation. Since the agreement has technically been approved, I suppose it could be executed by Ambassador Mohammed, especially if it were signed outside of Nigeria. Upon the full execution of the settlement, I could authorize the payment to Mr. Sterling, along with the distribution of your legal fees. All of Mr. Sterling's money, along with your fees, could be wired to your attorney trust account within the next few days."

Neil, sporting a huge grin and looking right at Norman, confidently remarked to Sanusi, "Well, what are we waiting for? Let's get this done. What's the next step?"

Once again, there was an uncomfortable silence, and then came the comment Norman knew would be next. "Neil, we have ways of doing things here. It's not quite that easy. We must always show gratification for this type of assistance."

Neil, who now had a mischievous 'I told you so' type expression on his face, looked at Norman as he pressed the mute button on the conference call telephone and said, "Here comes the shakedown!" He quickly disengages the mute button and addresses Sanusi's concern by saying, "Certainly, Minister, please tell me how we can assist."

"There are always inherent risks regarding accommodations such as what we will be requesting the ambassador to do on your behalf. Our ambassador normally would not undertake this type of risk during turbulent times such as these. It would be nice if we could offer our ambassador and his exceptional staff some gratification for their efforts. Wouldn't you agree, Neil?"

"I completely agree, Minister."

The minister, who now knew that Neil was open to take the bait, responded with, "Fine. I think $100,000 would be considered thoughtful and well-appreciated. Good, now that we understand each other so well, I will give the instructions and order everything in motion."

Neil, who was astonished at the amount of the bribe, calmly reacted by saying to Sanusi, "Excuse me, Minister, of course the gratification amount is acceptable to me, but as a courtesy, I must clear the $100,000 reduction in our fee with my law partner before I give you my final yes. He happens to be right here in the office working late tonight. So, please allow me a moment while I obtain his approval."

The minister, who was somewhat annoyed with Neil's request, said, "I will stand by, but there are many important people waiting to meet with me, so make the consultation with your partner swift."

"Yes, sir, I'll be right back to you. Thank you."

Neil, now in pressure mode, hit the mute button, looked at Norman, and blurted out, "The most I'm paying is $25,000. You got to be in for $75,000. Not negotiable, Paul. That's it. Yes or no?"

"Fuck you, Neil! I told you we're not paying anything!"

"Have it your way, Paul. I'm not going to cut my fees by $100,000 to get Sterling $7.5 million! I'd rather tell Sanusi to forget about forwarding all of your money but just send me my fees in full. I'm sure he'd prefer that deal over the one I'm arguing for. Final offer, I'll pay $50,000 and you pay $50,000. We don't have any more time. In or out?"

"You are a fucking, unethical bastard, Neil. You set me up to come here exactly for this reason. To mitigate the amount of money you were going to need to pay these gangsters. You calculated that you wouldn't be able to get it out of us after this call, so you tricked me into coming. Your sole motive was to scam Mr. Sterling into paying what we clearly told you we were unwilling to pay. You're a piece of shit, Neil!"

"Thank you, Paul, for your extraneous and irrelevant insults. I'll give you one extra second to answer me!"

Understanding that he had no option, Norman answered with contempt, "You're authorized to pay us $7.45 million in lieu of $7.5 million. I understand that there is a $50,000 administrative fee. Go ahead and tell your corrupt, asshole friend to proceed."

Without so much as even looking at Norman, Neil released the mute button and declared, "Minister, please make all of the arrangements. You may withhold from our fee $100,000. Please have the ambassador execute the settlement agreement, then forward our remaining legal fees along with the Sterling settlement funds to my trust account. It is the same account where you previously wired my retainer fee at the start of the case. Thereafter, consider this legal matter concluded in its entirety."

"Very well, Neil. The ambassador will sign within the next three working days. The funds will be wired to your trust account one business day after the ambassador's signature. Please pray for our country. Farewell for now."

"Thank you, Minister Sanusi. Our thoughts and prayers are with you. Best of luck, and goodbye."

Norman, who was livid, addressed Neil by saying, "You're a bigger con than they are! For Christ's sake, you're an American lawyer. We got laws and a state bar that regulates ethics and proper behavior. What kind of a man are you?"

Neil, who genuinely believed that he had done Sterling and Norman a great service, looked up at Norman and tempestuously responded by saying, "Don't talk to me about ethics. Your big boss entered into a bogus contract. Yeah, my clients seduced and scammed him. He is an experienced businessman who should have known better. When you conduct commerce in a foreign nation, like Nigeria, you need to play by the customs of their country. All I'm doing is playing by their rules. Now, what I just did has given Mr. Sterling a free pass to just under $7.5 million. So, instead of reprimanding me, you really ought to change your tune and start praising me for what a brilliant job I just accomplished."

Norman, who has calmed down, said, "I hear your explanation, but there's still no excuse for lying to me when you knew full well that you were setting me up to shake me down for the Nigerian gratification fees. That was unmitigated bullshit."

Neil seriously responded, "Was it bullshit? Or was it smart? I say it was smart, and reasonable men can differ."

Norman, understanding that it was time to go home, said, "There's never an excuse for straight-up lying, so, in my book, its bullshit and so are you. Anyways, I'll make the change on the settlement agreement regarding the $50,000 'administrative' fee, then I'll have Mr. Sterling execute the document. You'll have it later this morning."

Neil, gazing at Norman walking out of his office without shaking his hand or saying goodbye, shouted out to Norman, awkwardly joking, "Does this mean you won't consider working here as my partner in the future?"

Norman stopped in his tracks, turned around, and said, "Not even if you were the only firm practicing law in America. Make sure you get Mr. Sterling his money, then I never want to see you or speak to you again."

As Norman departed the elevator, he recognized that he must contact his boss as promised. Even though he was ashamed for having caved into paying a portion of the gratification, it was time to make that call. Sterling answered on the first ring and asked, "How did we do, Paul?"

"We won, Mr. Sterling, with the exception of $50,000. I was ambushed, and regrettably, I accepted a $50,000 administrative fee to get the deal done. As a matter of principle, I probably should not have agreed to the demand, but I felt like it was better to advise you that we will be receiving $7.45 million as opposed to 0. I apologize for not following your specific instructions and standing our ground, but I did what I thought was right."

Sterling, who was relieved to hear the good news, said, "When I asked you to take on this matter, I knew you would handle this challenge as if it were your own. So, if you tell me there was no other alternative, then there was simply no other alternative. I am certain that you have conducted yourself with the highest degree of integrity. You have demonstrated to me exceptional talent. I thank you for your splendid work, and I will forever be grateful for what you have accomplished here tonight. Go get some well-deserved rest. We'll pick up on this tomorrow."

"Thank you, sir. I appreciate the kind words. I was guided by your leadership, and I am honored to represent you. Good night, Mr. Sterling."

As Norman made his way to the car, he couldn't help but think about a night where he did not say one word to the minister during the Nigerian call, yet this may have been the most successful moment in his legal career. What a night!

Chapter 23

Sterling's first order of business the next morning was to call Mark in order to inform him they had a deal with the Nigerian settlement agreement. He stopped in his kitchen to pour himself some coffee and noticed a headline story in the newspaper. The story indicated that the Nigerian military had slaughtered hundreds of unarmed, innocent anti-government civilian protesters in Independence Square, near the city of Lagos. The United Nations and the United States had immediately condemned the killings and promised to take swift actions against the Republic of Nigeria's government. The article went on to predict that 'a civil war was about to erupt at any moment.'

Although the seriousness of the civil unrest was not news to Sterling, the timetable was rising to a boiling point and could explode at any second.

He finished reading the article, then quickly walked over to his office and placed a call to Mark, who answers the phone by saying, "I'm glad you called. The State Department is about to recall our ambassador. That place is a powder keg that's ready to burst. Nigeria is on the brink of disaster. Did Paul get the deal done with Neil?"

"That's why I'm calling, Mark. It's done!"

"Hallelujah! Is the settlement signed? When are they going to wire the money?"

Sterling, who needed to control Mark's anxiety, said, "Slow down! You got to relax. We just made the deal late last night. It's a miracle Paul got these bastards to agree to sign off on anything under these circumstances."

"I'm sorry, Boss. The urgency of this situation is driving me a bit nuts. Winning or losing could come down to a difference of minutes. Okay. What's next?"

"First of all, do not leave Washington until I give you the green light. About 7:00 AM this morning, Paul called to continue briefing me as to what to anticipate. According to Neil, the Nigerian ambassador will serve as the power of attorney and have lawful authority to execute the settlement agreement. I will sign the agreement later this morning. The Nigerian Ambassador will execute it within the next three days. Thereafter, our money will be wired directly to Neil's attorney trust account for distribution to us. That's the absolute fastest we can move. You're going to need to stay in Washington just in case we need you to act on something unforeseen related to the ambassador, who is right there in D.C."

"Elliot, I hate to be the negative guy here, but I think it's going to be too late!"

"Tough shit, Mark. That's the card we've been dealt. All we can do is push hard and control what's in our hands. Something tells me we're going to pull this off. Just keep your faith."

Mark simply responded with, "You got faith. That's all I need to hear. Now I got faith."

"That's the spirit! Be ready to act on a split second if we need you. Make sure you know where the Nigerian Embassy is located. In fact, change your hotel so that you are as close as possible to the Embassy. Stay in touch if you hear anything new and look for my call. We're going to get this, Mark. You'll see. Take good care of yourself."

Sterling was very concerned that the American State Department had decided to recall the US ambassador from Nigeria. What kept crossing his mind was the possibility that the Nigerians might retaliate and recall their ambassador to return to Nigeria. Sterling, of course, didn't give a damn about the diplomacy, he just needed the Nigerian ambassador to sign the settlement agreement before he left. With that in mind, he picked up the phone and called Norman. On the fourth ring, Norman answered and said, "I apologize for taking so long to answer the phone, but I just got off the line with the bank. Good news, Mr. Sterling, the bank has executed all of their settlement agreements documents with us!"

"Terrific! I guess I no longer own a company."

Norman, always the attorney, responded by saying, "Well, technically, it's still yours until you sign. But, as a practical matter, I'd say you're right. Anyways, I told them that you will be returning shortly from out of the country and that you would sign off within 72 hours. We can hedge the signing for three days, but no more. Upon your signature, they will release to you the net $2.5 million amount they owe us from the interest reserve account. The personal guarantee will be voided in its entirety and you will own your home free in the clear of any liens. The bank also agrees that you are entitled to any funds collected regarding the Nigerian contract or court case. Sterling Development Company will be entirely owned by the bank. You will be signing a grant deed 'in lieu of foreclosure,' recorded at the County Recorder's office, relinquishing the Sterling Development's ownership of our real estate. All of your personal stock holdings in the firm will be handed over to the bank. In exchange, you will be released from any and all liability associated with the company. The bank has selected a high-level real estate development executive to run the company, and they expect to continue managing Sterling Development with no business disruption."

Sterling, holding back his nostalgic emotion, said, "With the stroke of a pen, there goes a few decades worth of work."

"Look at it this way, Mr. Sterling. You walk away without an ounce of liability and they inherit a hurricane."

"I put my life's work into building that company, but as the French say, 'C'est la vie.' Such is life. I'll execute the bank settlement agreement today. Bring it to me this afternoon. I'm not sure what's going to happen with the Nigerian settlement agreement money. Maybe we get it. Maybe we don't. But let's say we receive it, by chance, prior to my having signed the bank deal, technically, as you always say, Paul, the bank might have a right to those funds. As you know, they do have a way of tracing collusion these days. Besides, we're done with the property development business. If nothing else goes our way, we'll at least have 2.5 million bucks along with my house free and clear. I'm confident this's enough to get the hedge fund started. Find a notary and I'm signing today!"

"Yes, sir. I'll get us the notary; by the way, you are correct. If the Nigerians fund the $7.5 million prior to us signing the bank settlement, they technically could have a legal right to claim collusion, lien the funds, or perhaps even withdraw their settlement. I should have thought of that probability. I guess I figured that this would never happen. This is precisely why you will always be my boss and I will always be answering to you."

Sterling, who was laughing out loud, said, "To be honest with you, I just want to ensure that we can have some working capital if everything else goes to hell. It's time for me to let go. You've been brilliant to get me out of all my liability with them. I do think the bank will regret not rehiring us to manage the company. They'll be begging us to come back within six months. I'll see you at my home in an hour to sign. Then, let's urgently get back on Nigeria."

Reflecting on the fact that Sterling had called him, Norman said, "I realize that you were attempting to contact me before I went off on the bank settlement. Did you need to discuss something regarding Nigeria?"

"Yeah, I do, but we're juggling too many balls. Let's put the bank agreement to bed, then we'll talk about Nigeria. Although it's urgent, I don't want to distract you. Let's stay on the bank matter. After I sign their settlement, we'll get right back to Nigeria this afternoon."

"That's fine, Mr. Sterling. I'll see you in an hour."

As Sterling was waiting for Norman to arrive, he turned on his flat screen TV in his office. After surfing the channels, he stopped at one of the news networks, which was reporting on 'The Crisis in Nigeria.' The experienced news anchor was outlining various egregious acts the Nigerian government was performing. The death of civilians was appalling. The aggressive government crackdown regarding civilian opposition was shocking. The civil rights of Nigerian citizens were being violated and the world was taking notice. The news show went on to demonstrate how many government official offices were temporarily being closed, which was starting to create some paralysis in the day-to-day function of the country.

The prediction of the news commentator pointed towards 'inevitable civil war.'

It seemed as if the hour had gone by in a flash. The doorbell rang and it was the notary that Norman had scheduled. A few moments later, Norman had arrived. They got right down to business. Norman pulled from his briefcase document after document and Sterling just kept signing document after document. He didn't even bother reading the pages. That's how much Sterling trusted Norman.

When the final document was signed and notarized, there was virtually dead silence except for the sound of Sterling extending his hand out to shake the notary's hand and saying, "Thanks very much for your assistance."

And just like that, Sterling had become the former chief executive officer of Sterling Development Company, which he had founded. This was not a happy day for this proud man, but it was a new beginning.

As soon as Norman returned from escorting the notary to the front door of the house, he said to Sterling, "Should I take these documents over to the bank now or do you want to continue with the Nigerian conversation? If I hand-deliver the fully executed settlement agreement today, we will get paid your $2.5 million cashier's check within two business days from this afternoon. Whatever your preference, Mr. Sterling."

"Sure. Take the documents to them now. Then circle back here as fast as you can. The sooner you get us our money and the lien released off my home, the better. I didn't check closely the agreement, but I assume the bank will take the $2.5 million left in the Sterling Development business checking account, which will serve as an accounting offset for the money we owe them regarding my home."

"Yes, sir. We settled it that way so that we'd forfeit the business funds in exchange for you personally receiving the $2.5 million. I'll be back here by 5:00 PM. Is there anything further that I can do for you?"

"No, Paul. Just concentrate on finishing the job with the bank. Don't think about Nigeria. Just finish your work with the bank. I don't want any mistakes. Concentrate on the task at hand, then get your butt back here as fast as you can."

Although Norman felt uneasy with the lack of discussion on the Nigerian matter, he answered his boss by saying, "That's fine, Mr. Sterling. I'll seal up with the bank and see you back here at 5:00 PM sharp."

The bank's offices were about a 15-minute drive from Sterling's home. Norman had called ahead to the in-house bank attorney and had advised him that he was on his way with the fully executed settlement agreement.

Upon arriving at the bank, he drove into the underground parking facility and parked in a specially-marked parking space for 'Bank Guests Only.' Norman grabbed his briefcase and walked to the elevator and takes the trip up to floor 30, where the bank's legal department was stationed. He introduced himself to a very pretty blonde-haired and blue-eyed receptionist who said, "We are expecting you. Mr. Clarence Levy and Mr. Walsh will be meeting you in the main conference room. Please follow me."

The receptionist took Norman into an impressive, over-sized conference room that could easily double as an auditorium. At first glance, the massive conference table appeared as if it could comfortably seat 50 around it. Norman couldn't help but think that this venue was selected by the bankers to intimidate him, since the meeting consisted of a total of only three people. Of course, if that was their motive, who cares, the deal was done.

Within a short time, the bank's experienced lead attorney and the young banker Mr. Sterling considered a contemptible schmuck

237

walked into the room, saying almost in harmony, "How are you, Paul?"

Norman cleverly answered, "Since we're turning over our company to you, I'd say not so well. Big thanks, though, for seeing me on such short notice. Mr. Sterling returned early and instructed me to get this painful moment over with."

Levy answered with, "Well, to tell you the truth, Paul, this takeover may be more painful for us than it is for Mr. Sterling. We're inheriting a fucking mess. Believe me, we'd prefer that you just pay us back than takeover this piece-of-shit company!"

Norman, biting his tongue, responded, "If you know anything about real estate, timing is an integral part of success. I'm positive that this 'piece-of-shit' company you now own will make the bank a significant profit once the economy turns around. Of course, that potential profit will have much to do with the management you put in place to run the 'piece-of-shit' company. Anyways, let's review the documents so that you can return to your busy schedules."

Young Mr. Walsh decided he wanted to chime in, he said, "Hey, Paul, I hear that Nigeria is about to go to hell. I hope Mr. Sterling isn't betting all of his limited marbles on those losers! Our senior bank directors have been sending me messages all day long congratulating me on what a smart decision it was to get Mr. Sterling's bogus Nigerian contract off our books. That's going down as a feather in my hat! At least I'm looking good. I just don't get how a guy like Sterling could have fallen for such a fake contract like that. You really ought to do your client a big favor and advise him to forget about suing Nigeria. You're not collecting a dime from these people. It's just not going to happen, Paul!"

Without responding to Walsh's ignorant and abusive comments, Norman turned to Levy and said, "Every document has been signed where indicated and we now have a deal. I will return in two business days around this time to pick up Mr. Sterling's cashier's check for $2.5 million, including recorded copies releasing the lien on my client's residence. Please leave the check and the release with that pretty young receptionist at the front desk. As of this moment, we now have a binding settlement agreement. Best of luck with our former company, and goodbye."

As the meeting came to a cold and abrupt end, Levy and Walsh stood and shook hands with Norman. The Sterling Development Company had been quietly transitioned to the bank. Mr. Sterling was now free to pursue new ventures for the first time in decades. The immediate challenge was access to capital, and Nigeria was the answer to that challenge. The money coming from the bank settlement, even if Sterling mortgaged his home, would fall far short of the capital required to start up a new hedge fund. Norman clearly saw the handwriting on the wall. Nigeria needed to pay up. First, the $7.45 million from Neil, then the $100 million from Stanley Roberts. That was the kind of capital required to meet the business model and goals for the new Sterling Hedge Fund.

Norman soon found himself back at the Sterling residence with only one thing on his mind: get the money out of Nigeria. Sterling greeted Norman, saying, "Were they smiling or crying at the bank?"

"I saw a little of both. Levy is worried and Walsh thinks he's smartest guy on the planet."

Sterling responded, "I think Levy has it right and Walsh is an idiot. So, are we done?"

"Yes, sir. I'll have your cashier's check in two days. You're released from all liability. You own your home without any liens. And we're now free to pursue Nigeria without the bank having any claim to the funds."

"Thank you, Paul. Outstanding work! Alright, let's get on the Nigeria contest. Take a seat. This is going to take moment."

Norman pulled out a yellow legal pad from his briefcase and said, "I'm all ears."

Sterling remained on his feet pacing back and forth as he said, "The United States has recalled our ambassador from Nigeria. I'm reasonably sure that Nigeria is going to retaliate against America by recalling their ambassador. That could happen at any moment. We need to get Ambassador Mohammed to sign the Nigerian settlement agreement by tomorrow, or I'm afraid it's going to be too late! Here's what I need you to do. First, make sure that Neil gets the fucking settlement to Mohammed today, if he hasn't already sent it. Second, Neil needs to make arrangements to have Mohammed officially sign the documents ASAP. Third, I want Neil to organize for the release of the fully executed settlement agreements to Goldman by tomorrow at the Nigerian Embassy. Mark will, in person, pick up the settlement and fly it back to us by the end of the day tomorrow. Fourth, insist that Mohammed confirm with Neil's Nigerian legal contact, Mallam Sansusi, that the settlement was fully executed and that the $7.5 million, along with Neil's legal fees, are wired to Neil's attorney trust account tomorrow. Any questions?"

Norman put his pen down and said with a smile, "I'm definitely going to be requesting a raise."

"You got it! Now, can Neil do this?"

Norman, with a much more serious demeanor, said, "I've got a confession to make. Neil and I are on pretty bad speaking terms. In fact, I think the last thing I told him before I left his office the other night was that I never wanted to deal with him again. Other than that, I perfectly understand the plan of action."

With an exasperated tone of voice, Sterling said, "Paul, what in the hell are you talking about? You just completed a complicated settlement agreement with Neil. The only reason he's getting his legal fees paid is because of us! You've got to be joking. Look, if you can't talk to him, I'm going to need to call him myself. We've got way too much money riding on this to worry about some macho thing going on between the two of you."

Norman, embarrassed about the circumstances, responded, "It's kind of a long story. I'll save it for after we get our money. I'll call him. He'll cooperate. This is the only way for Neil to get his fees. He'll play ball, but I better call him right now. I'm assuming Mark is in D.C."

A less irritated Sterling said, "Yes, Mark's waiting for our instructions. Go ahead call this bastard."

Without hesitation, Norman called Neil, who immediately answered. Without even saying hello, Norman got right to the point by saying, "Our State Department contacts are telling us that Ambassador Mohammed will be recalled back to Nigeria at any moment!"

Neil interrupted Norman, saying, "Wow. Those guys at State are really good! I just got off the phone with Sanusi and he tells me that Mohammed will be leaving Washington for Nigeria by tomorrow night. Sansui wanted me to inform you and Mr. Sterling of this glitch: Mohammed has the settlement agreement but cannot officially sign it until tomorrow morning, because it must be executed and witnessed before one of their notaries. That special notary will be witnessing many other Nigerian documents being signed by the ambassador as his final official business before the recall. Sanusi has assured me that he can get our settlement agreement in that final group of notarized documents."

A relieved Norman commented, "That's great news, Neil."

Neil continued with, "I'm trying to get on a 'red-eye' to Washington in order to pick up the settlement. It's possible the fucking ambassador could sign the damn agreement but not get it out of the Embassy in time. We can't take that risk. Once the agreement is officially signed by the ambassador, there is no reason the Embassy can't release the fully-executed document to me or any other courier. We just got to get it out of the Embassy the moment Mohammed signs it. I'm not going to risk having some incompetent courier fail to pick it up on time."

Norman placed his phone on 'speaker' without informing Neil so that Sterling could listen in on the rest of the conversation. Norman then went on to explain to Neil, in detail, the proposed plan of action that included Mark.

Neil, who loved the plan, especially the fact that he did not have to fly all night to Washington, enthusiastically responded with, "I knew you were smart the first day I met you. We'll make this plan work. Hell, I got $200,000 riding on this. You bet your ass we'll get this to work! Tell Mr. Sterling to have his associate pull up to the Embassy security gate at precisely 11:45 AM, Washington time. Advise your guy not to be one second late. He will be escorted to the ambassador's attache in the Embassy, who will hand your man the fully-executed settlement agreement in a sealed, unlabeled package. The moment he leaves the Embassy's grounds with the package, tell your associate to immediately call and say these words to you, 'It's a beautiful day in the nation's capital.' Once you hear these words, call me, and I'll make the rest of the arrangements with Sanusi to wire us the funds to my trust account. Mr. Sterling will have his money, minus $50,000, within 24 hours from the moment I give Sanusi the green light. You know what, Paul, even when you left angry the other night, I just knew we'd end up friends. What's the full name of Mr. Sterling's associate?"

Norman answered, "Mark Goldman."

"Alright, tell Mark Goldman to have a government-issued ID with him. A California driver's license will work. His name will be on the official visitors' list, granting him access to the Embassy compound. Tell Mr. Goldman to keep his answers to any questions very simple. Preferably as simple as yes or no. He'll be taken right to the attache, who will ask him to sign for a large manila envelope. Advise him to sign, but not to open the envelope. Tell him to just receive it, then get the hell out of there as fast as he can without looking rushed. The worst thing Mr. Goldman can do is appear nervous. These are trained diplomats, or should I say spies, who can detect anxious behavior in a hurry. Remember, these guys in the Embassy just got their boss recalled back to Nigeria. They are jumpy. Any little gaffe by our Mr. Goldman could cost us a fortune!"

Norman, who was listening carefully, said, "Mark is the right man for this mission. He has a military background and is very calm under pressure. He'll be at the gate at precisely 11:45 AM tomorrow."

Neil, who just couldn't help but be egotistic, responded, "This time, advise Mr. Sterling not to spend all this money I'm getting him on some stupid new venture. Well, anyways, at least I'm getting my fees out of all these bullshit maneuvers."

Norman, who was observing a disgusted look on Sterling's face regarding the narcissistic comments by Neil, decided it was wiser to appease Neil than defend his boss. "Thank you for your exceptional efforts. I'll inform my client of your astute work. You will hear from me the moment I hear from Mr. Goldman."

"Okay, Paul, let's get this done! I'll keep an eye out for your call."

As Norman hung up, he looked up at Sterling and began to explain why he did not come to his defense, but Sterling stopped him mid-sentence and said, "Perfectly handled, Paul. Enough said. Let me get on the phone with Mark."

Sterling then dialed Mark, who answered immediately, "Elliot, do we have a plan? The ambassador will be gone by tomorrow!"

"Yeah, Mark, thanks to the remarkable efforts of Paul, we're set. Here's what you need to do."

Sterling went on to outline the plan with extraordinary precision. He had Mark repeat it back to him to make absolutely sure that he knew what was expected of him. Once Sterling was unconditionally certain that Mark had gotten it, he asked Norman to get on the phone and fill in anything he might have missed. Both Sterling and Norman were satisfied. Mark was ready; he was the perfect man for the job. Now came the hard part: waiting until tomorrow for Mark's call to Norman.

The plan was set in motion. Norman said his goodbyes to Sterling and Sterling thanked his loyal attorney for his continued smart and hard work. Both men felt the pressure of the moment, but neither expressed anything other than total confidence in the activities that were to play out within the next 24 hours. Sterling decided he'd do the most relaxing thing he knew. He would spend the rest of the evening and the night with his loving and supportive wife Felicia.

Sterling had enjoyed a splendid evening with his wife. They ate dinner, played cards, and spoke to each other about their children and their future. Felicia and his kids were Elliot Sterling's life, and he was determined to continue to provide them with the kind of life they had become accustomed to. The night had gone by quickly in the comfort of his warm and gracious wife. The sun was rising, and a new, important day was about to begin. Before too long, it was already 8:45 AM in Los Angeles, which meant it was 11:45 AM in Washington, D.C. Now calmly settling into his private office to monitor what he hoped would turn out to be a successful day, Sterling began to envision Mark parked at the Nigerian Embassy gate.

In reality, this was exactly where Mark was parked. It was 11:45 AM on the dot when a muscular, armed security guard addressed Mark in what sounded like a British accent, "State your name and who you are here to visit."

Composed and confident, Mark responded, "My name is Mark Goldman. I am here to see your attache."

The guard maintaining constant eye-contact with Mark demanded, "Let me see your identification."

Mark handed over his pictured driver's license as his I.D. The guard looked at the license, then stared at Mark's face, then said, "Please park your car where I indicate. You will then follow me into the Embassy. At all times, you are to remain next to me until we reach the office of the attache. Please leave your cellphone locked in your automobile."

Following the guard armed with an automatic weapon, Mark cautiously drove his car into the compound.

As the guard was escorting Mark from his car into the Embassy, he couldn't help but observe that the diplomatic employees appeared to be busy shredding documents. It seemed as if the entire staff had been given an order to destroy every piece of paper in the place. The attache's office was on the second level of the building, which required walking up an elaborate staircase near the center of the first floor. Once on the second level, the guard showed Mark into the office adjacent to the ambassador's official executive suite. They entered an impressive workplace that included a large, curved sofa professionally decorated with an expensive, lush apricot-colored upholstery. The guard, who reminded Mark of a Nazi Fascist, directed him to, "Sit down," on the couch and then said, "The attache will be with you as soon as he completes his meeting with the ambassador."

Approximately 30 minutes later, a tall, elegant, gray-haired black man, resembling a diplomat cast in a Hollywood movie, walked into the room. He extended his hand, saying in a now familiar British-type accent, "Please accept my sincerest apology for the delay. These are very hectic times for the Republic of

Nigeria. I am aware that you are here to receive a package. Regrettably, I do not have it in my possession."

Maintaining a cool disposition, yet wanting to get to the heart of the problem, Mark said, "Fine. When will you have it in your possession?"

The attache, respecting the question, said, "That is not clear. The contents of your package have not yet been signed by the ambassador. This is a very busy man who cannot be rushed."

Norman, looking directly into the eyes of the attache, responded with, "Okay, so we'll wait."

The attache's frown spoke volumes, indicating a facial expression of disapproval. Then, came the words from the attache, "It may be a considerable period of time. Perhaps you can return later. We'll call you."

Mark, now having trouble maintaining his cool, said, "No, sir. I don't leave here without the package. I've got nothing but time on my hands. Besides, this is a very comfortable couch."

Again, raising his eyebrows, the attache used his graceful diplomatic skills by stating, "I'm sure you would make very good company, Mr. Goldman, but as you can see, we're very busy here. Besides, you cannot be seated in my office, for security and confidentiality reasons. I assure you, I will personally call when we are ready."

Mark, who didn't want to fly all the way back to California empty-handed and then have to face his boss and Norman in defeat, spiritedly stated, "Look, Mr. Attache, perhaps I'm not making myself clear. I don't leave the Embassy without my package. Where I come from, it is considered dishonorable not to keep your word. Besides, it's downright rude to waste a man's time, don't you think? So, go tell your busy Mr. Ambassador that I expect him to honor his word. Unless you want to arrest me, I'm going to continue sitting right here on your pretty little couch impatiently waiting for what I came here for. Do I now make myself clear?"

The attache, impressed with Mark's fearlessness, said, "You are either very courageous or quite loyal to whoever sent you. Let me be candid with you, Mr. Goldman. The reason your documents are not signed is in no fault due to the ambassador or myself. The ambassador is prepared to sign your settlement agreement, but his signature will not be valid without our official notary witnessing the signing. The notary's wife just gave birth to their first child."

Somewhat dazzled by the disclosure, Mark said, "Now what?"

The attaché responded, "Our notary is on his way from the maternity hospital. Apparently, he is experiencing significant traffic. The good news for you is that he will in fact be here. The bad news is that when he arrives, the ambassador must concentrate on executing more important time-sensitive documents regarding official diplomatic state business. Those documents will take priority over your settlement. The ambassador will get to your document when he gets to your document. Now, am I making myself clear?"

Glancing at his wristwatch, Mark responded with, "Yeah, you're clear. I'm going to wait right here for as long as it takes for me to leave with my signed documents. I read in a Washington newspaper that the ambassador is going back home to Nigeria tonight. Just make sure he doesn't leave America without signing what I need. By the way, your security guy forced me to leave my cellphone in my car. I need to make a phone call. Would you be good enough to allow me to use a phone?"

The attaché, who was somewhat bemused by Mark's assertive demands, said, "For a gentleman who holds absolutely no power over anyone in this diplomatic compound, you are rather contentious, Mr. Goldman!"

"Yes, sir, I am. There is only one reason I'm sitting here, and that's because you guys made an arrangement for me to be here at a precise time. I took care of my end of the bargain. It's your turn to make good on what you promised. Now, will you please show me where I can make a phone call?"

Returning to his familiar frown, the attaché said, "I do not appreciate your antagonistic tone of voice, but we will do what we can to honor our pledge. I will ask you to leave my office. You will be escorted to our diplomatic waiting room until we are ready for you. From that room, you will be allowed to make one call. Now, if you will excuse me, I must visit with the ambassador and carry on with my day. Good afternoon."

As the attaché left the office, the security guard entered and said, "Please, follow me."

Mark took a brief walk and then entered the dazzlingly-decorated Diplomatic Reception Room. He was instructed to take a seat at another one of the stunning couches that seemed to be the norm in the Embassy. Next to the couch was a table with a landline phone on it. The unpleasant security guard, who kept to a very limited vocabulary, stated, "You are to remain in this room until further notice. The attaché has authorized one phone call. The phone

245

line is now available. Dial the number 9, your area code, then your remaining numbers."

The moment the guard left, Mark rigorously called Elliot on a prearranged private cell. Way too much time had passed and he knew his friend would be worried. Sterling picked up instantly, blurting out, "What the fuck is going on, Mark?"

For fear of possible eavesdropping, Mark answered in code, "The tea party is taking a little more time than expected. So far, the nation's capital is not quite as beautiful as expected, but I have some more sightseeing to do. Anyways, I'm doing fine. Just wanted to say hello and let you know that I'll be in touch as soon as I've completed visiting the city."

A relieved Sterling said, "If needed, I'm happy to come guide you around Washington. I hope you enjoy your stay."

As they both hung up, it was clear that the encrypted dialogue between these two old buddies had worked to perfection. Sterling knew that Mark was not in any physical danger, but it was apparent that their plan with the ambassador was not proceeding as designed or on schedule. Although Sterling understood that this situation was not going so well, he took comfort in the thought that if anyone could get this mission done, it was Mark. There would be nothing further for Sterling to do except to inform Norman, who would in-turn inform Neil with a courtesy update. Thereafter, all Elliot could do was patiently wait for the next communication.

Two hours had slowly gone by with not even one human being having entered the Diplomatic Reception Room to give Mark an update. He would have been satisfied just to see the unsociable guard. The room was dead silent. Although Mark was comfortable in probably the most elegant living room he had ever witnessed, he was starting to get very antsy. As he got up out of the plush couch to stretch his legs, in came the infamous guard.

"You must come with me. The ambassador will now see you."

The first thing that crossed Mark's mind was related to why the ambassador wanted to visit with him. This certainly was not part of the plan. The next thought was that this could not be a good omen. The original deal was that the ambassador would sign the settlement before the official notary, then stick the fully-executed document into a package and hand it to Mark, the innocent courier. Nothing about this unexpected meeting felt right or innocent.

The guard brought Mark into the ambassador's magnificent suite. This was an impressive office, with its high ceilings, spectacular Baccarat Crystal chandelier, and impeccable decor. The ambassador was seated behind his grand desk.

The moment Ambassador Mohammed made eye-contact with Mark, he said, "Please have a seat, Mr. Goldman. You are my last meeting before I depart for my homeland. I do not have much time, so this will be brief. I have been informed by my staff that you are Mr. Sterling's senior associate and close friend from childhood. Therefore, I will get right to the point. We have a longstanding custom in the great Republic of Nigeria to thank our public servants for their efforts. The last official act this embassy is about to conduct will favor your colleague Mr. Sterling for many years to come. Of course, we at the Embassy are happy to accommodate him, but it is important to properly show your gratification to the many civil servants involved in this effort. Apparently, there was a misunderstanding as to the appropriate amount of gratification. The correct amount is $200,000. It's unclear to me why the figure of $100,000 was raised, but that is water under the bridge. Do we now better understand each other, Mr. Goldman?"

Mark, who was sick to his stomach listening to this despicable scam artist, responded, "Let me get this straight. You are increasing the 'administrative fee' your own attorney drafted into the settlement agreement by 100%? Sure, I understand. In America, we call this highway robbery. The rest of the world calls it extortion."

Now agitated, Mohammed said, "Call it whatever you please, Mr. Goldman. That is my final word on this subject. There will be no further discussion. If your answer is no, you are to leave the Embassy immediately without your executed settlement. If the answer is yes, you will leave here with the signed document. The gratification will be accomplished by your agreement to pay half the legal fees due to our American attorney. I believe that total amount is settled at $200,000. You will sign a side agreement on behalf of Mr. Sterling, agreeing to this condition. This will be your personal guarantee assuring us that our United States lawyer will be paid in full. Yes or no?"

Mark quickly calculated the numbers in his head. Norman had previously agreed to pay $50,000 towards Neil's fees, and Neil had accepted to chip in $50,000. The net new money that Sterling would be responsible to pay was a commitment of an additional $100,000, or a total of $150,000 going to Neil. Perhaps Neil could be persuaded to take less after an explanation regarding how this last-minute shakedown by the ambassador had taken place.

Mark intuitively knew that the ambassador held all of the cards. This was not negotiable, and no call would be permitted to ask his boss. Mark looked up at the chandelier on the ceiling, took a deep breathe, then looked at the bully asshole across the desk and said, "I've got a plane to catch." Then, conscious that their conversation might be recorded, he paused for a moment and completed his answer by saying, "So, could you please get your notary in here and sign my documents so that I can be on my way?"

Not exactly certain what the answer was, a confused-looking ambassador asked, "Was that a yes?"

Mark responded, "We will agree to pay for a part of your attorney's legal fees as a part of our settlement agreement. Now, I really mean it. I've got a plane to catch!"

Mark had no choice. He had to pay the ransom or go home with nothing. Within minutes after the ambassador gave his instructions over the phone to his legal assistant, a notary entered the room holding the settlement agreement and the amended legal side agreement. It was apparent to Mark that the ambassador had previously ordered the side agreement prepared, since it was instantly ready. Without any further comments, the ambassador signed two copies of the settlement and Mark signed two side agreements. The notary then proceeded to make the documents official, placed one full set in a large white envelope, and handed the envelope to Mark. The settlement deal was done!

The ambassador extended his hand across his desk and said, "Good luck, Mr. Goldman. Have a safe journey home."

Mark reluctantly shook Mohammed's hand, then without saying another word, grabbed his package and headed towards the door of the ambassador's suite. Instantaneously, the guard spotted Mark and demanded, "You must slow down! I will escort you to your automobile. Follow me."

As they made their way out of the building to the front portico of the Embassy, Mark observed a three-car motorcade parked at the entrance door with its engines running. Mark was abruptly instructed to halt by the guard, who turned towards him and said, "You must move to one side, stay still, and wait until I give you further instructions."

Initially annoyed by the guard's demand but simultaneously worried that something bad was about to happen to him, Mark moved to one side. Three immediate thoughts passed through his mind. The most extreme was that the Nigerians were about to arrest

248

him on some false accusation. Then, he thought that these guys were going to confiscate the package!

And finally, he thought that the guard and his cohorts were going to shake him down for some of that famous gratification before he was allowed to leave the Embassy compound.

None of those thoughts were even close. Within moments, the ambassador and his small entourage walked right past Mark and entered straight into the waiting shiny black limousines. Mohammed was apparently telling the truth when he expressed to Mark that his last official act before he left for his homeland was to sign the settlement. Of course, it was worth the wait for the sleazy ambassador, since he had just extorted $200,000 dollars.

Once the limousines were off the Embassy grounds, the guard received a verbal message in his earpiece authorizing them to proceed. Without any expression, the guard said, "You may now follow me to your car."

Once they got to the car, Mark couldn't resist a comment and blurted out to the guard, "I'm sorry, I never got your name." Receiving no response, Mark continued with a straight face, saying, "Well, anyways, thanks for showing me around." Again receiving no reaction, Mark held back a smile and said, "Since the Embassy is closing, you're probably going to need a new job. Hey, listen, if you ever need a reference, just call me, I'll vouch for you."

Finding absolutely no humor in Mark's sarcastic remarks, the guard, without any further words, just pointed towards the Embassy gates at the end of the long driveway. Mark backed out his car from the parking space, waved at the guard, and quickly made his way out the gates.

When free and approximately one mile away from the Embassy, it was time to make that happy call to his boss. Before making the call, Mark couldn't help but reminisce what a smart move Sterling had made to instruct him to stand by in Washington to ensure the success of this mission. This was the only way the settlement could ever have been signed. The Sterling-Goldman combination was successful once again.

What a pleasure it was for Mark to make the call, and as expected, Sterling answered right away, still remaining in code, saying, "How are you enjoying the city?"

Now came these exquisite words from Mark, "It's a beautiful day in the nation's capital. I'm on my way home!"

Sterling, grateful that his loyal friend was safe and the business deal was done, responded with only two words, "Thank God!"

Chapter 24

As Mark was making the voyage back to Los Angeles, Sterling instantaneously took over command of ensuring that the $7.5 million settlement agreement funds were wired swiftly into Neil's trust account. Given Nigeria's state of affairs, there really wasn't any time to waste. The moment Sterling got off the line with Goldman, he was on the phone with Norman pushing for the funds. Of course, Norman understood the timing pressure and was, without delay, speaking to Neil.

The consistently scheming Neil had already been informed by his Ministry of Legal Affairs contact, Mallam Sanusi, that the settlement had been executed by the ambassador. Neil had also been briefed by Sanusi that there had been a change in the gratification amount. The ensuing problem was that neither Norman nor Sterling were aware of the adjustment in the deal, because Mark, for security reasons, had kept his comments in code while on the phone.

Norman began the conversation by aggressively demanding payment. Neil responded ballistically by shouting, "That's old news! I know the deal is done, but do you know that your fucking associate gave away my fees?"

Norman, who was baffled by Neil's comment, answered, "No. I'm not. What are you talking about?"

"Your Mark Goldman signed a personal guarantee assuring the Republic of Nigeria that Mr. Sterling is obligated to pay my fees in full. The wire is only going to be for a total amount of 7.5 million. No legal fee money!"

Not quite sure what to believe, Norman said, "I assure you, this is the first I've heard of any such change in the deal."

Neil, likewise uncertain as to whether he could believe Norman, decided to follow his unscrupulous instincts and bluntly responded, "Do you realize that I can hold Sterling responsible for the entire amount of the legal fees I billed! Paul, you know that I earned fees well over $250,000, as opposed to the $200,000 they had agreed to wire me. In fact, the way I now see it, I don't think I'm even going to acknowledge the 50 grand I was willing to throw in for the fucking gratification. Let's face it, I didn't give my permission to your Mr. Mark Goldman to negotiate how my fees were to be paid. So, as far as I'm concerned, you guys technically owe me the entire $250,000. It's really your gratification to pay, not mine! I mean, come on, look at it through my eyes. You guys get well over $7 million, and I get a measly $250,000. Explain to me where you see fair equity regarding the payment of gratification. Paul, you know Goldman had no legal authority to play with my fees! Let me cut to the chase with my position, there will be no distribution of your funds until Mr. Sterling acknowledges that I'm entitled to the full $250,000. Before I release your funds, I will pay my firm $250,000 and send you the balance of $7.25 million. Actually, I don't even need your boss to legally acknowledge this. Goldman was stupid enough to take care of that for me. Lucky me!"

Assuming that Neil's version of the facts were true, Norman understood that this was a legal checkmate. Mark had been pressured and scammed into the unconditional obligation to pay for all of Neil's fees. With anger in his voice, Norman responded, "Neil, you are repulsive and literally turn my stomach! No gratification should be paid by anyone, period. You have no character. You're just an obnoxious asshole committing moral turpitude against a fellow lawyer. Since you're breaching your fiduciary duties, at least confirm that the $7.5 million is sitting in your trust account!"

Neil said, "Don't take everything so personally. This is just business. I earned my fees, as opposed to you guys playing nice with some bogus government contract. Don't give me some bullshit lecture on ethics. Yeah, I should honor our gratification deal, but I don't see any opportunity to make up any lost fees with Nigeria and I certainly don't see a future between you and me. I will acknowledge that it does sounds like Goldman probably had a gun to his head when he signed off on the new gratification deal, but he signed. You guys are getting a windfall amount of money, I'm just going to collect what's mine. I'm going to stick with the newly-written Goldman amendment."

Norman understands that he's dealing with a snake and returned to his question, "Do you have the money?"

Neil answered, "Yes, but I'm not paying you anything until we have a meeting of the minds regarding my fees. Do you hear me, Paul?"

"Sure, I hear you. Look, let us talk to Goldman. He's in the air and should land soon. We'll hear what he has to tell us and we'll get back to you. By the way, do you have a copy of what Mark signed?"

Surprised at how calm Norman was behaving, Neil cautiously said, "No, I don't have a copy, but Goldman will."

Now that Norman knew that the funds were in the trust account, he wanted to buy time to think through the best legal strategy to use with Neil. The urgency was no longer to get the funds out of Nigeria, it was to get the funds out of Neil's trust account and into Sterling's bank account. Confidently, Norman said, "Let me consult with Mr. Sterling and talk to Mark. We'll review Goldman's guarantee agreement and then I'll call you."

A pensive Neil closed the call by saying, "Yeah, sure, you do that. I'll be waiting for your call. I'm really not a bad guy, Paul. I'm just looking after my firm."

Upon finishing with Neil, it was time to explain the newest version of the Nigerian crime story to his boss. Norman reluctantly picked up the phone and said to Sterling, "We've been seduced and scammed again by these bastards. This time, Mark was the victim. I'm positive that Goldman had absolutely no choice, but he apparently agreed in writing to pay off all of Neil's legal fees. Neil is taking advantage of Mark's ambush at the Embassy and holding us to Mark's written guarantee amendment. If what Neil is telling us is true, it's going to cost us $250,000! I'm positive the amendment was extorted from Mark under severe pressure. In any case, I think they got us on the hook for the fees, even though Neil had previously agreed to a different fee deal. The good news is that Neil has all of the money parked in his trust account, ready for distribution."

Sterling, who was silently listening, reacted by saying, "I would expect nothing less from a crooked lawyer representing a crooked country. If Mark agreed, it's because there was no alternative. I have no doubt that Mark pulled off a miracle in getting us any money, so let's just be thankful with what he got. If Mark confirms the written existence of his guarantee, we're fucked! Get our $7.25 million out of Neil's possession as fast as you can. Perhaps once we take possession of our funds, you might be able to figure out a legal strategy to sue Neil based on the true intentions of our original written understanding concerning legal fees. First, get our money out of his hands!"

"Yes, sir. I agree with everything you just said. Once Mark attests to the facts and shows us the amendment, I'll do my best to obtain immediate possession of our funds. We'll worry about suing this asshole later."

Sterling responded, "I expect Mark to land shortly. I'm sure he'll call me once he's on the ground. Why don't you plan on getting to my office in two hours? Mark should be here by then. After we speak with him and you review the official guarantee amendment, you can call Neil and make final arrangements with this bastard. See you in a couple of hours."

Within about an hour, Sterling had tracked Mark's airline, confirming that his plane had arrived from Washington, D.C., at the Los Angeles International Airport. It didn't take long thereafter for Sterling's phone to ring. It was a frantic Mark apologetically yet angrily rattling off the details of how he had been bushwhacked by the Nigerian Embassy. Sterling composedly interrupted Mark and said, "Welcome home. You did great! Don't worry about a thing. Do you have the written guarantee amendment with you?"

Mark answered, "Yes."

Sterling then said, "I know you must be exhausted, but I need you to bring it to my office. Norman and I will be waiting for you. Once Norman looks at the amendment, we need to get our money out of Neil's trust account ASAP."

Somewhat surprised, Mark asked, "Neil already received the funds?"

"Yeah. They're sitting in his trust account waiting for us to agree to pay off his fucking legal fees!"

"Oohrah! Let me fetch my bags. I'll be right over."

It took a little over an hour for Mark to arrive from the airport to Sterling's home. Norman had previously entered the office and felt on edge waiting to review the amendment. Mark, looking understandably run-down, was greeted by a joking Sterling, who said, "You look like shit!" Then gave him a big welcome-back hug.

Mark responded by saying, "You try dealing with these pricks. They're just a bunch of ruthless, money-sucking, narcissistic thugs. In case you haven't figured it out, there is no way in hell we were going to get paid by these crazies without you sending me right into the Embassy, the way you did. I'm not sure where you came up with that strategy, but you got that one right! Hey, Paul, how you doing? Sorry about caving into them over the legal fees. There was just no other option for us. It got down to take it or leave it. I took it, or we'd have nothing. The ambassador actually left the Embassy compound before I did. That's how touch-and-go this got down to. Here's what I signed, but under severe protest."

Mark handed the personal guarantee amendment to Norman. As Norman grasped the document, he said, "We all would have done the same thing, Mark. Congratulations on saving our asses on the deal. I'll quickly look it over just to make sure there isn't any loophole for us. Welcome back, and thanks for your valiant efforts."

Feeling gratitude, along with a great sense of compassion, for the effort and risk his friend had gone through, Sterling said, "Take a seat while I pour you a glass of my best Scotch. In fact, let's make that a double."

By the time, Sterling pulled out the bottle of Scotch and grabbed a glass, Norman looked up at Sterling and Mark and said, "Neil has us by the balls. We're screwed!"

Without any emotion, Sterling responded to Norman saying, "Get us our money. Do not argue with Neil. Just get us our money. Instruct him to issue a cashier's check payable to Elliot E. Sterling and Felicia Sterling for $7.25 million. Meet him at his bank at 10:00 AM and personally collect our funds. Be certain that he reads no commotion on your face or body language. Just professionally walk into to the bank, receive the check, and get the fuck out of there. Once that mission is accomplished, I want you to meet Felicia and me at Felicia's personal bank in Beverly Hills. She and I will endorse the cashier's check and deposit it into her account. Felicia will then instruct her bank to wire seven million dollars to our newly-arranged bank account in Israel, set up by my good friend Benjamin Yaalon. Once those funds hit the Israeli account, the Sterling Hedge Fund will be capitalized and just waiting for Stanley Roberts to perform on November 2nd. So, go ahead and call this creep and tell him what to do."

Norman acknowledged his marching orders with a simple, "I got it. I'll call Neil right now."

Satisfied that his attorney understood him, Sterling made his way over to Mark and poured him a well-earned drink, then poured himself one as well. He raised his glass and said, "To the bravest man I know, and to my friend and brother. Job well done!"

In the background, they both heard Norman clearly and precisely instructing Neil as to what was expected of him tomorrow. Within moments, Norman joined Sterling and Mark, saying, "Neil will meet me at his bank at 10:00 AM. He responded like a lamb, as opposed to a beast. He has no idea where we're coming from, other than he thinks he's won. We'll have our money tomorrow. Now, Mr. Sterling, do you mind if I get in on this Scotch thing too?"

It was 10:00 AM the next morning and Norman was sitting in the lobby of Neil's bank, waiting for him to arrive.

Fifteen minutes later, Neil walked into the bank holding a document. He looked at Norman, and without even saying hello, or that he was sorry he was late, Neil said, "Here, take a look at this. I need Mr. Sterling to sign before I can issue you a check. It's no big deal, but it does assure me that you won't turn around and sue me after I give you your funds."

Even though Sterling had ordered Norman to stay calm, it was not possible to do so. Norman reacted with disgust in his voice, saying, "Why didn't you call me and tell me about this condition?"

"Because you don't call the shots, Paul. I do. Now, go get this signed by your boss and I'll see you back here in a couple of hours."

Norman glanced at the document and said, "You want us to sign a Release of Liability to you, personally, and your firm? You are not our client nor are you the defendant in our case against you. You're just a greedy asshole extorting money from us after you reneged on our gentleman's agreement regarding your fees. Here's my advice to you. Take that piece of paper and stick it up your ass. Now, let me tell you something else. If you do not issue us forthwith our cashier's check in the amount we discussed last night, I am going directly to the State Bar Association. I promise you that I am going to get you disbarred from practicing law, then I'm going to sue you, your firm, and your client!"

"Paul, every time we speak, you take things to heart. Relax. I'm just trying to keep things kosher. It's just business."

"Neil, look at me. I'm very relaxed. Now, escort me into the bank and get me my fucking cashier's check."

"I can't do that, Paul. I need Sterling's signature, or no check."

Without looking at Neil any further, Norman dropped the document on the floor and started his exit towards the front door of the bank. Neil, who was shocked that Norman was going to walk out on him, desperately shouted out, saying, "Paul, come back. We can work this out. I apologize. Let's go into the bank."

Norman stopped, then slowly looked over his shoulder and said, "No more tricks, Neil. Do you hear me? No more bullshit!"

Neil responded, "Okay. Let's go finish our business."

As Norman made his way back, he said to Neil, "When this deal is done, I suggest you take a long sabbatical. Your ethical compass is way off. For the sake of the legal profession, go fix yourself."

"I might just do that. Making money the ethical way is getting harder and harder to do here in America. Sorry about what I'm doing to you and your boss. I feel really bad about it. Anyways, I guess the fact that Goldman signed the personal guarantee amendment covers me well enough. I shouldn't have asked for anything further from you guys. Let me get you your check."

It was apparent to Norman that Neil was not curable. The most important concept that Neil processed was not the necessity to reflect on ethics, it was that Goldman's guarantee had his ass covered in the event of a lawsuit by Sterling. Neil was a lost cause. The only thing that mattered was to get the check and get the hell out of the bank.

It didn't take long for Neil and Norman to walk to the special department of the bank known as 'Private Banking.' This unit was specially designed to handle the bank's high net-worth clients. Effectively, it was a bank within the bank. As they arrive, a young banker dressed in a navy blue three-piece formal suit warmly greets Neil and Norman. After some small talk, he asked them to take a seat in his beautifully-decorated office, which contained freshly-cut flowers and professionally-coordinated furnishings.

The banker then addressed Neil by saying, "Your wire transfer in the amount of $7.5 million has now been released into your trust account. The funds are available for distribution. I understand that you have some instructions for me. How can I assist?"

Now playing the role of a sophisticated lawyer in front of the banker, Neil responded in his pompous manner, "Mr. Norman is an attorney representing a prominent businessman in Los Angeles. We will be issuing a cashier's check to Mr. Norman's client representing a full and complete settlement approved by the courts. A portion of the funds will remain in my trust account. Those remaining funds are legal fees charged by my firm but agreed to be paid by Mr. Norman's client as a part of the final settlement. Mr. Norman is here to collect his client's funds and to acknowledge to you that the balance of the funds may remain in my trust account. Go ahead, Paul, the banker will follow your instructions."

Norman was astonished by the audacity of Neil's comments attempting to force Norman into a quid pro quo. Neil was effectively trying to create the banker as his witness regarding the legitimacy of Neil's legal fees. Norman thought quickly, grabbed a hold of his emotions, and with swagger, gave his instructions to the banker, "Make one cashier's check payable in the amount of $7.25 million, payable as follows: Elliot E. Sterling and Felicia Sterling. Due to attorney-client confidentiality, I am not allowed to comment any further."

The banker, sensing a little discomfort in Norman's comments, simply responded by saying, "Yes, sir. I'll return with your check in one moment. Please excuse me."

With the banker out of the room, Norman became cold as ice with Neil. He doesn't say one word to him. He doesn't even look at him. Neil, who realizes there was nothing he could say to Norman to reconcile his continued foolish behavior, just decided to stay silent. Both maintained their complete absence of sound until the banker returned to the office with the cashier's check in his hand. The banker first showed the check to Neil, who nodded in approval. Then, the banker addressed Norman and said, "Please review the check. If you find it in order, please sign our copy of the check indicating your receipt of same."

Norman examined the cashier's check and made one comment, "Correct." Then, he signed the banker's receipt and placed the check in his briefcase. As he stood to shake only the banker's hand, he turned to face Neil, making sure that the banker could hear his voice, and said, "Make sure you send my office a full hour-by-hour accounting of your fee breakdown. Since you've never disclosed your statement, we may have some further questions for you. I'll see myself out. Good day, gentlemen."

Felicia's bank was within walking distance. Once on the sidewalk, Norman called Sterling and said, "I have the check. I'll be at Mrs. Sterling's bank within 15 minutes."

Sterling responded with, "Good job, Paul. We're at the bank, waiting for you on the second level. When you get off the elevator, turn to the right and we'll be in the Executive Conference Room. See you soon."

The walk along Wilshire Boulevard near Rodeo Drive in Beverly Hills was pleasant, because of its palm trees and well-maintained women shopping in ritzy boutique shops along the stroll. Norman spotted the bank and made his way to the second floor conference room. As he entered the room, he couldn't help but notice how gorgeous Mrs. Sterling appeared. She was wearing a charming dress and expressed a friendly smile towards Norman. He greeted Elliot, then said hello to his wife. Felicia then said, "Hi, Paul. My husband can't stop telling me what an outstanding lawyer you are. He tells me that you are hard-working and raves about the trustworthy work you have done for our family. Thank you for your efforts. They are greatly appreciated."

Humbled by her comments, Norman responded, "My boss is an extraordinary and visionary leader. Your husband is a man that I trust. I look forward to serving him, and your family, for as long as he will permit."

Felicia looked at Elliot and then said, "I'm sure I speak for Mr. Sterling. Stay with us for as long as you wish. The new Sterling Hedge Fund is going to become one of the biggest companies in the world by the time my husband is finished with his new venture."

Just as Felicia finished her upbeat words, her banker walked into the room. He gave his polite welcome to everyone, then got right to the point, "I understand you have a cashier's check for me. Additionally, I have been previously informed by Mrs. Sterling that we will be wiring almost all of those funds to a bank in Israel. Can I see the check?"

It was apparent to everyone in the room that the banker was not exactly happy, since virtually all of the money being deposited will be leaving the bank about as fast as it is stored. Without delay, Norman handed the banker the check.

The banker took a quick look at the check, then addressed Felicia, saying, "Please endorse the back of the check, and Mr. Sterling, I'll ask you to do the same. Unless you have any further instructions, I will deposit these funds into Mrs. Sterling's checking account. Once the funds have cleared the attorney's trust account and they are good funds, we will wire-transfer $7 million to your designated Israeli bank account. I have spoken to your Israeli banker, Benjamin Yaalon, and he has confirmed that the Israeli bank account is open and ready to receive your funds. It will take three working days before the cashier's check clears our processing. The moment the funds are available, they will be wired forthwith. Is there anything else, Mrs. Sterling?"

"Yes. Please move the remaining $250,000 to a 90-day time certificate of deposit at the highest interest rate you have available."

"Of course. Anything else?"

Sensing a very disappointed banker, Elliot stepped in and asked Norman, "Hey, Paul, what's going on with that other $2.5 million we're expected to receive on that other deal you're finishing up?"

Norman, preoccupied with Nigeria, had momentarily forgotten that the bank settlement funds regarding Sterling Development were due to be paid at any moment. He replied, "Yes, sir. Those funds might be available as soon as today."

Elliot then said to the banker, "As early as tomorrow, my wife will be depositing an additional $2.5 million, which will remain right here at the bank for the foreseeable future."

The banker appreciated the goodwill gesture and responded, "Thank you, Mr. and Mrs. Sterling. We're not a big bank, but we do take good care of our customers. The moment the funds are cleared, I will process the wire to Israel and set up your time certificate regarding the remaining funds. When the new $2.5 million funds are available, I will be happy to go to your home and pick up the check. You and Mrs. Sterling can give me your instructions from the comfort of your residence. Well, then, if there is nothing further, I wish you all a pleasant day."

On his way out of the conference room, Sterling turned to Norman and said, "I'm going to walk my wife to her car. Meet me in the lobby of the bank. I need to discuss something with you."

Norman responded by saying, "Sure. While I'm waiting, I'll call Clarence Levy or George Walsh at the bank to see if our bank settlement money is available."

Elliot and Felicia were hand-in-hand walking to her car. They both felt the old magic that had so clearly defined their life together. It was a combination of grace, intelligence, and street smarts. They felt the power of money again, yet without uttering a word to each other, they both understood that money was a commodity that could come and go, but that their love and respect for each other was the real power. Elliot kissed his beautiful wife goodbye, then turned around and made his way back to Norman.

It didn't take long to find Norman, who excitedly said to Sterling, "Levy confirmed that the bank's settlement agreement cashier's check for the $2.5 million will be available this afternoon at 3:00 PM. He claims Walsh left me a voice message to that effect. Seems like kind of our lucky day today, doesn't it?"

Sterling responded by saying, "I'm not so sure I believe in luck alone. I think we worked pretty damn hard for this day to come, but I guess I'd rather be lucky than good. Great news on the funds, and great legal work by you. Slowly but surely, we're getting back to some respectability. Make sure you pick up those funds at 3:00 PM. Then take the check to my private office. I may have Felicia's banker come to my home around 4:00 PM so he can get those funds cleared and in our account ASAP."

"Consider it done, Mr. Sterling. Now, what did you need to discuss with me?"

"Late last night, I received a call from Stanley Roberts' daughter ,who is attending UCLA."

Norman, somewhat alarmed, said, "What the hell did she want? I thought Stanley didn't want any further contact from us for the remainder of his life, with the exception of collection of his huge fee. This can't be good news!"

"I don't know what she wanted, because she didn't say. I didn't speak to her. She just left a message in that familiar Nigerian-British accent. She spoke in a mysterious code, saying she was attending UCLA and was the daughter of a friend of mine. The message said she'd soon be back in touch. She left no name, and the phone number was restricted."

Norman, at a loss for words, said, "Wow. Jesus!"

Sterling responded, "I felt the same way. Do you think I should find her in the dorms? Or should we just sit back and wait for her to try me again? I mean, we got a 100 million bucks riding on what this young woman has to tell us!"

Norman briefly thought for moment, then responded, "No. Do not call her or try to contact her. You cannot afford to breach the confidentiality arrangement you have with Stanley. Let her contact you in the manner she elects. I guarantee you that Stanley is secretly guiding her on each move. If and when Stanley decides that it is safe, she'll be in touch. When they have something to tell you, I promise you, you'll be hearing from them. November 2nd is only one week away. Stanley and his family have $5 million riding on this. Sit tight, we'll hear from her."

With a concerned look on his face, Sterling said, "You're absolutely right. But we need that $100 million. I know that you and Mark are realists. So am I. It's just not possible to start an important hedge fund without serious capital. We won't be able to compete on the world market without that $100 million. The big boys out there will eat us alive! You're right, though, we'll wait."

The loyal Norman answered his boss, "If it's not a hedge fund on a global scale, we can always scale it back domestically, if you choose. Please don't be concerned about Mark or me. We're all going to be fine. I'll deliver your bank settlement funds to your home by 4:00 PM. So, if you want to make arrangements with Mrs. Sterling's banker, go ahead and do that. I could be right or I could be wrong, but I'll leave you with this thought. If Stanley didn't have something up his sleeve, I'm pretty certain he wouldn't be risking his daughter's security, or his, just to deliver bad news to us. So, as a great man once said to me, 'let's plan for success.'"

Faintly grinning, Sterling said to Norman, "You're a good man, Paul. I'll see you later this afternoon."

Chapter 25

It was exactly 3:00 PM and Norman was working his way through the bank with the goal of locating the pretty young receptionist at the bank's legal department. Once he arrived, she immediately recognized Norman, saying, "I think you're here to see me." Pointing at a package, she continued, "I believe you're looking for this. Am I right?"

Making eye-contact with the receptionist, Norman answered, "Yes, ma'am, you are correct."

The spunky young woman said, "I'll tell you what. You sign the receipt Mr. Levy has prepared for you and I'll turn over the envelope. Deal?"

Norman, who was starting to take a liking to her, responded, "Here's my counter-offer to you. You turn over the envelope to me, I review the cashier's check and the documents enclosed, and if they are in order, I'll sign. Agreed?"

Feeling a comfortable rapport, she handed him the package and said, "Fair enough."

Norman opened the envelope and saw a cashier's check for $2.5 million, an official cancellation of Sterling's personal guarantees, a lien release on Sterling's personal residence, and so on and so forth. Levy had delivered everything as promised. The bank now owned a very clouded Sterling Development Company and Mr. Sterling got back his home, some needed cash, and his business freedom. The settlement was officially done.

Norman glanced at the young woman, built up some nerve, then awkwardly said, "It's all in order. I'll sign your receipt. I really should have just taken you at your word and signed earlier. I sincerely apologize. Can I make it up to you? How about we have some coffee when you get a chance?"

The sassy and very bright receptionist responded, "Well, if you're going to ask me out on a date, you really ought to first ask me my name. And since you feel so bad about it, I don't think coffee is enough retribution. At minimum, the crime deserves lunch, maybe even dinner. My name is Emma Adams. Nice to meet you."

Norman, who was getting more and more impressed by the second, said, "Glad to meet you, Emma Adams. I'm Paul Norman. How about dinner tomorrow night at 7:00 PM?"

The self-assured Emma answered, "I know your name, Paul. I typed it on the envelope. Remember? Yes, I'll have dinner with you. I finish work tomorrow at around 6:00 PM. Can you pick me up here at the bank around that time?"

Flashing a rare grin while signing the receipt, Norman said, "Sure. See you tomorrow at 6:00 PM."

Realizing that Mr. and Mrs. Sterling, along with Felicia's banker, would be waiting for him, Norman hurriedly said goodbye to his new acquaintance and made his way to Sterling's home, which was approximately 15 minutes from the bank's Wilshire Boulevard location. Norman arrived at the residence and found Mr. and Mrs. Sterling, their banker, and Mark sitting in the living room drinking tea waiting for him. Elliot greeted Norman, asking, "Everything good, Paul?"

Norman uncharacteristically answered, "It went perfectly, Mr. Sterling. Beyond my expectations," as he handed the cashier's check to Sterling.

Sterling, who looked at Mark, then back at Norman, asked, "How much better could it have gone beyond what we negotiated? Did we receive something we didn't expect?"

Realizing that he was overstating the bank settlement results while thinking about Emma, Norman said, "No, sir. We got everything we asked for. I've reviewed the documents and we're good to go, including all of the releases we settled on. The 'beyond expectations' comment is personal, but I'll talk to you about that later in private. So, if you don't need me any further, I'll show myself out."

Sterling, now looking at Felicia, then back at Norman, said, "No, Paul. Take a seat. We're meeting with Mark as soon as we finish here."

Sterling went on to endorse the back of the $2.5 million check, handed it to his wife, and said, "Go ahead and deposit these funds in your bank. Since you set up the other funds on a 90-day time certificate, it's probably a good idea to mirror that timeline. I've got to go meet with these gentlemen." As he was leaving the living room, Sterling shaked hands with the banker and said to him, "Take good care of my wife. She may develop into the best customer you've ever had!"

Mark and Paul followed their boss out of the room, knowing that something important was about to be discussed.

As they entered the office, Sterling closed the door behind him and said, "Before we start this meeting, I just want you both to know that as of today, you're on the payroll of the Sterling Hedge Fund. We are a legal entity in Israel and Benjamin Yaalon will be direct depositing into your accounts, once a month, the equivalent salary you were receiving at the Sterling Development Company. We'll revisit salaries, assuming we receive Stanley's wire from Nigeria."

Both Mark and Norman gratefully responded with, "Thank you."

Sterling then pointed a finger at Mark and said, "Tell Paul what your State Department guy told you."

Mark got right to it, "There is all-out civil war in Nigeria. The government is arresting unfaithful civil servants and government officials. Our contacts in the Department of State believe that Stanley Roberts may have been arrested. They cannot unconditionally confirm this as a fact, but they think so. Apparently, there is widespread corruption going on at the Central Bank of Nigeria and General Yemi Muhammadu ordered the arrest of Governor Wole Obasanjo and his entire staff, which probably includes Stanley."

Interrupting Mark, Sterling jumped in and said, "We think that's why Stanley's daughter is attempting to contact me. She called again, this time leaving a voice mail saying that it is urgent that I meet her on the campus of UCLA. She requested that I meet her alone at Drake Stadium, which is the home of UCLA track and field. I'm to meet her on the west side of the field at 8:00 PM tonight. She said she'll be wearing a yellow dress. I don't think there's any choice. My only fear is that she's not the real daughter and the Nigerians are trying to set me up. I doubt it, but it's crossed my mind."

Norman immediately responded, "You need to meet. I'm certain it's her, not a trap. We'll be cautious and prepare for a long-shot possible safety risk. We'll definitely arrange some security people to follow you under surveillance. This young woman has something critical to tell you and we need to hear it."

Mark stepped in and said, "I agree with Paul. I'll arrange for a two-man security detail to follow you undercover. My buddy runs the top security firm here in LA. He only employs former Israeli

Mossad and Special Forces security personnel. This group is the most elite in the country. I'll make arrangements to have his two best guys covering you tonight. When you leave for UCLA this evening, you won't even see them, but they will see you. Don't worry about a thing. These men know their business."

Sterling could not conceal the concern on his face. The concern was not due to a possible security risk, but more the anticipation of bad news. He realized that the $100 million wire was in deep jeopardy. He also understood that the Nigerians played hardball, and no matter what anybody said, something bad could happen on that field at UCLA. The question that kept swirling in his mind was whether to advise Felicia. He certainly didn't want to worry her, yet he felt she should know where he was going and the possibility of the risk. Sterling decided, right then and there, that he would inform his wife of the meeting with Stanley's daughter. He just wouldn't bring up the possible risk.

Elliot then announced his decision to Mark and Norman, "Yeah. I'll go. Here's how we'll do this. Paul, I want you to be on foot somewhere near Drake with a cellphone ready. Mark, go ahead and set up your Israeli tough guys. I'll leave my home at exactly 7:30 PM. As soon as I'm done, let's meet right back here to figure out our next step, if any!"

Sterling spent the balance of the evening enjoying dinner with his wife. He explained the importance of the meeting while trying not to create any sense of worry in her. Elliot clarified that the November 2nd wire was less than a week away.

Obviously, there was much at stake as to the outcome of this meeting with the daughter of the one person who could make or break the international future of Sterling Hedge Fund. As always, his wife gave him perfect advice. Felicia said, "Elliot, listen carefully to this young woman's words. Do all that you can to make this happen, but don't put this family or yourself in danger for any criminal or security risks. I know these are not good people you're working with. There may even be some security risk in you meeting with her. I'm assuming Mark knows that you're taking this meeting. If I know Mark, he won't allow you to go to this encounter without plenty of protection for you. So, go do what you need to do. If the overall risk no longer justifies your involvement, get out! We own our home without any debt. We just deposited nearly $10 million in the bank and have zero business obligations. We're the parents of two wonderful daughters who adore us. I'd say we're doing just fine. Elliot, when you finish talking with this man's child and your gut instinct doesn't feel right, promise me you're going to walk away!"

Looking into Felicia's eyes and appreciating what a wise and intelligent wife he was blessed with, Sterling responded, "You were right about Mark. Although Norman and Mark believe there is little to no risk, they are preparing two Israeli security guys to follow me undercover. I promise you I'll walk away if I sense any personal, criminal, or security risk to the family or me. I get that it's not worth a continuous threat. Norman, Mark, and I unanimously agree that she has something very important to tell me, or her father would not be putting his own daughter in any danger. It's almost 7:30 PM. I gotta go. I'll call you as soon as I'm done. I love you, Felicia."

As Elliot grabbed his coat, an uneasy Felicia kissed and embraced him, saying, "I love you. I'll be waiting for that call."

The UCLA campus was less than ten minutes from Sterling's home. It was a beautiful southern California night with not even a cloud in the sky. He entered the campus off of Sunset Boulevard and parked in a two-story concrete parking structure near the Drake facility. Before he exited his car, Sterling called Mark and told him that he had arrived. Mark responded by saying, "I'm aware you have arrived, because I'm the third guy looking after you. We got one guy already at Drake. He sees your gal. She's there waiting for you. It's actually not a yellow dress, it's more like some oversized, yellow jogging suit. Anyways, you'll recognize her. Our other guy is literally watching every move you're making. We got you covered, Boss. Good luck."

Upon hanging up with Mark, Sterling called Norman and asked, "Any final thoughts?"

Norman responded with, "You need to be all ears. She called for the meeting. Let her tell us what's on her mind. I'm near Drake, at Pauley Pavilion, where the Bruins play basketball. Let me know if you need me. I'm a few minutes away."

Very much at ease, Sterling made the walk from the parking structure to the Drake facility and was ready for the moment of truth. The track and field area was virtually empty, with the exception of some students either jogging or walking around the perfectly-manicured red-colored track. This was an excellent choice for a rendezvous. It was casual, yet cleverly discreet. Sterling quickly spotted Stanley's daughter wearing the very yellow garment that Mark had alluded to. Likewise, the young women recognizeed that it was Mr. Sterling walking straight towards her.

They met near the center of the track as she extended her hand and said, with a British accent, "I am Adeleye Roberts."

Sterling, recognizing the voice from the phone messages, said, "I'm Elliot Sterling. How can I help you?"

She responded by saying, "Would you mind if we take a walk along the track as we talk?"

Starting to walk, Sterling smiled and said, "No, I don't mind. I could use some exercise."

Adeleye went right to the heart of the reason they were meeting, and with a serious demeanor, remarked, "My father has expressed to me that I can speak freely and confidentially with you. He is in severe danger. All government and civil servant officials working for the Central Bank of Nigeria are under close surveillance. The governor has been arrested for treason and corruption, along with many on his staff. Although my father was not directly implicated, he is very worried that he will be rounded up and thrown in jail at any moment. Our family fears for his life. Nigeria does not have the same due process that America enjoys. There's a civil war going on and we are concerned that my father will be murdered along with all the rest. This is a brutal regime in Nigeria. They will take all measures to remain in power, including the killing of an innocent man like my father."

Sterling was very impressed with the intellect and poise of Adeleye. He decided to go right to the point of their meeting by saying, "What do you need from me?"

Adeleye stopped walking, stared into the eyes of Sterling, and said, "We require your assurance of two commitments. First, my father insists that you promise me to honor paying my family his $5 million fee, even if he is in prison or killed. Second, if he goes to jail, you must promise to confidentially help my family in assisting to set him free."

As Adeleye was speaking, Sterling was hearing the sincerity of the message, while simultaneously thinking to himself that there still remained a second part of why they were meeting. Obviously, somewhere in that message was the insinuation that the $100 million would in some way get paid. It wouldn't make sense that Stanley would expect Sterling to work on getting him out of jail if the wire wasn't going to be paid. Likewise, there would be no $5 million fee to pay if Sterling didn't receive his $100 million. There had to be more to this conversation.

Sterling decided to use his instincts. In a polite, sensitive, yet direct manner he asked the question on his mind, "Is your father going to wire my contract funds in the amount of $100 million on November 2nd?"

Adeleye was quiet for a moment, then softly answered, "I am prepared to answer your question, but I must insist first that you affirm to me that you agree and vow to honor the commitments we have requested of you. Do I have your promise?"

Without any hesitation, Sterling responded, "If I receive my money, I promise to pay you your money. The fee will either be paid to your father or to your family. As far as my commitment to assist you regarding the potential, regrettable incarceration of your father, I will do whatever I can to get him out. For the security of my family, you need to understand that I will never be in any way publicly identified with this assistance. But, I do pledge that I will use whatever political and other influence I have to seriously help you from behind the scenes."

With a tear in her eye, a grateful Adeleye expressed, "That is exactly what my father wanted me to hear. So, now I will inform you as to what my father has planned."

A thankful Sterling, gratified that he had compassionately chosen the right words to assure Stanley's daughter, said, "Please continue."

Adeleye, who appeared much more relaxed, divulged the plan, saying, "Four weeks ago, my father programmed and preset the Central Bank's computer to automatically enable your $100 million wire transfer to be sent by the Central Bank on November 2nd. There are only three officials in the entire country who have the codes to accomplish what my father has done for you. Although your contract is technically legitimate, the government does not want to acknowledge it, especially after you brought the lawsuit against them. You understand that my father faces grave consequences once those funds are detected missing. The government will figure out that the funds have been wired within three business days from the day they are deposited into your account. You may have an extra day or so, due to the civil unrest. Please be certain to inform your bank to lift the funds off the wire transfer and immediately deposit them into your account. My father sternly told me to make sure you understand exactly what I just said. Do you?"

Sterling said, "Well, let me summarize. Your dad was clever enough to program our wire in advance. We're going to receive it on November 2nd. The moment my banker confirms receipt of the funds, he needs to immediately get the money transfer off the wire and into my separate account. After that happens, I owe you folks $5 million. I think I get it."

With a slight grin, Adeleye said, "I think you have it, especially the part about the $5 million fee. But, seriously, let me conclude my father's message with his warning. He has done his best, given the conditions in Nigeria. He cannot guarantee you that someone in the Central Bank won't stop this transfer. We will learn our fate on November 2nd."

Sterling responded, saying, "Your father is a brave man. He is placing his family first, above all else. What he is trying to accomplish for all of us is nothing short of remarkable. Please pass on to Mr. Roberts that he has earned my trust. For now, all we can do is wait until November 2nd. When is your father planning to leave Nigeria?"

Adeleye, with a sad expression, said, "He is scheduled to leave on November 1st. Everyone at the Central Bank has known, for a long time, about his retirement from the government and his impending immigration to America. The fact that he has plans to leave the country on that date will not come as a surprise to any of his colleagues. My mother and my siblings are already living in the United States with their official immigration green card status. Our worry is that he will not make it out on time."

Sterling, to do his best to lighten up all the serious conversation, said, "By the way, what are you studying here at UCLA?"

Adeleye proudly responded, "My undergraduate degree will be in international relations. Just like my father, I plan to attend Stanford University to study law and become an attorney in this country."

Sterling leaned over to give his new-found friend a brief farewell hug and said, "Be sure to look me up after law school. Good luck to your father and all of you. If you need anything, you know how to reach me. It was a pleasure to meet you, Adeleye."

"Thank you, Mr. Sterling, and good luck to you too!"

The moment Sterling started walking back to his car, his cellphone went off. It was Mark, so he answered, "What's up, Mark?"

Mark firmly, yet calmly responded, "Switch directions. Do not go back to your car. Do you hear me? Do not go back to your car. We have a possible security situation. Walk briskly towards Pauley Pavilion. Look for Norman, then blend in with the small crowd of fans standing outside for the halftime basketball break. Paul is briefed and will advise you what to do. Move quickly, Elliot!"

It didn't take much time before Norman had taken custody of his boss. They looked at each other, but neither one discussed anything except for Norman's initial comment instructing Sterling to, "Follow me towards the center of these basketball fans." Within a few minutes, Norman received a follow-up call, which prompted him to say to Sterling, "We're heading to my car. We're advised to leave now!"

Once securely in the car, they were met by a tall, handsome and physically fit man wearing a black suit and black shirt.

The man opened the door, and speaking in a distinct Israeli accent, said, "My name is Yonatan. I will help you. Please drive the car away from the campus. Mr. Sterling, for security reasons, I want you to lie down so that your head is not visible or in the range of any of the car's windows. Mr. Norman, you are to drive to the Beverly Hills Hotel. We will meet Mr. Goldman and my associate there. You must move faster, Mr. Norman! You are driveing much too slowly!"

Driving east on Sunset Boulevard, it took about ten minutes to arrive at the hotel. Sterling was anxious to hear an explanation.

As he was about to exit the car, he addressed Yonatan and shouted, "What the fuck is going on here?"

Yonatan opened Sterling's door, looked right, then left, and said, "I will explain everything to you once we have you securely inside the hotel. When we enter the hotel lobby, we will turn to the right and walk straight to the corridor where the guest rooms are located on the ground level. Walk to the end of the corridor to room number 1111. Mr. Goldman and my associate will be waiting for us. Let's move quickly, Mr. Sterling and Mr. Norman."

Before he could even think of all the possible scenarios of why he was ushered here, Sterling found himself in a large Beverly Hills Hotel suite. The masterfully-designed room included a large living area with a dining room table, two perfectly-decorated sofas, and a well-stocked wet bar. Mark was seated at the dining table, while the second Israeli agent was pacing back and forth waiting for Yonatan.

A rattled Sterling did not greet anyone, and without even sitting, looked at Yonatan and aggressively said, "Will someone explain to me what the hell is going on here? Did anything happen to Roberts' daughter? Shit, I got to call my wife. She's going to be worried sick!" Looking straight at Yonatan, he demanded, "You go first!"

Yonatan, a prideful and globally-respected security professional, responded, "First, Mr. Sterling, do not talk to me in this way. We are here for your protection, not to be insulted. If you'd prefer we leave, we'll go now."

Sterling, who was accustomed to always being in control, gathered his composure and said, "Yeah, you're right, sorry about that. You're just doing your job. Let's start over. Tell me why I am here."

Yonatan simply said, "We detected a breach in your security. We never gamble with the life or safety of our clients."

Sterling reacted politely, "Thank you. Now tell me what happened. I really do need to contact my wife, but I'm not calling her until I know exactly what's going on here. Go ahead, Yonatan."

With everyone now seated around the elegant dining room table, Yonatan begun by saying, "My associate, Ariel, using very powerful Optik Laser Rangefinder binoculars, discovered that you were under surveillance by a heavy-set black man. He was stationed at the highest level of the Drake Stadium bleachers and screened off by what appeared to be some kind of media structure. Once we had him in our scope, we rapidly detected that this man was armed. Underneath his suit coat, we were able to assess that he was carrying a Dan Wesson semi-automatic pistol with long range capacity. At no time did he reach for the gun, nor was it visibly exposed. The moment your meeting was complete, the man left this location and began making his way towards the track. We acted on impulse by immediately informing Mr. Goldman as to what to do, who instantly called you. The Beverly Hills Hotel was previously prearranged with Mr. Goldman as a contingency location in the event of special circumstances such as the one we just encountered."

Sterling, who was very grateful for all the meticulous surveillance and thoughtful security planning, said, "Wow. You guys really are as good as Mark said you were! Very impressive! Thank you, Yonatan and Ariel. And thanks very much to you, Mark and Paul. You guys were just great! I feel pretty stupid yelling at everybody. Please forgive me for the dumb behavior. What's your assessment? Am I in danger?"

Yonatan, without any emotion, said, "If the Nigerians wanted you dead, we'd all be sitting at the UCLA Hospital or the morgue, as opposed to this hotel. We acted quickly and decisively because we err on the side of caution."

Interrupting Yonatan, Sterling urgently asked, "Are my wife and children safe?"

Understanding Sterling's concern for his family, Yonatan said, "Allow me to first assess the situation, then I will answer your question with my best opinion. There are three scenarios we are facing. One is that the Nigerians are trailing you because they want to gather enough evidence against Mr. Roberts to prove that he is in conspiracy with you to commit some kind of crime, perhaps financial fraud against the government or possible treason. The second theory is that, in order to assist her father with avoiding imprisonment, Ms. Roberts was wearing a wire with the goal to get you to state, for the record, that you are willfully prepared to defraud the Republic of Nigeria. And the last is as simple as Mr. Roberts having hired a security company, just like mine, to keep an eye on his daughter, due to the dangerous and ruthless behavior of the Nigerian government. Mr. Roberts could be as concerned about his family as you are about yours. Based on my experience, and my opinion, it is the third option. It appears that Mr. Roberts is doing his best to keep his family safe. The man we detected was sloppy in his work. Typically, when a government agency is involved, they will have more than one person carrying out this type of operation. They are much more cautious than this guy was. Additionally, we did not observe Ms. Roberts' behavior or demeanor to be consistent with a person trying to incriminate you. So, go ahead. Call your wife. Advise her that everything is fine and that you are concluding your business while enjoying a drink with Mr. Goldman and Mr. Norman at the Beverly Hills Hotel."

A reassured Sterling, no longer feeling distressed or anxious, said, "I'm going to call my wife. Make yourself at home. Pour yourself a drink. I'll be right back and we'll talk some more. By the way, I'd bet my life that Adeleye was not wired."

Yonatan, in his distinguishable Israeli accent, responded, "You just did, Mr. Sterling."

Sterling spent about 20 minutes speaking to his wife in the privacy of a separate bedroom section of the suite. Initially, it took a few minutes to calm Felicia down. She was angry that it took Elliot so much time before he informed her that all was well. As opposed to what Yonatan had advised him to say, Elliot just told his wife the whole story, and that was that. Felicia was the kind of woman who did not tolerate lies or sugar-coated half-truths. She wanted to make certain that her husband was safe and that her family was not in any danger. Felicia understood her husband's explanation, yet she told him to go back into the hotel living room area and ask Yonatan whether the Sterling family would continue to be safe, should Roberts actually succeed in wiring the $100 million. Elliot agreed that he would discuss the topic in detail and brief her later when he got home.

The first to spot Elliot re-enter the room is Mark, who whispered, "Everything good?"

Elliot turned to his friend and said, "Yeah, but we need to talk some more to your James Bond guy. Can you get me a glass of whatever you're drinking and let's have a pow-wow with Yonatan."

Everyone moved from the dining table to the the more comfortable living room as Sterling started the serious, yet necessary conversation by saying, "I think everybody here believes that the Nigerian government was not hunting me down tonight. I'm sure it was Stanley's guy looking after his daughter. I'm not going to worry about what occurred tonight. What I am concerned about is whether my family will ever be safe in the event that Roberts pulls off getting me the $100 million. Once those bastards see that the money is missing, and that the funds were wired to me, all hell will probably break loose. Roberts is going to be a dead man walking, unless he gets out of Nigeria in time. And even then, he's most likely going to be a dead man walking in America!"

Yonatan, who was pleased that Sterling was bringing up the subject, interjected by saying, "You are very astute, Mr. Sterling. This is the heart of the security issues facing you and your family. Please, go on."

Sterling continued, "For the moment, I'm not going to worry about Stanley. This is a choice he made, and he will need to make his own arrangements. I'm speaking about my daughters, my wife, and myself. I think the Nigerians are going want revenge. We need to plan for the very real possibility that someone in my family, most likely me, will be at serious risk. Yonatan, why don't you go ahead and describe those risks to us."

Yonatan looked first at Ariel, then glanced at Mark and Norman, then directed his assessment towards Elliot, saying, "These people will kill you for a lot less than $100 million. Also, there remains a threat that they could abduct a member of your family, or perhaps even you, and ask for ransom just to see if they can recover some of the money. Assuming your actual receipt of the wire-transfer, it is my opinion that you and your family will be at significant risk. All of you will require continuous protection for at least one year, perhaps beyond. Much could happen in your favor, such as the current regime is overthrown in the civil war or just steps down from power. If that should occur, your security risk will drop to a much lower level. As far as tonight's incident, I agree, I wouldn't give it any more thought."

Everything Yonatan mentioned had, in one way or the other, previously passed through Elliot's mind, he said, "I accept your assessment as accurate. Here's what I want from you. If I receive the wire, Sterling Hedge Fund is going to hire you to do two things. One, protect my family and me. Two, become our consultant regarding security matters. Our first business account is a major military arms transaction. You're going to come in very handy regarding that deal. We want you to start on November 3rd. What do you say, Yonatan?"

Without giving the topic thought, Yonatan responded, "Our fees will be much too high for you to contract us for a year, plus we do not consult on business deals. We're security professionals, not businessmen. I'll research who can assist you and get back to you."

Now smiling, Sterling said, "Perhaps I didn't make myself clear. We're going to buy your security company outright! If you agree, you're going to be on the payroll of Sterling Hedge Fund. We'll be able to use your expertise and contacts, not only for our business dealings, but we will be offering worldwide security operations as a profit center for the Fund. Simultaneously, you will be protecting my family, and of course, personally be in charge of keeping me alive. Don't give me your answer tonight. Think about it, then come up with an honest number you think your firm is worth, along with a reasonable salary for you and Ariel. Please get back to me or Mark within a couple of days. If the Nigerian money wires on November 2nd, I need our security in place. I believe what I'm proposing is a win-win. Again, thanks very much for taking great care of me tonight."

"I appreciate your generous offer, Mr. Sterling. I'll give you my answer within 48 hours. I don't think what you propose is for me, but I will speak with Ariel and give it some more thought. In the interim, just in case it's not for me, I'll try and figure out which might be a reliable security firm that will take good care of the Sterling family," Yonatan concluded with a wink and an affable expression.

Ariel, who had virtually been silent the entire night, almost on cue said in his thick Israeli accent, "Okay, I'll escort you back to your car, parked at UCLA. We don't expect any incident, but as a precaution, once I drop you at the car, I will trail you back to your home and maintain surveillance there until 6:00 AM. At that point our job will be done."

Within less than an hour, Sterling had returned safely to the serenity of his home. As he entered the front door, he was met by Felicia, who didn't say anything. She just hugged her husband and kissed him. Finally, Felicia said, "I'm frightened, Elliot. I'm scared. I don't want us to live this way. Get rid of these awful people. Their money is going to bring us nothing but trouble. Please, Elliot, let them keep their money!"

Elliot grabbed his wife's hand and led her into the kitchen so that they could both enjoy some tea while they talked. Felicia brought a plate full of homemade Rugelach, then poured her husband and herself a cup of Chamomile tea as the complicated conversation began.

Elliot started by saying, "I can't stop the wire. Stanley Roberts has preset the wire to automatically be transferred on November 2nd. If he says anything about it, the Nigerians will arrest him right on the spot. Probably kill him for committing treason. I can't say anything about it, because they'll accuse me of conspiring to defraud their government. On top of all that, those guys are in the middle of a bloody civil war. There's nothing we can do. It is possible that the wire transfer will be stopped by someone in the Nigerian government at the Central Bank. If that happens, well, God save Stanley's soul, but we're off the hook. We won't receive a $100 million, but you won't need to worry any further. Let's concentrate on our circumstances if the money does get wired."

Felicia, listening carefully to the husband she trusted with all of heart, said, "Alright, I'm done feeling weak and I won't be a coward. How do we protect our family? Help me understand the reality of the situation."

Proud of the strength displayed by his wife, Elliot got right to the issue, saying, "There are only two scenarios here. First, they wire us nothing. Game over. No money. We quit. No more worrying, except we start a new business way undercapitalized. Second, they wire us $100 million. We're very rich, but we inherit serious risks."

Feeling the strength of Elliot and knowing that her family was in the best of hands with her husband, Felicia responded with her quick wit, saying, "Walk me through the 'very rich' scenario."

Elliot bluntly outlined to his wife all the serious risks discussed earlier with Yonatan. He painted a realistic picture of what the family would be up against if the $100 million were wired. Sterling went on to explain that he was prepared to pay well over a million dollars to Yonatan, or some other high-level security firm, to ensure the protection of Felicia and their daughters. It was perfectly clear to Felicia that if the money was wired, the Sterling family way of life was about to be significantly altered on November 2nd.

Felicia remained silent for a moment, then said, "Okay, I get it. We'll be rich, but we'll need big-time security. Since we don't have much of a choice here, this is what I want. You're going to buy us a big, comfortable home in Israel with a big security wall all the way around it. Make sure to arrange Yonatan, or someone as good as him, to come with us. Let's talk to Stanford University and make arrangements allowing our daughters to study abroad and attend an Israeli university for the upcoming semester. We will keep our home in Bel Air, and when it is good and safe, we will return to Los Angeles, if we choose." As she finished her instructions to her husband, Felicia simply fist bumped her husband as her symbol of giving her approval and understanding of what is to come.

Elliot affectionately took ahold of his wife and said, "I love you. We'll make this successful, one way or the other. I'll get Benjamin Yaalon working on a possible Israeli home right away. The good thing is, we'll know where we stand with the wire transfer within a few days. I'm glad we talked. I'll start making preparations either way. Hey, who knows, you might even like living in Israel!"

Although relieved that his wife was fully understanding and supportive, Sterling was still very concerned for the well-being of his family. Perhaps the wire transfer would be stopped, or maybe the current government in Nigeria would fall. But, if the money was sent, one thing was clear, meticulous security preparation would be the key to maintaining their well-being and Yonatan was the man he needed for the job. Although Elliot could not predict the future, he understood the need to plan successfully for whatever might happen next.

Chapter 26

Two days had gone by with no response from Yonatan. Sterling could not stop thinking about security for his family.

All protection arrangements needed to be in place and ready to go in the event the $100 million wire-transfer made it out of Nigeria. So, this would be the day that Sterling would contact Yonatan to obtain his answer. The night before, Felicia's banker had confirmed that Neil's cashier's check for $7.25 million had 'cleared as good funds.' The banker further told Felicia that he had wired, to their designated Israeli bank, the $7 million she had instructed him to specially handle. The only step pending was Benjamin Yaalon's confirmation that the Israeli bank had in fact received the funds.

Sterling's first business move of the new day was to call Benjamin.

"Hello, Benjamin, this is Elliot. How are you?"

Benjamin, delighted to hear from his friend, said, "Shalom, Shalom, Elliot! Good to hear from you. I was just going to contact you. We have your $7 million. We're in the routine process of confirming that the funds have cleared. I have taken the money off the wire and placed them in the account we had previously set up for you and Felicia. Although, technically, we are obligated to wait a day or two, I authorized the funds to be immediately credited to your account. The money is available to you at your discretion."

Elliot responded in Hebrew, expressing, "Todah Rabah!" (Thank you very much!). Then, he went on to say, "Please, leave the funds in the checking account until we determine the status of our impending November 2nd wire-transfer."

Yaalon then asked his friend, "So, Elliot, do you believe this big Nigerian wire is going to happen?"

Sterling gave him an honest answer, saying, "I don't know, Ben, I just don't know. It is preset to transfer on November 2nd for the entire $100 million. As you have probably read or heard, Nigeria is in the midst of a serious civil war. There is a whole bunch of chaos over there. Two days ago, a messenger from my contact in the

Central Bank of Nigeria confirmed that we are on schedule to receive the money at your bank. Anything can happen due to that country's pandemonium. Nevertheless, we need to plan for the successful receipt of the wire. If it gets stopped, well, it gets stopped. We did the best we could. So, here's what I've been told. The moment you confirm that the wire has arrived at your bank, instantly remove the funds off your wire and into my account. Do not wait even a minute. On that day, November 2nd, the only work you should do is monitor this transfer under the microscope until you see it on your wires. Then, like a bat out of hell, get those funds into a safe bank account. Ben, do you understand me?"

Yaalon, who heard Sterling's very serious voice, said, "My only job that day will be to search for the wire, then immediately move the money into your account. Either myself, or my trusted assistant, will remain in the bank 24 hours around the clock in order to ensure that we don't miss it. You have my word that the second we get it, we will process the funds."

All the way back to his college days, Sterling had known Benjamin to be as reliable as any man he had ever met. Sterling responded with, "Thank you, Ben. I know you'll take care of this for me. You've always been a great friend to me, and now, finally, we're going to do big business together! Okay, I've just got one other topic for you. I'm moving to Israel. Can you help me find a home?"

Ben, somewhat stunned, said, "What did you just ask me?"

Elliot answered his friend, "You heard me. I'm moving to Israel with Felicia and my daughters. If the $100 million is wired, my family and I will be facing a major security risk. We're going to be in danger. We'll need a spacious home in the most secure place in Israel. The residence must be located in a gated neighborhood that includes 24-hour security, along with a guardhouse at the entry. Felicia insists that the home must have a wall all the way around it. We'll need up-to-date security cameras throughout. I think you get the picture."

A concerned Yaalon reacted, saying, "This doesn't sound good, Elliot. When are you planning on coming?"

Elliot, continuing with the hard truth, said, "The threat and danger are very real. The ruling Nigerian government is unaware that the wire will take place on November 2nd, even though the payment for my contract is approved and legal. They just don't want to pay me what they owe, especially given all the civil unrest. Once the officials figure out we've been paid, they're going to be livid!

They probably want the money for themselves, in case they need to flee the country. Anyways, I got a man in the Central Bank who is authorized to legitimately wire us my funds. He legally, yet clandestinely, preset the wire to fund on November 2nd. Now, he's not doing this out of the kindness of his heart. I'm paying him a fee of 5 million bucks to do this. I'll fill in more details in person. So, now you understand why I'm taking all these extraordinary precautions. I'm not going to risk the lives of my family. Oh, yeah, and the answer to your question is that we plan to move in by December 31. Once you get me possession of the home, we're there!"

Understanding the gravity of the situation, Ben said, "I know the perfect home! Should I prepare a security firm here?"

Sensitive to the security matter, Sterling addressed the issue by saying, "I'm actually in the process of hiring a security expert based in Los Angeles who happens to be an Israeli. I'm guessing this may cost upwards of a million dollars to keep us all safe. Obviously, security expenses for my family will be a necessary line item in the foreseeable future. Let's just call it a cost of doing business. I would greatly appreciate your recommendations on hiring the correct security people for me in Israel. As long as I'm living in Bel Air, I can continue to retain the people I'm working with now. Once we arrive in Israel, I could possibly transition to one of your recommendations. That might be the most practical way to go. So, yes, Ben, go ahead and locate the right people in Israel. Now, tell me about this perfect home."

The very efficient Yaalon quickly responded, saying, "I'll have the security name, along with their annual budget, by the end of next week. If the home is still available, you will need to buy it sight unseen. I will visit it on your behalf, but I guarantee you, there is no better residence in all of Israel for your needs. The estate is being sold by a major customer of my bank due to a death. It is not on the open market, but I can get it for you, assuming someone hasn't already bought it. The home is located in an exclusive residential compound where the current prime minister of Israel maintains his private beachfront residence. Imagine how much attention to security is paid in that neighborhood. It's got the entry security guardhouse, the gates, the walls; you name it, it's got it. The house is located in Caesarea. I am told that the residence is very spacious, with an excellent floor plan, featuring high ceilings. It has six bedrooms and seven bathrooms. The French architecture is gorgeous, and you, my friend, please be prepared to pay a lot of

278

Shekels in order to own it. It's going to cost you millions of US dollars, but if it is available, grab it! This home will always go up in value. I'll inquire as to availability and price. If it's obtainable, I'll make sure you're in the number one position with the seller to buy it. We'll need to submit a written purchase agreement on or before November 3rd."

Very impressed with his old college buddy, and soon to be business associate, Sterling said, "Sounds very good, Ben! Please inform me as to the price of the home and the budget for the Israeli-based security firm. We need to get a purchase agreement prepared in the event the Nigerian wire arrives on November 2nd. That should give us plenty of time to purchase the home, then make the move by December 31. Go get that house for me! Once we control it via written contract, either Felicia or myself will go to Caesarea during the month of November to walk through the residence in order to better prepare for our move to Israel. In the interim, we'll be protected by my Los Angeles security people until we move. By the way, Ben, make sure someone pays you a big commission or a fat finder's fee if I do end up buying the house. I'm not kidding. Get some money out of this!"

"Thank you, Elliot. You're my friend. I wasn't assisting you for money. It didn't even cross my mind. But, since you mentioned it, here's what we can do. Make the offer through your attorney. In the offer, place a three percent commission payable to the buyer's broker and/or attorney. If you end up buying the home, this will generate over $100,000 in commission paid by the seller. I'll return half to you and I'll retain the other half. Fair?"

Elliot responded, saying, "I haven't even moved there and I'm already making money with you. Let's talk tomorrow. My warmest regards to your wife. Thanks very much, Ben."

As he hung up the phone, all Sterling could contemplate was how fortunate he was to have a trusted friend like Benjamin Yaalon.

Sterling kept thinking about what a great privilege it would be to work side-by-side with Ben at the new Sterling Hedge Fund. What a formidable company it was developing into, with astute men like Goldman, Norman, and Yaalon. Within a few days, the suspense would be over and the new reality for everyone would arrive.

Sterling understood that the capitalization of a powerful international hedge fund hinged on the success of the wire-transfer by Stanley Roberts. He also knew that life for the Sterling family was about to change, with or without the transfer.

Since he couldn't do anything about the wire, Elliot decided to focus on the protection of his family and called Yonatan, who answered on the first ring, saying, "You beat me to the call. I just concluded my meeting with Ariel and was about to contact you. This is what we can do for you. I'm not going to sell you my firm, but we will protect you and your wife for as long as you live in Los Angeles. Your daughters at Stanford University will be watched over by our security associates who operate out of the San Francisco area. We'll take over whenever they are in the Los Angeles. If any of you should travel to different parts of the United States or abroad, we'll cover you. Our fee for 24-hours around-the-clock security will be $80,000 a month, plus expenses. It takes a lot of security people to watch every move you make day and night. This arrangement will go month-to-month until you tell us to stop. In my opinion, I don't believe you need to start our services until about one week after you receive your funds. The Nigerians won't even discover the money missing until two to three days later. Then, they must investigate what happened, who was involved, along with other details. Once they figure out you received the funds, but you're not willing to return the money, then it will be, as you say in America, game on!"

Sterling, who agreed with Yonatan's analysis, said, "Let's see if I got this right. Assuming the wire hits on November 2nd, you'll start your services for my entire family on November 9th. So long as I'm based out of Los Angeles, you're going to charge me 80 grand a month, plus expenses, until I tell you to quit. Any one of us can travel anywhere in the world and our security will be in place. Is that it? What about being my business consultant?"

"Yes, Mr. Sterling, that's it on your security. As far as business goes, I'll tell you what I know when asked. No extra charge."

Without another thought, Sterling responded, saying, "You got a deal, Yonatan. Send me your retainer agreement. Just so you know, I'm seriously considering moving to Israel for about a year until the dust settles on all of this. Are you okay with that? What happens to our agreement?"

Yonatan instantly said, "You fire me, then hire someone in Israel. If you need a referral, I'll give it to you."

Sterling continued by asking, "Will you be assigned to me? Here's why I ask. If I'm in a business deal someplace around the world and you're with me, I may require your advice on business matters. If you're guarding me all of the time, well, it's possible that you and I could be talking about my hedge fund deals quite a bit. Will that be considered within the scope of our agreement?"

Very direct with his words, Yonatan simply answered, "Yes, I will handle you, and yes to your second question."

Impressed by this man, Sterling said, "Subject to my receipt of the Nigerian wire, please prepare to start on November 9th." As he's about to complete the call, Elliot finishes by saying, "I still think you're going to end up working full-time for my company. Anyways, I'll look for your retainer. Thanks again, Yonatan."

Sterling hung up knowing in his heart that he was in very good hands with Yonatan. There wasn't too much left to prepare, except to wait for Benjamin's answer regarding the potential Israeli home. Of course, November 2nd would define Sterling's direction. Even for an experienced and veteran businessman like Sterling, the wait for that day was beginning to make his stomach in knots. The next few days would prove to be the most anxious of his life.

Although Sterling felt stressed, the days seemed to go by uneventfully until the morning of November 1st, when a call came to his cellphone and was marked 'restricted' on the screen. Normally, Sterling did not pick up calls he did not recognize, but today, he decided to accept the call.

Elliot immediately recognized it as the distressed voice of Adeleye, who sounded hysterical and on the verge of tears. Elliot compassionately interrupted her and said, "Calm down, Adeleye. Calm down. What's going on?"

Slightly better composed, Adeleye began telling the story that Sterling was fearful might happen. She began by saying, "My father's sister contacted me from Nigeria. Regrettably, she has information that my father was arrested. We do not know where he was taken or whether he is even alive. My father's loyal colleagues are trying hard to gather more facts. Obviously, I wanted you to be told immediately. I spoke to my father about 12 hours before he was abducted. He was preparing to get to the airport and make the journey to his freedom in America. He was excited, yet concerned that something like this could occur. My aunt believes that it was his driver who deceived my father by delivering him to the brutal governing regime. One comment I do want you to know is that he confirmed to me that your wire was set to transfer. Should my father survive, my family will be very grateful for your promised assistance to rescue him out of Nigeria. And of course, we will require all of the money he so dearly earned from this endeavor."

Sterling, who was emotionally touched by Adeleye, responded, "I'll help you whether the transfer is made or not. Your father risked his life for his family and for me. If he's alive, I'll get him to

281

America. I'm going to set up a different method of communication. It is best you do not call me at this cell any further. You will hear from one of my people. He will identify himself only as 'a friend of the family.' He will be your liaison to me from this point forward."

A much calmer Adeleye softly said, "Thank you, Mr. Sterling. Here is my private cell number where you can contact me. I have great faith in you. I will advise my mother that you will do all that you can to help her and my family."

A reassuring Sterling then said, "You tell your mother that not only will she receive the money your father earned with me, but with the will of God, she will see the day that your father will be here in America dancing at your wedding! You'll hear from me soon. Take care of yourself, Adeleye."

Upon disconnecting the call, a realistic Sterling was focused on whether the ruthless government holding Roberts would viciously torture him, forcing him to disclose the existence of the wire-transfer. How easy it would be for the government to obtain a written confession out of Stanley, make the 'crooked' American Mr. Sterling the scapegoat, then murder the witness anyways. If Stanley broke down and told them the truth, not only would his family never receive their $5 million, but he'd never make it out of that country alive. On top of that, the Nigerian government would have legal cause to chase Sterling without him having the resources of a $100 million. This was a serious crisis in the making, and his instinct was to call Yonatan for unemotional advice.

"Hello, Yonatan, this is Elliot. Something just came up. I need your advice. Adeleye just informed me that her father, Stanley Roberts, has been arrested! She's fearful he may be dead. If alive, I think the Nigerians will pressure him for information that will not only lead to his own death, but stop my wire and make me a criminal. What should I do?"

Yonatan, the consummate professional, answered, "Nothing. You do nothing. Tomorrow is November 2nd. First, we wait to see if the money is wired. Once we determine that fact, we'll know how to react. Call me with the answer."

Sterling, amazed at how quickly Yonatan came up with precisely the right advice, said, "You're gifted at that this stuff, but you know this, don't you? You're a security mastermind. How the hell am I ever going to live without you? You are absolutely correct. There is nothing to do until the wire is defined. The moment I hear something tomorrow, I'll be in touch. I really appreciate the sage advice."

Soon after he completed his call with Yonatan, Sterling's cellphone rang. It was Benjamin Yaalon calling from Israel to say, "Mazel Tov, Elliot, I got you the house! We owe the seller a purchase agreement by November 4th. The best and final price is $4 million. I think this is a fair deal. It's one of a kind. Felicia is going to love it, and it's safe as hell for your family. I still don't have a final quote from the security firm here in Israel, but just settle on spending a lot of money for around-the-clock protection for four people. I should have something for you within a couple of days."

Sterling elected to closely follow the advice Yonatan had recommended, and for the moment, decided he'd disclose nothing about the tense situation concerning Roberts' arrest. Instead, he concentrated directly on the good news regarding his potential new Israeli home by saying, "Excellent job, Benjamin! If we get the wire, buy the home. I knew you'd find a way to deliver the house. You always win! I don't know whether it's charm, intellect, or persistence, but for as long as I've known you, you always end up coming out on top. Thank you for all the hard work on this. I'll send you my attorney's version of the purchase agreement. You can amend it to fit the Israeli legal format. You'll have it by November 3rd. It will be forwarded to you directly by Paul Norman, my lawyer. If you have any questions, call Paul directly at the contact number he'll provide you. Obviously, no wire, no deal. But, if we get the Nigerian transfer, you're authorized to pay for the house from the $7 million in the bank account we have with you."

"Very good, Elliot. I'll take care of this."

Sterling then reminded Yaalon, saying, "Make sure you get the seller to pay you the three percent commission. It's worth $120,000! We'll write it into the agreement. You just make sure you collect it. Also, keep me posted on the security guys. We'll need them operational by the end of the year. Hey, Ben, tomorrow is a big day for us. Keep a sharp eye out for the wire. If you get the money, put it in a safe spot, then call me at any hour of the day. I'm excited just thinking about living in Israel and working with you. Let's hope for the best tomorrow. Thanks for everything, Ben."

All the planning was done. There was nothing further to do but wait for the final results of the infamous wire.

Everything else had been reduced to final paperwork and some pending questions. Would Sterling remain in Bel Air or move to Israel? Would his family be safe? Would Stanley Roberts live or die? If he lived, how would Sterling fulfill the hope he had given his family of freeing him from prison? How could he afford to pay good men like Goldman, Norman, Yaalon, and Yonatan without that wire? Would the Nigerians chase Sterling for the rest of his natural life? These were the difficult questions, and starting tomorrow, time would begin to tell the answers.

Elliot decided to spend the remainder of the day with his lovely wife. Although Sterling was experiencing worry, unease, and nervousness about the uncertainty of the wire-transfer outcome, there was no one else he wanted to be with other than his wife. Felicia would bring him peace of mind and the strength to face whatever was coming his way. They would spend the rest of the evening doing what they always did, give each other comfort just knowing that they had each other to rely on for the rest of their lives.

Attempting to sleep that night proved to be very difficult. It seemed as though Elliot kept checking his cellphone and the digital clock on his nightstand every 20 minutes. He was very aware of the fact that Israeli time was ten hours ahead of California.

It was now 4:00 AM in Los Angeles on this fateful November 2nd day and 2:00 PM in Tel Aviv. There was still no word from Benjamin. Too antsy to lie in bed, Sterling abruptly stood up, grabbed his cellphone, and made his way to the kitchen to make some coffee. It didn't take too long before Felicia joined him in the breakfast nook.

Sounding uncharacteristically dejected, Elliot said to his wife, "I'm not so optimistic, since we haven't heard a word by now. I guess the good news is that we won't require a bunch of bodyguards. I feel ashamed that I won't be able to start up the international hedge fund I promised to deliver to good men like Mark, Norman, and Ben. I cherished the thought of leading such an important new fund. Oh, well, I guess I should be grateful we'll be left with a decent amount of money and this home paid off. I'm going to brace myself for the worst and see what kind of plan God has in store for us. I'm prepared to live with the consequences either way. I do feel horrible for Stanley Roberts and his family, especially if the wire is dead."

Felicia, partially sympathetic with her husband, although a little bit upset, said, "Elliot Sterling, I didn't marry a pessimist! I fell in love with a man who saw no obstacles, just solutions. You are a guy who has always seen the world through pragmatic eyes but have remained forever an optimist. Give Benjamin more time. If I know Ben, he won't call you until he is absolutely certain that the wire is either safely secure in our bank account or the transfer is unconditionally canceled. I'm sure we'll hear something by the end of the bank's business day. So, in the meantime, I'm going to make us some breakfast and you're going to get yourself ready to react aggressively in either direction. Deal?"

With those simple words of wisdom coming from his wife, Elliot was right back on track. He looked at Felicia and said, "Yeah, deal. Now, how about a couple of eggs, a sesame bagel, some tomato slices, and a piece of that expensive imported Swiss cheese you only serve to our guests?"

It was 6:00 AM as they were finishing their breakfast and 4:00 PM in Israel. Still no word from Yaalon. Trying to remain optimistic, Sterling said, "The Israeli bank should be closing around this time. I'll give Ben another 15 minutes. If I don't hear from him, I'll just go up and take a shower. As you said, he'll call when he's ready to say something. Great breakfast! Great wife! Whatever happens, happens!"

The 15 minutes came and went as Sterling got up off his breakfast table seat, stretched a bit, gave his wife a kiss, and said to her, "I'm going upstairs to get dressed." Just as he made his way out of the nook, the cellphone rang with the screen name reading Benjamin Yaalon. Elliot glanced at his wife and she glanced right back, saying, "Aren't you going to answer it?"

Sterling composed himself for the moment of truth, cleared his voice, and said, "What's the answer, Ben?"

Benjamin excitedly said, "We received the wire-transfer, Elliot! The money is here! We have it in your secure account. You're home free, Elliot, you're home free!

Elliot, who was overwhelmed with emotion, placed his hand over his eyes, then stared at his wife and said, "We got it!"

This was the type of ecstatic moment that perhaps those few individuals who have won huge lottery amounts experience. Or maybe the euphoric feeling a baseball pitcher senses when winning the seventh game of a World Series championship. There are just no words to describe the moment. Felicia, without saying anything, jumped out of her chair with an indescribable warmth towards Elliot and clung on to her husband as he attempted to continue the conversation, which had momentarily gone silent, with Yaalon.

Sterling, still feeling somewhat dazed with the news, asked, "Did you receive all of it?"

Yaalon, who had been Sterling's close friend since their college days and is thrilled for him, responded by laughing out loud, saying, "Yes, Elliot. All $100 million!" Benjamin, feeling excited to the point of disorientation, continued with, "I've been inside the bank for over 24 hours straight. I've got to go home and get some sleep. Congratulations, my good friend! I'll call you tomorrow."

As he was about to hang up, Elliot completed the call of his life by simply saying to Ben, "I love you, man!"

With his wife hugging him while she was simultaneously breaking down in tears of joy, Elliot couldn't help but think about how ironic it was that this intriguing story, which began on an Israeli airplane en route to Tel Aviv, had ended, at least for now, right where it had begun.